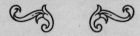

I LOOK LIKE A PANTHER, she thought. No, not a panther. One of those snow leopards. She had seen them in the market in the middle of Shanghai. One particular snow leopard had caught her attention. It was attached to a rope in the hands of a Tibetan musician. Although the animal was captured, Sophia had noticed the haughty look in its eye. Nobody, the look said, can truly capture a snow leopard. The beast's intense eyes glared at Sophia, who felt for it an instant empathy.

Now those same eyes stared back at her. That's what I am, she whispered to her image in the mirror. I am a snow leopard. . . . Tonight I am reborn.

Erin Pizzey

The Snow Leopard Of Shanghai

Harper Paperbacks

Harper & Row, Publishers, New York
Grand Rapids, Philadelphia, St. Louis, San Francisco
London, Singapore, Sydney, Tokyo, Toronto

This is a work of fiction. The characters, incidents, and dialogues are products of the author's imagination and are not to be construed as real. Any resemblance to actual events or persons, living or dead, is entirely coincidental.

Harper Paperbacks a division of Harper & Row, Publishers, Inc.
10 East 53rd Street, New York, N.Y. 10022

This book was first published in 1989 in Great Britain by William Collins Sons & Co. Ltd.

Cover photograph by Herman Estevez. Cover illustration by Michael Herring. Snow leopard pin courtesy of Van Cleef & Arpels, New York, N.Y.

First Harper Paperbacks printing: May, 1990

Printed in the United States of America

HARPER PAPERBACKS and colophon are trademarks of Harper & Row, Publishers, Inc.

10 9 8 7 6 5 4 3 2 1

DEDICATION

This book is dedicated to Hedi and Garston Grant
and to Troy for their friendship, in memory of Hurricane Gilbert; to Eston and Jewel Scott, who take care
of us; to everybody at the airport, Nat, Tom, Lona,
Tony, and Bud, who like our explosive pizza; to
Melvin MacFarlane, who cares for our eight dogs and
three cats; to Mr. and Mrs. Tracy Hunter for all their
kind help; to Henley, Norma, and Richard (who will
review all serious applications for the position of
wife) Scott for providing us with fish and lobster; to
Mr. and Mrs. Frankie Bodden and to Eva, who are
always smiling; to Cliff and Jean Quimby, and Durl
and Amelita Grant for making our lives more comfortable; to Maggie Tatum, whose bright face at
Tiara Beach we see at the end of a day's writing; to
Nola and Steve Bodden for their continuing help; to
Karen Fraser and to the pyramid which she imagined
and made a magnificent reality; to Cayman Brac itself, unique and beautiful, where we live so happily.

To our friend Peter Lavery, with unforgettable
memories of Alphonso; to Keita, Amber, Shauna,
James, and Randy, and the children of Cayman Brac,
with love.

To David Morris, John Elford, Alan Cohen, and
John Faure, who are always our friends and protec-
tors; and of course to Christopher Little, who is end-

lessly patient; and to Marjory Chapman, my editor and friend.

A special mention needs to be made to the Public Library on Grand Cayman and to Susan Miller, our librarian and dear friend, who looked out and supplied hundreds of books on the histories of Russia and China. Without her I would have been lost.

To the staff at my parents' house and to my amahs whom I remember from my childhood in Shanghai; to those of us who escaped on the *Gripsholm*, the last boat out of China, and to those who did not escape.

Finally this book is dedicated to my beloved husband, Jeff Shapiro, who makes me so enduringly happy.

God bless you all.

Does the road wind uphill all the way?
Yes, to the very end.
Will the day's journey take the whole long day?
From morn to night, my friend.

CHRISTINA GEORGINA ROSSETTI
From *Up-hill*, 1861

QUESTIONS

"Come in." The door to the cottage was held open by an old man with kind eyes.

Natasha stood on the front step and hesitated. She was nervous. Interviews did not usually make her nervous, but this was different. A cold winter wind blew off the sea in the Cornish village of Cawsand. It was mid-morning on a blustery gray day. The small cottage sat immediately on the shore, so close to the sea that Natasha felt a breath of salty spray tingle on her cheek. Strands of her blonde hair waved before her eyes. She pulled her woollen coat tighter around her body. "Good morning," she said. "I'm Natasha Waldbauer. Are you the gentleman I spoke with on the telephone?"

"Yes, yes." The man, whom Natasha assumed to be a butler of sorts, seemed eager to close the door against the wind. His hand made a circling motion as if to pull her inside. "Come in."

Natasha stepped into the warmth.

He shut the door behind her and hung up her coat.

Natasha followed the man up the narrow corridor that led through the cottage. It was a small cottage, furnished just as Natasha had expected it would be. A chintz sofa and two comfortable-looking armchairs sat either side of the coffee table in front of the fireplace in the sitting-room they walked past. English carpets cushioned their steps up the hallway. On the walls hung anonymous paintings of ships and seascapes. The man put his hand on the knob of a closed door at the end of the corridor. He raised his eyes to hers. "Tea?" he asked suddenly.

Natasha smiled and nodded. "Thank you."

The man seemed gratified by her answer. He returned the smile and bowed his head before opening the door. He held out his arm, waiting for Natasha to enter. "Please," he said.

Natasha felt her heartbeat quicken. She breathed deeply. "Thank you," she said again, wondering if her breathy pulse could be heard in each word. She entered the room.

The room was a surprise. The walls and ceiling were painted a strong Oriental red. From the molding at the top hung long scroll-paintings of birds singing to craggy mountains in mystical moonlight. The furniture was heavy dark teak, carved with intricate Chinese patterns, and waves of red and gold silk—spread over a table-top on which stood a porcelain vase, ivory statuettes and jade carvings, and draped from the ceiling in a kind of Eastern canopy over the bed—glistened and sparkled in the light. The room, which gave Natasha the impression that she had walked into some intimate corner of an Oriental palace, bore no relation to the rest of that unexceptional cottage or, for that matter, to the damp, gray-stoned coastal town of Cawsand. Natasha had the strange magical feeling that, in an otherwise drab world, she had chanced upon an ornate jewel-box and, opening it, found it full of light, heaped with treasures, with gems that glinted and rings that shimmered.

The bed itself was a priceless, Chinese red-lacquered piece, carved with gold-leaf dragons. In the bed, propped against cushions covered in smooth silk, lay the woman Natasha had come to meet. Her hands lay atop the thickly padded feather duvet that covered her body. The woman was old, into her eighties. Her silver hair was long and still beautiful. Well-brushed and smooth, it lay over the shoulders of her embroidered robe. Her face was wrinkled, though the skin had not lost its softness nor its radiance. But it was her eyes that most captured Natasha; wide eyes, their color dark and powerful, that seemed almost to slant upward in their outer corners. "You're the Snow Leopard?" Natasha began. She framed the words with difficulty.

"I am," the woman said. "What do you want?" she asked in a voice that held faint traces of some Continental origin.

"My name is Natasha Waldbauer," Natasha said firmly. "I'm a writer for *European Woman* magazine. Have you seen it?"

"No." The woman was obviously unimpressed. Natasha reached into her large floppy handbag and pulled out three glossy-covered back issues. Offering copies was usually a reliable ice-breaker. Natasha smiled, holding out the magazines. "I've brought you some recent editions, if you'd like to have a look through later."

The woman was silent, and just stared at her. Natasha felt foolish. This woman did not look like a reader of magazines. "Put them over there," she said at last.

Natasha understood her to mean a nearby table-top and put them down with a sigh of relief. "I've come from New York to do an interview with you. My editor said . . ."

"I know who you are and why you've come," the woman said without smiling.

Of course, Natasha thought. The man I talked to on the phone would have told her. However, this was not proving easy. Ordinarily the people she interviewed treated her like visiting royalty, so eager were they to see their names in print. And she was no foot-in-the-door journalist out to dig up dirt. She worked for a respectable magazine and tended to write sympathetically about anyone she chose to interview. But this woman, Natasha sensed, was intent on remaining close-lipped. And how articulate would the woman be, even if she did agree to the interview? It was quite possible that age had got the better of her mind.

"I'm not well," the woman spoke suddenly.

"I'm sorry. Did I come at an inconvenient time?"

"You could say that." A smile started to form on the woman's lips. "I'm dying."

Natasha gasped. "Oh. I'm so sorry. Is it . . . ?"

"It's none of your business. Dying is a private affair."

"I didn't mean to intrude."

The woman's eyes narrowed to what looked like an accusing stare. "I've breath enough to say what I want to say. If I want to say it."

The woman was silent again. Then she said, "Sit. In that chair, where I can look at you." She lifted a hand and indicated a carved chair on the other side of the bed.

The chair had looked hard but was surprisingly comfortable, supporting Natasha's back and arms perfectly. She nestled herself into the chair and smiled. "Thank you," she said.

The woman's eyes remained on her in an unsettling gaze.

"Do you mind if I smoke?" Natasha asked.

"It's your life," the woman said with disinterest. "Smoke will not harm a dying woman." She raised her hand again and pointed to a brass dish on a table beside the chair.

Natasha pulled the ashtray closer. She took her cigarettes and lighter out of her handbag and, before retracting her hand, pressed the record button of her cassette tape-recorder. She sat back, lit up, put the cigarettes and lighter on the table, and inhaled deeply.

"Natasha Waldbauer," the woman said, pronouncing the W as a V, in the German manner. "Let me see." In silence, her eyes appraised Natasha, resting longest on Natasha's long golden hair that fell naturally into generous curls, taking in the young woman's stylish boots, purchased at an expensive New York store, the fashionably cut tweed skirt, the cotton shirt open at the neck, and the well-tailored jacket. The eyes lingered on Natasha's face, a face thought by men to be beautiful, with wide expressive eyes and a full pleasant mouth.

Natasha did not know what to do while she came under such scrutiny. She wanted to project the woman she felt herself to be: professional, intelligent, confident, thoughtful. Finally, she allowed herself a pensive half-smile that would not show the deeper insecurities and nervousness that lurked beneath the practiced veneer of self-assurance. She was glad she had not put on lipstick and hoped that her mascara was not too heavy.

"Natasha Waldbauer," the woman repeated, finishing her inspection. "Tell me, Natasha Waldbauer. What have you heard of me?"

Natasha was relieved that talking had begun. *"European Woman,* like all magazines, has contacts with news services around the world. It seems that a journalist from a local Cornish newspaper found out that you were living here. An editor at our offices suggested that you would make an interesting story and so here I am."

"An interesting story," the woman echoed with a small nod. "And what did they say about me?"

"That you were a remarkable woman." Natasha smiled. "That you were called the Snow Leopard but no one knew your real name. That you had lived for years in China, though you were originally from Russia. That you became an important dignitary in China before you were forced to leave because of the Cultural Revolution."

"Dignitary, indeed!" said the Snow Leopard, visibly offended. "You make me sound like a functionary, like some bureaucratic busy-body!"

"I didn't mean it like that. But please, I'm hoping you can tell me the story in your own words."

The woman looked unmoved. Some soothing was in order. Natasha said, "The wire said that you had actually lived the history that the rest of us have only read about. I wanted to meet you. So I flew here . . ."

"All the way from New York." Natasha could hear a mocking note in the woman's voice.

"All the way from New York." Natasha laughed.

"And what do you want from me?"

"I want to find out more about you. There's so much you could tell me. Like why you're called the Snow Leopard, for instance."

"It's just a name," the woman said dismissively. "That's all it is. A name to hide behind." With her eyes fixed on the wall at the foot of her bed, she spoke as if to herself. "Everybody hides behind a name. What does it matter which name? The Snow Leopard was a name I invented when I was a young woman. Silly, don't you think? A child's imagination. And then I had to become the name. For a while at least."

The woman paused, as if deliberating, then shook her head. "I don't like this," she said. "I don't like this at all."

"What don't you like?"

"You come as a stranger and you ask me to tell you my life, my secrets. Why should I?"

Natasha felt she had been getting close, but now the woman was pulling away. Before she could speak, the man who had shown her in entered the room, bowed to Natasha, and put the tea on the table next to her. She inhaled the steam from the tea and smelled the perfumed scent of a strong-steeped Chinese blend. "Mmm," she said, glad of the momentary break from the woman's stern intensity. "Thank you. Smells lovely."

The man bowed again and stood at the foot of the bed, raising an eyebrow to ask if the Snow Leopard would like a cup. She shut her eyes and shook her head. The man pulled the door shut behind him, leaving them alone together.

"Why should I?" said the Snow Leopard as if their conversation had not been broken. "You, a total stranger, come here and I am supposed to tell you my whole life, knowing nothing of you? Why should I allow you to extract from me my secrets?"

"I would tell you about myself," Natasha said calmly, aware that she was about to breach an unwritten professional code, according to which the journalist, like the psychoanalyst, must reveal nothing of herself to the subject. "But there's not much to tell."

"You could tell me how old you are, for a start."

Natasha did not want her answer tape-recorded. As far as her editor knew, she was thirty-two: magazine journalism today was a young woman's business. She returned her cigarettes and lighter to her handbag. If, in order to gain the Snow Leopard's confidence, she must talk about herself, there was no reason why her editor should eavesdrop. "Let's just say I passed my thirtieth birthday a while ago." She switched off the tape-recorder.

"And your thirty-fifth, I would imagine," the woman said.

Natasha tilted her head from side to side in an I-won't-say-yes-and-I-won't-say-no gesture.

"You must be honest with me," the Snow Leopard insisted, but her hard accusing expression had softened. Her face, when relaxed, was warm. "But I'll let you lie about your age. I like that. A woman may always lie about her age."

"And your age?" Natasha risked.

"You're not telling, and neither am I." The woman smiled. "I am as old as this century, and a few years older. How many, I won't say."

"Fair enough." Natasha grinned back.

"Are you married?" the Snow Leopard asked.

"Was. Once. Ten years ago. That's how I came to have the name Waldbauer. But it didn't work. We were both too independent for each other, maybe for anybody." The old woman's eyes seemed to express genuine interest. Natasha found this to be a face she could talk to; this was a woman who understood a lot, having been through a lot herself. "His idea of independence," Natasha continued, "meant other women. Mine meant work, a job, being a person in my own right. Not tied down." She shrugged her shoulders. "We divorced a year after we were married. End of story."

"But not the end of men, I should guess." An almost impish light shone in the old woman's eyes.

"No," Natasha confessed with a soft chuckle. "Not the end of men. I've traveled a lot—before I ended up in New York and got the job at *European Woman,* that is. I was born and raised in England . . ."

"Ah," said the Snow Leopard, "so that's why your American accent is not very strong . . ."

"And after I finished school here," Natasha continued with a nod of agreement, "I lived in Barcelona—that was when I was married to Michael—and after we split up, I got a job at a newspaper in Portugal, then my first magazine assignment in Paris, then Florence . . ."

"A woman of the world!" The Snow Leopard laughed. She had a delightful laugh, throaty but infinitely womanly. "And a lover in every port?"

Natasha, too, laughed. "It's funny, but my memory of each city is completely centered around the man I was with at the time. Barcelona *was* Michael, and Lisbon *was* Antony, and Paris, Adolph, and Florence, Angelo." She shook her head and smiled a far-off smile. "Oh, Angelo."

"And who is New York?"

"New York," Natasha leaned forward, the way she did when she chatted with her friends back home, "is Colum."

"Colum. An interesting name."

"For an interesting man. He's a musician. Very successful. Last month he conducted his own composition at Lincoln Center."

"You must be proud."

"I am." Natasha's face was aglow.

The old woman's expression changed to something resembling cynicism. "And if you and Colum should part from each other, then it would be time to leave New York, as you've left every other city in the past?"

"Perhaps." Natasha lowered her eyes to her hands in her lap. "But I hope this one lasts."

"Then why aren't you married? A young woman like you should be married."

Natasha was flattered to be called young. For years she had felt anything but young.

"Yes, you are young," the Snow Leopard said, reading her mind, "particularly to an old woman like me."

Natasha was startled to be reminded that the vibrant woman in whom she was confiding was indeed old.

The woman continued unperturbed. "If you love the man, marry him."

"It's not as simple as that," Natasha said seriously. "We're both afraid to commit ourselves. Colum's the first to admit that he's terrified of commitment, and I'm not sure I want to give up my independence again. I just . . ."

"Puh!" the Snow Leopard snorted. "The curse of people today. Listen to you. You talk of commitment as if it could kill you: marry each other and the world might end. The difficulty is that there are not enough problems in your life. In my day we had revolutions to think of, and wars. *Real* problems. If you found someone to love, you did not worry about the dreaded risks of commitment.

You were grateful to be alive and to have each other." She looked severely at Natasha. "You are a spoiled generation."

Natasha blinked. She knew the woman was right, but not altogether right. "I've been touched by war, too," she said sadly. "I had no father, not one I ever knew. My mother fell in love with a young Englishman just before the War, and when she got pregnant, he disappeared. They were never married. They were children themselves really. That's what the family solicitor told me years later.

"After I was born, my mother and I lived in the country mostly, not all that far from here. And the rest of the time we'd go up to London and stay with my great-aunt and -uncle." She lifted her eyes to the ceiling. "I had just been sent to boarding school when it happened. I was still a little girl. My mother was in London with her aunt and uncle. It was toward the end of the bombing. It was nearly over. But a bomb hit the house, a direct hit, and killed them all. I spent the rest of my childhood at school and out of term-time at a holiday home. When I came of age, the solicitor handed over the inheritance. But it's not the same as having family. So you see, I do know something about loss and suffering."

"My God." The woman's face was pale, her lips trembling. "My God," she repeated, shaking her head.

Natasha felt exposed. This was most extraordinary, entirely unprofessional, opening her soul to a total stranger. "I don't know why I'm telling you all this," she said.

"Because I understand." The old woman was very clearly upset.

"Well," Natasha said, "I've told you my story. Will you tell me yours?" When the woman looked as if she was about to speak, the professional side of Natasha came to the fore. She pressed the button of her tape-recorder, switching it on once again. But she was careless. As she pulled her hand away, she inadvertently knocked the tape-recorder out of the bag and onto the floor.

"What's that?" the Snow Leopard demanded.

"It's nothing," Natasha said, quickly trying to tuck it away.

"Don't lie to me! I will not be lied to. What is it?"

Natasha held out the machine. "It's a tape-recorder. It's just a memory aid for me when I sit down to write the story."

The Snow Leopard stared at the tape-recorder as if it were a loaded pistol pointed at her. "So that's it, is it?" she said bitterly. "And I thought I could trust you." She lay back against her pillows and shook her head decisively. "There have been many," she said, "who have wanted me dead. Many who wished to kill me. And now you come, you, the writer, to assassinate me with your pen?"

"I'm sorry." Natasha felt sure she had lost this interview for good. "I didn't mean to upset you."

The Snow Leopard turned and seemed to take an interest in the machine. "A tape-recorder, you say? And it's so small. So easy to conceal. We never had such machines when I was young. It would have been very handy."

"Yes, it is. But I don't have to use it." She put it back into her handbag, the record button still depressed.

The Snow Leopard turned away again. "No. It won't do. You do your interview, I tell you my life, and you leave me to die alone, all my secrets gone, stolen from me and given to the world? No. I cannot accept this."

"That's not the only reason I came," Natasha said slowly. She lit a cigarette. She had not planned to say what she was about to say, but she recognized it was her only hope. "There's more. A personal reason. Any other journalist from the office could have come out here instead of me, but I asked to come. There was something I had to find out. You see . . . oh, I hardly know how to put this . . . you see, as I said, I was raised by my mother and her aunt and uncle. But nobody would tell me about my grandparents. They said I was too young. Then after my mother died, the solicitor said that he didn't know a thing. All I was ever told was that I had a grandmother who lived in China. And she had been born in Russia. So when I read the news wire about you, I thought . . ." She paused and took a puff from her cigarette. "But it isn't possible. How could it be? But I had to come anyway." She looked into the face of the mysterious woman lying on the magnificent Chinese bed. Her heart raced, as it had when she walked to the cottage, when she stood at the bedroom door. "Are you my grandmother?" she said at last.

The Snow Leopard lay silent. She was still upset, but color had returned to her cheeks. "My God," she said to the canopy over her bed. Then she turned to Natasha and her face relaxed. "Natasha," she said, her voice more gentle than it had been since they met. "Drink your tea." She smiled. "And I will tell you a story."

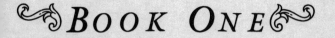

BOOK ONE

The
Nightingale

CHAPTER 1

Sophia was hunting wild pig with her father. At such times in her life she could have burst with happiness. She, dressed in a blue riding habit, cantered beside him. Her father, who loved his clothes, wore a riding doublet and hose, his feet shod in the smooth polished leather of riding boots. Behind them the courtiers kept a respectful distance. The air was light. Little shafts of sunlight pierced through the thick canopy of the dark pine forest. There was a smell of autumn and pine needles. Sophia loved the forest. As the hunting party passed the huts of the peasants who lived on the estate a few miles from St. Petersburg, the peasants touched their foreheads—while no one starved on the Oblimov estate, there were terrible tales of starvation and cruelty elsewhere in Russia.

Sophia sometimes bitterly envied the young children as they ran free in their serfdom. They worked in the fields, but they knew a freedom she did not, for the life of a young countess in the court of the Tsar was highly regimented and very lonely. Often she felt like a caged bird. The ribs of her cage were golden and the drinking cup made of silver, but still it was a cage and she was eternally bound by rules of conduct.

Her thoughts were interrupted by the long wailing sound of the horns.

"Sophia." Count Oblimov grinned at his beloved daughter. "Are you ready?"

Count Oblimov's horse was an ebony stallion. The huge arched neck was straining at the reins and the fierce wild eyes rolled. Sophia was riding Wild Bird, a small bay but fast.

"Let's go!"

She felt her horse tense under her, and then came the glorious moment when she and her father bounded across the forest together, joined in their mutual excitement of the hunt.

The forest suddenly filled with the sound of drumming hooves. "This way! This way!" called the huntsman. The hounds bayed with one voice.

Sophia stood paralyzed behind the thick velvet curtains in her father's library and listened to her father making love to his present mistress. The countess reached a sobbing crescendo and then both partners lay silent. "Petruskova, my darling," she heard her father whisper, "you're so lovely." Sophia thought she would faint. Peering out from behind the curtains, she saw her father rise from the long sofa. She heard the swish of silk and the sound of footsteps receding, and then the bang of the big black library door shutting out the daylight. The long low-ceilinged room was now empty, the air slightly perfumed. Sophia heaved a sigh.

Alone now in the library, she remembered the moment of the boar's death in yesterday's hunt. Pinned to the ground by shafts of steel, the boar lay helpless, his tusks useless, his legs broken. There was fury in his wild yellow eyes and Sophia thought she saw regret. Then with a last twitch he was dead, the eyes no longer alight . . .

Feeling the sudden need to find Elena, Sophia ran out of the library and down the long unlit corridors until she arrived breathless in Elena's bedroom.

"Where have you been, Sophia? Mother's been looking for you."

Sophia hung her head. "Oh, in the library. Reading." She raised her dark eyes and stared at her twin who, like herself, was in the early bloom of young womanhood but had yet to lose fully the smooth and unblemished face of childhood. The girls' features were identical, their eyes set wide apart above strong cheekbones. There was a hint of a slant to the corners of their eyes, the trace of some early Mongolian ancestry. But while Sophia's hair was so brown as to seem almost black, Elena's was soft and golden, the color of orange-blossom honey. Perhaps it was the luminous waves of Elena's hair that gave her a gentler, more peaceful appearance than Sophia, who looked intense and mysterious. Often Sophia thought that should she herself die and become an angel, shedding the dark colors of earth for a brighter, more heavenly radiance, then her resemblance to Elena would be complete.

Elena saw her sister's stare and she smiled. "You're always reading. Anyway," she said, "we have to get ready to go shopping."

Sophia slumped her shoulders. "I hate shopping. Can't you do it for me?"

"Mother says you have to come. We must choose material for our ball-gowns."

"Balls, balls, balls," Sophia said, collapsing into the soft pillows of a chaise longue. "Really, I'd much rather hunt than dance with silly vacuous boys at these beastly balls everyone keeps giving."

"But Sophia," Elena laughed, "that's where you will meet your future husband."

Sophia shrugged. "I am not getting married. I want to do something with my life. It's all right for you, Elena. You just want to get married and have six children. I want adventure." She walked to the large square window of the castle. The walls were thick and warm from the sun. She put her hand on the deep window sill and looked out. Outside, men were rolling the grass between the castle and its fortressed ramparts. Seen from above they looked like a swarm of ants. Faraway dots moved in the fields against a sky that grew dark and cloudy at the horizon, threatening an autumn storm. It was harvest time, with hay wains and apple smells. "For us nothing changes," Sophia said. "Nothing. Outside, people live and die, seasons change. We just go on eternally the same. The same balls, the same people, just a change of clothes."

"Oh, don't be so morbid," Elena said with a light laugh. "It's really not as bad as all that. I hear Mother coming. And you know how much she loves to shop."

Countess Isobel Oblimova opened the door. From the day they were born, the twins had taken two different paths. Elena had been a sunny, plump, loving baby, Sophia, a tense, sometimes wild, child. From the beginning, Elena's affection had gravitated toward her mother, Sophia's toward her father. Now as she considered her two daughters, Countess Oblimova smiled. She said, "I don't suppose, Sophia, you are looking forward to a little shopping. But I have a consolation surprise for you." Sophia looked into the gentle gray eyes she had so often caused to look hurt. "We're going to have dinner with Grandmother."

Sophia gave a whoop of joy. Elena frowned. Elena was a little frightened of her grandmother.

"Let's go!" Sophia shot down the stairs, sliding down the banisters and landing in a breathless heap on the floor of the great hall. Ha! she thought. Grandmother. That's more like it.

A very long time ago, Sophia had pledged her fierce young heart to her grandmother. Her grandfather was dead, assassinated many years ago by a revolutionary who believed the only way to deal with aristocrats was to kill them. Grief at his loss lined her beloved grandmother's face, which so resembled her own. Whenever Sophia was unruly and badly behaved, Countess Oblimova called in the child's grandmother. As she slowly descended the stairway, the Countess said, "Sometimes I think Sophia was bred by the devil."

Sophia hopped into the carriage and leaned back against the seat. Dinner with Grandmother. She felt hungry already.

As the carriage set off toward St. Petersburg, Sophia gazed eagerly out the window and watched the long streets race by, while Elena sat demurely beside her. Countess Oblimova smiled. Here were the two prettiest girls in all of Russia. Her girls.

"I want to wear black." Sophia was in an obstinate mood. "I'm tired of blues and pinks and silly pastel colors. I want to wear black."

The Countess had had this discussion many times in the past. "Darling, you cannot wear black. Black is for mourning or for widows."

"Please, please, Mother. Let me wear black. It suits me. Look." She took a swag of black silk and bunched it under her chin. "See how it makes my eyes light up?" She twisted her sinuous body into the coils of the material. "Watch." Sophia swept up the narrow corridor between the shelves stacked high with fabrics from China, Tibet and Europe. She turned to face her mother and her sister. "Let me wear black."

Both the Countess and Elena were shaken by the look on Sophia's face. Behind the innocent mask of a teenage girl they could see the woman she was going to be. Her hair, a raven wonder, fell to her waist. Her eyes, slanted like her grandmother's, spoke of strong unawakened desire. Her mouth was almost cruel in its sensual outline, her body slender and curved like the fluted glasses from which she drank.

Her mother shuddered. "Sophia . . ." she said.

"I will wear black," Sophia said in a tone that brooked no objection.

"You'll be the talk of St. Petersburg," said Elena. "They'll all gossip about you."

"Let them. Why should I care?"

"Oh, Sophia, why can't you be like everybody else?" Countess Oblimova's tone was despairing. "Why must you always embarrass me?"

"Mother, I did not come into this world to be like everybody else. I am Sophia Oblimova and I am different." She smiled. "Anyway, it's decided. Let's go and have dinner. Grandmother will understand."

Elena trailed behind her mother and her sister, carrying the material she had chosen. I wish I could be like that, she thought. I always feel so gray when Sophia is about. She has such life in her, and no doubts. I doubt everything . . .

Elena's material was a soft shade of pale blue. She knew it would bring out the fair coloring of her skin. Although as comely as her sister, Elena believed Sophia to be the more beautiful. Elena's beauty was shy and reticent, a beauty which she herself could not perceive. But other people saw her loveliness, which had the quality of spring in the countryside, or of a crescent moon. The mere sight of her gave joy to her parents, particularly her mother, although her deeply sensitive nature occasionally irritated her father: her concern for all living things, her care for the children on their estates, her tears when a baby died. Yet in the poise of her body and in those gentle slender hands a fierceness equal to Sophia's lay dormant, still unguessed at by she who possessed it.

Unlike Sophia, Elena had no need for adventure. All she wanted was to fall in love and to live happily ever after. Why was Sophia not content, Elena wondered as she followed her sister out to the carriage. They had everything anyone could want: loving parents, a life rich in leisure and culture, balls, dinners, boys who were interested in them, and girl-friends with whom they could giggle. She shrugged as her footman helped her into the carriage. Only Sophia did not giggle with them. Elena gazed at her sister's enraptured face. Why did she have to live life so vehemently? Elena lay back her head and closed her eyes. Sophia so tires one out, she thought.

❦ CHAPTER 2 ❧

The road to the Countess Anna Oblimova's residence was deeply rutted. The rain that had been hovering on the horizon had come down on the city of St. Petersburg with sudden wilful force. The carriage bumped and crashed through the mire. Through the gilt window the girls saw the thin shivering figures of the starving men, women and children who lived and died on the city streets.

The family's religious confessor, Father Ivan, had told them that these unfortunates deserved to die and that they were doomed to an eternity in hell. Had these people regularly attended the Russian Orthodox churches, said their prayers, eaten only fish on Friday, their lives might have been otherwise.

Sophia did not know what to think about these paupers. They half-frightened her, the way they ran after the carriage, their skinny arms outstretched and long-taloned hands raking at the windows, the men cursing and spitting as the footmen beat them off with their whips. Ten years ago, only one footman clung to the back of the carriage to guard the passengers. Now two rode in the front and three at the back. Elena found all these trips deeply distressing. She loved the peasants who worked for the Oblimov family and cared deeply for her people—this was how she thought of the workers on the estate. She and her mother fed, clothed and visited each family. They were both much loved; so too was Sophia, but many of the workers were a little alarmed at Sophia's moods. Elena they regarded as a saint, like her mother.

Now Elena watched and winced. There was trouble brewing—not just the usual trouble that always existed between the poor and the rich. Now there was the possibility of an imminent revolution. In recent years there had been rumors and arrests. Bodies blackened by decay regularly swung in the main square of St. Petersburg. Elena could not bring herself to look at them, but Sophia stared. So that was what it was like to be dead. Hideous faces stared back at her, the sockets empty where ravens had torn out the eyeballs. Sophia was fascinated by death. She read all she could about it and from her grandmother she learned the art of the poisoner.

Now on the way to the Oblimov mansion, she recalled the poison that once had been the talk of the Russian court: a toxin taken from a pufferfish was rubbed on the victim's skin, causing the victim to fall into a state of suspended animation. Believed to be dead, he was taken away by the grieving family and buried. Several days later the poisoner was able to dig up the body and then administer a powerful datura potion that brought on unimaginable mind-twisting hallucinations. From then onward, the victim became one of the legion of the damned, with no will or mind of his own, forever doomed to obey the will of the poisoner.

Grandmother had one such near victim in her household, a dwarf called Misha. She had heard of his poisoning and burial from a maid. The maid was in tears because her cousin Misha had upset an eminent physician at the Tsar's court. Old Countess Oblimova, who had heard of the practice in her travels abroad, hurried to the grave with her attendants. She had saved the dwarf's life and now in return he shuffled and scraped along behind her, his powerful arms nearly brushing the floor, his bulging eyes gazing at her with adoration.

Sophia loved Misha. Often, when she was troubled with her mighty rages, it was Misha who could comfort her. He stroked her with his long arms and hugged her. He dried her tears and told her stories and made her laugh. She was looking forward to seeing him again.

At last the mansion gates came into view. Sophia relaxed. The contrast with the grim crowded streets when the carriage swung into the great courtyard always seemed to her miraculous. One moment all was death and dying, the next the world reformed into the calm elegance of a well-ordered mansion.

It was a contrast that tended to give Elena a headache. "Are you all right, my dear?" Her mother leaned forward, took Elena's hand and squeezed it. "I know," she said, understanding her daughter absolutely. "I know how you feel. The times are dreadful. The Russian nobles have lost touch with their own people. While we, as a family, are at one with the people on our estate, it is not like that any more on other estates. The aristocrats have forgotten their duty to serve. Now they think of nothing but drinking and dancing. So sad, so sad." She frowned, thinking of the troubling early-morning talk she had had with her husband. He was worried, and Boris Oblimov was not a man much given to worrying. Isobel felt a shiver race down her back.

Elena pressed her mother's hand. "Come," she said, "let's try to forget the world for the moment and just enjoy the evening."

Sophia threw her bonnet and gloves at one of the servants who had come out to greet them, and ran into the mansion. "Grandmother! Grandmother, I'm here!" As she flew across the hall and up the grand staircase she was joined by Misha. He had been waiting for Sophia all day. She gave him a rapturous hug and hand in hand the little shambling dwarf and the young girl ran to find Countess Anna Oblimova.

Father Ivan rarely left Anna's side. He had much to thank her for. He was the son of a poor trader on one of her country estates. Forty years earlier, Anna had seen the small boy who was Ivan running like a wolf-cub in the wake of her carriage. He had asked for nothing. He merely ran because he loved to run. When her carriage drew up at the country house she owned, he stood there, bright-eyed and puffing. Anna sensed a challenge from this child. He was ten. They exchanged inquiring glances and then Anna invited him into the house. The boy looked about him and then startled Anna by saying, "When can I come and live with you?"

Anna was so surprised she said, "Any time you are ready."

"Good," the boy said and ran off into the forest, returning with a small bundle of clothes. He had little to leave behind. Both his parents were dead of typhoid. He lived with an old uncle. "One less mouth to feed" was his uncle's grumbled good-bye.

From then on Ivan lived as a member of Anna's family. It was Ivan who comforted Anna when her husband died and who stayed with her in those dark months when she did not believe she could survive the pain. To Boris, the son Anna had borne so late in life, Ivan was like a brother. In later years Boris would confess his womanizing to Ivan, and Ivan forgave him on behalf of the Lord. Ivan himself had no time for women. His love for Anna was a pure and holy love for a woman who had in her time achieved greatness.

When the Tsar called Anna "the Golden Salamander," he was only half-joking. Like so many men before him, he was in love with Anna. After the death of her husband many men aspired to marry her, imagining that the legendary woman would need a man to replace the one she had lost. But Ivan knew that this would never be so. Whatever fire and passion had fueled her marriage to her husband now was extinct. Her beauty had not faded, nor did her humor leave her. But a hint of sadness in her eyes and a certain cooling of her vivacity made Ivan realize there were some men who could never be replaced. Instead Anna lavished all her love on her two granddaughters.

Today Anna spent time with the cooks ordering the girls' favorite dishes. Chocolate for Sophia, sorbets for Elena, and, for her daughter-in-law Isobel, lobster. She hoped that Boris would arrive in time to sit down to dinner, a rare treat these days when the news was so bad that Boris's chair, inherited from his father, was often empty.

Boris arrived after the lobster had been served. Isobel was relieved to see that her husband looked considerably more cheerful than earlier in the day. Having kissed his mother, then his wife, Boris slid into his chair. "What's the next course?" he asked. "I'm starving. I've been sitting all afternoon with the Tsar and that dreadful wife of his. She's completely mad, you know. Since when did women run this country? I tell you, she will be the downfall of us all." A silence followed this remark and hung over the table.

"Darling," Anna said, "shall we leave politics outside the door?"

Boris grinned. "Come on, Mother. You know that as soon as the girls leave you'll grill me."

Anna nodded. "But until then, shall we enjoy the food?"

Footmen entered the dining room with huge silver salvers of roast chicken, duck, mutton and lamb. A contented quiet fell upon the room. Sophia cut choice bits of meat from her plate to feed to Misha, who sat contentedly on the floor by her chair. "So," Anna asked her granddaughters, "what are we wearing to the Kolinsky ball?"

"Black," said Sophia, knowing her grandmother doted on her and would approve of anything she said.

"I see." Anna raised her eyebrows. "We are going to look different, aren't we?"

Sophia laughed. "Yes, but then remember the ball you told me about when you were just eighteen and they carried you in on pillows made of gold cloth and you were painted gold with nothing on?"

Anna smiled. "Yes, I do," she said. "Oh my! The court whispered of nothing else for days! My mother was furious. That was when your grandfather fell in love with me, you know."

The girls nodded. They knew well the story that

had become part of the rich tapestry of court history. Elena was not so sure that she approved of her grandmother's conduct, but she smiled. No wonder Sophia is so wild, she thought. Grandmother only encourages her.

Isobel also smiled, secretly hoping that Anna would not suggest her daughter behave in the same way. "Madame," she said respectfully, "please don't fill Sophia with any more ideas than she already has. We have trouble enough with her as it is."

Boris nodded. "Mind you," he said, "she is a wonder to ride with." Sophia turned to her father. She was at that golden age in a young life when a father knows he will lose his girl to another man. In Sophia's face Boris saw such passion, such capacity for pain and for power, he was frightened. He also knew of the warmth within her, that part of her that remained innocent, for all the sophistication she believed herself to possess (really just precociousness, he told himself). She was like a brave yet fragile bird with a proud song and a quickly beating heart. Who would hold his little nightingale? Now, in the warm room filled with people who loved both girls, he hoped with all his heart that the threatened revolution would recede into the darkness whence it had sprung and leave his beloved Mother Russia to continue on her course. But he knew that the Tsar was weak and ineffectual. He knew the Tsarina Alexandra to be a wicked and cold woman who cared nothing for her people. The future did not look good.

Count Boris Oblimov sat and joked with his

mother, patted his wife's hand, and laughed with his daughters. I'm a lucky man, he thought. Elena, his bright shining moon, his consolation when he was depressed, his archangel, smiled at him. He felt blessed indeed this day. The tension left his neck and shoulders and he undid his belt after the sumptuous meal.

Isobel and the girls left the room, with Misha following. Boris and Father Ivan sat alone with the Countess, who leaned forward on her elbows. Ivan sat beside her, his long legs outstretched. "What's the news?" Anna's voice was terse and questioning.

"Not good," Boris reported. "Everything seems to be crumbling. The heads of Central Europe become more restless by the day, but the unrest here is even worse. Discontent is growing all the time. We should have learned our lesson seven years ago on that awful Sunday at the Winter Palace. We had our moment then. I still think Witte's plan for civil liberties would have worked, given half a chance. What a fool His Royal Spinelessness the Tsar was to bring in that murderous bastard Piotr Arkadevich Stolypin and put down the Duma that would have given the people their only opportunity to have some say in the government of their country. I tell you frankly, mother, I smiled all the way through Stolypin's funeral last year. I wished I could have given his assassin a medal. But, of course, such things cannot be said openly.

"The Tsar's pig-headedness will get us all killed. And behind it all stands his damned wife." A grunt escaped the Count's sadly smiling lips.

"It's that woman. Really, Mother, I wish you could concoct some potion or poison to take care of her."

"Don't think I haven't thought of it myself." Anna laughed. "Many times. But she is too well guarded. The kitchen staff taste everything before the food goes up, and then the court physician tastes everything again before it passes her lips."

Boris made a face. "She will be the death of us all if she is not stopped. She has no feeling for the suffering of the people. How can any woman be so heartless as not to see the dreadful famine in her own country? So many of the landlords leave their estates to rot and the peasants to starve. They make no attempt to care for anybody. Their lives are devoted to pleasure. They are nothing but drunken bloated animals. This is not the Russia I once believed in.

"Mark my words: Bloody Sunday will prove to be just a small taste of what is to come. But this time the rebels will be far more organized. People are arriving from America, from England, people who will institute a reign of terror. These anarchists with their misguided ideas about freedom—who is to pay for all this freedom? And these Bolsheviks who want to organize everything down to the last rusty nail—they preach no freedom, just a new kind of enslavement to the state. I can only pray the Russian people won't stand for any of it." He frowned.

Ivan nodded. "Well, we may get a dictator out of all this, a man prepared to use force and to see blood run in order to subdue a nation like ours. I wouldn't want to live to see it, though."

Anna put her hand on Ivan's arm. "Whatever happens now, we must think of the girls. They must have a future."

"What do you mean, Mother?" Boris's tone of voice changed.

"Darling," Anna replied, "we all must see our destiny through. It is our duty. But if it gets too dangerous, we will have to send the girls away. That is our duty to them."

The idea of life without his girls was unthinkable for Boris. "Perhaps I've been too pessimistic," he said suddenly. "It's not nearly that serious yet."

"No," Anna agreed. "Not yet."

❧ *CHAPTER 3* ❧

The room was now empty, the dishes cleared, the lights lowered. Anna was in bed. Boris kissed the dear familiar face. "Good night, my darling," he whispered tenderly, feeling the pang in his heart of a man who loves his mother more deeply than he could ever love any other woman, except his daughters. Anna was incomparable. Other women faded into pale insignificance beside her, the fabulous Golden Salamander, the beautiful, imperious, joyous creature who was his mother.

She was drowsing as he left the room and

walked quickly down the well-remembered corridors of his boyhood to his waiting family. The carriage pulled away, the footmen well armed and watchful. St. Petersburg was no place for the rich at night.

As they left, the head cook was selling off the piles of uneaten food at the back door of the kitchen. The bins outside the mansion were piled high with the day's food and the wretched and the despairing were snarling and snatching among the sodden remnants for an evening meal.

All over the city starving wretches scrabbled for something to eat. Women with breasts puckered from lack of milk scavenged with the ferocity of the gutter animals that competed with them. For the poor, rats were often a staple, and cats too—anything to assuage the pains of hunger that led people to kill over scraps of food. Meanwhile, in the palaces and the great houses of St. Petersburg, the rich slept replete.

All except for the Tsar's wife, who lay awake, turning over in her mind the meeting that day with her adviser Grigori Efimovich Rasputin, the mad monk of Russia. The Tsarina Alexandra was still infatuated with Rasputin, after he had made great show of healing her hemophiliac son, the Tsarevich. Today, despotic maniac that he was, the dark monk had prophesied war in Europe.

"War," the Tsarina murmured. "Let there be war."

War, Rasputin advised her, would distract the people, the insane, monstrous evil of war uniting all it threatened. Russia, faced with a war, would forget its divisions and cheer itself onto the spiked guns of its opponents. The trouble-makers could be sent to the front. Whatever the outcome of the conflict, millions of the cities' poor would die.

The Tsarina fondly recalled the priest's smile as he kissed her hands, the blood of millions of Russians on his lips.

As day broke, at last she slept.

Sophia was feeling impatient. All day long she lay about her bedroom. The morning finally passed, but the afternoon seemed to drag on as if a mule were tied to the back of time and refused to budge. Ivan came to tutor both girls most mornings, but this particular morning he was called away by the Tsar. There had been a big uprising in the north, leaving many dead. A division of the Tsar's soldiers were talking of mutiny. They were refusing to turn and shoot their own people.

Neither girl was thinking about the poor. Tonight was the Kolinsky ball, for Elena an opportunity for triumph, for Sophia a chance to tease a little the young men of her acquaintance. "I need a much older man, you know, Elena. I am too bored by these young men with no chins and spots on their faces."

"Oh, come now, Sophia. They don't all have spots on their faces."

"I see, you're talking about that frightfully proper Englishman, Sir Edward Gray."

"No, I'm not," said Elena. "Anyway, he really is too old for you."

Sophia looked at her twin sister, her eyes full of laughter. "Dare me. Go on, dare me."

Elena shook her delicate head. "No, I won't dare you. I don't need to. You're going to chase him whether I dare you or not, aren't you?"

"I suppose so. Anyway, I need to practice my English."

And for the next hour the girls spoke to each other about this and that in their best English with their finest British accents. Having been tutored since early youth by private teachers, Sophia and Elena could switch from Russian to English and from English to French or Italian as easily as two musicians finishing a piece of Handel might continue with a work by Corelli or Rameau. The girls spoke each language correctly, with no lack of fluency but with the most charming and subtle trace of the throaty speech characteristic of the Russian tongue.

But even when they had finished practicing their languages for the evening's party, still too many hours remained before ball-gowns could be donned and perfume applied to freshly washed necks. Sophia ran up and down the corridors, in and out of rooms. She bullied the maids and the servants. "Bring me tea." "Bring me bread." "Hurry, hurry, hurry." Time refused to yield.

She ran out to the stables and saddled her bay mare. "Let's go!" she yelled. "Let's go." The farm workers saw her go by. Horse and rider looked as if they were on wings. She galloped down the main highway into the forest. Finally the horse stood winded in a clearing in the thickest part of the forest. Before her squatted a small hut. A young woman stood at the door with three children clinging to her rags. She was wringing her hands in fear. "I won't hurt you," Sophia said gently. "What's the matter? Why are you so frightened?"

"Some people have just been this way, my lady. They talk of bad things. Of guns and revolution . . ."

Sophia snorted. "It's only talk," she said, longing to get away. Why, she thought, must life always be so full of unhappy contrasts? What started off as a fantastic gallop in the beautiful countryside now ended in front of a sour-smelling peasant's hut. Why was life not like the bucolic paintings that hung on the walls of the palace? There the peasants looked fat, pink and happy.

Turning her horse, Sophia waved goodbye and rode home. She was gratified to find that the time had edged forward by several hours. Now she could curl up in the library with a forbidden book. Boris had several shelves of literature that he considered too advanced for Sophia's young eyes. The name Théophile Gautier was strictly unspoken, but today Sophia was determined to read *Mademoiselle de Maupan.*

Underneath the shelves were cupboards closed and clandestine but Sophia knew the contents. Figures of men and women carved into lustful juxtapositions. Breasts, buttocks, thighs, all straining in a permanent frenzy of lust. How does it really feel? she wondered. Today however she was going to explore the new book.

Hoisting herself behind drawn curtains onto her

favorite windowledge, Sophia began to read. She failed to hear her father's footsteps as hurriedly he entered with a crowd of men. Sophia peeped through a slit in the curtains. "I tell you," her father was saying angrily, "the Tsar must leave or we cannot be responsible for what may happen. If we can just get them out of the country for a while, the fighting might stop."

"But we need him if there is to be a war," said another voice, quiet and hesitant. "Besides, where can we send them? All of Europe is taking up arms."

This was the first time Sophia had heard a tone of despair in her father's voice. Trouble among the peasants had been a common occurrence in her life, rather like the measles or the typhoid that scourged region after region in this massive sprawling country. Now, listening to the voices, urgent and prophetic, Sophia felt afraid. She waited until the men had moved to another room and then she quietly slipped the grown-up book back onto its place on the shelf.

In her bedroom she rang the bell for Katrina, her nurse. "Hot water," she said, "and lots of it." After her bath she would emerge like a moth from a chrysalis and pour herself into her beautiful black ball-gown, and then she would become the fabulous Sophia Oblimova, the toast of the ball.

She shut her eyes and admitted to herself that it was Elena who was usually the toast of the ball. Dear, good, kind Elena gracefully swam into ball-rooms like a beautiful goldfish. One flicker of her gentle eyes and men were reduced to quivering heaps of longing, filled with a pure love. Many a young man secretly imagined himself asking Count Oblimov for his daughter Elena's hand in marriage. Sophia knew that most of the young men, though they flirted with her, would never dream of a life with Sophia Oblimova, nor she with them.

Sophia lay back in the clear water glistening with bath oil and dreamed of the day when a man would love her with a true and eternal love.

🦢 CHAPTER 4 🦢

Really, Sir Edward Gray thought, bowing his way down the receiving line. The Russians can be such a bunch of barbarians. Sir Edward winced as yet another member of the royal court received his hand and blew garlic in his face. Coldly Sir Edward's hooded eyes glanced around the room. And then he saw Anna accompanied by the rest of the Oblimov family. He beamed. Anna was the one Russian woman whom he wholeheartedly admired. They had known each other for years, and Boris and he shared a passion for hunting. He could see also that the two young girls were growing up to be a credit to their grandmother. He pushed his way through the thronged ballroom and took Anna's hand.

"My, Sir Edward." Anna smiled. "Where have

you been for the last six months? We've missed you."

"I had to return to England for further instructions." Sir Edward caught Boris's eye. They both knew what those instructions were, but tonight was no time for pessimism. Sophia curtsied and imagined herself in Sir Edward's lingering embrace. He was tall and slim. His dark eyes twinkled with amusement and his mouth was firm. He had a quality not to be found among the Russian men of Sophia's acquaintance. His calm and formal manner belied, so she believed, a warm and passionate heart. Besides, he could ride. How he could ride! Sophia often hung out of her bedroom window to watch Sir Edward and her father set out to go hunting, her father dressed in his gorgeous silks of red and gold, and the Englishman riding in a black jacket and a hard black hat. Somehow her father, his head uncovered, shouting with pleasure to the rest of his entourage, looked a little flamboyant compared with the quiet trim figure whose only show of emotion was to tap his riding crop on the elegant leather of his boots. Oh, to be thrown across the saddle by this man, and to ride into the night with him . . .

Sophia realized that her grandmother was laughing at her. "Come along, little one," she said. "You're dreaming again."

Sophia arched her eyebrows and nodded. "You're right, Grandmother. I am dreaming. I shall always dream, until I am old enough to do what I want. And then," she looked up at Sir Edward from under her long lashes, "I shall be free."

The musicians began to tune up for a waltz. There was an excited flurry as the men claimed their dancing partners. Elena stood next to her grandmother, watching her mother and father take the floor.

How diverse were the people of Russia, she thought. She saw that the guests included Muscovites, Turks, Ukrainians and Georgians (such a different people, big and bear-like); Novgorod, Smolensk and Jaruslav were also represented. Elena shook her head. How on earth could anyone whisper of a revolution that would combine all these different peoples into one united entity?

Elena marveled at the glitter and beauty of the ballroom. She knew that each ball of this kind occupied many working hands, months before the great castles opened their doors. Silversmiths and silk merchants as far away as Tashkent, vendors of furs and of leopard skins from Tibet, of diamonds from Siberia, gold from the east, and rubies from India.

Sir Edward bowed in front of Elena and said, "Shall we dance, my pretty little one?" He took her by the waist and they floated into the crowd.

Anna, with Misha clearing the way for her, moved to a small throne-like chair. Her dancing days were over, but the music and the excitement in the air had brought two bright pink spots to her cheeks. Once she was seated, Misha looked about for a glass of champagne for his mistress. Anna sipped and watched her granddaughters: Elena, so small and fragile in Sir Edward's arms, and then Sophia in the arms of a young Russian guardsman,

looking splendid in his red uniform and cummer-
bund. Sophia danced like a wild bird. Anna sighed.
She had no worries about Elena, but Sophia . . .
She knew her granddaughter and she also knew
that much of Sophia's passionate rebellious ways
were hers.

Misha crouched by Anna's chair, watching over
both girls intently, particularly Sophia. This young
man means no harm, Misha assured himself,
though he did not like the potential cruelty that
flashed in his eyes.

Anna sat quietly. For years she had been a close
confidante of the Tsar. Recognizing him as weak,
diffident, and deeply dependent on his wife, Anna
had tried to help him, but to no avail. The deep
love that Anna had for her people did not strike
a common chord with the Tsar. She worried now,
thinking of the girls' future. For her, at eighty-five,
time was now to be counted not in years but in
months, and soon in days. The future of Russia
would be in the hands of men such as Boris and
Sir Edward.

Anna watched Elena and Sir Edward finish their
waltz. Sir Edward bowed as the music ceased;
Elena dropped a shy curtsy. Together they walked
back to Anna's chair. Anna hoped she could as-
sume that Sophia too was being escorted back to
her place within the family. Misha looked up at
Anna and she nodded. Joyfully Misha bounded off
to find his young mistress.

"Oh, Misha, do leave me alone! I am having
fun." Indeed she was. For all that she liked to complain about the lack of real men at balls such as

this, Sophia was now surrounded by a group of the young guardsman's friends and could not help but enjoy their attentions. "I'll be along in a minute."

Misha would have none of it. "Now, now," he insisted. "Come now." He pulled at Sophia's hand.

"What's that?" One of the young men pointed at Misha.

Suddenly Sophia was furious. "Don't you dare speak of Misha like that! You or any one of you silly idiots! Come, Misha." Taking Misha by the hand, she ran back into the stultifying safety of her family.

And the night whirled on. For a while Sophia sat next to her grandmother, watching the carousel of dancers and diners, lovers and mistresses. Sophia saw her father's latest mistress fly by in the arms of another man. What a stupid way to live, Sophia thought: always depending on a man to keep you, always waiting like a goat with a tether around her neck, vulnerable and afraid. For now, Petruskova could bask in the knowledge that she had an Oblimov for a lover but soon, Sophia knew, Boris would tire of her and then the months would go by when she was no longer received. The footmen would politely refuse her entry and letters would be returned to her unopened. What a way to live.

Sophia promised herself that when she grew up she would not owe her freedom to a man. Her freedom would be hers and hers alone. And when she did look for a man, she would choose a mature man like Sir Edward, not a young fool like the guardsmen over there, some of whom were already quite drunk and causing a disturbance.

Then the Kazakhs, the roughest of the officers, yelled a challenge to the Georgians. Two chains formed and the men began to dance and sing. They sang from the depths of the blackness and sorrow that was the Russian soul. Only Russians can sing like that, thought Sir Edward.

Sophia stood on tiptoe, straining to see, and then caught her father's eye. He, knowing his nightingale, nodded and Sophia started to sing. It took time for the assembled guests to realize what was happening but soon ears began to listen. She was known in St. Petersburg for her glorious singing. Nor was it out of place tonight. As the men danced and sang, her pure strong voice soared above theirs. She was no longer Sophia; she was the voice of Russia.

As the last notes of her song died Sophia relaxed into her father's arms. "What a child," he said, looking down at her.

Sophia smiled. "I am not a child any longer, Father. I am a woman now."

Boris was startled. "I think," he said, "it is time to go home." All the way home he wondered what sort of woman this child of his would become.

It was late that night when he was ready for sleep. In his mind he saw a picture that he would take to his grave, of Sophia singing in her pure strong voice.

In the bedroom of her own mansion, Anna said

good night to Father Ivan. "And you know, Ivan, Sir Edward was quite taken with Elena."

The priest laughed. "You are a wise old woman, Anna, but isn't he a little old, and she too young?"

"Of course," Anna said. "Yet the heart knows little of age. Good night, dear one."

"Good night."

Anna was tired, but not too tired to remember to pray. Misha took his place on a fur on the floor beside her bed. Dear, dear Misha, who grunted and snored during the night, chased away the awful loneliness. She fell asleep before finishing her prayers.

Both girls lay on Sophia's bed. The bed was a wide mahogany four-poster. The tapestries, fashioned by her mother and grandmother with the help of sewing women, depicted fat rosy cupids and a variety of women lolling about in their boudoirs, pink and white shoulders rising out of ivory robes, garlanded girls leaning against trees. The tapestries gave the room a vernal look. The moon, high in the clouds, shone down on the girls and cast its milky light on their limbs. Their clothes lay discarded on the floor, a heap of frothy silk that stirred slightly in the breeze from the open window. Sophia lay with her back cradled to her sister's side, her knees tucked up to cover her belly. Sophia often needed the comfort of her sister's warm body. Rarely did she sleep alone in her bed. Usually it was she who crossed the corridor to climb into her sister's bed, but tonight both girls had been in Sophia's room, discussing the evening's events. Elena, tired, had fallen asleep first. Sophia, however, was restless. Her singing had discomforted her. Why can't I be like Elena and take things calmly, she thought.

Finally she did sleep. Night owls hooted in the bushes outside. "Trust the night," they seemed to call. "Trust the night."

❧ CHAPTER 5 ❧

Nurse Katrina walked into Sophia's bedroom the morning after the ball. She often found the girls lying together, their arms wrapped around each other. Quickly she twitched a cover over them and bent to retrieve the clothes flung so casually on the floor. Katrina was a big, six-foot, plump woman from Georgia. Like all Georgians, she felt superior to other Russians. The Georgians were a proud earthy people, living on rich fertile land.

Katrina had loved her girls from the moment she set eyes on the pair, years ago. I love them as though they were my very own, she thought as she stood holding the ball-gowns in her heavy hands. Katrina never thought of love for herself, never imagined marriage. Like so many of her impoverished women friends, her future was to serve the rich. Katrina was not bitter about this. She had her own room here, something she had not dreamed of as a child living in the one-room shack that had been her family home. There had never been any attempt to educate her. Had she stayed with her family, the chances were that her drunken violent father would have sold her off to one of his cronies or exchanged her for a cow. She would have been beaten and abused and forced into unwanted pregnancies. The women in such marriages rated lower than the beasts of burden they cared for. Beating, even killing, was not uncommon. No one questioned a man's authority over his wife and children. Katrina knew she was much better off here.

Elena stirred in her sleep. A deep child, that one, Katrina thought. Much deeper than anyone realizes. As a young girl, if Elena was hurt she showed little sign of it on her face. But Katrina, who would pick her up and straighten her skirts, could feel the soft flutter of distress run through the child's small body. Sophia took any fall personally and kicked and screamed defiantly. Sometimes Katrina could hardly believe they were both born of the same mother, never mind at the same time.

Today was Sunday and it was Katrina's job to get the girls ready for the Russian Orthodox service at the cathedral in St. Petersburg. She woke her charges. Sophia was cross and petulant, Elena resigned.

Father Ivan's sermons could be guaranteed to rivet the good burghers of the city to their seats. Ivan, who heard all the confessions of St. Petersburg's most eminent citizens, withheld from public knowledge none of the goings-on of the truly rich and powerful. Many a flushed face would stare at the prelate, hoping that no brother or sister in Christ would identify him with the sins being denounced from the pulpit.

The girls stood piously by their mother in the family pew and nudged each other as they tried to match the sin with the slice of gossip they had picked up the week before. Today, Sophia looked about her at the straining faces. How marvelous, she thought, to have all that freedom to sin at one's leisure! How unutterably boring to have to plod one's way through one's childhood as she was doing.

The stained-glass windows shaded and paled as the sun rose higher and higher. As the ceremony proceeded, clouds of incense filled the air and the tall hats of the Orthodox priests bobbed and swayed. How different was the singing the night before! Then a great animal was unleashed; today's hymns went out of the cathedral and onto the highways to find that beast and return her in chains of virtue. Sophia sang, but without the welling passion of the previous evening, and for this she was glad.

She walked beside Elena and her mother out into the autumn cold sunshine. Winter would soon take Russia in its annual embrace, planting on it the hoary kiss of an old bearded man whose beard was yellow with mud and slush, whose breath was icy and treacherous. But as yet only the flying of the great birds across the skies told of his coming.

As Sophia stood dazzled by the sun on the steps of the cathedral, she looked to see if Sir Edward would appear at the doors with the English contingent. There he was, tall and self-assured, dressed in a morning-coat of pale gray. He saw the Oblimov family and raised his whip to his top hat and smiled. Sophia captured his smile and treasured it in her wild young heart. If only it had been for her alone.

As winter approached, both girls found that time hung heavy on their hands. Father Ivan tried his best to interest the girls in Russian literature. They studied the magnificent parchment copy of the Gospels made by Deacon Grigory for Ostromir, once lord of Novgorod. He taught them the skazki tales, history, geography, languages. Elena listened with a dreamy smile playing on her lips as she remembered Sir Edward's arms around her when they danced . . .

Whenever Sir Edward came to visit her father, she called Sophia and they would watch him descend from his horse or his car or his carriage and sweep into the large library, then the door would close. Sometimes both girls had tea with Boris and his guest. Elena loved these occasions. Sitting decorously on the stuffed sofa in the library, where the fire roared and glowed almost too hot to bear, she would watch the big brass samovar glisten and bubble. The hot, brown, brackish tea was poured into thick glass tea-cups. Sir Edward had his tea served from his own small silver tea-pot, with a Coleport jug of milk and a matching bowl for sugar. Both girls were trained by Sir Edward in the art of pouring the tea. The last time it had been

Elena's turn and she felt her hand tremble as she passed the cup to a man she loved, though she was far too shy ever to admit the fact even to herself. "Very good, Elena," Sir Edward said. He smiled at her and she blushed. "Tea first, milk after. Well done."

"I know, I know," Sophia interrupted rudely. 'Manners maketh the man.' You always say that."

Isobel frowned. "Please, Sophia, don't be so ungracious."

Sir Edward smiled at Sophia's angry face. "Really, Sophia, manners are all that life is about. Without them there is no diplomacy, either at home or in the outside world. There must be a time and place for everything."

"What about passion? What about living, or loving?"

"Ahh . . ." Sir Edward looked across at Boris.

Boris shrugged, which made Sophia even more angry. Her father, of all people, should know about passion, furtive and illicit. Sir Edward looked at Elena. He saw her recoil from Sophia's anger. Gently he took Elena's hand and held it captive in his long slim fingers. "Elena, you will know all these things, but they will remain private between you and the man you love." He turned her hand over and kissed the back of it.

For a moment there was a sense of great happiness in the room, and a silence pregnant with hopes for the future.

Then Sir Edward laughed. "Whoever marries you, my dear, will be a lucky man indeed." He turned to Sophia. "As for you, my little one, whoever marries you will need a whip and some sharp spurs."

Sophia's eyes flashed white with rage. "You forget, sir, I may be a better rider."

"Indeed, you may." Sir Edward's eyes were shadowed with sadness. Perhaps, he thought, I know what the future holds for this child I have known so long. A light chill touched his heart. As a diplomat he was trained to sense the slightest nuance in any situation.

"Come now." Isobel brought the tea party to a close. "Your father and Sir Edward must have some time to talk alone together. Sophia, you must practice your piano-playing. Elena, come with me to the sewing-room." Both girls curtsied to the visitor and walked slowly out of the library.

Alone at the grand piano, Sophia felt a black misery engulf her. Why did she have to be so jealous of Elena? Why did she have to blurt out unwelcome questions? Why did Sir Edward reach out for Elena's hand? She played a Chopin mazurka fast and with fire.

Katrina was informed by the footman on his way past that the little madam was in one of her rages. Katrina knew those moods well. "Better let her play her heart out," she said.

CHAPTER 6

Snow shrouded the city of St. Petersburg. Dead bodies lay frozen in the streets. Men came and removed them, throwing them onto carts that took them to be buried in unmarked graves. Young men left the city to join the Tsar's army, the only way in which they could be sure of earning a few roubles to feed the wives and children they left behind.

Isobel was considering the prospect of exile as the grip of war tightened on their lives. How would she cope without the girls? With sorrow, as any mother would. With much pain and grief, but with the certain knowledge that her girls were safe. Looking down onto the street, she could see a few of the new-fangled automobiles making their way through the snow. Now Boris had one of these strange contraptions . . . But if the girls were to leave, it would have to be by sledge. The roads to the west of Russia were barricaded and fortified against the European threat. Europe itself was divided and England was preparing to go to war: it was no place for the girls. Elena would be all right; wherever they sent her, she would adjust . . . But Sophia? Sophia would be a problem no matter where she lived. Isobel's heart ached for Sophia, her little broken-winged nightingale.

The Countess could see Boris entering the gates and hurried to greet him. Boris had been away for many nights and Isobel experienced a familiar joy at seeing his beloved face, gray and strained from the worries of state.

In the nursery Katrina was serving tea. Peace and calm reigned. The big rocking horse stood to attention, his ears alert, his nostrils aflame, his hoofs raised to race with either girl into her childhood dreams. In the early years he had carried Sophia in her imagination to the circus, where she tumbled with the clowns and walked the high wires with the acrobats, while Elena had ridden into the arms of her prince. Still the girls dreamed their dreams—Sophia of adventure, and Elena of her prince.

Now Elena had found her prince. Tonight, as the city lay silent beneath the snow that pressed against the window panes, she pined for him with misty eyes and lowered eyelashes. Sir Edward was going away. Today her mother had said he had been posted to Shanghai. He was to go into exile from Elena's loving. She said nothing but Sophia made no attempt to conceal her anger. "What? Going off to Shanghai? Why can't he refuse?"

Katrina laughed her fat-bellied laugh. "Don't be a goose, Sophia. He has to do his job. And war is coming . . ."

"Oh, don't go on about the war, Katrina. We talk of nothing else. Where is the war?" Sophia leapt to her feet and ran to the window. "Can you see it? I see nothing, just snow and more snow."

Katrina refilled Elena's glass and handed it to her.

"Drink up, *dushenka*," she said. "Drink up. You'll get over it."

Elena flushed. Katrina knew her so well.

"Get over what?" Sophia said crossly. She grabbed Elena's long hair. "Get over what, pussy-cat? Do you have a boyfriend I don't know about?" She pulled fiercely. "Go on! Tell me!"

Elena pushed Sophia away. "I don't have to tell you everything, Sophia."

"Yes, you do. We're twins. You know you have to tell me everything or you will go to hell and"— she paused for effect—"you will burn in the eter-nal fires of damnation."

Seeing the tears in Elena's eyes, Katrina inter-vened. "Don't bully your sister, Sophia. She's just tired. That's all. Now go on, both of you, go off and amuse yourselves until bedtime."

"What is it, Elena?" Sophia felt remorseful.

"Nothing," Elena said, feeling guilty. She had never kept a secret from her twin before. Lying in bed, she looked at the ceiling. *Oh Lord, is it possible for me to love a man like this? Will I ever see him again? Please, Lord, if I do Your Will, please make it possible for me to see him again. Maybe I can't marry him, but I'll never love another man* . . . She turned her face into her pillow and the tears, long held back, rolled down her cheeks.

Downstairs in the drawing room Isobel was sob-bing.

"I had to tell you," Boris said wretchedly. "I've spent six months trying to stop her contacting you."

Isobel was so dazed by Boris's confession, she

did not really hear what he was saying. She was aware only that he was talking quickly and furiously, his hands waving in the air, as though trying to prevent himself from saying these awful things. She remembered his hands from their first night together, when they had stroked her thighs, and pressed her breasts, and touched her nipples with such gentle loving passion; the hands that had joined with hers when they made their vows together before the high altar in the cathedral; the hands that held her face after the birth of the twins when he had pledged timeless faithfulness. These hands had betrayed her. So too had the mouth, the eyes, and the body that stood before her. They had shamelessly and repeatedly betrayed her. Isobel could bear it no longer. She fell to the floor in a faint.

Boris was beside himself. He rang for Katrina and then he drove off in his new shiny car. He pushed away the chauffeur and he sped recklessly into the icy black night. He wished he had never been born. All he could see was the hideous wounded look on his beloved wife's face. "Why?" he whispered to himself. "Why did I do it? What were those women to me, after all?"

He was on his way to see his mother. At a time like this, a man needed his mother. He drove through the hushed and shrouded streets, his heart breaking. Isobel must forgive me, he thought, I cannot live without Isobel. She is my rock and my anchor. For the first time since he was ten, since the day he lost his puppy, he found himself crying. "Damn!" he muttered, and put his foot down.

A curious peasant watched the car from his shack at the side of the road. Hmm, he thought, they might not live like us, but they die like us.

❧ CHAPTER 7 ❧

Misha heard the Count's footsteps as he came flying up the central staircase. He uncurled himself from the rug on which he had been lying, tugged Anna's hand, and said, "My lord is coming."

Anna was awake instantly. Like the salamander, Anna never really slept; she rested her eyes, half-awake. The slightest sound would rouse her. "Lie still," she said to Misha.

Boris came into the room and fell into his mother's arms. "Mother, Mother!" he sobbed. "I've lost Isobel."

Anna, pinned to her bed by her son's huge body, breathed a sigh. So, he had confessed. She shook her head. Of course, he would have to confess, the dear boy. Such a conscience. "There, there." She stroked his head. "Don't take on so. Come, let me sit up."

Boris rolled over and lay face down on the big double bed. "She'll leave me."

A smile caught the corners of Anna's lips. "Misha," she said, "a bottle of Dom Perignon.

And make sure you choose a very good year. Hurry!

"We'll have a glass or two together," she said, patting Boris on the back, "and tomorrow we will go back to see Isobel. I don't think for one minute she will leave you. Isobel isn't that sort of woman. Anyway, women don't leave the Oblimov family. Besides, there are the girls to think of."

Misha, beaded with sweat, arrived with the bottle and two glasses. Boris drained his first glass. He suddenly caught sight of himself in his mother's mirror; a middle-aged man, his face distorted with sorrow. He drank a second glass and then a third.

Within no time the bottle was empty and he was fast asleep, curled up beside his mother, who was still sipping her first glass of champagne. Anna lay back on her pillows. She looked at Misha and then she handed him what was left in her glass. Misha grinned gratefully. "Boris should learn how to keep a secret," she said. She closed her eyes and regretted the day to come and the journey she would have to make.

Sophia was worried about her mother. All morning Isobel stood by the drawing room window, her cheeks sunken, looking suddenly very old. "Mother," Sophia called across the room. "Where's Father?" And then Sophia knew. "It's Father, isn't it?" she asked, at once at her mother's side. "What are you going to do?"

"I don't know." Isobel's voice was soft. "I really

don't know. I hope your grandmother will bring him back. He would go to her with his troubles."

Sophia felt very angry with her father. Why run off sniveling to his mother? Her thoughts were interrupted by the opening of the gates.

Isobel could see the upright little figure of the Golden Salamander sitting in the back of the car. She felt relieved: at least she had a negotiator. Some of the pain lifted. "Go upstairs to the nursery, Sophia. And don't say anything to Elena."

Anna, her head held high, bore down on her daughter-in-law. "I have sent Boris off to change and have a bath," she said. "You and I need to have a little talk."

Isobel stiffened. A little talk, she thought. Is that all my life means?

"Now sit down, and listen to me, my darling daughter," said Anna. "I, of course, knew nothing of Boris's peccadillos, silly man, but,"—she raised a delicate forefinger to her nose—"men don't grow up until they are in their forties. And most never grow up at all. Unless you are very lucky they remain children. Boris," she said with a sigh, "has finally grown up."

Isobel gasped. "You mean I am to forgive him his affairs? Just like that?"

Misha peeked out from behind Anna's chair. So far he had remained hidden behind his mistress in case the storm became too intense. Now his face peered up at Isobel and his huge trusting eyes throbbed with sympathy for Isobel's plight.

Anna smiled and shrugged. "Do you love him? That is the only question."

Isobel nodded slowly. "Yes. I love him."

"Well!" The old lady was sharp. "If I were you I would forgive him. But only after making him feel thoroughly guilty. Demand furs, jewels, perfume, anything you want. Insist he buy you one of those shiny new cars and learn to drive it. Scandalize him. Every time you go out in his jewels, wearing his perfume and the silk underwear he has bought for you, make him wonder where you are going. Isobel, learn to play the game. There is a game between men and women, but you have always stood in the wings. *Men* have to be kept on a short leash. I should know." Anna's nostrils flared. "I kept my husband guessing for years."

"I don't think I'd be any good at all those feminine wiles," Isobel said.

Anna laughed. "And that's precisely why Boris loves you," she said. "Forgive him and let him treasure what he has. I must go now. Come, Misha." And she swept out of the room, leaving Isobel to think about what she had said.

Watching from her bedroom window, Sophia saw her grandmother go. Sophia knew her mother would forgive her father. But had she been in the same position, would she have been so forgiving?

CHAPTER 8

A week later and Isobel appeared herself again, with maybe a few extra lines of apprehension around the eyes, but otherwise just as gentle and loving as before. Perhaps, Sophia thought in the quiet of her room after Katrina had exited in a flurry of sheets and towels, perhaps it is being able to make love that keeps them together.

Elena remained serenely oblivious to all the family drama. Wrapped up in her love for Sir Edward (or simply Edward, as she secretly thought of him), her days were filled with golden fanciful dreams. "Really," said Katrina when she reappeared carrying clean fresh linen, the fragrance of the sheets promising a blissful night's rest, "your sister will dream her life away."

Sophia smiled. "Elena is the lucky one," she said. "Everybody likes her. I'm too sharp at the edges."

Katrina chuckled. "We have a Georgian saying: 'Those born in a shed have no front door.' You, Sophia, are like one born in a shed. You may live in a castle but you're too open. Now take Elena. She has her own front door, which she knows how to shut. She keeps her secrets to herself. You would do better to do likewise."

"I know." Sophia was penitent. "I do try. Really I do. All week I've been dreading tea here, dinner there, dances with Nicholas and his three brothers, church on Sunday . . . There must be more to life than this, Katrina. There must."

"There is, little one, but you must be patient."

All winter long the two Oblimov girls had been virtual prisoners, their outings carefully supervised by the staff, if not by their parents. Katrina knew of Sophia's night excursions during the summer and she allowed them to happen. Being a light sleeper, she would hear Sophia slip out of the house. Often, when not taking a wild ride on her bay, the young girl would visit the nightingale tree to listen to the birds vying with each other in song.

Katrina could understand Sophia's impatience. "You are fast becoming a young woman, my dear. I know it's hard, but you have your whole life ahead of you. Don't be too eager to rush into the world of adults before the time has come. Now into the bath with you, my girl. You need an early night."

Isobel bought new clothes and began to discover that she actually enjoyed wearing them. Boris bought her a large white ermine wrap, and new dresses. Now he went shopping with her, and for the girls he bought gold watches and perfume.

Gradually the hurt faded with the coming of spring, and slowly the ache receded from Sophia's heart.

Spring was always Sophia's favorite time of the year. She forgave her father and went riding with him again in the forest. Spring sowed a carpet of wild flowers—in bright reds, blues and yellows—on the forest floor. Later, as the summer bullied its way into the forest, the wild flowers would droop and die, but for now all was pregnant with the promise of abundance. Sophia, suspended between childhood and womanhood, galloped faster and faster.

"Summer is a-coming in!" she sang loudly, and her father laughed and sang with her.

CHAPTER 9

The girls' birthday party marked the end of any pretense that war was not now on their doorstep. As spring gave way to summer, rumors, and rumors of rumors, swirled around St. Petersburg. Throngs of men, all the able-bodied, were rounded up, put into uniform and sent off to the front line which extended right across the Russian border with Europe. The women left behind tried to maintain some form of family life . . . Boris was glad the Tsar kept him in the city to help plan the defense of Russia, rather than having to take his place at the battle front.

Nightly, he and Isobel discussed their plans for the girls. Isobel would not agree to leave Boris. Russia was her country too, she argued. And had Sir Edward not written from his new post in Shanghai to say that he would act as guardian for the two girls until all danger was past? Shanghai was safe from the war. Many of their friends were already there. Boris begged his wife and his mother to leave. Anna, her face like parchment in the light of the candles on the dinner table, shook her head. "I could never leave Russia," she said. "Russia is my blood and in my bones. Better that I die sooner than leave St. Petersburg."

Sophia and Elena listened open-mouthed, Elena with tears in her eyes at the idea of leaving her parents and her grandmother. But Sophia, in spite of her sorrow, felt her heart pounding. Shanghai! *Freedom*, she thought. My life will begin in Shanghai.

The girls kept quiet during these conversations. Upstairs, however, all of it was recounted to Katrina. "I'll come with you," she offered.

Sophia smiled. "And Misha. Grandmother says Misha must come, too."

"What an adventure we will make of it!" Katrina said. She threw back her head and laughed, her big hands beating on her broad thighs. "Who would have thought it?" she cried. "Katrina in Shanghai! Come girls, let us dance." She scooped both the girls into her arms and stamped and swept around the room until the rafters shook and the two girls were delirious with laughter.

"We would have to take the sleigh through Siberia," Elena said later that night. They were sitting in their white shifts on Sophia's bed. The moon was full.

"Yes." Sophia was thoughtful. "I'm glad Misha is coming with us," she said slowly.

"And Katrina. I shan't be afraid if Katrina is with us. Anyway, Grandmother says it's not for long. After the war is over, they will come and fetch us. In a year or two maybe." Elena smiled at the moon and thought of her Edward. "I do hope the wolves don't get us."

The moon cast a reassuring silver light on the two girls as they lay in each other's arms, Elena's long fair hair entwined with Sophia's dark mane on the freshly ironed pillow. Only the long faint cry of a hungry wolf, its head silhouetted against the moon, disturbed their dream-filled sleep.

CHAPTER 10

The Sarajevo assassination of Archduke Francis Ferdinand prompted the adults in the Oblimov family to take the final decision to send the girls to Shanghai. They waited six months in the hope that the war would quickly be over but by winter it was clear that it would drag on. Sending the girls westward was out of the question, for all European borders were now closed. Only the roads to the East remained comparatively passable. Rail travel was ruled out, for Russian trains had been commandeered for the transportation of military personnel, supplies, and arms.

A family sleigh was made ready. All gold ornamentation was removed and the sleigh repainted a plain sober black. Bandits abounded across Siberia, so there was to be no ostentatious evidence of wealth. The mink coats and blankets were not worth stealing, for mink was plentiful in the countryside. Baskets of provisions were stowed at the back of the big sleigh. In a secret compartment, known only to Misha, money and jewels were stashed also, sufficient to keep the girls for several years—at least for the two or three years while the war was fought and won, until the signal was given to come home.

There were so many goodbyes to be said, with more teas and dances and little presents for the departing girls. Now Isobel made a point of visiting the girls' rooms to kiss them good night. They did not see her tears; they saw their mother and father somehow strengthened through this ordeal.

Katrina was pleased with the large mink coat which the Oblimovs gave her for the journey. "I look like a pregnant whale!" she said. "But a wealthy one!"

Sophia laughed. "You know the old Russian legend: it is the whale that supports the earth on its back."

"And if the whale moves," said Elena, "we get earthquakes."

Katrina stopped jigging about and sighed. "Well!" she said. "Whoever would have thought of old Katrina going to Shanghai? Not I, not in a million years." Then she wandered off to her own room and shut the door.

A moment later Katrina heard the sound of leather boot soles tapping quickly up the hallway and recognized the footsteps as Sophia's. Many times in nights gone by Katrina had heard those steps as Sophia rushed out to seek her secret magical places in the night-time forest. Katrina never followed. She felt she had to allow the girl her privacy, and time to be alone with her thoughts and imagination. But never on such nights did Katrina close her eyes in sleep until she was sure that Sophia had returned safely.

Once outside, Sophia began to run. Her warm boots sank to half-way up her calf in the crunchy snow, but Sophia felt weightless. She envisioned herself flying as she rushed among the trees on the forest's edge, cutting a path between the snow-laden pines. The bright moon made the snow all about her glisten with a cool electric blue. The trees near her, whose strong branches needed only a sudden wind or an extra ounce of fresh snowflakes to make them dip groundward and shake off their burden of crystal powder, were clear and distinct in the moonlight. It was the far-away trees, growing closer to each other in the distance, that made deep purple shadows and crowded each other in hidden blackness. In her childhood this same forest had been the home of nymphs and fairies, the domain of the Snow King and Snow Queen from Hoffman's Christmas tale, *The Nutcracker,* which, years before, she had seen performed at the magnificent theater in St. Petersburg. But now she needed no storybook characters to bring the forest to life. The reality of the snow, the trees, the shimmering star-filled sky and the moonlight was itself more mystical and beautiful than any fantasy.

Sophia ran on. The icy air prickled her cheeks. Her lungs began to burn at the coldness of each breath, which turned white in the cold when she exhaled. Then she reached her destination. Panting, she stood beneath the tree, her tree, the nightingale tree. Tonight it was empty. The stiff brittle branches held no leaves and no bird sat waiting to serenade her. The nightingale, she knew, had gone away to distant Africa, to a gentler climate that would not chill its fragile body. And I'm going away, too, Sophia thought. Did the bird know where it was going, each autumn, with the first wing-beats of its great flight?

But the nightingale would return, drawn by migratory instincts beyond its comprehension. After the winter, spring would arrive and with it would come the nightingale, back to the forest, back to this very tree, back home. Sophia, however, would not be here next spring to welcome the little bird, nor was she likely to be here to visit at night in the summer and to listen to its recounting of its winter adventures. Will I ever come home? Sophia wondered.

For many moments Sophia stared at the upper reaches of the tree. She listened to the whistling of the wind through pine branches and could all but hear, once again, the nightingale's melody. There, on the highest branch of the tree, the bird would point its beak to the sky and begin his warming-up trills. Gradually it would find its voice and then sing the song of Sophia's life, of a destiny to be fulfilled, of dreams not yet imagined, of a future still unknown.

A gust of wind caught a branch behind her, dislodging its burden of snow. I am the nightingale, Sophia thought as she turned from the tree and started to walk back to the house. And I too must leave this land.

She walked slowly, savoring the clean cold air, the warmth of her hands in her soft fur-lined mittens, and the sound of her boots breaking the crisp ice-crust that covered the softer snow beneath. She must cherish each instant, each step in the frozen night.

Hearing her footsteps going up the hall and into Sophia's bedroom, Katrina at last shut her eyes and slept.

⤴️ CHAPTER 11 ⤴️

While the girls slept and Katrina sat guard over all the baggage for the next day, Misha was spending his last night with his adored mistress. Misha knew he would never see his beloved Anna again. In Misha's cross-starred world, he often knew things far more acutely than normal people did. In the world of the half-maimed and misshapen, one survived the tortures of life because one lived forewarned. Misha lay on his familiar fur rug watching Anna's face. "Goodbye, my faithful Misha," Anna whispered.

"I fear I will never see you again, my lady," he sobbed, his head bowed in prayer over her hand, which he held in his.

"But you will, my darling," Anna said. "I'll see

you and you will see me. When you need me, call for me and I will be there. I want you to guard my grandchildren with the same love as you have guarded me. Take special care of Sophia. She is going to need you more than Elena."

Misha knew this was true. "I will," he promised. "You mustn't worry."

"Misha, sleep now. You leave in just a few hours."

Obedient in everything, Misha slept while Anna gazed upon her friend, praying that God would guide this little caravan to safety across the wicked Siberian wilderness.

CHAPTER 12

At the dead of the night, after the midnight ange-lus, when the wolves were quiet and howled no more, and the moon cast long enveloping shadows on the snow, Anna tearfully said goodbye to her grandchildren. She shook hands with Katrina, then put her arms about her favorite friend and hugged his little knobbled body. Locked in the embrace of those old bones, feeling her dry skin against his cheek, Misha thought his heart would burst with pain. Big tears rolled down his face, but he knew he had to go with the twins. He pulled back and stared long at her beloved face, memorizing the lines around the mouth, the sparkle in those intelligent eyes.

Then Anna smiled her warm angelic smile. "We are eternal souls of God, remember," she said, trying to comfort the forlorn little man. She put her hand under his deformed chin. "My body is only an old withered envelope," she reminded him. "I, Anna, will always be beside you. When the moon is full, call for me and you will not be alone." Misha nodded. He had no reason to doubt her. He sighed and rubbed his eyes. "Go now, Misha." He bowed and with a last look at Anna stumbled out of the room.

In the hall Boris and Isobel were saying their goodbyes. "A year or two and all this nonsense will be over." Boris sounded confident, but he knew his promises were hollow.

Isobel agreed with her husband. "Look on it as a great adventure," she comforted the girls. Elena was crying and clinging to her mother.

Sophia felt the distress of the moment, but tried to follow her parents' example of maintaining a brave countenance despite everyone's fears. She put her hand on her father's arm. "Look after yourselves," she said. "I'll take care of Elena. Don't you worry about a thing. We'll write regularly and we'll see that we don't get into any trouble."

Boris smiled and shook his head. "That'll be the day, Sophia."

"Take care of my horse, won't you?" The only regret that Sophia felt she could safely allow herself was that she had to leave behind her bay. But she could cope with the thought of missing her horse. She would also miss her parents; miss them so much that . . . She stopped herself pursuing such thoughts. She would be back in a year, two years at the most. And then she would take her horse for more rides and be sure to bring it even more treats of carrots and sugar lumps. She kissed her parents and moved toward the door.

Katrina was already in the sleigh. All the food and clothes were neatly arranged in the back. Misha and Katrina were already seated and now both girls took their places, well wrapped in fur. Two drivers—the most villainous-looking pair of drivers employed by Boris—sat on the front bench, and at the very rear of the sleigh, behind the provisions, two expert hunters armed with rifles stood guard. Boris was pleased: the four men were unsurpassed shots. Should there be any bandits, the girls would be well protected. Quietly the driver shook the reins. No bells on this trip; no happy shouts of farewell. They were leaving quietly and secretly. In hearse-like silence they pulled out of the big gates.

Both girls turned their heads for a last look at the castle and a final wave to their parents. Somehow Boris and Isobel looked so small and vulnerable standing on the steps. Behind them stood Anna, holding the door slightly shut to protect the hall from the icy wind. Elena whispered, *"Au revoir. We will return,"* into the wind.

What felt like a cold dry hand brushed Sophia's cheek, causing her to gasp.

"Are you all right?" Katrina asked.

"Yes, yes." Sophia's voice was tense. "I'm fine." She turned her luminous eyes toward her nurse's face. "Katrina," Sophia felt compelled to say very quietly and in a hoarse whisper so as not to upset Elena, "do you really think we will ever see them again? I mean, Grandmother and my parents? I don't know why, but I have a strange feeling that something awful is about to happen." Sophia looked up. "Look, Katrina." They both gazed in horror as a large gray owl flew into the waning moon. For a moment outstretched wings seemed to cover the face of the moon and its body obscured the light for what seemed an unnaturally long instant.

Katrina laid a warm steady hand on the young girl's shoulder. "It's only a bird, darling. Don't panic. Of course you'll see them all again."

Privately Katrina was as shaken as her charge. An owl against the moon boded no good. And Katrina was aware the dangers that lay ahead needed no supernatural augury. Beyond the perils of war lurked the growing threat of the Bolsheviks. The entire Oblimov family, as far as she was concerned, should have left months before. Katrina understood their responsibility to the Tsar and his family, but in Katrina's view the Tsar and his wife were doomed. The Oblimovs, however, were not the heartless aristocrats the Bolsheviks so loved to caricature. But, should the Bolsheviks ever have their day, individual virtues could well be washed over by the tide of revolution. She wished they had all found an escape long before Russia was overtaken by war. Still, she reminded herself, her job was not to sit in judgment but to escort the girls to safety.

Misha sat silently beside Katrina. All his life, at least as far back as he could remember, he had loved Anna. From the day he had realized he was not dead, when his eyes opened on Anna's face leaning over him with warm broth and towels. The spades had ceased their scraping, then his cousin had lifted him from his shallow grave and set him upright on the ground. At that moment he had truly been born again, no longer Misha the object of scorn and ridicule, but Misha the respected subject of Anna's court. Now he was losing her. His gaze was fixed on the back of the twins' heads, one blonde and the other dark. Sophia carried her head in the same imperious way that Anna did. Hers was the head of a woman who gave orders and expected to be obeyed. Elena's neck bespoke a calm and submissive nature. Elena would make some man very happy, Misha thought. And thinking about the girls, his heavy heart lightened. It was wise for him to accompany them. Only a year or two, he prayed, and they would be back. Then he could be with his beloved mistress again.

The four men clung grimly to the sleigh. They knew a difficult journey lay ahead, but they were loyal to Boris and, in their rough way, they loved the two young girls. Not everyone wanted war or revolution. Many of the people who worked in privileged conditions in the palaces of the rich privately wondered how they would manage if the rich were stripped of their wealth and thrown out of their homes. Would a new class of people take their places? Would the bedroom of a prince and princess fall to a fat functionary and his wife, just as cruel and oblivious as their predecessors might have been? No matter now, for the four taking their leave of Russia. Boris had promised them the sleigh and a bag of gold each. They had a new life to look forward to in Shanghai.

The sleigh sped past shacks and hovels, the buildings along the roadside becoming fewer as they traveled on and deep countryside surrounded them. "We're heading toward Moscow, then on to Sverdlovsk, my darlings. We have weeks of journeying ahead of us." Katrina was tired. "Sleep now, girls." All four of the passengers, warm in their furs, were lulled by the hissing of the blades as the horses pulled them onward.

Sverdlovsk was grim and gray in the wind that blew icy snowflakes onto the sleigh. Still, it was the first city they reached after Moscow—which, armed for war, felt to them like a shrouded jewel— on the immensely long and wearying journey. During the daytime the girls could read for entertainment. Sophia read her Bible and books by her favorite author, Count Tolstoy. She could see herself as Anna Karenina . . .

Elena read poetry of the rather turgid kind. Katrina knitted endless, large, shapeless cardigans, which she forced on the girls. "This will keep you warm," she announced as day after day they traveled across a seemingly unending desert of winter snow. Ramshackle, uncomfortable country inns between the cities were their nightly resting-places. The small towns they pulled into each evening were not to be lingered in; they were simply places to unscramble legs, stretch backs, wash, eat, sleep, then the little party of travelers would pile into the sleigh once more and go on. Soon the girls felt haggard and gray—gray as the mud-splashed snowbanks beside the road. Occasionally trains passed, big hooting monsters, into the frozen landscape, pulling soldiers back and forward, gathering up men who had lived on this arid route all their lives, taking them westward to Moscow, to other cities full of what to the peasants would seem metropolitan wonders. Facing certain death in the trenches, these men sang en route to their end.

The days and weeks were long and monotonous. Cities and towns passed in a blur of snowy whirlwinds: Omsk, Irkutsk . . . Lake Baykal, a huge frozen expanse, broke the tedium of their journey for a while, being a sight delightful to behold, but soon they moved on again. All of them, each in his or her own way, became adept at the many tricks of distraction of which the mind is capable to keep from brooding on those thoughts it most wants to dwell on: thoughts of everything—the people, the places, the love—they had left behind.

CHAPTER 13

Having traveled around the southern tip of Lake Baykal several days before, the sleigh pulled up one evening in front of an inn at the town of Verkhne-Udinsk, the great railway intersection which, for the sleigh on the open snow as well as for many trains that ran on the rigid rails, marked the point at which their easterly journey across Russia veered southward toward Urga, the heart of Mongolia. The day's travel had been long and the darkness of evening was already a deep black when Misha, Katrina, and the two girls climbed down from the sleigh. They stretched, shook their legs to loosen stiff muscles, and stepped inside the inn.

What they found was a bright oasis of warmth, cleanliness and comfort. Unlike other inns they had rested in so far, this old farmhouse had freshly painted walls and smelled of good food, a pine-wood fire and clean sheets, instead of the usual mixture of must and wet wool. Though by no means luxurious, its simplicity and tidiness made the house feel like a palace to the tired travelers. "Yes," said Misha as he paid for rooms. "This is much more like it."

The horsemen and the guards were given lodging in what had been the stable—horses now spent the night in an adjacent barn. The stalls had been converted into meager but spotless rooms, and a large central stove heated the building adequately. Misha was so impressed by the cleanliness of the place, he decided they should treat themselves to two rooms, one for the girls, and a separate room for Katrina. He would take the bedding from the spare bed in Katrina's room and curl up outside the door of the girls' room. Even in sleep he would guard his charges.

Dinner was a satisfying winter-vegetable stew served at the long table in the open-hearthed, pot-simmering, onion-smelling kitchen. When all had eaten as much as they could eat, the guards and drivers, exhausted by the drive, retired to their beds in the stable. The innkeeper, a young woman whose husband was far away fighting in the war against the Central Powers, cleared away the plates, while Sophia, Elena, Misha and Katrina sat at the table, their chairs pushed back, their stomachs happily full. All were tired, but none was eager to leave the kitchen, to break the magic of this moment, the peace of sitting calm and safe in the glow of the big fire and the well-polished oil lamps.

No one spoke. Each sat silently with thoughts and memories. Something in the atmosphere reminded Katrina of the Georgian kitchen of her childhood home, which had been poorer, and had always required great efforts with a broomstick to ensure that rapacious rats did not invade the sacks of grain and flour, but the very *homeliness* of this kitchen was reminiscent all the same.

Misha thought of his mistress. He stared into the flames burning in the hearth and saw Anna's face. She would have seemed perhaps out of place in such a humble house—opera halls and palaces were far more her natural domain, but then again, he thought, she does have a knack for fitting in, wherever she is; not by lowering her standards to suit others in her company, rather by elevating the hearts of all around her, creating the illusion that by some mysterious transformation they were her peers. She could sit with a lowly stable-boy or tenant farmer, and, listening to her stories of her great escapades, of the wondrous places she had been, even a serf could laugh at her tales and feel himself privileged to be in the presence of such a radiant personage. Misha shut his eyes and offered up a prayer that the months would not be many before he could again sit beside her and treasure her every word.

Sophia and Elena exchanged glances, and in that unspoken communication peculiar to twins, they knew each other's thoughts: If only their parents were here. If only Boris, who loved a good stew, could have shared their meal. If only Isobel, who always took a compassionate interest in other people's lives regardless of their station, could have talked with the innkeeper and comforted her in her fears for her husband. If only their parents could be at the table now, Boris with his black leather belt loosened a notch, Isobel with her mouth curved in a smile that said all was well; if only they could sit together as a family in the contented silence of the room . . . Then the girls' happiness would be complete. Sophia and Elena could see this scene of contentment in the depths of each other's eyes.

And then Sophia began to sing. She sang a song

from childhood, an old courtly song about the longing in a young prince's heart for the maiden he loves. It was a simple song, but its clarity and beauty caused all eyes in the room to turn toward Sophia. She did not rise from her chair; she looked into the fire while she sang. The notes were pure, like the song of a bird. The melody shifted from the minor key to phrases of lightness and joy, then back to the melancholy loveliness of the minor. Her voice grew stronger and reached out past the white walls of the kitchen, out into the cold air, across the cobbled barnyard. It drifted over the sleeping heads of the guards in their beds and was heard in the stable by other more wakeful ears.

When she finished her song, silence spread a blanket over the room. Then Misha smiled. "Beautiful," he said.

"Very beautiful," Katrina added with pride.

Misha put his hands on his knees and hopped down from his chair. "And now," he said, "we had better get to bed. There's a long way to go tomorrow."

Katrina went off to her room and the girls to theirs. Misha lay his bedding in front of the girls' room and was soon asleep. On the other side of the door the girls, snugly tucked up in separate beds, enjoyed the deepest sleep yet of their vast journey.

"Don't scream. Don't make a sound."

Was this a dream? Sophia, feeling herself slowly tugged from the emptiest and blackest of slumbers, could not be sure. Her head, still muffled in the dense cotton-wool of unconsciousness, felt a hand over her mouth. The hand was cold, yet moist in the palm. Elena? No, Elena was in another bed, and the hand was too strong to be Elena's.

"I heard you singing and I knew it was you," the nervous voice said. The speaker's quickened heart-beats seemed audible in his words.

Sophia felt as if drugged. Why could she not shake off her sleep? With a great effort, she forced her eyes to open. Pressed close to her own was a young man's face. His eyes were wide and desperate. Feeling a cold wind against her cheek, she turned her eyes and saw the open window. Surely, she told herself, she must be dreaming.

"Don't tell me you don't recognize me," the man said in a hoarse whisper that sounded surprised. Then, having found his own answer, his face changed to malice and he said, "No, but you wouldn't, would you? Your kind never do."

Who was this man? It was a puzzle to Sophia. Strangest of all was the fact that with her eyelids still so heavy and the desire to sleep still so strong she was not awake enough to feel fear. She felt only curiosity, an analytical desire to identify this man, to ascertain whether he was real or only some phantom in a dream.

"My name," he explained, pressing his hand tighter on her mouth until her lips were pressed against her teeth and began to hurt, "is Yevgeny Piotrovich, though you never bothered to ask. I was a guardsman in the Tsar's army. Do you recognize me yet?"

Fighting hard to keep her eyes open, Sophia

looked at the face. The chin needed a shave. The breath was sour. Certainly no guardsman would ever be in such a state. But the nose, the high-bridged nose did look rather familiar . . .

"Don't be stupid!" he spat, though his voice never rose above a whisper. "The Kolinsky ball, in St. Petersburg! You remember."

She did remember. The ball . . . The music . . . The young guardsmen . . . Yes, the horrid guardsman who had been rude to Misha.

"You sang that night and I remembered your voice. I had never heard such a voice." His eyes squinted and he shook his head as if in a loving reverie. "And I heard your voice again tonight. And I knew. I said to myself, 'She's here! Countess Sophia Oblimova.'"

Her name sounded obscene on his lips. Sophia wanted to move, to raise her hands, to run away, to scream, to do something, but her limbs had no strength and his body lay heavy on hers.

"And suddenly," he continued, "my heart was full of excitement and full of hatred." His eyes flared wildly once again. "The enemy, I knew, was here." His tone brightened. He raised his eyebrows. "I ran away, you know," he said almost casually. "Deserted, they call it. But don't you see? For me it was a matter of conscience. The bugle woke me in my tent one morning and I realized I was fighting for the wrong side. What was I, Yevgeny Piotrovich, doing, fighting for the Tsar? What had all the Tsars ever done for me and my family except keep us poor and in slavery?" His eyes wandered from Sophia's, for he was talking more to himself. "And there I was, fighting against the Germans when my real enemy was in St. Petersburg. The Tsar, the Tsarina, the Imperialists, the loyalists, the Oblimovs!"

He stared again into Sophia's face. "So I ran away, back to home. I'm from Khabarovsk, you know, hundreds of miles east of here. Still a long way to go. But I'll be there on the day the revolution comes." His eyes hardened. "I'll be there to fight and get rid of your kind once and for ever. You who dance at balls and don't even remember dancing with a soldier like me! You who can sleep in a soft bed like this while I lie like an animal in the barn! Do you hear me, Sophia Oblimova? Yevgeny Piotrovich can bear it no longer!"

It was then that Sophia felt something sharp at her neck, the needle-sharp point of a dagger began to press the soft skin of her neck. And suddenly the choice was made for her. With no thought what might happen if she made a noise, with no conscious decision at all, a scream came up from inside her, a huge scream that shut her eyes, pushed open her mouth and tilted back her head. Frenzied, blindly, in an oblivion of fear, she screamed.

Yevgeny Piotrovich was frightened. He jumped back and waved his hands frantically over Sophia's face to stop the noise. Sophia's eyes snapped open while she shrieked and all she saw was a blur of movement. Something flew, and miraculously the weight on top of her body disappeared. She blinked her eyes to focus.

On the floor beside her bed, Misha was

crouched over a motionless body. He removed a knife from the man's back, wiped it clean on the man's shirt, and slid it back into its scabbard inside his boot. Katrina, a look of terror on her face, appeared at the doorway. A bewildered Elena sat up on the other bed and stared. Sophia began to cry.

The next moment Misha was explaining to the innkeeper that the dead man had tried to harm one of the girls. The guards and horsemen were summoned to prepare the sleigh, while Katrina held Sophia in a big rocking hug, murmuring "Shh. You're safe now," and Elena, over Katrina's shoulder, kept asking, "What did he want, Sophia? What was he doing to you?"

"I don't know," Sophia cried. "I don't know what he was doing or what he was going to do. I just . . . I . . ." And the tears came again in relief at the ebbing horror.

Before Sophia had time to think, she found herself once more in the sleigh, speeding away from the inn into the night. Elena clung to her on one side and Katrina, with an arm around her, held her on the other. Misha, who sat beside Elena, kept leaning across to look into Sophia's face and check that she was all right. To be away, far away from the inn, from death, fear, danger! But Sophia felt danger everywhere about her and sat wide awake as the sleigh sped on. It was because of my singing, she told herself. I sang as a child, but now it's not safe to sing. I'm no longer a child. I will never sing again.

❧ CHAPTER 14 ❧

At last they were over the border into Mongolia. They noticed a change in the people they passed. The sharp Russian face had given way to more eastern features and wide smooth cheeks. "Look," Elena pointed out a group of peasants who stood, clad in sheepskin, staring at this strange caravan. "They have our eyes."

No one was in the mood to take up the comment. Since fleeing the inn at Verkhne-Udinsk, none of the foursome had discussed what had happened. Sophia was withdrawn, which worried Katrina, for Katrina had never known the girl to be so long silent before. Misha suffered remorse, not for killing the man—he deserved to die—but for not having heard him sooner, when he first stepped through the window, before his filthy hand had touched Sophia. Elena was shocked by what had happened to her sister and hardly knew what to say. It was a relief to have crossed into Mongolia. The last taste of Russia had been bitter. Now they began to realize that they were approaching a very different life.

Misha was torn. Though glad to have the brutality that had become Russia behind him, the pain of separation from his Anna still felt as if an invisible steel wire was attached to both their souls, and that wire was stretched to an agonizing tension. The pain was very real and at times almost unbearable. Now, as he looked into the light golden faces with the eyes that seemed to reach the tip of the ears, he remembered her. His beautiful Golden Salamander, alone in her bedroom at nights, his fur bed now lying empty across the floor.

They reached the ancient city of Urga where, for centuries, travelers through the region had met to trade stories as well as goods. The sleigh drove in silence past the Da Khure monastery. Here, it was said, lived the monk revered throughout Mongolia as the Living Buddha. So holy was he that his devotees claimed him the perfect embodiment of Nirvana on earth in this, his final, incarnation.

Sophia had studied the town in an old book she had found in her father's library. Now the pages of the crimson-colored leather-bound volume came to life, the images taking on color, and smell, and depth. She heard a gong sound from deep within the monastery walls as the sleigh slowed at a crossroad. Straining her eyes to peer through a gateway, she beheld a column of monks walking in meditative procession. She had seen Russian Orthodox monks in the past, but they, though indisputably holy, seemed very much part of this world. Their black robes were earthy and their long frizzled beards definitely manly. These Buddhist monks had an altogether different aspect. Their shaved heads and red and orange robes gave them an appearance neither male nor female. Even the distant sight of their silent steps conveyed to Sophia a sense of ineffable tranquillity, of liberation from earthly preoccupations. They began to chant; no recognizable song or melody like the Russian Orthodox chants, but a single strong sound with many parts, one moment unified, the next in antiphony.

The serenity of this vision touched something profound in Sophia. She watched and felt a peace and quietude she had not known for days, ever since that awful night in Verkhne-Udinsk. But suddenly she realized she had survived that ordeal. It was an unpleasant experience, but it was over now, and she had come through it, almost as if it were some bizarre initiation rite.

For the first time, she began to feel the excitement of being in the East, of getting to know this vast new world she had come to. They were nearing China, and she found herself eager to learn about everything—the food, the people, the mysticism of which she had just had a glimpse through an open monastery gate. She began to feel happy.

The sleigh started again with a jolt. Misha had not noticed the monks, nor had he slipped momentarily into a realm of ethereal peace. He was suffering a particularly bad bout of missing Anna. He let out a groan.

Sophia heard him and she turned. "Misha, we'll only be away for two years. That's not long. Grandmother is in good health. Don't worry. The worst part of the journey is over."

Misha saw the excitement on Sophia's face, the familiar vivacity, and knew that all would be well with her. Taking her hand in his, he smiled.

The rest of the journey to the Chinese border passed far more agreeably than the earlier Russian leg. Their safety, now they were out of Russia, was assured. Such delicate matters as bathrooms and the private cleansing of bodies became the priority. Once again the inns were often shabby and bug-ridden. But as the weeks went by, a rough camaraderie sprang up between the guards and their passengers. They would all make conversation to shorten the hours, telling each other stories of what they expected Shanghai to be like. Enjoyment was found in the spotting of buildings among high mountains or of villages along a snowy tundra. Sightings of animals were a treat. They saw wolves, who tended to stand in a group and watch the sleigh pass by. And once, a pair of snow leopards ran snarling into the dusk.

As they crossed from Mongolia into China, the faces changed again. The broad flat faces of the Chinese peasants did not have the same frightening demeanor inherited by the Mongolian descendants of Genghis Khan. Now the faces were rounded, the eyes less elongated, the cast of the visage more questioning and gentle. Their bodies were smaller; they kept their hands tucked away in their sleeves. Pigtails hung down the backs of the people of China.

Finally they came to their first city-stop in China, in the outskirts of Peking. Both girls were filled with joy. Instead of bowls of greasy soup, they were offered fragrant dishes of red-cooked chicken. Each meal was a revelation.

"If this is the food of China," Sophia announced, "I think I'm going to like living here."

Katrina laughed. Misha wiped the grease off his

chin. "Very good, very good," he said. For a moment he almost forgot his pain.

Elena was attempting to eat with chopsticks. "Here." The Chinese waiter showed her how to hold them between her thumb and third finger. "You try," he instructed her. "Hohoho!" He covered his mouth with his hand, lest he show his teeth and offend the little party.

Elena managed to pick up a small strip of duck in a heavy plum sauce. "Delicious!" she said. "Utterly delicious! I wish Mother was here to see us now."

All four of them smiled, no spoken agreement necessary. Tonight the girls were to sleep in real beds and—a miracle!—they were to have a proper leisurely bath.

"I never imagined," Sophia said solemnly, "I could want a bath so badly. Funny, isn't it, how all those things you take for granted become so important when you don't have them?"

Katrina smiled, pleased to see Sophia acting exactly like her old self. She knew how important all those things were and never took anything for granted, but, yes, the girls had already learned a lot on this trip. They had been heroic in the face of difficulty and fear. Though once she might have thought them spoiled, their ability to face danger with equanimity was admirable. She knew their parents would be rightly proud of them.

Later that evening she poured hot water into the big white bathtub adjoining their hotel bedroom. "Oh, Katrina! How wonderful!" Sophia came in first and she dipped her toe into the steaming water. Katrina watched her affectionately. She had seen her grow from babyhood to young womanhood. "Jump in," Katrina said, "and I'll wash your hair."

Elena walked in as Sophia's head was bent under the heavy weight of her hair and the water. "Will you wash mine, too, Katrina? An itchy head is a feeling I never want to have again."

Soon Katrina was squeezing and rolling Sophia's hair up onto her head in a thick white towel. "Your turn, Elena."

Elena got into the tub and sighed. "What a pleasure!" she said as she slid into the hot water. Immediately her soft white skin went pink.

"You look like a blancmange." Sophia laughed.

Elena grinned as the water descended over her head and she could see her sister through the cascade of crystal beads. For a moment Elena wished she and her twin could sit in this bath for ever. With Katrina close by, and the hot water and soap suds gently caressing her body, she felt that mystical union with Sophia known only to twins who have shared the same womb for the first nine months of their existence. Now, enwombed again, they were safe.

Sophia stepped from the bath and Katrina took a big towel from the towel rail and began to rub her dry. For Sophia the rubbing awakened memories of childhood, when she used to lie in Katrina's lap, until she was old enough and tall enough to stand. At first she had resented the vigorous drying, but now she enjoyed it. It made her tingle. It made her aware that she was alive. She was grateful to feel herself clean again.

She ran into the bedroom to put on her long flannel nightgown. Elena soon joined her and together they climbed into the big double bed. Feeling scrubbed and content, they kissed each other a soft good night on the lips as Katrina put out the lights.

✤ CHAPTER 15 ✤

Dawn spread a pink hand over the stone-gray streets and buildings of Peking. Elena sat up in the wide double bed, with its feather-filled mattress, and for a moment she was still at home in her own bed.

Morning brought the city to a frenzied bustle. People, carts, oxen and horses streamed into the city through the narrow streets. Elena moved to the window, where her blue-gray eyes widened in amazement. Never in her life had she been so close to the street-life of a city. True, she had visited peasant huts with her mother and shopped in the streets of St. Petersburg, but that was different. There she was immediately deferred to. Her fine clothes and furs made the people in the streets afraid and mindful of their station. Here, in this modest hotel, the girls were just part of the teeming crowd. That's the difference, thought Elena.

St. Petersburg was a beautiful but desolate city, filled with hunger and resentment. Peking was a city full of life.

The smell of noodles, garlic, and jasmine tea reached her even through the closed windows. Elena returned to her bed and picked up her Bible. A psalm for comfort, she thought. "The Lord is my shepherd . . ." She read on.

Eventually Sophia stirred. She stretched luxuriantly, like a cat on a satin cushion, and she opened her eyes and gazed at the ceiling. "Where am I?"

"In Peking at the Rising Sun Hotel."

Sophia sat up and hugged her knees. "How long have you been up?"

"For ever. I saw the dawn break over the city."

Sophia yawned. "Sounds lovely. But for me it's too early in the morning for aesthetic appreciation. Let's get dressed and go out for breakfast. This is fun! This is adventure! Imagine having breakfast in a room full of people we don't know."

Elena stared at her sister. "You're right, you know. I never thought of it that way. I've always accepted that people like us never mix with people on the streets, except to help them or take them food."

Sophia laughed while dressing herself. "Well, I've thought about it a lot and I can't wait to enjoy this new freedom."

"Oh, Sophia," said Elena with a smile. "You're always so extreme."

They could hear Misha shuffling about outside the door. "Misha!" Sophia shouted. "We need breakfast! We're famished." Then both girls linked arms and danced out of the room, down the stairs, where Katrina was waiting for them, and out onto the pavement.

At first the little foursome felt as if a huge tide of human bodies was about to sweep them away. Yoked oxen ambled solemnly down the center of the road, while the sun began to warm the gray cobbles underfoot. The weather was cold, but nowhere near as cold as St. Petersburg. The Chinese wore quilted coats—predominantly blue—and other nationalities wore regional dress. Uygurs, Mongols, Uzbeks, Tajiks and Kazakhs passed by. The girls watched fascinated.

Misha was fussing, trying to keep his brood safe. Katrina noted the girls' faces, alive with interest and curiosity. Yes, she said to herself, this is quite an education for my little countesses. Dressed by Katrina in unassuming gray dresses with matching gray coats, the two girls still drew admiring glances. Elena with her madonna smile walked quietly; Sophia's eyes were alight.

For a moment the tide receded, giving the group a chance to join the flow and work their way across the road and around the corner to a restaurant, there to sit and study this amazing phenomenon.

"Noodles?" Misha asked in despair.

"Not just noodles. No, no, no." The waiter was eager to please. "Not just noodles. We have porridge."

Misha's bulbous eyes showed relief. The girls were happy with noodles. Katrina ordered jasmine tea.

Porridge turned out to be a thin gruel with a great deal of garlic. Resolutely, Misha bore his disappointment with a brave face. After all, food was food. He hoped he would be able to survive without the strong Russian tea he liked so much. The girls, using chopsticks for the second time in their lives, turned in a creditable performance with the noodles.

All around them people sat talking and laughing. Small children played about the feet of their families. People slapped each other's hands in agreement and hid their mouths when they smiled; there was much nodding of heads and general good humor. The inhabitants of St. Petersburg, Sophia thought, seemed miserable by comparison, like heavy Russian bread, whereas there seemed to be some special kind of leavening in the Chinese. Sophia knew there had been revolution here. From Father Ivan she had learned how Sun Yat-sen had led the insurrection against the Ching dynasty, creating the newborn Republic of China, and still a sort of revolution bubbled, not open civil war, but a perpetual simmering of different political factions. Even so, the Chinese national character, or what she had seen of it, seemed basically optimistic. In spite of evident poverty and the lack of certain items in the shops, the babies were fat and well fed. No one lashed out at them as they played and rolled on the floor. People picked them up and passed them about, one to another.

Sophia leaned back with her tea. Her eyes shimmered as she looked at Elena. "I'm going to like it here," she said. "I already feel Chinese."

"We are part Chinese, you know," Elena said slowly. "Mongolian, really, from a long time back."

"I just want to get to Shanghai."

Katrina took out her purse and stared at the unfamiliar loop of Chinese coins, strung together like a necklace of discs. Misha was silent, brooding on his plan to unpack the sleigh, for now they were to complete the journey by train. The Chinese snow was beginning to melt, making further travel by sleigh impossible, and there was no longer any reason not to travel by rail. Misha admitted to himself he had enjoyed much of the sleigh-ride, snuggled close to the girls he loved . . . Now he had to collect their bags and retrieve the jewels. "All right," he announced. "Let's get back to the hotel and then we must make our way to the station."

The rest of the morning they spent reorganizing their baggage.

The train awaited them at the grand Peking station, and they climbed thankfully into the first-class carriage booked for them by the sleighman. Waving goodbye to the guards who had accompanied them across Russia and now stood with their hats clutched to their chests, both girls sank into the deeply upholstered chairs. Sophia gazed around the compartment. Beside her chair was a small table on which stood a lamp with a bright-pink shade. The bunks were made from a very red mahogany, and in the corner stood a little bronze basin, with a mirror hanging above it. Sophia rose and went over to peer in the mirror. "Surprising," she said. "We don't look too awful, Elena, despite infrequent baths."

"Misha says we have several more days without a bath coming up. He says the journey will take at least four, possibly five, days."

"I guess we'll have to strip and wash. But this carriage is so lovely, I don't mind." Indeed, Sophia felt she could happily live on this train for the rest of her life and never set foot on firm ground again.

Misha was leaning out of the adjoining sitting-room, buying food sold in bamboo baskets by vendors on the platform. "Tiger prawns," he said, lifting a lid. "Good, good. And we'll have some of that duck!" Hearing his voice through the open window, Sophia laughed gently. Misha cared for them and fed them with such diligence. And if he hadn't rescued her at the inn . . . No, there was no use going over that again. Misha had been there and for that she was truly grateful.

A man thrust his basket under Misha's nose.

"Ahh!" Misha sighed. "A duck to die for." The delicate strips of pink duck lay upon a bed of green spinach, dressed with a red sauce and a few slivers of almond.

"Misha seems happy," Sophia said.

Elena nodded but said nothing. She walked from the bedroom into the sitting-room, which reminded her of Katrina's sitting-room at home. It was small but comfortable, with a little dining table and four chairs. At the far end was a door leading to two other bedrooms and a small lavatory. Dreamily Elena sat down and contemplated the strangely isolated life of a traveler. All four of them had been together now for many weeks. St. Petersburg, her home, and family were finally beginning to recede for her into a hazy distance that only longing could reach across.

Looking out of the window, Elena saw Chinese soldiers boarding the train. The sight of them made her shiver. Why must so many people die in war and revolution?

The train puffed and blew out steam. Katrina smiled to see the girls apparently settling so quickly in such foreign and unfamiliar surroundings. They had been well trained. *Noblesse oblige* had been drummed into them from when they were tiny. The hallmark of an aristocrat, as Anna often reminded them, was that you are at home anywhere and with anyone. Katrina had a vision of Anna's face reflected in the window, nodding in approval.

"Eat, eat, eat!" Misha was ravenous after what had been for him an unsatisfactory breakfast. The girls sat down at the table as the train pulled out of the station. *Shanghai-Shanghai-Shanghai* puffed the train. *Who-who-who?* screamed the wind. Rocking in their carriage, the girls ate the fragrant delicacies. Misha's sore heart was assuaged. He had found his perfect duck.

❦ CHAPTER 16 ❦

For four days the train wound its caterpillar way along rivers and gorges, meandering across flat fertile plains, then climbing precipitous mountains. Sometimes Sophia feared the train simply could not carry its great burden up the rocky inclines. After a particularly perilous climb, she said, "I do hope we make it to Shanghai."

Elena looked amused. She did not have her sister's vivid imagination. A calm radiated from Elena, a resignation much envied by Sophia. "We'll get there," Elena said. "I reread my favorite psalm this morning: 'The Lord is my shepherd.' It goes on: 'Yea, though I walk through the valley of the shadow of death, I will fear no evil . . .'"

"I really must read my Bible more often," said Sophia. "The valley of the shadow of death," she repeated. "What a horrible thought. Elena, do you think Grandmother and our parents will be all right?" She looked out of the window and for a moment she thought she saw bodies strewn everywhere.

"They'll be fine."

"How can you be so sure?"

Katrina broke the moment's silence by saying, "Come along, girls. Let's do some sewing. You need to practice your needlework. And once we're settled in Shanghai, I can teach you to make your own dresses."

"Do you think our parents will be all right, Katrina?"

Katrina offered a warm reassuring smile. "Of course, girls. Your parents know what they're doing. If they were really worried, they would have left Russia too. Wouldn't they, Misha?"

"Of course," Misha said. "No question." Both Katrina and Misha knew they were lying, but there was no point in telling the girls that now, even as they traveled, the situation in Russia was worsening; that Misha, during their days in Peking, had met other Russians fleeing into China. Many of them were wealthy exiles; some were from the Bolshoi Ballet. All were on the run, trying to get away from what they saw as an approaching holocaust. There were at least fifty Russians on this train, all seeking safety in Shanghai.

Whenever the train stopped, Misha would run up and down the platform asking for news. One source of news was a young woman called Maria. Misha was much taken with her. On the second day he brought her to the carriage to introduce her to the girls. "We have company," he said gruffly. Misha was always gruff when he felt amorous. Though his diminutive stature prevented him from acting on his feelings, Misha possessed a proper admiration for beautiful women, particularly if they had long hair. Maria's bright red hair was even longer than Sophia's.

Maria stood in the doorway, smiling. Life, one felt looking at her, was just a huge joke, never to be taken seriously, always to be laughed at and celebrated with a good bottle of champagne. She had just such a bottle in her hand. "So early in the morning?" Katrina inquired. She certainly was not going to take on trust any Bohemian-looking young woman whose background was unknown to her. Katrina realized how difficult life was going to be from now on: before, she had only to consult a few of the servants and she immediately knew the pedigree—or lack of one—of any person approaching her girls. Now she would have to rely on her instinct to protect her charges from harm. Katrina's instinct was to lock the girls up for the next few years and bury the key, but it was too late for that now. She scowled at Misha, who smiled back benignly.

He knew Katrina well enough to expect her to scowl. Well, let her. The girls needed the company of someone closer to their own age. Maria smiled gracefully and glided into the carriage. Both girls were quite overawed by her striking appearance. How beautiful she is, thought Sophia. I wish I could walk like that, thought Elena. "Let's have a toast!" said Maria, swiftly pouring champagne into the five glasses supplied for the occasion by Misha. "To the Tsar and his family."

Sophia took a mouthful of champagne. The bubbles tickled her throat. Elena sipped her champagne slowly and a quick vision of Sir Edward raced into her mind.

"To those we have left behind," said Katrina sharply, in a reproving tone. Maria giggled. Her long red hair waved like a flag and her deep green eyes flashed. Where did she get those eyelashes, Katrina wondered. She checked the woman's hands. Never done a day's work in her life, I expect . . . Katrina was getting cross. Those emeralds on her fingers looked more like evidence of an old man's lust than a young man's offer of marriage. "Are you traveling alone?"

Maria let out a small laugh. "Yes and no," she said. Then she hurled her glass against the wall. "Goodbye, Mother Russia," she said. Sophia detected anger and hurt in her voice.

"Come," she said, touching Maria's hand lightly, as Misha went off to get a brush to clean up the mess, "let's sit down. I'm desperate for outside news."

Elena sat opposite Maria. "I'm almost afraid of news from outside. In here no one can hurt us."

"But we can't stay on a train for ever," said Maria and laughed, revealing a glimpse of perfect pink gums and white teeth.

"Do you get off in Shanghai," Sophia asked, "or are you traveling on from there?"

"No, I'm going to Shanghai to stay with friends until all this trouble is over back home."

"Did you want to leave?" Sophia fished for information. Romantic preoccupation was meat and drink to Sophia. Sophia was in love with the idea of being in love, and who better to imagine being in love with than Sir Edward, the man who waited for them in Shanghai. All her thoughts about Sir Edward centered upon his ability to inspire romance in the shape of passionate kisses, hidden nights of love, bunches of roses strewn with jewels . . . Maria, Sophia hoped, was in the same position and they could compare notes.

Maria was silent for a moment and then said hesitantly, "In a way I had no choice." She could see Katrina listening avidly. This was no time to be careless with words. "I am an actress. I have just finished playing in a Turgenev play. I have no family. I was brought up in a convent. My mother offered me to the nuns before she died; in return for my education I was to become a nun myself."

Sophia listened eagerly. How romantic!

"But things didn't turn out like that. I was, well, I was too independent. So I left the convent and struck out on my own."

Katrina sniffed. Not on your own for long, she thought, if those jewels on your fingers are anything to go by. Humph. This young woman will be putting ideas into Sophia's head—and Sophia has enough ideas of her own.

"Go on," Sophia said. "What happened next?"

"Next? I found lodgings and then I approached the theater. Some people were kind to me along the way and I was one of the lucky ones. Moscow is full of people trying to be actors and actresses, but I didn't take long to reach the top. And the top is a dangerous place to be in times like these. So I left.

"Now you know all there is to know about me, but I know nothing of you. Where are you from?"

"St. Petersburg," Misha said eagerly. "The most wonderful place in the world." His eyes grew moist with emotion.

Sophia leaned over and put her hand on Misha's head. "Hush, Misha," she said gently, feeling suddenly very grown-up. She turned to Maria. "Who are you traveling with?" she asked.

"A group of ballet dancers. They're nice

enough, but like all ballet dancers they think only of themselves and their bodies. They talk of nothing else but ballet. I don't know how it will be in Shanghai, but many of them will never dance again. And I wonder what chance I'll have to act. Who knows? There's a big Russian community there, I'm told. Maybe we'll all end up doing plays and ballet for each other."

The four members of the Oblimov household were silent. None had any idea of what lay in store for them. All they knew was that their future lay in the very capable hands of Sir Edward Gray.

Maria changed the subject. "Did you know," she said, "there is a new fashion in hairstyle this year? I learned it in Moscow. Shall we give it a try, Sophia?" For the next few hours Maria and Sophia did and undid each other's hair until Katrina thought she would scream. Try as Katrina might, there was no way of shaking Maria off. For the first time Sophia had a friend, someone she actually liked. For the rest of their journey Maria was in and out of the carriage all the time. And on one never-to-be-forgotten occasion, Katrina lost Sophia for a whole afternoon. Like an invincible ship, she stalked the corridors, peering into all the carriages as the train swayed and chuntered along its course, and finally spotted Sophia in a second-class carriage with a crowd of Russians. She could hardly see the girl through the smoke from the cheroots. The women in their silks and satins looked like a clutch of dragonflies. Their clothes clung to their limbs in an indecent fashion, Katrina noted. Sophia sat among them as if she had known them all her life. Every so often one of the crowd would stand up and stretch a leg or bend to the floor and touch an ankle. They'll be filling her head with nonsense, thought Katrina, pulling open the door. "Countess Oblimova, you will come with me immediately."

Sophia was mortified. She wished she could drop through the floor of the train. Not only had she been exposed as a countess—which might not go down with her new friends—but also she suddenly felt like a baby with a nanny. Why could Katrina not leave her alone? Katrina grabbed Sophia's protesting hand and dragged her from the carriage. The last Sophia saw of her friend Maria was her amused glance, and she heard her shout, "I'll see you tomorrow!"

"Not if I can help it," muttered Katrina. "How dare you run off like that?"

Sophia was angry. "How dare you embarrass me in front of my friends?" she screamed back as they struggled up the corridor. "Let go of me! Let go of me!"

"Certainly not!" Katrina retorted. "Those are not the sort of people your mother would want you to know."

"I don't care." Tears were streaming down Sophia's face. By now the row had attracted an audience. Bored faces, bored no longer, peered around compartment doors. Katrina forged ahead, towing an irate Sophia in her wake. "Those are *my* sort of people!" Sophia screamed. How could Katrina do this to her, the one time she had finally found a group of people who interested her?

When they reached the carriage Sophia threw herself into Misha's arms. "Misha," she wept, "Katrina is going to stop me from seeing Maria."

"Oh no, she is not," said Misha, "I'll see to that."

"Misha," Katrina said, "I am in charge of the girls."

"So am I. Come. We'll talk." Misha opened the door to his room and pulled Katrina, easily twice his size, inside.

When they came out Misha was beaming, while Katrina scowled. "You can continue to see the woman," Katrina said, "but only here in this carriage. Anyway," she added triumphantly, "we only have tomorrow, then we'll be in Shanghai."

Misha smiled at Sophia. "Never mind, little Nightingale." He stroked Sophia's hair. "I will find her for you." And he winked. "You are like your grandmother. You need your flighty friends."

Sophia sighed. "I think I would die if I had to live the way we did in St. Petersburg. I don't like respectable people. I really don't. They live awful lives, trying to be like each other. If one woman has a blue dress, they all want blue dresses. If one girl ties her hair up, they all tie their hair up. It's a dreadful way to live. I want to live like Grandmother. Her house was always full of . . . of . . ."

"Bohemians," Katrina said drily. "And they deserve their awful reputation. They steal the silver and have dirty habits," Katrina announced emphatically.

"I'd rather lose the silver," Sophia countered, "and lead an interesting life than keep the silver and die of boredom."

"All this talk of dying." Katrina decided a retreat was necessary. "If you concentrated more on your needlework, you'd find interest enough."

That night, Sophia dreamed of her new friends and their exotic lives, while Elena dreamed of her Edward. Misha's snores only just outdid Katrina's, but the snoring seemed to make the world a safer place. The train hooted into the cold, cold night. Only the puffs of smoke kept the seagulls warm as they drifted off course from the sea at Shanghai. Nearly there! they yelled. Nearly there!

❧ CHAPTER 17 ❧

Sophia stared out of the window of the train as it slowed to edge its way into the city through the crowds that stood, sat, or squatted along the railway line. "Fabulous, fabulous," she kept whispering.

Elena was not so enchanted. Many of the Chinese who squatted were performing their morning ablutions and, without modesty, defecated where they sat. She noticed that the little children wore trousers with open flaps at the back. Men, pushing carts, collected the steaming ordure as if it were a prized possession. Carts piled high with fruit and vegetables passed by. "I hope we've come to the right place," Elena said nervously. "I mean, what if it's absolutely awful?"

Sophia did not take her eyes from the window. "I love it, Elena. It's all so alive and busy." She thought back to the St. Petersburg streets so empty of stalls, the lack of food in general, and the grim faces of the peasants in Russia's capital, trying to keep body and soul together. "It's much better here," she said. "I promise you we'll be happy."

Katrina noted the vegetable carts outside the window and was pleased. Already she imagined cooking the vegetables for her girls. Misha just smiled. He didn't mind where he was, he decided, as long as the girls were happy.

The train finally pulled into the gigantic station. Bedlam broke loose. Through it all Sophia recognized the tall figure of Sir Edward Gray waiting for them. Before him lay a red carpet and beside him stood several officers of his staff in full uniform: red coats with gold cummerbunds, swords at full salute. "Ah!" Sophia laughed. "We are to have the red-carpet treatment!"

"Of course," Katrina replied. "You're daughters of the great Oblimov family and you are to be officially welcomed."

Elena had eyes only for Sir Edward, becoming less of a blur and more of a reality. She held her breath. Had he changed? Did he look older? Then the train stopped. She breathed freely. No, he had not changed. He was exactly the same as when she last saw him. She gazed at him, her large blue eyes filled with admiration. Sophia, forgetting all her mother's training, flew out of the train and ran into his arms. Sir Edward hugged her and laughed. "Now, now, Nightingale," he said. "You mind your manners." Etiquette. The officers stood, their swords pressed to their noses, at a loss for a command.

Elena stepped out of the train. She extended her hand to the station manager who had been obsequiously hovering around the door of their compartment. The manager, much relieved that he had a role to play, took her hand gratefully and walked her up the red carpet to where Sir Edward stood. Gravely Elena curtsied. "Thank you so much, Sir Edward, for meeting us. You are very kind."

Sir Edward nodded, and from that moment his heart was completely lost to this slim girl with her gentle manners and quiet ways. Much as he loved Sophia in an avuncular fashion, he adored Elena deep in his heart. Edward, for many years a bachelor, had never found a woman he could love and trust. Certainly he had had liaisons with a number of women, but never had he found himself completely engaged in the flirtations and the carrying-on. He had always prayed that one day he could safely entrust his heart to a woman who would not play polo with his emotions, a woman who would stand behind him in his career and beside him at the many receptions, cocktail parties and banquets that played such an important part in his life. Elena, he knew, was such a woman. A girl now, but soon to be a woman.

Edward motioned to Misha and Katrina to proceed with a coolie to the waiting limousine. Having saluted the girls, the officers sheathed their swords. They marched off while the girls followed Sir Edward to the car. Sophia was entranced. There had been cars in Russia, but this was a gleaming leviathan made by Rolls-Royce in England. Misha and Katrina were squeezed into the back with a mountain of luggage. The girls sat either side of Sir Edward. As they turned out of the station, Sophia could see her friend Maria going off with her troupe of compatriots. Sophia waved through the window. She didn't worry because Misha had the address of the lodgings where Maria would be staying: she was not going to lose her. Maria was too important to her.

Elena said nothing but leaned back, feeling very protected and comfortable now that her Edward was here. Sophia gazed at Sir Edward, studying the long line of his upper lip. She smiled at him. "At last," she said, "we've arrived."

Edward inclined his head. "Yes, at last. And I want you to be a good girl and behave yourself."

Sophia grinned. "I? Why, Sir Edward. What can you be thinking?"

Sir Edward did not smile. "Sophia," he said, "life right now is rather a grim business. We have a war in Europe and troubles here. I've heard from your mother that, since you left, St. Petersburg has been renamed Petrograd." He shook his head.

"It's not the war I fear most for Russia. It's the Bolsheviks. That madman Rasputin is virtually running the country, which gives the Bolsheviks all the more reason to push for revolution. It's all very troubling."

"Have you news about Mother and Father? How are they?" Elena suddenly spoke.

The Englishman took her hand reassuringly. "They are fine," he said, so much wishing he could take her into his arms. "They are very well indeed."

"And our grandmother?" Sophia interjected.

"She sends her love as well. I have letters waiting for you."

The car nosed its way through the city throng. Shanghai was a gloriously painted lady. Much of the color came from the blue suits and jackets. The days were growing warmer and the people were beginning to leave the dim shadows of their shops and come out in the mornings onto the sidewalks. Cages of birds sang to the passers-by. Little cooking stoves supported woks of bubbling soup. It was breakfast time and thousands and thousands of people squatted around the warm braziers, brandishing chopsticks and chattering. The girls' eager ears were met by the sounds of children carrying satchels, on their way to school, old people making ready for a new day. Poles of clothes hung out of windows and lines stretched over alleys. A veritable forest of trousers, skirts and blouses danced in the wind. Sophia thrilled to the pulsating energy of the city. The car passed through the different concessions: first the German concession. Apart from a tutor from Munich, Sophia had only met a few Germans in her lifetime at court. Most of the men seemed very stiff, with little sense of humor, their wives fat and complaining. And now they were the enemy. Certainly the German concession seemed more orderly than the Portuguese quarter. Big houses loomed in the streets. Huge gates clamped protectively around the occupants. They passed through the French concession and Elena brightened up. "Look, Sophia, dress-shops." Sophia made a face, remembering hours of tedious fittings at St. Petersburg dress-shops while seamstresses, their clenched lips full of pins, fussed about the hemline.

Finally they were in the English concession. The road leading to their new home was long and wide. Trees and houses stood to attention on both sides. The car pulled into a drive that swept up to a huge, Gothic, Victorian-style mansion dreamed up by an imaginative architect for the greater glory of Queen Victoria and her consort Albert. Sophia loved the house. It was wonderfully monstrous with turrets and gables. "This," said Edward, "is home." Elena smiled quietly. At the back of the car Misha felt a definite thrill. He had always wanted a turret, a high place where he could pretend he was an eagle and no longer crippled. Katrina was just glad the months of journeying were over and both girls were safe and sound, and now in the care of Sir Edward. "Thank God," she murmured, crossing herself. She leaned back and smiled at Misha. "We made it," she said.

Misha nodded happily, and hopped out of the car.

✑❧ CHAPTER 18 ❧✑

The news reaching the Oblimov Palace was terrifying. Stories of servants killing their masters were no longer mere rumors that could be dismissed as scaremongering. The spirit of revolution was spreading and what had been a dream for some and a dreaded nightmare for others was fast becoming reality. Mobs of Bolsheviks went on nightly rampages, overturning the edifice of the Russian aristocracy. Frantically Russia's rulers struggled to keep their hold on the country, like a shaky-handed surgeon trying to resuscitate an all but dead patient. But in February 1917, St. Petersburg, now called Petrograd, fell to the Bolshevik workers who first had crippled the city with strikes. By mid-March the Tsar was forced to abdicate and his family were taken as prisoners to Tsarskoye Selo palace, leaving behind a succession of provisional governments to try to run the country according to a new order.

Boris, with both his mother and wife to look after, and worn out by the task of protecting two households at once, decided they should all live together. He and Isobel arrived by car, and additional carriages were immediately dispatched to gather up Isobel's entourage and servants and bring them all to the safe and fortified walls of Anna's palace.

Anna sat in her chair beside the fur vacated months before by Misha. Misha, she thought. Oh,

Misha! It has come to this: the royal family in captivity, aristocrats fearing for their future, and a band of lunatics and barbarians running the country! But there was no rough head to fondle, no intelligent brown eyes in which to find sympathy. Instead Boris paced the room, while Isobel sat in a chair by the window silently weeping, only a hiccough of a sob occasionally disturbing the cold air.

"We've done what we can," Boris said. "If we manage to withstand an attack tonight, we may be able to make a run for it tomorrow. Think, Isobel, if we follow the same route as the children, we may be able to get to Shanghai and be reunited much earlier than we ever thought possible."

"I won't go, Boris." Anna stood up and walked across to Isobel. "Darling, I'm too old to rush off to another life. My world is here. After all this is over, everything will settle down as it always does. The people of Russia are individuals. They won't want their new masters to chain them to the state, any more than they wanted to be bound by the Tsars. In the long run, I believe in my people, their sanity, their honesty and their love for our country. I prefer to wait here. But, Boris, I think you should go, and go now." Anna felt tremors threaten to shudder her small frame. If I can persuade them to go, and the Bolsheviks come tonight, I can hold them off long enough for these two to escape, she thought. Smiling, Anna said, "The snow is still deep and my sleigh is already loaded with provisions for such an emergency as this. Don't trust any of the servants. When it gets dark, put on old clothes and drive away as if you were seeking food or firewood. God knows, there is nothing to eat in St. Petersburg."

Boris shook his head. "But we can't leave you here."

"You must, Boris." The Golden Salamander was firm. "I order you to leave, to save your life and that of Isobel, the girls' mother. I have Ivan with me. We'll be all right. But the girls need you, especially Sophia." Anna put her hand out. "Elena will be fine, but Sophia can be so difficult. Life isn't easy for her. She needs your influence or she could well take the wrong road and find herself in trouble. Go now. Get ready. I will rest for a while. Go."

Boris took Isobel's hand and gently kissed it. Deep within himself, he realized just how much he had come to love and respect this quiet gentle woman who had stood so coolly by his side all these years. The throbbing moments of lust and passion shared with other women, the torrid nights of sweat-soaked sheets wrapped around other women's bodies, nights also of tears and recriminations, all counted for nothing. The love Isobel gave him was pure, and the nights they shared left him cleanly slaked. His waking was without guilt or an aching head. His light touch on her long white back was always rewarded with a lovely devoted smile. "We must go," Boris said. "Mother is right. This is our only chance."

They climbed the long staircase to the room where they slept. Boris opened the door and then impulsively picked Isobel up in his arms and carried her over the threshold as he had when she was his young bride. Softly he laid her upon the bed and, sighing, she wrapped her arms tightly around him. He made love to her for, he felt, the last time. She responded to his want with all the passion she could muster. Their union was so complete they would for ever be part of one another. With his head lying upon his wife's soft breasts, Boris began to contemplate their nightmare journey out of St. Petersburg. Isobel thought of the twins. "How surprised they will be!" she whispered.

"Yes," her husband said. "We must hurry, darling." He lifted himself up on his elbow. He looked down at his wife and smiled. "Come along," he said. "Let's put together a few things and then we'll go."

They rose out of the warm safety of the bed and began to pack. Two valises, Isobel thought. Two valises is all that remains to us of our lives together. She wandered about the vaulted room. She touched the brocade curtains. She looked at the carpets from Persia. All this we must leave behind, she thought. She would take her jewels in her jewel case and a few clothes. What will happen to the horses and the dogs? she wondered. What would happen to the peasants on their estates, to old Rushka who was ninety-two and could no longer feed herself. "What will become of us, Boris?" Isobel asked urgently.

"I don't know," he answered. "Only God can answer that question. But for a while Russia will be no place for us or for our children." He put his arm around his wife's shoulder. "Who knows for how long?"

They were standing at the window overlooking

the city that lay in darkness. Gone were the nights of balls and banquets, when torches and lanterns lit the skyline in beautiful glistening celebration. Most of the shops were long out of food and boarded up. The bigger shops had holes in the windows after looters had run wild down the streets, screaming "Death to the bourgeoisie!" Some of the shopkeepers had been beaten and others killed. Great mansions and palaces stood empty, their owners fleeing abroad or to their country houses.

"Come, Isobel," Boris said. "It's time to go."

Downstairs Anna was waiting for them. She pointed to a small door in the hall. "Leave quietly," she said. "I will go upstairs and make a noise to distract the servants. You stand in the shadow and then slip outside. The sleigh is there and the gates are unguarded."

"Unguarded?" Boris looked alarmed. "They can't be unguarded."

"I called off the guards so that you could leave unnoticed." She was pleased to see the anxiety in his eyes vanish.

"Oh," he said. "I was worried they had defected."

"No," Anna lied to her only son. "Our guards would never defect. Go now," she said, wanting the next hours to be over as quickly as possible. The guards were gone and she sensed the Bolsheviks getting closer. Before long she would hear the dreadful tramp of determined footsteps, the angry shouts of an unruly mob ready to loot and rape and kill, all in the name of justice. Tenderly she took Boris into her arms and kissed his face. "Take care, my beloved boy," she whispered. "Get there safely and kiss the little ones for me." Anna embraced Isobel and then pushed them into the shadows. Silently she glided upstairs and then loudly rang the bell in her bedroom.

Only the cook heard the bell. He had watched all day as the serving maids hurriedly left. Now he was alone in this huge, empty, echoing mansion with only one determined old lady and her priest. The cook had long wanted to get even with this woman whom everyone feared and loved. He feared her, but he didn't love her. He hated her and all her kind. He too was waiting for the tramping of feet and the stench of blood on his insurgent friends—those who had ruled the poor and treated them like scum deserved to die. If some that died by the sword or the cudgel were killed needlessly, so much the better. The rich never discriminated between the deserving poor and the villainous, or the uncomplaining peasant and the troublemaker. Let them all die!

The cook watched as the sleigh pulled away from the house. "The Count and the Countess," he whispered to himself. "Huh! How long do they think they've got before we catch up with them?"

"Ivan," Anna said, "you must go."

The priest shook his head. Anna had taken refuge in her drawing-room. She sat in her customary chair by the hearth. Tonight she had laid her own fire. She knew that the cook alone remained, and that he stayed for a reason. Ivan stood beside her chair and watched her anxiously. "I will not leave you," he said. "I cannot leave you. If they come, then we must hold them at bay for as long as we can to give Boris and Isobel a chance. Believe me, Anna, I have seen this moment coming for years." He saw Anna's face whiten, the delicate blue veins in her temples throb.

"I, too," she said. "Now I feel inexorably sucked into a future that has no future. This time will pass. A new generation will be born who will seek liberation from the tyranny that is to come." Anna gazed into the fire, her eyes focused on some distant vision. "Ivan, I see many long years ahead. A violent dictator, his hands dripping with blood, stands over Russia." Her voice rose. "Do you see him, Ivan?"

Ivan shivered.

Anna's face relaxed, and she shook her head. "This is not the way I want to live," she said. "Ivan, if you won't leave, we must prepare ourselves for what must come."

The middle hours of the night found Anna sitting motionless in her chair. The fire was still burning and the heat intense, but Anna was cold, in anticipation of the nightmare to come. She wore all her jewelry, her diadem of diamonds on her head, enormous gems on each finger—rubies from Burma, emeralds from Africa—and ropes of pearls lay on her breast. She sat upright in her throne-like chair, her small slippered feet resting on a gold embroidered pillow, and waited.

In the library Ivan was at prayer. He knelt at a

small prie-dieu, the fingers of his white hands locked in supplication. Ivan was not praying for his life. That he knew he had already lost when he made the decision to stay with Anna. Rather he prayed for his soul and for Anna's, that they might be united in all eternity. He prayed for Isobel and Boris, that they might reach Shanghai and be reunited with the girls. He prayed for Russia, that she endure her long agony. He prayed for all mankind and offered up his death in return for the saving of some poor soul. He knew the cook would lead the Bolsheviks to him first and then to Anna.

And suddenly he saw lights in the courtyard and heard the pounding of excited feet. Then the cold hallway rang with the sound of men shouting and women cat-calling, of sticks and swords striking glass and hacking at furniture, of paintings being slashed, of marble busts toppling to the ground. Leaving a trail of destruction in its wake, the mob spread through the house urged on by the cook, his fat face distorted with the orgasmic joy of despoliation and desecration, his tongue hanging out of his mouth, slobbering with the urge to kill. Behind him men and women raced, panting, their eyes bulging, their hands knotted around weapons. Running, running, running. Then the cook pushed open the library door and smiled an obscene smile. Ivan rose to his feet and drew the sign of the cross. His fingertips touched his forehead, his heart, his left shoulder and the right. He finished with his fingers touching his lips. "Into thy hands . . ." he murmured. The mob pressed into the room and the cook, raising an old revolver, shot Ivan in the chest. As Ivan slid to the floor he finished his prayer ". . . O Lord, I commend my spirit."

He saw a bright white light before him and a hand reaching out to him. Ivan smiled and the crowd swayed nervously. A man going to meet his death smiling? the cook thought. Surely not. The cook wheeled, afraid the crowd might get superstitious. "Come on!" he bellowed. "The old bitch next!" For a moment he sensed the hesitation in his followers. He fired several shots into the hangings on the wall. "Revenge! Revenge!" he screamed. The crowd began to tear down the library, pulling bookcases from the walls, swinging on the curtains, smashing the chandeliers. The cook seized the big Bible that always lay on the library table and tore the illuminated pages from the binding, throwing them through a shattered window out into the night air.

The rabble regained its revolutionary fervor. It was ready to kill again.

Anna sat and waited. Like Ivan, she was praying. She was not praying for herself but for Ivan. She knew he was dead. She heard the shots even through the thick walls. Ivan was far from the fray now and in a moment she would join him. All her thoughts rested on the sleigh, as if by an act of will she could get Boris and Isobel to safety.

The cook led the charge to the upper floor, but having spent all his bullets, he now held a sword in his hand. The thought of running the old bitch through with a blade excited him.

They did not need to break down the doors to the drawing-room. They were open already. As the cook paused momentarily on the threshold those following him gasped, for they did not find the cowering pleading aristocrat they had expected. They saw Anna imperiously sitting at the far end of the room, her chair facing the door. The fire's embers burned demonically. Anna saw the wild-eyed rabble and smelled the stink of sweat and blood. "You!" she said, addressing the cook, her voice contemptuous. "Vile dog. I curse you."

The cook ran forward, his sword extended. "Bitch! Whore!" he screamed, plunging the tip of his sword into her heart. Instantly blood welled from the wound, but Anna's eyes never flinched. Wide open, they stared straight at the cook, whose own eyes rolled in fear. Filled with a superstitious dread, he pulled the sword out of her body, and it was as though it had been drawn from his own breast. He fell in a dead faint to the floor.

The crowd stood disconcerted. Anna sat in her chair, blood flowing down her breast, her face now like stone, but her eyes still staring. Her jewels gleamed in the light from the fire. The room was hot and still. The crowd were silent until one man at the back said, "I'm off. I don't like this at all." He could be heard running down the marble corridor to the main staircase. Others shuffled after him and slowly the mob melted away.

Eventually the cook stirred. When he opened his eyes, Anna's gaze was still upon him. The look chilled him to the marrow, penetrating him as deeply as the cold blade had pierced her. In a panic he fled.

CHAPTER 19

The sleigh hissed through the night. The horses' hooves were muffled. Boris would have preferred the speed and protection of his car, but on a night like this, with the rabble crying for blood, the car would have been far too conspicuous. Isobel was pressed close to his side, her face white and drawn in the light of the moon. Tonight the moon was no friend to the fleeing couple.

Soon the sleigh pulled past the main square and Boris tugged on the reins. The horses obediently turned down a small back alley. It was a risk Boris knew he had to take to avoid the crowd ahead that he could hear screaming and shouting. The alley led to a side of the city that was quiet.

Isobel, too, heard the screams of the crowd and saw the red pall cast over the city by the fires. "I do hope Anna is all right," she whispered softly.

Boris pressed her hand. "She'll be fine," he said. "She was not called the Golden Salamander for nothing, you know. She'll find a way out of this trouble. She always has."

Isobel managed a strained smile. "Can you believe," she said, "that we are fleeing our own city? I never thought a time like this would come." She shook her head. "Imagine, the Oblimovs living as fugitives. Still, the girls are safe."

The sleigh passed quietly down a deserted street. Boris felt the tension subside. Nearly out of danger now. Shadows from tall trees helped to hide them. All was silent. Not even a wolf howled. They were approaching the edge of the city when Boris saw what he had dreaded to see. "Damn!"

Ahead of the sleigh, coming toward them, was a long stream of enraged people. On seeing the sleigh, they broke into bloodcurdling whoops. Boris was horrified to see the tail end of the crowd detach itself and run around to circle the sleigh. "We'll be trapped," he muttered. For a moment he felt numb with fear. The crowd had been waiting for the moment when they could tear him and his wife to pieces. Well, he would not give them that satisfaction. The fear left him, and suddenly Boris was filled with a calm resolve, and knew what he must do.

He pulled the sleigh to a stop. The horses stood, puffing and blowing. The crowd advanced. He could see the blood-lust in their eyes and the hatred on their faces. Isobel did not stir. Trained never to show fear, she watched them as they approached. Boris drew Isobel into his arms. His mouth came down on hers. They kissed a long, sad, intimate kiss, gazing deep into each other's eyes.

Isobel did not hear the shot that took her life. "Goodbye, my darling," Boris whispered, his eyes full of tears as she slumped in his embrace. He waited until the leaders of the mob had almost reached the horses, then raised the pistol to his mouth and pulled the trigger.

The crowd howled with rage, frustrated in their urge to kill. Boris and Isobel lay for ever at peace in each other's arms, the stars above indifferent witnesses to this night's violence.

In his turret in Shanghai, Misha shifted and moaned, then awoke with a start. He got up and shuffled over to the window. "Something is wrong," he murmured. "Something is dreadfully wrong." Way above his head four stars winked at him. Misha prayed for Anna and the Oblimovs.

Not until daybreak, when the familiar early-morning noises of Shanghai began to fill the streets, did he finally manage to sleep again.

ᔥ CHAPTER 20 ᔥ

The news of the rampant killing of aristocrats traveled slowly. The official version lay in a letter on a slow and interrupted train.

Because of the great distance between St. Petersburg and Shanghai, and the disruption caused by war and social upheaval, letters from the Oblimov parents to their children and vice versa had been rare. All chronology turned chaotic, all replies utterly disjointed from questions that passed them in transit.

Elena had written to her mother, telling how well they were all settling in Shanghai, in the lovely house they shared with Sir Edward. She wrote of her great affection for Sir Edward himself. But Elena was worried, she explained, because Sophia seemed to show an interest in him, too. Nevertheless, should Sir Edward ever ask for Elena's hand in marriage, would her parents give their consent? The letter ended with many assurances of how much both she and Sophia missed Isobel, Boris and Anna, and a brief reference to the fact that Misha seemed to have found himself a good companion in the person of Mei Mei, the Chinese wash-amah who was no taller than he.

And somewhere en route to St. Petersburg was a letter from Sophia to her grandmother, full of love for the woman Sophia yearned to see again. A surprising number of Japanese soldiers could be seen in China, Sophia reported, but their new life in Shanghai was as peaceful as it was fascinating. Sophia told her grandmother about her beautiful friend Maria, and of Maria's circle of acquaintances: struggling artists, starving painters and thin-faced poets from Moscow, very much the sort of people she knew Anna could spend hours talking to. She assured Anna that Misha, though he missed her, was in good spirits. Indeed, a little romance seemed to have entered his life, and she went on to describe Mei Mei, who "giggles a lot when he is around." Sophia, writing from her four-poster bed in her lovely new bedroom, was happy. She told her grandmother about the view from her window, which looked out onto a courtyard that had a small pond with clumps of bamboo growing at the edge—inside the pool swam giant goldfish. She explained how she was getting to know the city, and taking lessons in the Mandarin language and Chinese calligraphy. "I love the way the characters represent the words," Sophia wrote. "The character for the wind actually looks like the wind blowing . . ." Sophia signed off with lots of love.

She never received a reply.

One letter that did arrive came from Isobel:

Darlings,
Your father is very tired and has lost much weight. The situation here is rather desperate, though nothing for you to worry about. We are thinking of leaving and joining you, if we can persuade your grandmother to come with us. I am sorry that we shall miss your birthday, but when we are together again we will have much to celebrate. The war is making life very difficult, but strangely it is in our interests to keep it going, your father says, rather than allow the war to end and the Reds to come to power. What a time we live in, when war is the best alternative to revolution!

Give our regards to Katrina and to Misha. We both hope they are looking after you.

With prayers and love,
Your mother

There was a short postscript from Boris:

I dream of the day when I'll be able to hold you both in my arms again. Your loving father, Boris

Both girls pored over the letter. Elena had another letter pushed under her mattress. It was an earlier note from her mother, and for once she refused Sophia the right to read a letter addressed to her. "It's mine, Sophia," she said firmly, "and I don't want to share it." Sophia was hurt and baffled. What on earth could be in that letter? She intended to find out.

Misha's eye was caught by the red of the temple roofs ornamented with great green black-eyed dragons that writhed and swirled, and seemed to grin at him as he and Mei Mei bowled along in a rickshaw, having spent the morning shopping together. Did he really love her with a passion he had never felt before, or was it that he saw something of his mistress, Anna, in this tiny woman? Her chin was imperious and she carried herself as one nobly born, with a pride lacking in the slouching figures about her. She never spat on the floor or picked her nose. She never smelled of sweat and garlic. She had laughing eyes and her hair hung long and black to her knees.

Nor was Misha's love—if love it was—unrequited. Not that Mei Mei said anything specific. His protestations of affection were met with a quiet smile, a down-fluttering of eyelashes, and a demure tremble of her very kissable lips.

Still, Misha consoled himself this hot spring morning six weeks after Isobel's letter to the girls had arrived, I know she loves me, because she cooks special dishes just for me. Any man knows that when a woman is interested in him, she tries to please his stomach, Misha reminded himself.

The elderly rickshaw man was in a good mood.

He was glad that his passengers were so light. His last fare had been a portly drunken gentleman. But these two were a pleasure to pull. "Surely your children will be small," he joked.

Misha blushed and looked sideways at Mei Mei. She lowered her lids and smiled.

"A pair of lovebirds, eh?" The rickshaw-runner grinned. "Nothing like love to take your mind off troubles. I hear that bastard Chiang Kai-shek is setting up a new government in Canton. Nothing good will come of it, mind you. The Manchus were bad enough, but Chiang is no better."

By this time the rickshaw had arrived at the servants' entrance to Sir Edward's house. Misha helped Mei Mei down and paid the fare. He gave the man a fat tip, so grateful was he for his welcome words on the subject of love. The rickshaw man laughed. He looked down at the dwarf and said, "Love makes beauteous all that it touches." And Misha, loaded down with straw baskets, beamed. "Marry her," the rickshaw man said. "Marry her. She is a good girl."

Mei Mei had run into the house, her heart skipping and jumping. I will make Misha the best Peking duck he has ever eaten, she vowed to herself. She loved the luminous brown glow in his eyes. She loved his tousled hair—which she had plans to cut so that it would curl nicely over his collar—so different from the plaits that hung down the backs of the Chinese peasants. She had heard recently that there were men in the North who had cut off their pigtails in defiance of the new government and insisted that they were free men. They are certainly brave men, she thought.

Katrina was in the kitchen when Misha finally stumbled in. The moment Misha set eyes on her, he knew something bad had happened. Katrina sat at the huge old mahogany table, her head in her hands, too choked to speak clearly. "They're dead," she blurted. "All dead."

Misha stared wide-eyed but unseeing at the mouth that had uttered such a dreadful piece of news. "How?" he asked, hoping there had been a mistake.

But there was no mistake. "Sir Edward heard today." Katrina swallowed. Her face was gray, etched deeply with lines of loss and sorrow. She looked ten years older. "I should not have left," she said.

Misha put his arms around her waist and tried to comfort her. "There was nothing we could do to save them, Katrina. We promised to take care of the girls." He didn't want to know any more details. His beloved Anna was dead. Never again was he to see her face. Never feel her arms about him, or see her smile at him with that lovely smile. The thought of his loss caused him to rock and shake and finally to howl. Misha wailed for the whole house.

Upstairs Sir Edward held both girls in his arms. He had kept the details to himself. "They died as bravely as you would have expected them to. They suffered very little."

The rest of that black day was spent by the grief-stricken trying to make sense out of a darkened universe. Maria arrived, sensing the desolation in the house as soon as she entered. Sophia clung to Maria, while Elena held fast to Sir Edward. "I shall never see their grave!" Sophia sobbed.

"Who will bury them?" Elena asked.

"I have written to ask," said Sir Edward, "but I am fairly sure that some of the servants who stayed loyal will have seen to it that they were properly buried."

Elsewhere in the house Mei Mei took Misha to his room, where she lay down beside him with her head on his shoulder, listening to his anguished outpourings. Katrina too was devastated. Her world had been the Oblimov mansion in St. Petersburg. Her life had been devoted to Boris and Isobel. She had always imagined that, when the time came for her to retire, she would live out the rest of her life in a little cottage on the estate, sitting by the window, watching the seasons go by . . . All these thoughts rambled through her head, keeping worse thoughts at bay. Katrina knew how a mob behaved. Be it English, Chinese, or Russian, a mob kills, because humans on the rampage behave worse than animals. Wolves at least kill to eat; humans kill out of envy, for revenge.

With the onset of evening a silence descended on the house. It would be many weeks and months before those within smiled again. Sir Edward, who had seen so much war, knew that nevertheless such a day would come. And then he would make known his intentions to Elena. For the first time in his life, Sir Edward was truly in love, and this fact comforted him as he, too, grieved for his friends. He sat up alone in his room late into the night.

BOOK TWO

The Snow Leopard

❧ CHAPTER 21 ❧

It took the stifling summer and a wet and muddy autumn before some sense of harmony was restored to the girls' anguished souls. During the days they were kept busy with their lessons and outings. Elena tried to distract herself with shopping trips. Katrina would follow her along the crowded jostling streets, in and out of emporiums. Elena's small face still betrayed her sorrow but she kept her back straight and her shoulders set in defiance. She knew her mother would expect it of her. For Elena, the loss of her grandmother and her father were just bearable by now, but she would never get over the loss of her mother. Elena and her mother were soul sisters, and with Isobel's death something had gone out of Elena's life that she knew she would never find again. While Sophia could always find comfort in Anna's receiving arms, it was to Isobel that Elena always turned in moments of need, and it was she who had been able to comfort Isobel in her darkest hours. So Elena shopped and sewed in an attempt to assuage the pain. Sophia hid her rage and her pain by going to parties.

Lots and lots of parties. So wild and so wicked that she caused many a frown on Sir Edward's face, when he saw her yet again going out on the arm of one of the many young Russians only too willing to escort a beautiful young countess anywhere she wished to go. Only Maria understood.

Sophia cornered Maria one day toward the very end of autumn. "Tell me the truth, Maria," she demanded. They were taking tea in the great Shanghai Hotel. Surrounded by white marble walls and servants running about with white towels over their arms, the place all hurry and scurry, the two young girls sat in idle splendor, their legs crossed neatly at the ankle. Her eyes flashing at the men who passed by, Maria said, "I'll try, Sophia. I promise. But remember, if I tell you my truth, it might not be the truth you want to hear. You may prefer your own truth, so you mustn't get cross if you don't like what I say."

Sophia said she understood, then leaned forward earnestly. "I've been watching Elena with Sir Edward. Have . . . you know . . ." Maria arched her eyebrow, encouraging Sophia to go on. Her great virtue was that she was an excellent listener, which was why men found her so attractive. "Do you think Sir Edward is in love with Elena?" Sophia blurted out, finally giving expression to the fear that had been haunting her ever since Elena had received the letter she refused to show Sophia.

Maria, not much older than her friend but infinitely wiser, made a move. "Good heavens, Sophia! I wondered when you were going to wake up. Anyone can see that they're wild about each other."

Sophia flung herself back in her seat. She felt as if a knife had been pushed into her breast. Her eyes filled with tears. "But I love him, too," she said in the hurt voice of a little girl.

"No, you don't, you goose. You just like the idea of being in love with him." Maria took her friend's hand. "You'd be bored with him before long. He's too safe for you. Leave him to Elena. They suit each other." She leaned back. "Besides, I've lined up a treat for you this afternoon."

Sophia smiled through her tears. "Then I'll have my treat now and worry about Sir Edward and Elena later."

"OK," Maria said, using the American slang expression she had picked up from a certain young American naval officer with whom she went dancing. "Okey-dokey. Let's go."

Sophia signed the chit and they left the hotel. The Rolls-Royce glided along the road that ran down to the Bund. Colonnades shadowed the doors to numerous shops. Soon the car turned into a small dark alley off the Nanking Road. A giant wooden door barred the dead end. On the door was a golden dragon. "Hoot your horn four times. Loudly," Maria instructed the chauffeur.

The chauffeur looked fearfully over his shoulder. "I no go there, missie," he said. "That bad joss house."

"No," Maria answered. "It's a good joss house."

Hissing to himself, the chauffeur hooted, and on

the fourth hoot the gates swung open, revealing a courtyard in which there was a large pond filled with sacred carp and surrounded by little waterways and trellises. The sound of the running water was soothing to Sophia's recently jangled nerves. "Why is the driver frightened when it's all so beautiful?"

"The Gorgon has a terrible reputation among the local population of Shanghai. They are afraid of him, but I don't want to prejudice your meeting with him, so I won't say anything until you've had your audience."

Sophia felt a flicker of fear. "He won't hurt me, will he?"

"No." Maria was reassuring. "But you'll understand when you've seen him."

The car drew up at a moon-shaped door and the two young women stepped over the lip of the big round hole. Sophia felt she had just entered the inner ring of hell, or heaven—she couldn't decide which. The walls were lacquered in Imperial red, with a gold-leaf design superimposed. Jade statues lined the hall. She recognized one figure as that of the eternally laughing Buddha. He stood fully her height with his face turned to the sky, his mouth huge and his belly fat. Just to see him made her smile. They walked self-consciously down the corridor to another door at the far end. Maria knocked. Maria has obviously been here before, Sophia thought. I wonder why she kept it to herself. Maria's ways were incomprehensible to her sometimes, but Sophia was looking forward to this interview. "Is he a soothsayer?" she whispered while they waited for the door to open.

Maria shook her head. "He's a monk, a very ancient monk."

"Oh. I see." She remembered the monks of Urga and felt a growing excitement. The door swung open.

A young man in monk's robes ushered them both into a comfortable sitting-room. The room had European chairs, which was a relief, for Sophia found squatting on her heels very uncomfortable. Not so Maria, who folded herself down on the floor. "Is the Master ready yet?" Maria asked. The young monk gave Maria a lascivious smile and she grinned back. Huh, Sophia snorted to herself. Maria's been at it again.

Then the inner door of the antechamber opened and a small thin figure stood before her, blinking. He looked as if he had been preserved for thousands of years. His hands were pressed together in greeting. He bowed his head. "Ho ho," he chimed softly. His voice rang like windbells through the room and into Sophia's bones. "Ho ho. This way."

Sophia shot a look at Maria, who was smiling. Maria motioned with her chin. "Follow him," she said.

Sophia trailed after the little figure, feeling big and awkward. They entered a room half in shadow. A bed was pushed into a corner. Not really a bed, she noticed. More of a plank with a wooden neck-rest. Thin filaments of sunlight filtered through the green bamboo slats that covered the skylights. "Sit," the old man said. Sophia saw a straw mat at her feet and she sat down. She hoped she could sit still long enough not to disgrace herself in front of this elderly man who looked like some delicate antique. "Legs hurt?" He smiled. Sophia nodded, startled. How would he know? "Child," he said, "you have come here from many times ago." Sophia felt the blood behind her ears turn to ice, a sensation familiar to her whenever she was frightened. "I am Lau Tchi," the man said. He was wearing a long robe, the cowl of which he pulled up over his head. "Look into my face and begin your journey. Hold your fingers so." He held up his four fingers on both hands and Sophia did exactly as he said. "Now touch your thumb with your third finger and hold them in front of you until I see you again."

As Sophia felt her thumbs touch her fingers, she was suddenly hurtled out of the room, sliding down a tunnel that whistled her through the ages. Before her eyes she saw the pyramids still under construction. She saw Moses in his bulrush basket, and the shape of a man beside him. Out of the desert rose another huge figure, that of a goddess. A door between the breasts of the figure was open. Sophia hesitated. The desert was hot and oppressive. She looked down at herself. She was wearing a blue silk robe. Around her waist was a twisted belt of pearls and her feet were shod in embroidered silk sandals. The open door was inviting. It looked dim but cool inside. Walking carefully with her arms extended, she approached the door. Beside it she noticed a scarab, an ancient beetle hammered out of copper. She walked up the narrow hall lined with sarcophagi. Goosebumps tingled all over her flesh as she approached the back of the hall.

Sophia came to a halt. She stood in front of a purple silk hanging. A cool breeze from nowhere made the silk ripple and shimmer. A voice, also emanating from no visible source, said, "Pull back the curtain," and she did. Sophia found herself face-to-face with a bird. The face was that of an eagle and the claws that clung to the golden perch were strong and thick. It was the eyes that drew Sophia's attention. They were clear green, made of emeralds, yet seemingly alive. "Who are you?" she asked breathlessly.

"I am your mentor," the voice cawed. "I am with you always. I speak to you through Lau Tchi. You have been chosen to do great things with your life. I have called you this once to tell you to prepare yourself for a life of service. This is your destiny. Your only choice is to accept it or not . . ." The voice faded. "I will come again when you need me. Now go your way and return whence you came. Remember," the voice faded more, "remember, I shall always be with you." Sophia felt a wind suck her back through time.

And then with a jolt she felt herself once more in her own body on a mat, sitting before a very old man who was smiling at her. "Are you a wizard?" she asked.

Lau Tchi shook his head. "I am one of the ancient ones," he said. "I am the last of my dynasty. The history of China, the history of the world, is written in my soul. It is my destiny to guide China through the coming struggle. And you have been chosen to help me, Sophia. Now," he said without moving from his place, "go. I will see you again."

Sophia stood and left. How long she had been in the room she could not say.

CHAPTER 22

"Was that all a dream?" Sophia stared out of the car window.

Maria laughed. "It depends on what you believe. I have always studied the occult. I've read widely about all the religions that exist." She stretched and yawned. "Lau Tchi is my master. If I need him, I call him. He has given you the great honor of his time. He acknowledged you. Now it's up to you. You can accept his gifts or not . . . But then, knowing you, Sophia, I don't see you backing away from unusual experiences."

The car drew up before the little gray door that led to Maria's lodgings. For Maria they were a great source of embarrassment. They were poor and shabby. For Sophia a visit here was a delight. She could sit on Maria's bed and watch Maria and her friends giggle and gossip. The samovar was always bubbling. Today, however, she did not want to go in. She had too much to think about. What had just happened, for one thing. But she also needed to come to terms with the idea that Elena loved Sir Edward.

Sophia sat in the back of the car, having kissed Maria goodbye, and tears rolled down her face. She felt lonely and orphaned. Most of all she felt betrayed, a feeling that had first assaulted her when she watched her father making love to his mistress in the library, long ago. His betrayal made her wary of love of any kind. Love can be given, she thought, nestling in the luxurious car, but love can always be taken away. When love is betrayed, the pain is like that of a wound left unstitched.

For the first time, Sophia had to face the fact that Elena loved Sir Edward as much, or even more, than she loved her sister. When the car stopped at the house Sophia leaped out and rushed up the stairs calling for Elena. She finally found her in the music room. The soft strains of a Mozart minuet fell soothingly on Sophia's ears. Reluctant to destroy the harmony of this beautiful music, she waited, her eyes fixed on her twin. Elena sat in a haze of golden light. The piano too was golden. Bird's-eye walnut, Sophia guessed. Watching her beloved sister with her gentle smile and soft blue eyes, Sophia in her heart of hearts knew that Elena would be happy with Sir Edward. Both were reserved and self-contained. So, Sophia told herself, she must put aside her own love for the man and content herself with announcing that she knew Elena's great secret. "I know," she said as the piece came to an end. "I know all about your loving Sir Edward."

Elena sat with her hands poised above the keyboard. "And you're not cross?"

"No. Of course not, silly. Why should I be cross?"

Elena stood up and flung her arms around Sophia. "You're still my twin, you know. No one can ever take that from us."

"I know." Sophia felt her sister's warm slim back as they stood breast to breast. In a way, Sophia thought, this is a farewell. Once there were only two of us, and now there will be three. We have to grow up, she supposed, but for the moment she wished they never would. One day I won't be able to share a bed with Elena. She will have her own bed with Sir Edward. Who will be with me in my bed? "Did Mother know?" she asked, with a slight stammer on the word mother.

"Yes." Elena nodded. "She did know, even without my saying anything. I mean I wrote to her about it—about Sir Edward—but I don't think she ever received my letter. But Mother knew me very well, and she sent a letter saying she approved."

"The letter you wouldn't let me see?"

Elena's eyes clouded. "You were grieving over their deaths, I didn't want to hurt you any more. So I hid the letter until we all had the strength to face life again."

"Oh Elena! I should have known you weren't being selfish. How could I have misjudged you so?" She hesitated, then decided to share her secret with Elena. "You'll never believe me when I tell you what happened to me today." They walked down the corridor arm in arm while Sophia tried to find words to describe her experience with Lau Tchi.

"There. You see? I don't know if it was a dream or if I actually did fly back in time."

Elena was sitting in the drawing-room beside her twin, her brow furrowed. "You don't really believe in things like that?" she said.

Sophia snorted. "Why not, Elena? It says in the Bible, if you check it carefully, that God made the *worlds.* Not just one world, but *worlds,* plural. Who's to say that we are the only civilization? Why shouldn't there be lots of other galaxies? Time is a man-made illusion. Perhaps there is no time, just a continuum, and we are all living at once. Maybe all our lives run parallel, and there is no past, no future, only now. And perhaps occasionally we accidentally bump into ourselves in another dimension. 'Good heavens,' we say to ourselves. 'Fancy seeing you here.' " She could see incomprehension on Elena's face. "Anyway," she said, putting the subject aside. "Enough of all this mystery. My brain aches with it."

Katrina came bustling into the drawing-room. "Really, Sophia. You and your raffish friends! A man arrived at the door with this parcel for you. What on earth it is, I cannot think." She sniffed and handed the small package to Sophia.

It was wrapped in thick brown paper and tied with hemp. Sophia was intrigued. Who on earth could have brought it? she wondered. Quickly she untied the string and tore open the parcel.

"Huh," Katrina opined. "Tear the paper, tear your heart."

"Mine is already torn," Sophia replied. Inside was a small box the size of a pocket book wrapped in a black silk scarf.

"Oh, hurry!" Elena whispered. "This looks interesting."

When the wooden box was opened, there lay a deck of cards—not playing cards, like the ones the girls used to play snap, but a different kind of cards altogether. Sophia took them out of the box and gazed in awe at the figures depicted on them—figures representing love, life, and death. "Tarot cards!" Katrina said with evident disapproval. "Give them to me, child. You don't want to be doing with that sort of thing. In the old days you could be killed for even possessing such cards."

"No!" Sophia was adamant. "The cards are for me. They're mine. I won't part with them." At the bottom of the box was a tiny book with instructions on how to use them. "Come on, Elena, let me tell your fortune."

"Do you think we should?" Elena giggled.

"Nothing good will come of this," Katrina said and she stormed out of the room to tell Misha.

"Miss Sophia is up to her usual tricks," she announced to everyone in the kitchen. "Misha, she has tarot cards."

Misha looked at Mei Mei. "Maybe she can tell our fortune," he remarked.

"Oh Misha, you're impossible." And Katrina retired to her room, grumbling and rumbling.

Elena's future, judging from the notes in the

booklet on each upturned card, looked bright. There was a man in her life whom she loved and who loved her. The card of strength lay between them, and money appeared in abundance. The answer to the question card was clear: yes, she would marry Sir Edward. Elena was delighted.

Sophia's own spread of cards put her in a bad mood for the rest of the evening: many men in her future, the crumbling tower, signifying destruction. "Dear Lord," she prayed as late into the night she spread the cards on her bedroom floor, trying to come up with a brighter prophecy, "save me from my future." Looking into the red embers in her fireplace, she saw again the great beast with the luminous emerald eyes. But now the eyes were opaque and offered no comfort.

ॐ CHAPTER 23 ॐ

"Sophia! Wake up, Sophia!" Elena was knocking on the door. She let herself in and leaned over Sophia's bed.

"What's the matter?" Sophia said sleepily. "I was dreaming and . . ." She stretched and rolled over. "It was such a lovely dream, too. Bother you, Elena. What do you want?"

"Are you sure you don't mind me loving Edward?"

"I'm sure." Sophia shut her eyes. "I'll just have

to find myself a lover. After all, Maria has a lover. Awful man, called Vassily. *Very silly,* I'd call him, but Maria says he's good in bed."

"Sophia, you won't do anything foolish, will you? I mean, you're not hurt, are you?"

Sophia opened her eyes again and contemplated Elena's worried face. "Of course not, darling," she said. She put her arm around Elena's neck and pulled her down beside her. "Why should I be hurt? And I won't do anything foolish. Rash maybe, but certainly not foolish." She thought of her father again, and then tried to imagine Maria with no clothes on with this Vassily person. Well, she thought, I might as well get on with life. Everybody else seems to be. Even Misha is in love. That only leaves Katrina and me. She kissed Elena and then sat up. "I need a good hot bath, and then I'm off to Maria's house to look for a lover."

"Sophia!" Elena's voice was incredulous. "You can't just go out and look for a lover. It's not like shopping for something. You must wait until you fall in love."

"Fall in love?" Sophia snorted. "That sounds like something to be avoided, like falling ill. Definitely not. I am my father's daughter . . ." She did not complete the sentence because Elena had no knowledge of her father's amorous escapades.

Sophia finished the rest of the sentence to herself as she lay in her bath, relaxing in the hot water. She washed between her legs with the big yellow sponge from the spongebag that had been a Christmas gift many years ago from her parents.

A familiar fevered feeling stretched from the middle of her spine and tingled down her legs. Ahh, she sighed, I will be famous in Shanghai as the lover of many, just as my father was in St. Petersburg. I shall have many men. I have an appetite for love. I know I have.

The sponge had a rhythmic life of its own. And finally Sophia let herself go to the rhythm and the lapping of the hot bath water. Ecstasy, sheer ecstasy.

When Sophia was ready to leave the house she sensed a glow of contentment. Freed of her childish infatuation with Sir Edward, she was ready to take on the world. And where better to start than Maria's lodgings?

On the way there in the car, Sophia, wearing a blue silk gown and carrying a small parasol, fanned herself with a black silk fan, and practiced looking over the edge of it with seduction in her eyes. Not bad, she thought. Not bad at all.

Maria greeted Sophia in the hall. "Darling," she said, "you look quite different. What has happened to you in the last twenty-four hours?"

"Tea, Maria. I am dying for some tea. Quick, let's go to your room."

Maria's room was at the top of a long flight of stairs. The house was tall and tenanted by a large group of young people. Open doors revealed unmade beds, with bottles and candles everywhere. On some of the beds, and even on the floor, lay entwined bodies. Two very old amahs doddered about the building sweeping and cleaning and moaning about the occupants. How they live! Sophia thought joyfully as she followed Maria up the stairs. Some day, she vowed, I shall live like this: free, able to do anything I want.

"Maria, you were right," Sophia said as she sipped her tea. "Elena will undoubtedly marry Sir Edward. They are such a straight couple. But for me life has to be different. You know, when I was traveling back in time, I felt as if all my life I've been stagnating, just sitting and waiting at a window while real life hurried by. If I'm not careful, I could end up an old maid left on the shelf."

"Ah, Sophia!" Maria laughed the affectionate nostalgic laugh of an experienced woman conversing with a virgin. "Sophia, my dear, you see yourself as quite the woman of the world." The inside of her mouth was bright pink and her tongue rolled back as she chuckled.

Sophia was mildly stung. "What's so funny?" she asked sheepishly. "Do I sound silly to you?"

"No, of course you don't. Not at all. Don't worry. You have all the makings of a worldly woman, if anyone does."

Sophia, though unsure, felt reassured and flattered. "Then why do you laugh?"

"You just reminded me of myself a few years ago when I was your age. A bit younger than you, actually. I decided to get rid of my virginity, so I found a cowherd who had massive thighs and broad shoulders. I persuaded the poor man to make a bed out of sacking in the cowshed and I gave myself to him."

"What was it like?"

"Wonderful. Absolutely wonderful. He was big and lusty and we lay on the hay. I lay there thinking, 'Is this really me?' " She sighed dreamily. "I enjoyed every moment of the adventure."

"Weren't you worried about getting pregnant?"

"Not really," Maria said. "I tried the old trick of using a piece of cotton soaked in vinegar. Anyway, since then I have had many lovers, but that was my first man. I never saw him again. But I'll never forget him. Listen, little one, I'll give you a tip. When you choose your first lover, find one whom you will never want to forget. Don't just grab the first man to come your way. Make sure it is an affair you will remember with affection. I've had some that make me blush with regret when I think of them."

"How about Vassily? How will you remember him?"

"Oh, Vassily! He'll be here soon. We can all go out for lunch. Vassily is just a stop-gap until I meet the love of my life." Sophia heard the edge of sadness in these words. "I've waited for so long for the love of my life." She got up and moved to the window to watch the crowds below swirling past. "I hope there is a love of my life. I'm not the compromising type. I can't imagine just putting up with someone for the rest of my life without being passionately in love. Can you see me living in a small house by the river, having babies? I can't cook, and I hate housework. All I can do well is to make love."

"And you can act," Sophia added.

"Yes, there's always my acting. But there's no real need of actresses here."

"Then you'll have to marry someone rich like my father. He wasn't faithful, you know."

"Most men aren't. Sex doesn't mean much to them. A quick sneeze below the waist, and they run off home to their wives. But what matters is if the man has given you his heart. He may be unfaithful, but as long as you have his heart he will always come back to you. My last lover gave me his heart, but I handed it back to him. He got much too settled in his ways. I was fearful that he might arrive one day with his slippers in one hand and sit the whole evening smoking his pipe and reading a newspaper."

Sophia finished her tea and gazed at Maria. "That sounds just like how Elena and Sir Edward are going to end up. They'll spend evenings reading poetry or she'll play the piano for him—he loves listening to her play. They'll sit for hours discussing the day's events. Even now, they both drive me mad with boredom. I want adventure. I want to go out there," she said with a sweeping gesture, "and really live."

"That will all have to wait a bit," said Maria gaily. "I hear Vassily and he's bound to be starving. He always is."

"By the way," Sophia said, "did you send me some tarot cards?"

Maria shook her head. "I didn't send you any cards. But now that you've been introduced to the Gorgon you must expect many strange things to happen. My life has never quite been the same since I met him."

Vassily burst into the little room, filling it with his presence. "Come on, girls," he said. "Let's eat. Quick quick."

Maria sighed and winked at Sophia. "It's always quick quick with Vassily. Too quick."

Sophia felt herself blushing. She caught the sexual innuendo in Maria's last remark. I'm definitely growing up, she thought as they left the house and battled their way up the road to a local restaurant where the Marias and Vassilys of Shanghai could be surrounded by their own kind.

❧ CHAPTER 24 ❧

By the beginning of winter Sir Edward felt confident that sufficient time had passed since the girls' bereavement to allow himself the great joy of proposing to Elena. Sophia seemed to be eternally busy with her friends and her social life. Elena still mostly stayed at home and occupied herself with running the house. Misha and Mei Mei took charge of the kitchens. Misha was in his element, ordering the menus and supervising the cooks. Only Katrina couldn't settle. Try as she might, even in the company of other Russian servants who looked after their titled families, Katrina missed Russia. "But it's no longer the Russia you knew," her friend Agatha told her. "Now everybody is equal. The war is ended, the Tsar is dead . . . Everything has changed. There is nothing of the life we knew to go back to."

"Yes, there is," Katrina said. "There are the mountains and the hills. There's no peace here. There are too many people, too much rushing about, here, there, everywhere. Agatha, do you remember the smell of the pines in the forest? And the smell of the trees when the leaves begin to turn?" She breathed in as if in so doing she could re-create all that she missed. "Here all I smell is dust, and I hate the food. Rice served with little bits and pieces is no substitute for a good Russian meal. What about a huge roast wild boar? Or real borsht. Oh, Agatha, I think about the cabbage soup with vinegar . . ." Katrina shook her head. "Once my little one is married, I think I'll go home. Sophia doesn't really need me any more. She's a wild thing and I have no control over her now. Yes, I think I'll go back to my home town in Georgia. There," she said, "I never thought I'd live to hear myself say that. I must be getting old, Agatha. I really must. Recently I've been dreaming of the Georgian mountains and of the wine."

"I doubt they still drink wine in our godforsaken country!" Agatha retorted. Then she softened. "Maybe we'll all go back one day. Who knows? Maybe there is something to be said for the new way. You and I are lucky. We've worked for good families. Others have not been so fortunate . . . Maybe it's a good thing that everyone can now run their own lives . . ."

"Which reminds me." Katrina laughed. "Look at the time! I must get back to the house. I have the girls' ironing to do, and Sophia goes through so many clothes."

While Katrina was making her way back home, Sir Edward found Elena in the library. "What are you doing, my dear?" he said, suppressing an urge to drown her in kisses.

"Just reading. Turgenev's *Fathers and Sons*. The critics, both conservative and liberal, still haven't forgiven him for writing that book, although I do think their criticisms unfair. I think Turgenev was even-handed and accurate in portraying the younger generation as well as the old. And his critics have made life so difficult for him, putting him on trial for his work, and . . . Oh, what am I saying? Who am I to challenge the thoughts of the great intellectuals?"

Sir Edward smiled. Elena's cheeks were pink. She didn't usually express such forceful opinions, but he and she had read so much to each other over the last year that now she was beginning to have her own ideas about things. "I take your point, Elena. He suffered such great poverty, and I don't believe that's good for a writer. I'm not one of those who subscribe to the notion that poverty must be the mother of a writer's creativity."

"Poor soul," Elena said, looking down at the book in her hand.

"Elena," Sir Edward began, mustering his courage. "Elena, I have something of a private nature to ask you."

Elena looked up at Edward's face. She could see the love brimming in his eyes and the nervous quiver of his upper lip. She simply smiled at him, confident that this was the long-awaited proposal. For a moment there was a hush in the library, with only the ticking of the great clock solemnly counting off the minutes as they passed away for all eternity.

"Elena, dear," Edward began nervously. Suddenly he was no longer the urbane, sophisticated, much traveled man of the world; he was like a young and inexperienced boy, uncertain and hesitant, but so much in love. "Wait a minute," he said. "I must get something." He was gone, leaving Elena alone.

She sat, perplexed but patient, her hands clasped loosely on her lap. Soon she heard the sound of Edward's footsteps coming back into the library. He had one hand behind his back and a package in the other. "Presents?" Elena said, smiling.

"Oh, Elena!" Edward whispered. He was so afraid she might say no. He crouched down on his knees beside her. "Elena . . ." and then he forgot everything he had ever learned about the art of love. He thrust the bouquet of roses at her and dropped the box of chocolates on her lap. "Please marry me, Elena. Please. I implore you."

Elena laughed, secure in his love. "And if I don't?" She smelled one of the long roses. "What will you do?"

"I'll die, I swear it. Elena . . ."

She bent her head and kissed him shyly on the

cheek. Edward crushed her into his arms as he had been waiting to do for so long and kissed her as though his life depended on it. He kissed her with such force and ardor he left her gasping. Before she had time to recover, Edward drew a box from his coat pocket. "This is for you, a pledge of my undying love."

Elena opened the box: three perfect diamonds, set in white gold, mounted on a gold ring. "They're beautiful! Oh Edward," she said, for the first time abandoning the use of his title, "how did you know I've always wanted an engagement ring just like this?"

So Edward was to be her lover and her husband. The thought made her catch her breath. Although she too had experienced sensual yearnings, unlike Sophia she had curbed those feelings; the sexual side of her nature remained dormant. But now the man she loved was kneeling before her, the ring on her finger a binding promise, and Elena felt a rush of excitement.

She stood up and laid the roses and the chocolates on the table next to her. She and Edward leaned toward each other, as if drawn by an invisible thread, and fell into each other's arms. Then she kissed him with all the pent-up passion she possessed.

"Come! Let's call the servants and announce our engagement!" Edward was so relieved that Elena had agreed to marry him, he wanted to tell not only the servants, Sophia, and his friends of his good fortune but the whole world. Today he would have to be content with telling the servants.

Tomorrow he would arrange for the news to be published in *The Times:* "The engagement is announced between Sir Edward Gray and the Countess Elena Anna Borisovna Oblimova. The wedding will take place within the year."

Holding hands, the couple walked down the stone stairs to the kitchen. Katrina was just coming through the servants' entrance when she saw them. "Elena, my baby!" Katrina screamed and fell upon Elena in such an orgy of kissing, Edward felt quite nervous. "Ah, Sir Edward! My prayers are answered. My little Elena is going to be married!" She took Elena's hand and examined the ring with a very practiced eye. "Good, good. Nice ring. Very valuable." She pumped Edward's hand with a strong grasp. In vain he tried to withdraw it.

Misha, upon hearing the commotion, came running in with Mei Mei at his heels. "How happy we are!" He beamed. He put his arm around Mei Mei. "What a wonderful day!"

Edward beamed back, a shared masculine understanding between two men who have the woman they love on their arm. "Tonight there will be champagne for everyone," announced Edward. "I will call everyone together to toast our engagement and to drink to our future happiness. Get busy, everyone! We have a feast to prepare."

"It appears that I'll be able to leave sooner than I thought," Katrina mumbled to herself, and she went upstairs to the sewing room and a pile of clothes that needed mending. That cheered her up.

Sitting forlornly by the pile was a rather wan-looking Sophia. "So," she said accusingly, "they're engaged. He didn't waste much time. I mean, I expected it, but not so soon. In a year or two maybe . . ."

"Well, Sir Edward took us all by surprise."

"I guess I can call him Edward now," Sophia sighed. "He will be my brother-in-law. I don't know, Katrina." She looked at her nurse with sudden earnestness. "I think I'm destined to go to my grave a virgin."

"Oh, you do say such silly things!" Katrina laughed. "But there are worse things in life than dying a virgin."

"No, there aren't." Sophia was serious. "Think of all that unspent passion going to waste!"

"Sophia!" Katrina was beginning to feel uneasy.

"Never mind," said Sophia, catching the turn in Katrina's tone. "We'll have a party tonight, and you and I, who are two old maids, can toast the happy couple."

And with that she went off to her bedroom and her tarot cards. "No good," she told herself. No decent men in the spread at all, except the Fool, and she could do without one of those. "Damn it," she cursed the cards to their upturned faces. "Send someone to love me!" And she tried again. This time she got the Hermit, all hooded with his lamp over his shoulder. Just my luck, she thought. I get the celibate Lau Tchi. She thought she could hear him chuckle. "Remember, I am with you always," he reminded her. "Oh no, you're not," Sophia replied firmly. "I have my own life to live." She lay back on her bed and awaited the inevitable arrival of her twin sister.

CHAPTER 25

"Well?" Sophia was lying on her bed with her arms under her head. "I hear he proposed to you. A bit sudden, wasn't it?"

"Yes." Elena smiled. "It was far sooner than I expected, but, oh Sophia! I am so happy." She threw herself down beside her sister. "Look at my ring." Sophia stared at the glittering stones, then burst into tears. Elena held her in her arms. "What is it, Sophia?"

"I'm going to lose you. And then I really will be an orphan. No mother, no father, no sister."

"Hush," Elena whispered. "You aren't going to lose me. Edward and I will always be your family."

Sophia could not stop crying. She felt as if she had been outlawed from the universe, as if she hovered alone in the cosmos, suspended by only a tiny thread. Her relationship with Elena had been exclusive, hers alone to be treasured. Sophia longed for the certainty of Elena's life. She wished she could take delight in the small things that entranced her sister. Why must I chase the exciting, the different? she wondered.

Slowly the sobbing subsided and she fell silent in Elena's warm embrace. "I'm happy for you, Elena," she said after a while. "Really I am." She pushed the hair away from her forehead. "I must look terrible. I'd better go and wash my face."

Katrina came in as Sophia walked out. Seeing the tears still wet upon her cheek, Katrina looked sympathetically at Elena. "She'll get used to the idea."

"I feel terrible," Elena said. "I'd never want to hurt her. But, Katrina, I'm so in love with Edward."

"He's a good man," Katrina said, "and you will be very happy. Our little bird will be sad for a while, and then," Katrina grinned, "she will be happy again. Try not to worry too much. Now, I'm off to get ready for the party tonight."

Elena slipped away to her own room.

So far she had hardly had time to think. The proposal, the announcement, and Sophia's tears were all jumbled up in her mind. Elena drew a chair over to the window and contemplated her new position. Just imagine, she thought, soon I will share a room with a *man*. How, she wondered, does one walk about in such circumstances? With clothes or without? I have a dressing gown, of course, but then what about the bathroom? With Sophia, we've shared beds and baths since we were born. How odd to share with a man instead of another woman! How will it feel? She felt a twinge of fear. My life from now on will be totally different. She looked at her ring. The diamonds twinkled back. Funny, she thought, leaning her head against the rail of the chair. In many ways Edward is very much the man of the world, but emotionally I feel almost stronger than him. She remembered his pleading face. He really needs me. This thought pleased her so much that she jumped to her feet and began to dress. After tonight—well, by tomorrow morning—I will be different, she promised herself. I will make more effort at running the house and I will learn to give dinner parties. Not parties like Sophia's, where her friends lie about and argue about philosophy and *avant garde* art, and drink like fish. No, I will give proper dinner parties for Edward and his colleagues, and I will prove to him that, though I'm young, I can be the perfect wife and hostess.

The gong for dinner sounded and Elena flew downstairs, where she found Edward waiting in the library. She ran into his welcoming arms and buried her face in his chest. "I'm so happy, darling," she whispered.

"So am I," he said.

Sophia walked in as they kissed. "Oh dear," she said. "Am I going to have to put up with endless romantic embraces from now on?"

Edward smiled. "Come here," he said, "and give your brother-in-law-to-be a kiss."

Sophia smiled. "Oh well, if Elena has to be bourgeoise and get married, she could do worse than you, I guess."

Edward swept Sophia off her feet. "I see," he said, putting her down after a full turn, "the

Countess Oblimova does not approve of the thoroughly bourgeois pastime of getting married."

Sophia sniffed. "It's all right for some, I suppose," she said in a teasing tone. "But soon," she said, "the rest of us are all going to be equal. Women are going to be liberated."

"Liberated from what?" Elena looked puzzled.

"Not from what, from whom. From men. Women like me won't have to get married any more. We won't have to be men's slaves."

Elena laughed. "Since when has Sophia Oblimova ever been a slave to a man?"

Sophia blushed. "Never." She had run out of cheerful jokey things to say.

Elena put her arms around Sophia's shoulders. "You'll get used to the idea soon. You will, darling, won't you?"

Sophia raised her head and made herself smile. "Of course. I'm just being boring. Come on. Let's call in the servants and get on with the toast."

Edward chuckled. "That's our Sophia," he said. "Calling for liberation one moment and for the servants the next." He followed both girls out of the library, watching them walk ahead of him, arms linked, heads together. It will take some time, he thought, before they are ready to separate. Elena will learn to lead her own life . . . But in his heart he was worried about Sophia. Still, he reassured himself, once I'm married to Elena maybe I can be more of an influence on Sophia.

He heard Sophia laugh at something Elena said, and knew then there was nothing that could be done with her. She would go her own way.

The servants were summoned to the dining-room for the toast. Sophia eagerly sipped her champagne while waiting for the formalities to begin.

Edward raised his glass when Number One Houseboy had filled all glasses in the room. "All be upstanding for the loyal toast," Edward called out. "His Majesty!"

"The King!" the room reverberated in unison. None of the celebrants but Edward had ever seen the King, but in each heart there lay a love for the distant figure so far away.

"Now it is my pleasure," Edward announced, "to propose a toast to my bride-to-be. Elena," he said, looking at her with such love that Sophia thought she would burst with jealousy. "To my darling fiancée, Elena," he said. "A long happy life for us both."

Sophia swallowed her glass of champagne in a single gulp. Misha saw her wild face and desperate eyes. "Come, Mei Mei. Let's go and talk to Sophia. She's taking this engagement rather badly." Misha reached up to rest his hand on Sophia's shoulder. "Sophia," he said gently.

"You, too?" she whispered, feeling the first heady effects of the champagne. "You'll leave me, too?"

Mei Mei looked terrified.

"Never," he said. "I'll always be your Misha. Mei Mei and I will never leave you." Inwardly he groaned. Wait until she hears that Katrina is going home, he thought. Poor girl, her world is disintegrating.

In the general bustle and chatter Sophia drank two more glasses of champagne and soon began to feel uncomfortably dizzy. Misha saw her sway. "Here," he said, guiding her by the arm. "Why don't you lie down for a while?" He walked her into the hall.

She looked up the stairs and saw what a long way to the top it was . . . Misha caught her in his strong arms as her body went limp. His eyes were full of concern. "I'll take her up to bed, Mei Mei," he said. "Go and tell Elena that Sophia is tired and needs an early night." As Misha carried Sophia up the stairs and along the long corridor, he talked to her, hoping the sound of his voice would somehow comfort her. "My little pet," he said. "Don't you remember the days at your grandmother's house when I comforted you? Don't you remember having tea with your grandmother when I sat beside your chair and held your hand? How could you think I would leave you?" The celebration this night had pained Misha. Somehow the happiness in the room contrasted so sharply with his vivid mental picture of the terrible events that had happened in St. Petersburg not so very long ago. As he looked down at Sophia's white face, he could see many resemblances to that of his beloved Anna. "Don't worry, little one," he said upon reaching her room.

He carefully laid Sophia on her bed and covered her with a light blanket. "Sleep now, my child, and tomorrow you will be happy. I give you my word that you will not be alone."

Misha left Sophia adrift on a sea of unhappiness.

In her dreams she saw the Hermit in the distance; even he was walking away from her. She briefly opened her eyes, but the room was swinging around and around.

In a way Elena was relieved to hear that Sophia had been put to bed by Misha. She had feared that Sophia, with enough champagne inside her, might fly into one of her tantrums and spoil the evening. She stood beside Edward, feeling the heat from his body and relishing her role as his châtelaine.

After the servants had all congratulated the couple, they filed out. "Come, my dear," Edward said. "We can finish this bottle of champagne in the drawing-room."

Elena placed her arm around Edward's waist. How strange, she thought, to feel the thickness of a man's hard body instead of Sophia's slim waist. How odd to feel the stiff material of a man's jacket instead of the silk of her sister's dress. For Edward, the feeling was quite different. He sensed the tenseness in Elena's body, unfamiliar with his gait and height. She really has had no experience of men, he thought, then realized with a shock how deeply glad he was that she was his, in all senses of the word. The idea that he must initiate her into the adult world of sexual delight made him feel very humble. For a moment he felt disgust at the many women he had dallied with and the many beds he had lain in. Why didn't I wait for Elena? he wondered. He felt unclean and unworthy. I will make it up to her, he promised himself. I'll be gentle and patient.

Later, with the fire stoked and Elena sitting on his lap, he lay back contented. They kissed softly and then more passionately, but Edward knew he would wait for his wedding night, and even longer if need be. Elena was quite satisfied to lie in his arms and gaze into the fire. "I do wish," she said with a sob in her throat, "that Mother and Father and Grandmother could have been here tonight."

"I know," Edward comforted her. "So do I. But just think how happy they must be where they are now."

"In Heaven," Elena said without hesitation. "All three of them. And Father Ivan."

Edward smiled at her. "I love you, darling," he said. "And I will always take care of you."

Elena sighed, comforted. Upstairs Sophia lay alone in her misery. There was no one capable of comforting her.

❧ CHAPTER 26 ❧

For Sophia the ache of loneliness did not go away. "You *will* get over it," Katrina assured her too many times to count.

Privately Katrina realized she could not leave Sophia at this point. "Misha, I'm really worried about the girl," she sighed, her elbows on the kitchen table.

"When have we not worried about her?" Misha

replied. "Mei Mei and I are doing all we can to keep her company, but she feels like a watch whose spring is broken."

Mei Mei, folding table napkins, agreed. "Lovely blossom fallen on ground. Ground hard, and blossom not rest."

Two months later Elena was ready to give her first dinner party. "I'll be the best hostess you've ever seen," she said nervously to Edward.

"Darling," Edward smiled, "you're so beautiful, you could serve water and everybody at the table would think they had eaten with the gods."

Sophia was unwillingly roped in to help. "Who's coming?" she grumbled.

"Three couples, so altogether there will be nine for dinner. The Marlowes from APC, the Jeffreys from BAT, and the Harringtons from the Hong Kong and Shanghai Bank."

"Oh no," Sophia groaned. "Not the awful Mrs. Harrington. Honestly, that woman is a freak. Can't I at least have Maria and Vassily on hand to keep me sane?"

"You don't really think they'd fit in, do you, Sophia?" Elena was chewing on her pen. "It would be impolite to put them in a situation that's bound to make them feel awkward."

"Then what do you want me to do at this wake you're organizing?"

"Really, Sophia, sometimes I think you're just too spoiled."

"And sometimes I think you're in danger of becoming a real petite-bourgeoise."

"How can I be a petite-bourgeoise when I am a countess?" Elena replied.

"You think like one, that's the problem." Sophia rose from her chair. "I am going out to see Maria. At least she makes me laugh."

"And that's your problem, Sophia: all you think about is having a good time."

"If this is what engagement, let alone marriage, does to a person, I'll never get married!" Sophia yelled as she stormed out of the room.

"The way you behave, no man would have you!" Elena shouted back.

It was so unlike Elena to have the last word that Sophia was quite taken aback. The last sentence stung.

"Do you think any man would ever want me?" she asked Maria.

"Of course, darling," Maria consoled her. "Listen, you be good about your sister's dinner party and I'll take you to the celebrations for the winter solstice in the Heavenly Park. That's a promise, but you have to go now. Vassily is arriving to pleasure me."

"Just like that?" Sophia was interested. "Is he on a timetable or something?"

Maria grinned. "I'm a liberated woman. I make my own decisions."

"Whew!" Sophia whistled with delight. "Maria, you're marvelous!"

"Run along then, but first give me a kiss." Sophia offered her cheek, but Maria made her turn her face, and kissed her on the mouth. Sophia leapt back as if bitten. "It's nice between women, too," Maria said, looking deep into the younger girl's astonished eyes.

As Sophia walked slowly down the stairs, her hand touched her mouth still wet from the kiss. Sophia was shocked, but honest enough with herself to recognize that she had felt a moment of sensuous enjoyment. For a second she tried to imagine lying in bed naked with Maria rather than chastely dressed in nightgowns with Elena. She felt her nipples harden and realized how sexually arousing she found the idea . . .

Maria knows all about sex and how to give people pleasure, she thought. I don't know anything at all. And once again she felt very lonely and abandoned. Still, she comforted herself, the winter solstice will be fun. I guess I'll just have to endure the damn dinner party.

All week Elena ran about the house issuing orders, with Sophia tagging along behind. "Good heavens, Elena," Sophia moaned. "Anybody would think you were entertaining royalty. Remember who's coming! Ghastly Mrs. Harrington is going to bore us with her distorted perceptions of literature, and you're all going to go rhubarb rhubarb rhubarb at each other and shovel food down your throats and guzzle wine. And then it's down with the filthy napkins, kiss kiss kiss, and off they go into the night, and the servants have to stay up late to clean up after us."

"Don't be cynical, Sophia. I like Mrs. Harrington. And she's very well qualified to talk about literature. After all, she's a professor of English."

"I know, I know. Don't remind me. She finds a way to drop that fact into every conversation."

"Could you check that Misha has ordered all the food? And would you take a look at the menu? I've handwritten it and I'm so nervous that my handwriting's shaky. Make sure that I remembered to add that it's black tie; no decorations."

Sophia found the menu in the silver pantry and ran a jaundiced eye down the list. Sherry and lobster bisque. Hock with the fish course, white entrée, followed by a brown entrée, various puddings, grapes, and cheese, and a selection of sweet wines followed by coffee. And brandy for the men. Hunh, Sophia snorted to herself. Once we have liberation, we won't have to leave the men in order to discuss fashion and gossip about our friends. Sophia found her life unbearably claustrophobic. A free-thinker like Maria would never have anything to do with Mrs. Harrington, with her little boot-black eyes and her four chins and her fat pudgy hands that stabbed at the air when she talked. How could any grown woman wear ankle-socks?

Then it was Saturday, the day of the dinner party, and it poured with rain. The roads turned into rivers of mud and the coolies wore their pointed hats. Looking from her bedroom, Sophia marveled at the invincibility of the Chinese. In Russia the peasants worked because they had to. If they didn't work they were flogged and beaten, some to death. Here in Shanghai the peasants always seemed to smile and joke. Even the poorest went about their business industriously. In an odd way, after more than a year away from Russia, Sophia felt very at home in China.

She was standing in her room naked, waiting for her bath to be filled by Katrina. She had a big smile on her face: she was going to play a trick on Elena. She had borrowed a cheong-sam from Maria, which she intended to wear that evening. Elena would be horrified, because the slit in the black silk dress ran right up to the top of the thigh, and the garment was so tight-fitting it looked as if it had been painted onto Sophia's body. The only jewelry she planned to wear was a magnificent pair of diamond earrings. Elena might be engaged, she might organize a dinner party, but Sophia was going to make this evening her own. I am my grandmother's granddaughter, she reminded herself.

Standing in front of a full-length mirror, she pulled a long tress of hair over her shoulder and, shielding her pubic hair with her small hand, mimicked the well-known painting of Venus standing in a shell. Her pubic hair felt thick and soft in her palm. "Now, now, admiring yourself in the mirror again?" said Katrina as she bustled into the room, carrying hot water to pour into the bath.

"Go away, Katrina. I want to have a bath on my own."

"Hoity-toity!" Katrina remarked. "Sophia, you are getting *very* rude."

Sophia rolled her eyes. Then, seeing that she had actually hurt Katrina's feelings, she became contrite. "I'm sorry, Katrina. I know I've been rude and bad-tempered lately." She hugged her old nurse. "I'm just upset. I really didn't expect I'd mind so much about Elena getting engaged, but I do. I feel there's no room for me any more."

Katrina smiled. "I understand. Sophia, the little nightingale, is growing up. You'll have to find another name for yourself. Your grandmother was the fabulous Golden Salamander. What will you be?"

"I don't know," Sophia replied. "I'll sit in the bath and think."

She climbed into the tub and set her mind to the task of renaming herself. Picking another bird of song was out of the question. She had not sung for a very long time. The reason for this was by now embedded deep within her psyche. No longer was there a conscious decision not to sing. The habit and the urge to sing had simply left her . . . So, if not a bird, then what?

Usually, when she sat in the bath, inspiration came to her, but not this time. Determined to be late so that Elena could not send her back upstairs to change, Sophia consulted her tarot cards. She could hardly believe there was a time when she didn't have them. She was obsessed with them. If God can communicate through burning bushes and pillars of fire, she reasoned, maybe he could speak more directly to me this way. Every morning after reading her Bible she laid out the cards. She knew each one individually. They were her friends. Shut up in the house for hours with nothing to do, she found that these people spoke to her. The Fool was Vassily; the Queen of Discs—which stood for money—was Maria. The Knight of Cups—a man riding a horse holding a chalice with a malignant crab in it—was her lover-to-be. He looked dangerous but thrilling. If only I could capture his heart, she thought, hearing the sound of the gong reverberate through the house. Good. Cocktails are over and the dinner-party guests will be moving into the dining-room.

Quickly she ran to the cupboard and took out her cheong-sam. She wore no underclothes so as not to ruin the line of the dress. She pulled it over her head and slowly stroked it down her body. The dress was so tight it took several minutes to fall into place. She put on the earrings and slipped into a pair of black high-heeled shoes. Sophia turned her back to the mirror and looked over her shoulder at her reflection. Yes, that worked wonderfully. The fluid line of her back, her shapely tight buttocks, and the heels lifted her small feet. No makeup, except on her eyes, which she had outlined with kohl. The eyes stared back at her from the mirror. They looked fierce and mysterious.

I look like a panther, she thought. No, not a panther. One of those snow leopards. She had seen them in the market in the middle of Shanghai. One particular snow leopard had caught her attention. It was attached to a rope in the hands of a Tibetan musician. Although the animal was captured, Sophia had noticed the haughty look in its eye. Nobody, the look said, can truly capture a snow leopard. The beast's intense eyes glared at Sophia, who felt for it an instant empathy.

Now those same eyes stared back at her. That's

what I am, she whispered to her image in the mirror. I am a snow leopard. Or maybe by some magic Lau Tchi has turned me into one. *The Snow Leopard,* that's who I am. She shook her head at the image. I'm no longer my father's nightingale. Tonight I am reborn.

She walked slowly to the door of her room. Her walk changed from that of the former hoyden to the walk of a mature woman. Her hips, she found, had a rhythm of their own and her hands hung by her side. Sinuously she descended the stairs. Around her the air was electric. The Snow Leopard of Shanghai went down to meet the world.

❧ CHAPTER 27 ❧

As she walked down the familiar stairs Sophia felt irked by the placidness of her surroundings. Around the front hall English furniture stood solid and impervious to the cold weather. I would much have preferred Chinese furniture, she thought: mysteriously carved chests with great boats plowing up rivers and dragons seething and snarling; carved screens; a tall Buddha with a friendly stomach to pat and rub . . . She walked slowly across the hall and stood in the open door of the diningroom. She smiled and threw back her head.

"Oh dear!" Mrs. Harrington let out a shocked

gasp and put her hand to her mouth. "My dear Elena, your sister has gone native."

Elena, embarrassed at the criticism, smiled sweetly. "No, that's just Sophia. She's eccentric, you know." Then, turning toward Sophia: "Do come in, darling. You're a bit late."

Sophia grinned. She was enjoying the looks of absolute horror on the faces of the women and the men's eyes riveted on her tightly encased figure. "Sorry, but I took a little longer to dress than I imagined." She ran both her hands down the cheong-sam and slid into her seat beside Mr. Harrington. She waved the lobster bisque away. "No, thank you, Ah Ling. I'll just have the sherry."

Edward was neither amused nor horrified. "You look very pretty, Sophia," he said diplomatically.

Sophia was furious. The *very pretty,* she felt, was an implied rebuke. "Do you think so, Edward?" Sophia breathed. She let her thigh rub up against Mr. Harrington's bony shanks. She was delighted to see the banker turn pink and then deep red. Across the table Mr. Jeffrey, the British American Tobacco representative, was gazing at her bosom with an enraptured smile on his face. "How unusual . . ." he muttered. He was silenced by a knife-like scowl from his wife.

The tension was broken by the arrival of the trout fillets cooked in champagne. "Hock?" Sir Edward inquired. Ah Ling filled the glasses.

Sophia, who until now had consumed alcohol but never much savored the taste, suddenly realized that she very much liked hock—its lightness on the tongue and its fruity bouquet. She turned her head and admired her own reflection in the window. After all, she thought, if Maria and her friends can wear cheong-sams, why can't I? I am not going to be *like everybody else*. I leave that to Elena.

She observed the rest of the table as if she were suspended from one of the fat little angels in the moldings on the ceiling: Mr. and Mrs. Harrington, both prematurely wrinkled by the hot Shanghai sun; Mr. and Mrs. Jeffrey from BAT; and next to them sat the APS couple. Don't even bother with their real names, she silently snorted to herself. BAT, APS, and H & SB. They would work and live with their titles and then retire to Charmouth or Bournemouth or some other—mouth to spend their last years lamenting the old days in the Far East. Old China hands was what they were doomed to become.

She looked at her beloved twin sister, so beautiful and so young. She's like an orchid, Sophia thought, one of those air orchids that blooms and subsists only on oxygen. She felt sorry for Elena who obviously enjoyed the company of these old crabby people. "You see."—Mrs. Harrington was giving yet another of her lectures—"one simply cannot translate Tolstoy, as I told my class at the university. One must read him in the original."

Sophia tried not to yawn, wondering whether or not the woman really could read a single word of Russian.

Elena was alight with interest "Oh?" she said.

Then Sophia did yawn, much to Elena's embarrassment. It was one of those huge engulfing yawns that seemed to crack her jaw. Why was an English woman lecturing two Russian countesses on the virtues of untranslated Russian literature anyway?

Edward frowned. "Really, Sophia," he said. "I don't see why you cannot be interested in literature."

Should she, who had spent hours digesting books in her father's library, bother to meet this challenge head on? Sophia swallowed hard and replied, "Actually, Edward, I would rather live life than read about it."

Mrs. Harrington smiled. "She's young yet, Edward. Maybe, when she's older, she will learn to appreciate books a little more."

"I've always loved books," Sophia retorted, "probably not in the same way as you. To me they speak of the author's passions, and loves and disappointments and dreams. To you they are specimens to be dissected beneath a microscope."

"Sophia!" Edward said tersely. "Please don't be rude."

Sophia spent the rest of the meal gazing lasciviously at the two men across the table. She enjoyed watching their discomfort. Elena, busy in her role as hostess, forgot her sister and chattered away graciously. By the time the lemon sorbet arrived, Sophia was drunk. The table kept slipping away into the darkness and the room spun around her. She knew the only thing to do was to get upstairs as fast as she could. "Do please excuse me," she whispered.

Edward nodded. He had been watching her drink. Her face was white. "Good night," he said.

Sophia left the room, walking as steadily as she was able, and then clung to the wall as she made her way up the stairs. Katrina, who had been lurking in the hall waiting for the guests to finish dinner, found Sophia sitting on the top step. "Come," she said. "Come, darling." She smelled the wine, now rancid on Sophia's breath. "Ach, my baby, you've had too much to drink." She put her arms around Sophia and helped her to her room. She wisely procured a bucket, anticipating that Sophia was going to be sick, and held the young girl's head while Sophia vomited, feeling she would die. "Poor little one. You feel everything too much."

Sophia cried heartbreaking orphaned tears, weeping for her loss and for her loneliness. Somewhere out there, she said to herself yet again, there must be somebody for me. I can't live alone like this. "Please, God," she prayed into the black unknown. "Let there be somebody just for me."

❧ CHAPTER 28 ❧

The Son of Heaven, purified by fasting, knelt to worship the original creator of his house. With him, in his huge entourage, was Elter Betzelheim. Quite who Elter Betzelheim was, the Son of Heaven did not know or much care. The man played a good game of cards, gambled well, paid his debts, and often helped out the Son of Heaven with a bag or two of gold. As far as the hungry Son of Heaven knew, Elter represented the German government at all levels, and lived in state in Shanghai's German concession.

Elter was hungry too, as he had obligingly observed the ceremonial fast to support his friend, but at least he would not have to get down on his knees to knock his head on the white marble pavement. He remained erect while he watched the supplications to the Imperial Heaven and the Supreme Emperor, and then the offerings of incense, jade, silk, broth and rice. The Son of Heaven continued to knock his poor head until he reached the all-magic number of nine.

Elter was bored. This was the seventh time he had witnessed this scene. He yawned as the cars poured out of Shanghai and made their way to the Heavenly Park. Elter missed Germany. Above all, he missed German girls. Big robust wenches . . .

Sophia was electrified. Maria and Vassily had picked her up in Vassily's little car. "My goodness, how beautiful!" Sophia breathed. Indeed there was great beauty in the scene: three concentric marble terraces, each terrace rising upward toward the temple at the summit, with a marble staircase in each of the four sides of the ascending edifice, marking the four points of the compass, surrounded by the great stone walls of the Park. It was the night of the winter solstice. *Solstitis brumali verimus,* Sophia recalled her Latin tutor's words from a world ago. Sophia remembered how, on first hearing those words, she had felt a shiver of recognition.

She could see the Son of Heaven in his black silk robe kneeling penitently on the floor of the temple and touching his head to the stone. High above him shone the stars. One particular star burned particularly bright. "Maria, my star is up there!"

"Shhh." Maria smiled. "Be quiet." Sophia gazed at the group who stood around the man who humbly begged his forefathers for acknowledgment of his work on this earth.

She found herself staring at the back of the head of a tall man. He was thin, as far as she could tell. It was difficult to be certain, for he was wrapped in a long gray military coat. I wonder, she thought idly, if one can fall in love with the back of a neck? Then, with a sudden sense of shock, she realized one could indeed, even if one had never seen the face. "Who's that?" Sophia whispered.

Vassily followed Sophia's pointed finger. "Ha!" he said. "Elter Betzelheim. Don't go falling in love with him. He's bad news."

"It's too late," Sophia whispered.

Maria spoke without taking her eyes from the prostrate Son of Heaven. "Whatever you say. But don't forget, Little Nightingale, we warned you."

"I am no longer the Nightingale, Maria. I am the Snow Leopard."

Maria looked at her friend. "My, my. We *are* growing up, aren't we?"

Sophia hugged herself. "We are. And I am going to have Elter . . . What was his other name?"

"Betzelheim," said Maria.

"Elter Betzelheim," Sophia repeated.

"Yes, that's it. But do be quiet. I want to watch this."

Sophia was quiet. She was in a heaven of her own with a dream of her own. She watched intently until the group of priests, assistants and devotees turned to go. Then Elter's eyes were boring into her. She felt as if she were being irradiated. His eyes burned blue as hoar frost, blue like a streak of lightning in the mountains. The electricity tore through her body. She and he stood staring at each other, though many yards apart. Elter moved swiftly. He seemed to glide through the crowd between them. And then he was before her. His face was hard and lined, his hair cut close to his head. He took her hands in his. "Who are you?" he said.

☙ *CHAPTER 29* ❧

Sophia's mind reeled. She saw the mighty tiers of marble behind the man who boldly took her hand. Time stopped and her hand felt as if it had merged into the man's body, as if it were a hand now more his than hers. His wide shoulders reminded her of her father. The set of his head and the slight premature graying of his hair made her long to throw herself into his arms. "For better or for worse," she heard her now familiar inner voice prompt her. *Yes,* she whispered to her heart. *Yes, friend. For better or for worse.* "Until death us do part," the voice prompted again. *Yes,* Sophia nodded, *until death us do part.* She looked into the man's eyes and—like a terrible prophecy—for a moment she saw death returning her stare. Death smiled a hideous rictus, then disappeared. She found herself gazing into a pair of uncompromising gray eyes, the gray of the Whangpoo River, almost a non-color but full of light.

He smiled and rolled her hand over in his palm and, bending, kissed her fingers. He said, "You're a shy creature, aren't you?"

Sophia grinned, hoping that he did not realize how her knees were trembling and her body thrilling. She felt like a bird whose foot is tied by silk and flies over the head of its owner. "No, not really," she said. "My name is Sophia Oblimova."

"Ahh! You are of the Oblimov clan."

Sophia knew that he must have known the story of her parents' deaths, but he was too sophisticated a man to discuss such a purely personal matter on a first meeting. Sophia dipped in a small curtsy, and the man bowed at the waist. "I am Elter Betzelheim. At your service, mademoiselle. I represent the German Diplomatic Corps here in Shanghai. May I ask if I can call on you?"

"You'll have to ask my guardian, Sir Edward Gray, for permission."

"So. I will arrange to meet with Sir Edward. Now I must go with my friends." He clicked his heels together and bowed again. "Good night, my dear. I will see you again soon."

The two of them appeared to have been isolated

in a private world, like a silkworm in a chrysalis. Elter moved away and Sophia imagined she could see long thin strands of silk trail from his hands and his neck. She too was caught in the silken trap, but was content to stay within the cocoon they had made for themselves . . .

"Come on, dreamy. We've been waiting for you." Maria loomed into the shadow of the event.

"I don't want to move," Sophia whispered. "I just want to stand here for the rest of my life and wait."

"Wait for what?" Maria asked curiously. "Really, Sophia, you're dreadfully dramatic. We're all dying to go and get a drink, and you talk about spending the night freezing to death just because some man kissed your hand."

"Not *some* man, Maria. Not just any man, but *the* man, the man I've waited for all my life." She shivered and wrapped her arms around herself. "I feel so cold now he has left, and so alone." Before her on the stone lay the offering of food the Son of Heaven had just made to his ancestors.

She knelt down beside the blue-and-white bowl filled with brown sweet-smelling soup. Nervously she took the bowl in her hands and held it up to the sky. "To my love," she said, and drank a sip.

Vassily and Maria were quick to disapprove. "You can't do that," Maria said. "That offering is for the gods."

"There is only one God," Sophia said soberly, "and He understands." She lifted the red and gold silks that lay on the ground and, twirling them about her, danced in front of the marble temple.

Maria watched her, still uncertain. There was a part of Sophia that could be utterly disconcerting. It was as if she lived her life just teetering on the edge of a high wall, reckless and unafraid. Maria envied Sophia her position in life, but she did not envy her the naivety with which she rushed into situations. Maria knew all about danger, and danger was best faced with one's eyes wide open.

She watched Sophia dance. Trained years ago by one of the finest ballet tutors in Russia, Sophia danced the opening steps of *Swan Lake,* mentally hearing every note of the music. Then Vassily, caught up in the magic of the moment, joined her in dancing out the tragic story of the beautiful swan who died of love. Maria shuddered. She very much hoped that the dance was not prophetic.

She was worried about her instructions concerning Sophia. But then, the old, old voice whispered, we need a young girl of high birth. Her last meeting with the Gorgon had been a long one. "As you know," he said in soft tones, his breath smelling faintly of jasmine tea, "I wish for us to go back to our old ways. I wish for the great Chinese dynasties to reappear. Centuries of living under Manchu overlords have weakened us. And the European devils seek only to take from us and suppress us. Let us send them back to where they came from. Let us reclaim our lands and return to our old ways."

Maria had heard all this before, but it comforted her to be reminded of the goals. "The Tongs and the Triads control Shanghai. We must work even with them, for they negotiate with the foreigners.

Britain gave us opium; now we in turn supply the world." He laughed, a scratchy little sound, like a piece of wire dragged across a piece of tin. "You know the past as clearly as I the future. Where there is yin, there is yang. Darkness cannot exist without light, nor light without darkness. Activity by nonactivity." He cocked his eye at Maria as she crouched by his feet. And she remembered the touch of his light hand on her back. "Don't worry," he said, "about the little one. She is strong. She has a destiny only I have seen."

Watching Sophia tonight, Maria grew calm. The Gorgon was right. "Come on!" Maria yelled. "Come on, both of you! I'll drop if I don't get a drink. Let's go."

All the way back in the car, Sophia was unusually quiet. Once the car stopped outside the house, she kissed Maria and Vassily goodbye. This is the happiest night of my life, she thought as she raced up the front steps. "Misha?" she called. "Misha, where are you?"

Misha came shuffling out of his room. "What is it, Sophia?"

"I found him, Misha. I found the man I love. I saw him tonight. He is going to call on Edward. Oh, I'm so happy!" She grabbed Misha around the waist. Misha was grinning a dear, lop-sided grin.

Before going to bed, Sophia sat in a chair watching Elena brush her hair. "You will never guess how handsome he is, Elena. And I love him so."

Elena looked up in the mirror at her twin. "You've only met him once. How can you say you're in love? You don't know anything about him."

"Oh yes, I do. I know *all* about him. He's a German. He's in the diplomatic corps, and he reminds me a lot of Father, especially around the shoulders. He has gray eyes, like waves. You can look into them and see . . ." She stopped. She did not want that memory to mar her moment of happiness. ". . . things," she said quietly.

"There you are," Elena interrupted. "You don't really know him at all. He might be married for all you know."

"No." Sophia shook her head. "He hasn't been married. Ever."

"But how do you know?"

"Because men who are married have a certain resigned air about them. Like Edward. Edward now looks like a rather old lion who has been tamed. Elter isn't like that at all. He's fierce and independent. He's a loner, like me. He lives for himself, by himself, and he needs someone like me for a mate. Tomorrow I am going to find out where he eats, or if he goes down to the Long Bar for a drink in the evenings. I can't wait for him to get around to calling on Edward. I want you and Edward to take me to the Long Bar tomorrow."

There was no arguing with Sophia in one of her bossy moods. "All right, dear. If it will make you happy, I'll talk to Edward."

"It would." Sophia kissed Elena and then went into her own bedroom.

Now she no longer felt alone in her bed. She had her man who could join her, if not physically, then in fantasy. Imagining love-making, with her hands around his broad neck, she gave herself up to the feel of his lips on her nipples. Floating away on an urgent flood of desire, she gasped until her body went limp.

Not so far away the old man, lying on his wooden bed, wrapped in his robes, smiled. The flame is lit, he thought, and the little moth comes close. Slowly, slowly the web will entwine her. Elter Betzelheim, he thought, is also trapped. He smiled a thin smile. Maria, Sophia and Elter. That was sufficient work for the day. He rested, his eyelids permanently open. His eyes fell back into his head until only the whites showed. The room was silent and the moon high. The leafless trees outside raised their silent supplicating arms to the sky.

↬ *CHAPTER 30* ↫

If Edward was perturbed and his breakfast utterly ruined, he did not let Sophia see his discomfort. Beside him Elena sat tense, awaiting Edward's response. "I see," Edward said, lifting a spoonful of porridge to his lips. His enjoyment of the porridge was seriously impaired by the fact that the subject under discussion was Elter Betzelheim.

"We met at the Heavenly Park last night and he introduced himself to me and kissed my hand."

Edward raised an eyebrow. "That was very forward of him. You're not a married woman. He had no business, er, kissing your hand." The very thought of Teutonic lips kissing the hand of his unruly ward made Edward very cross.

Elena put her hand on his arm. "Don't be cross, Edward. Sophia's only met him once. We'll probably never hear of him again."

"I want to go down to the Long Bar to see if we can find him," Sophia said, remaining firm. "He must go for a drink somewhere in the city. Of course, there's also a chance he may dine in the Hong Kong Hotel. Perhaps you could telephone him."

"I most certainly will not, Sophia. What do you think I am, a procurer?" Edward's voice was dry and resolute. "If he wishes to call, I can't stop him, I suppose. But I shall have to think seriously about your future." The rest of the meal passed in a rather strained silence until Edward left for the office.

"Well," Sophia sighed, "he didn't seem too pleased, did he?"

Elena shook her head. "Edward takes your future very much to heart, and I don't think this man has a good reputation."

Sophia snorted. "But I wouldn't want a man with a good reputation. He would be so boring."

Elena shrugged. "What's boring to you might be bliss to someone else."

Sophia giggled. "What is it Mother used to say? The best use of culture is to talk nonsense with distinction."

Elena smiled. "Not everybody wants to live as if tied to a railway line and the train about to cut them in half. Some of the people you call boring get just as much delight in reading the newspaper as you do in dreaming of mysterious men who kiss your hand."

"No doubt." Sophia felt restless. "I'm going to get Katrina and go shopping. I feel a rather urgent need to be surrounded by noise and bustle."

She left the room.

Elena sat alone at the table, slowly finishing her cup of tea, her mind many miles away, back in the magical childhood they both shared in Russia, long before dark shadows had encompassed them all in a nightmare. In her mind's eye, both girls stood poised and innocent on the threshold of life, framed in the doorway of their dacha. She remembered with a smile her shy face gazing calmly into the future, her mother standing behind her, and Sophia leaning back against her father. She remembered the Russian pines that stood behind the house, and the high golden corn, full of promise . . . The telephone rang and she jumped.

"I've been thinking, darling." Edward's measured voice gave no hint of the alarm he felt. "I've heard of this fellow Elter Betzelheim. He's what we call a rum cove and I'm not at all happy about his calling on Sophia. Now Katrina wants to go back to Russia—she really isn't happy here. So I've made an appointment with a Miss Emily Trublood. She's calling at my office after luncheon and then, if I feel she would make a good chaperone for Sophia, we can interview her tomorrow at tea-time."

"That's a good idea, Edward. But Sophia seems determined to comb Shanghai to find this man. What do you know about him?"

"Not much. British Intelligence here are keeping a close eye on him. He appears to have business connections with the German Army, Amsterdam, and the Triads. I don't know about the Tongs. But then I really don't like poking my nose into such a dangerous business. The less we know the better, I say. My field is diplomacy, not murder and drugs."

"Well, we will have to appease Sophia and go looking for him this evening, darling. I promised Sophia you would take us out for a drink at the Long Bar."

"Better we go with her than she go alone, I suppose." He hesitated, then his voice brightened. "I wouldn't mind a gin and tonic. Goodness knows, the weather is nippy. I wish the spring would come."

"It will, darling." Elena's voice cheered in response to Edward's tone. "Spring will come and by next winter we should be married. I can't wait, Edward. I really can't."

"Neither can I." Edward found himself with a smile on his face. There was no guile in Elena. He had never felt so secure in the love of a woman. She honestly and openly adored him, as he did her. Edward was even prepared to put up with Sophia and her man-hunt for Elena's sake. "I'll be back around six."

Seven o'clock found the girls and Edward sitting at a table in the dining-room of the Hong Kong Hotel. They had passed through the Long Bar in an abortive attempt to find Elter and now Sophia was prodding at her ginger chicken. "Come on, Sophia." Edward was impatient. "Maybe he's had to go off on a journey. You can't sulk and pick at your food because he doesn't appear within the next twenty-four hours. What ever happened to the days when men chased girls?"

"They're gone," Sophia retorted. "We're a different sort of woman. We get what we want."

Edward grimaced. "Not this again. Listen, Sophia, if you become one of those hard new-fangled women, that's just what you will get, only you'll be surprised to learn the true meaning of getting what you want. Good men don't want pushy bossy women."

"Perhaps, but I don't want this 'good man' you all rave about. I want a real man."

Edward began to get angry. "I suggest you find out more about this German fellow *before* you get involved with him."

"I *will* find him, Edward. Don't you worry, I will." She sat in a sulky silence.

Edward looked across at Elena who was serenely eating her fish. Very well, he thought. If Sophia wants to sulk I had better really give her something to sulk about. "Anyway," he announced in his most measured Foreign Office tones, "I am recruiting a chaperone for you, Sophia. I feel you need a good woman to keep you out of trouble. Otherwise you will continue to occasion gossip."

"And do you already have such a paragon of virtue in mind?"

"Yes, as it so happens. I interviewed her this afternoon. I find her to be a woman of high moral tone, a woman eminently suited to take on the job of looking after you, my dear." Edward was inwardly tap-dancing for joy at the thought of Miss Emily Trublood putting Sophia firmly in her place. He couldn't wait to see Sophia's face at tea-time tomorrow.

Tea was served in the drawing-room when Miss Trublood was announced. Sophia and Elena heard a loud voice trumpeting down the hall and then the door crashed open as a very frightened Ah Ling attempted to get to the knob first. "Don't bother. I've opened doors for myself all my life and I don't plan to start a new habit now." The heavy oak door swung open and banged against the wall. Miss Trublood slapped Ah Ling heartily on the shoulder. His eyes clamped shut. "There you go," Miss Trublood said firmly. "On your way . . . Ah! Sir Edward!"

"Indeed. What a pleasure to have you for tea. Do sit down."

In the slightly stunned silence that followed, Elena took stock of Miss Trublood. She was pleased with what she saw.

Sophia also appraised Miss Trublood and was very displeased. She had the nose of a bloodhound, the shoulders of a Cossack sergeant, and the voice of a bugle with a bad cold. She looked well into the middle years of her life and as virginal as the day she was born. Sophia sensed that Miss Trublood was not the type to be of much aid in her schemes to track down Elter.

"Don't mind if I do," said Miss Trublood, ensconcing herself in a rather delicate chair that sagged under her considerable weight. She grabbed a large piece of cake with her huge hand and crammed the morsel into her gaping mouth.

Elena, misjudging her moment, inquired, "What part of America do you come from, Miss Trublood?"

"Des Moines, Iowa." And she was covered in a flurry of crumbs.

"Oh." Elena backed away and attempted to brush them off her blouse. "How nice."

"Only to someone born and raised there." Miss Trublood finished her cake with a noisy gobbling sound. She stared for a moment at the tea on the tray and then looked pleasingly at Edward. "I can't drink that darn stuff, Sir Edward. Could I ask you dear people to get me an honest cup of coffee?"

"Of course," said Elena, flustered. "I'll ring and ask Ah Ling to bring you some."

"Thanks, dear. I can tell I'm going to like it here. You see, my folks passed away, and I lost the farm, so here I am in Shanghai as a missionary, trying to teach the little boll-weevils the Good Lord's truth. And believe me, it's hard going, what with them being so used to worshiping idols and all." She shook her head. "I'm just about ready to try my hand at a different country, and then along comes the Lord and taps me on the shoulder and says, 'I've got this poor motherless girl for you to look after,' and then He led me right to you, Sir Edward. So here I am. All I possess is sitting in my little old suitcase in your lovely big hall." Miss Trublood beamed a big irradiating smile that encompassed her Lord, her world, and now theirs.

Sir Edward glowed back. He liked this sturdy straightforward woman. And Sophia would have a hard time getting around her 250-pound bulk. Even Elter might be intimidated if he had Miss Trublood tracking him like the hound she resembled. "Have you ever considered marriage?" he asked evenly. Only marriage could prise a woman like Miss Trublood away from her responsibilities.

"Never," she replied. "Never have, never will. No man is ever going to get into my pantaloons. I can promise you that."

Sophia's heart fell. Miss Trublood's heavy tweed skirt resembled a mail chastity belt. Anyway, no man would wrestle passionately with Miss Trublood and live to tell the tale. Oh no, Sophia thought. I'll die of embarrassment if I have to drag her around with me. She glared at Sir Edward. "Maybe Miss Trublood might not like to stay in Shanghai, with the Japanese poised to kill us all, and if not the Japanese, how about the Tongs and the Triads? Do you know what the Tongs are?" she asked of Miss Trublood.

"Oh them. Murderous thieves and heathens, the bunch of them. Don't you worry about them, young lady. I can look after myself. I just pray for their souls and tell them about the Good Lord and remind them that their feet are on the road to the eternally burning lake of fire unless they change their evil ways. That usually sends them scampering."

Indeed, Sir Edward mused. Should I be set upon by Miss Trublood in full missionary flood, I too might take to my heels. The thought of Elter getting long missionary lectures delighted Edward. "Well," he said decisively, "I think you'll be an excellent addition to our little family. Welcome." He put his elegant slender hand into Miss Trublood's bear-like paw.

"You betcha," Miss Trublood said, and she squeezed his hand until his fingertips were quite blue.

Elena removed her hands from the table, hiding them in her lap.

Miss Trublood had tears in her eyes. "Gee," she sighed, "I'm no longer an orphan. Thanks, guys."

"I'll ring for Ah Ling to take your bag." Elena smiled.

There was a short silence following Miss Trublood's exit. All three felt they had been in the path of a cyclone. "I think she's very nice, Edward," Elena said, looking at his crushed hand.

"So do I," said Edward faintly. "As long as I never shake hands with her again. Lord," he said fervently, raising his eyes toward heaven, "you have a devout servant in that one."

Sophia scowled. "She's common, vulgar and loud."

"Yes," Edward agreed. "And she'll follow you everywhere. That's precisely why I chose her."

Sophia rose from her seat. "We'll see about that," she said, storming out of the room.

Elena sat back in her chair and grinned. "Well done, Edward," she said. "Well done."

Edward smiled. "Thank you, my dear," he said with great satisfaction. "I'm inclined to agree."

CHAPTER 31

Elter was nowhere to be found. "He's gone to ground," Sophia told Elena. "Just like the foxes I used to hunt with Father."

Sophia's spirits were heavy. At breakfast Edward had broken the news that Katrina was planning to leave for Russia. At first Sophia refused to believe that her beloved Katrina would actually leave her, but it soon became clear she was going to have to get used to the idea, because it was true. She felt she was the only one in the house without a future to look forward to. Elena had Edward, Misha had Mei Mei. "Everybody has somebody except me," Sophia complained.

"You have Miss Trublood," Elena reasoned.

"I do not *have* Miss Trublood. I'm *stuck* with her, and that is an entirely different matter." Sophia had declared war on Miss Trublood, who appeared oblivious of the fact any such war had been declared.

Miss Trublood had settled into the household alarmingly fast. Her voice could be heard all over the house booming out, *"Well, I never."* When feeling particularly happy, she would burst into religious odes of joy. Her favorite was a ditty entitled "When I am twenty-one," which entailed a lot of tuneful spelling out of the word twenty-one. For the first few weeks the servants were suspicious, particularly Ah Ling, who flinched whenever he came upon her ungainly person rushing up and down the corridors looking for Sophia, who would disappear at any opportunity. "Ah! *There* you are!" bellowed Miss Trublood, not a bit put out. Finally the servants recognized her kind heart and well-meaning ways and grew to like her.

Ah Ling managed to get over his fright and even enjoyed the long biblical discussions about this man who was the only man in Miss Trublood's life. "He your brudder? *And* your fadder?" the discussions would begin. Ah Ling thought the Americans must be the most insane barbarians in the world, but this particular barbarian had been brought in to make Miss Sophia behave herself, and he admired her for that.

Katrina soon came to regard Miss Trublood as a godsend. "I'm grateful for your arrival," the old Russian peasant told her new-found friend. "Without you, I would have been unable to return to my country."

Miss Trublood nodded. "I get your meaning. I'll look after Sophia. You know, I do understand her, the poor motherless little thing. It can't be easy to lose your family and then have your twin sister getting engaged to be married."

"My worry," Katrina said, easing herself into a proferred chair, "is that Sophia will end up with an unsatisfactory man. She imagines herself in love at the moment with a man called Elter something-or-other, a German who, Sir Edward says, is no good. She's such a wild child, you know. So very wild. And I'm also worried about her friendship with that young hussy Maria. I know more about Maria than I would want to tell an innocent girl like Sophia. Sometimes I wonder if we have sheltered the twins too much. Misha says not. He says girls should keep their innocence, but I wonder. Maria," she fixed Miss Trublood with a very long stare, "is known to be a loose woman. But I can't tell Sophia that because she has no knowledge of such things."

Privately Miss Trublood thought that Sophia knew a lot more than she was letting on, and was not quite the innocent Katrina believed her to be. Sophia did know desire, perhaps not the slaking of desire, but desire, definitely. There was a fire in those big slanting eyes that spoke of knowledge. As if, Miss Trublood deduced that Sophia had seen the Tree of Knowledge of Good and Evil, though she had as yet not touched the fruit. But the fruit hung before her. Miss Trublood would not destroy Katrina's illusions, but she—Miss Trublood—would double her efforts to protect Sophia from falling into wanton ways.

Miss Trublood took Katrina's hand and patted

it reassuringly. "Don't you worry, Katie. I'll take care of her as if she was my own." Katrina could see a genuine caring in Miss Trublood's round blue eyes. "I may look like an old horse, but underneath it all, I'm good with people. I really like it here and I like the family. You get along home and I'll write to you with all the news." She smiled a warm toothy Des Moines smile.

Katrina's eyes were full of tears. "You do understand why I have to go back?"

"Yep," Miss Trublood said. "Yes, indeedy. Sometimes I get so homesick for my home town I could fill a bucket with my tears. I feel worse than chicken spit, I feel so low. But then I haul myself up by my boots and I say a prayer to the Good Lord and I get on with life. If, at the end of my days, I can find my way back to Des Moines, I will. Best place on this earth. I keep thinking how spring will be there soon and I picture the green of the leaves, the sound of birds—American birds, not Chinese birds."

Katrina was amused. Who would have thought the huge tough-looking woman possessed a poetic soul? She was glad; Sophia needed such a soul. "For me it is the pine trees I miss. Big pine trees, not the twisted Chinese kind. Everything seems so small. I feel like a giant here. I am so very homesick for Russia. Russia is my country. The Russian people are so different from the Chinese. In Russia we talk all the time. We hug, we kiss, we are like one big family." Katrina's eyes were bright. "You cannot imagine how beautiful Russia is. The most beautiful land in all the world. And even now, in these days of turmoil, there will be a place for me in our village. I hear they have collectives now, so my village will make a space for me. I know I can do much good work in my village. I can garden. I love to grow vegetables. Here I cannot garden. The Chinese gardeners forbid me even to put in a few flowers. There I can be among my people, the Georgians. Joseph Stalin, the General Secretary of the Communist Party, comes from my village, you know. I knew his mother years ago. She was devoted to him." She sighed and started to rise from her chair. "But I must get on with the laundry and I must go and talk to the girls. I dread this talk, but I can't put it off any longer."

On impulse, Katrina hugged the American woman. "Take good care of her for me."

"The Lord's will be done," Miss Trublood prayed. "And may God grant you a safe journey."

"Amen," Katrina replied in Russian.

With a weighty heart Katrina pushed open the door to Elena's room. Both girls stared at her, Elena with sympathy, but Sophia's eyes were puzzled. "How could you desert me?" Sophia asked. "How could you, Katrina?"

Katrina was taken aback. "I'm not deserting you, Sophia. You have plenty of people to look after you . . ."

"Think of Katrina, Sophia," Elena interrupted. "What happens if you get married and go off? What happens to Katrina then?"

"She can go back to Russia when I get married."

"That sort of selfishness doesn't help a girl to find a husband."

Hurt by her sister's tart criticism, Sophia replied, "In that case I'll need Katrina even more, if no man will ever have me. Don't go, Katrina. I'll die if you leave." And Sophia began to cry.

Katrina took the girl into her arms and sat herself down on the rocking chair. "I must go, my little nightingale. I must. I can't bear to live here any longer. I'm so homesick for Russia. Only another Russian would understand why I am so homesick."

Sophia stopped crying. "I'm Russian and I don't understand."

"Ah. No, child. You wouldn't understand, either of you. You lived the life of the rich in Russia. You were isolated from the real life of the country, from the village and the peasants and the way we all loved and hated each other. That is the tragedy of the very rich."

Sophia remembered envying the peasant children as they ran barefoot through the fields.

"You're right," Elena said. "And it's the same here. I've suggested to Edward that he let me do some voluntary work at the Shanghai Medical Union. I could roll bandages with some of the other women."

Sophia looked up. "Roll bandages with the other women? With the same old faces we see week after week, month after month. Why don't you do something really worth while, like actually nursing the sick?"

"That's an idea." Elena smiled. "I'll discuss it with Edward."

"I'm sorry I was so selfish, Katrina," said Sophia. "I do see how you must feel so far away from home." She sighed. "I can never go back to Russia. I couldn't bear to see what has happened there."

Katrina hugged her. For as much as she loved Elena, it was Sophia who held her heart. "I know, my little darling, my baby. But maybe when you are much older, and you understand more of the history of our country, you will be able to forgive. It will all be for the better in the end."

Sophia had no reply to that.

"I leave in two weeks. And if you'll excuse me now, darling, I have some shopping to do." With that, Katrina hugged Sophia and left the room, accompanied by Elena.

Left alone upstairs, Sophia leaned against the window and watched the milling crowd in the street below. How to escape from Miss Trublood's clutches . . . Sophia began to plan.

❧ CHAPTER 32 ❧

Plotting to escape from Miss Trublood was one thing; actually succeeding was quite another. Miss Trublood followed Sophia around with the determination of a rhinoceros charging into a bamboo thicket. No matter how often Sophia slipped down a side road, hoping Miss Trublood would steam off in the wrong direction, she never once managed to shake her off for very long. "I really will have to pray for your soul, Sophia," Miss Trublood finally said in exasperation.

"Don't bother." Sophia was petulant. Miss Trublood had galloped after her and tracked her down to the bar in the Shanghai Hotel. Sophia had been sitting on a banquette in the front hall where she could see the passers-by. She kept gravitating to this hotel, hoping against hope that Elter would appear. Last week she had waited unchaperoned in the shadows of the great clock in the foyer, watching to see who came in and out. Spring was in the air and, for many of the couples who approached the staff at the high white desk for reservations, so was romance. How Sophia envied them their breathless smiles, their joined hands! She imagined the bedrooms, with huge double beds, in which the lovers could satisfy their lust and celebrate their passion with champagne. How she yearned, how she shivered, how she burned with desire!

Now, sitting once again in front of this big woman, she sulked, her soul black with despair. "I'm never going to find him," she burst out, surprising herself. Although Katrina had told Miss Trublood of Sophia's great love, the subject had never since been discussed.

Lately Sophia had taken to reading a lot of poetry. She borrowed the books from Elena and nearly drove her sister mad, because she would leave the books face down on the table, she dogeared the pages, and underlined in pencil the passages she found most meaningful. Of all the poets,

Sophia's best-loved was Christina Georgina Rossetti, that beautiful proud woman with the long auburn hair. Sophia yearned to be like her, dressed in maroon velvet. Today she was wearing a Rossetti hairstyle, having spent most of the previous night crimping her long silky black hair with the hair-presser.

"Does the road wind uphill all the way?" she now intoned.

To her amazement, Miss Trublood replied, *"Yes, to the very end. Will the day's journey take the whole long day?"* Miss Trublood stopped and waited for Sophia to finish.

"From morn to night, my friend," Sophia sighed.

She looked at Miss Trublood, who smiled and then quoted, *"For each ecstatic instant/We must an anguish pay/In keen and quivering ratio/To the ecstasy.* That one's Dickinson," Miss Trublood informed Sophia.

"What do you know of ecstasy?" Sophia asked.

The question was not meant rudely, and Miss Trublood did not take it so. "Let's find a table and I'll tell you." The large American woman rose to her feet and lumbered through to the dining-room where she ordered coffee, while Sophia opted for tea.

Small elegant cups were rushed to the intimate table for two. Sophia loved tea. She loved the cucumber sandwiches that scrunched so nicely between the teeth—and then the sip of hot tea. Seen through the dining-room windows, the nearby wharves on the Whangpoo River and the great tea hongs squatted along its banks seemed desolate.

Sophia found her thoughts drifting slowly like the river . . . But Miss Trublood had a story to tell, and Sophia was beginning to think that it might be more worthwhile treating Miss Trublood as a friend than regarding her as an enemy.

"It was a long time ago," Miss Trublood began. "I was young and he was handsome, the most handsome boy in Des Moines, or maybe in all of Iowa. My, my." The years seemed to fall away from her face and Sophia could see in her the once slim girl, young and beautiful, with long blonde hair and the very distinctive blue eyes found only in the northern races. She could imagine the young Miss Trublood and her handsome love running together in a golden haze of wheat.

"Did you really love him, Miss Trublood?"

"I did. I loved him with every fiber in my body. I loved him to the ends of the earth. I didn't know or think of anything else but Will. He was tall as me. He had brown hair with a cowlick that fell over his eyes. He grinned like a watermelon and his eyes were hazel and full of humor. I can see him now as I talk."

"Where is he?" Sophia interrupted.

A cloud of sadness drifted across Miss Trublood's face. "I don't know," she said. "You got me there. But it didn't work out for us. His mother wanted him to marry another girl whose father owned the grocery store in town. We were a missionary family, and we were so poor you wouldn't believe it. We slept on the floor and dressed from the old pork barrel that was kept for the poor in the grocery store. And I suppose, I gotta admit it, the girl was pretty and had the best dresses in town. On the night of the senior prom, just before graduation, I had nothing to wear. So I didn't go. But I did sneak up to the tent to watch the dancing. And there he was—my Will—dancing with her and whispering in her ear. I decided then that I would . . ." Her voice faltered. "I would never risk falling in love again, or feeling the bitter, sharp hurt that came with it. For six months after that night I suffered. So you see, I do understand."

There was a lump in Sophia's throat. She reached out and took Miss Trublood's hand in hers. "So then you became a missionary yourself?"

"I went to missionary school and became a missionary, just like my father. Except I didn't get married and have a passel of kids. I love the Lord with all my heart and soul, so I never get lonely."

"I wish I could say the same," Sophia confessed, then added, "but I do say my prayers."

"Well, that's good. You keep on doing that." Miss Trublood smiled. "He hears them, you know. You may have a hard time finding God, but He has no trouble finding you. Now let's bow our heads and pray like crazy that God keeps you out of the mess you're trying your hardest to get yourself into."

Sophia was startled by the bluntness. "You know what I'm doing?"

"No point keeping secrets from me, honey."

"I do want to find him, Miss Trublood."

"Well, I can't help you there."

Sophia was silent for a moment, then said, "But will you stop me?"

"If I'd been in Eden, could I have stopped Eve from taking her first bite? Listen, Sophia. I'm going to keep on doing my best to see you're safe. And you're going to keep on wanting to do what you want to do. And God's going to keep on loving both of us anyway, no matter what. So can we say a word or two to include Him in the discussion?"

Both women quite unself-consciously shut their eyes, held hands across the table, and prayed. "Lord, protect Your child from harm," Miss Trublood said aloud.

"And help me find him," Sophia said silently.

The Chinese waiters looked on amused. The Western barbarians with their fantastical religious beliefs were a long-standing joke among them.

Sophia, oblivious to the amusement, squeezed her eyes even more tightly shut. "Please, dear Lord," she entreated, "*please* just let me see him."

"That ought to do it," Miss Trublood said, opening her eyes. "Come on. Let's get you home."

❧ CHAPTER 33 ❧

"Daisy, Daisy, gimme yer answer do. I'm arf crazy, all fer the love of you!"

Elena smiled. She was attempting to button a

gold stud in Edward's sleeve. "Stand still!" she said.

But Edward could not resist a flying kick at the end of his ditty. "My nanny taught me to sing that," he laughed. Edward was in jovial mood. "Nanny Boots. That and lots of other things that my parents would have sucked in their cheeks about if they'd known the half of what I was learning. Cockney rhyming slang . . ."

"I thought England was all quaint, pastoral melodies," Elena said. *"One is one, and all alone, and ever more shall be so,"* she sang.

"There are many Englands," Edward said. "When we go home, we'll live in a lovely England, the most beautiful of all, for me, anyhow. Rolling acres of England's pleasant pastures, cucumber sandwiches served with tea, soft pink roast beef. But other English people live in different Englands, not all of them lovely." He scratched his head and chuckled to himself. "But they have their good points to recommend them. I remember when I was a young officer in the Army—before I got into the Foreign Office—I had my first real dose of all the many English. And the men sang songs that were the furthest thing from the quaint pastoral melodies you'd expect." He took Elena by surprise, clasping her body to his and twirling her around in a lively dance. *"As you walk along/The Bar de Bullong/With an independent air,"* he sang, *"You 'ear the girls declare/There goes the millionaire,/The man wot broke the bank at Monte Carlo."*

There was a knock on the door. "Are you ready to go?" Sophia came to inquire.

Tonight her sister was wearing a more traditional evening dress, Elena was glad to notice.

"Come along then, girls." Edward smoothed his
hair down, glancing at himself briefly in his
dressing-room mirror and pleased with what he
saw. "We make a handsome couple," he remarked
to Elena as they walked down the stairs together.

Sophia followed, hoping and praying that
tonight was the night she would find her lover.
Perhaps, she thought, he'll be at the party on the
frigate. After all, invitations would have gone out
to all the embassies, legations and large busi-
nesses and no one refused an invitation to a party
of this kind. Tonight the frigate would be bristling
with guns to remind the Japanese that English
gunboats would blast any invading army or navy
out of China. In spite of intense fighting between
all the factions in Shanghai, the British colony remained serene.

The big black tender carried the family across the
bumpy water to the frigate. Dressed with flags of
welcome, the vessel swung and swayed with the
pull of the tide. English sailors hung off the gangplank to help the visitors on board. Pipes heralded
the arrival of Sir Edward and his party. Sophia
searched among the guests in vain. Elter was nowhere to be seen. Maria had only laughed when
Sophia told her about the party. "You'll find him
when you are meant to," she said. "You can't
hurry fate." Tonight, though, Sophia felt lucky.

Elena, the perfect fiancée, was talking to an admiral and his dried-up prune-faced wife. "I'm

nursing at the hospital now," she said, "and we have several cases of typhoid."

"You're nursing Europeans, I trust," Mrs. Admiral said sharply. "Otherwise, goodness knows what you might catch."

"No." Elena shook her head. "I tend the children mostly."

Mrs. Admiral perceptibly pulled away. "Oh dear. Why must you young things go native?"

A young man dressed in a rich yellow corduroy suit, and wearing red flowing locks, leaned forward. "Because we, madam, must break with convention and be Bohemians."

The old admiral put his monocle very firmly in his right eye and brought his thick gray eyebrows into an outraged frown. "And who might you be, young sir?"

"I am Rollo. Rollo St. John, at your service." And he clicked his heels and bowed. Sophia grinned.

"What you need, young man, is a haircut and a few years before the mast." The admiral and his wife swept off up the deck, muttering to themselves about impertinent youths. They puffed and blew until they hove to in the lee of a familiar like-minded couple, and all four turned their shocked faces to stare at Rollo.

Edward smiled. He knew Rollo and his fast set of painters, poets and musicians, who scoured the world in search of adventure. Rollo's family had money—lots of it—so he had imported several of his most impecunious friends to brighten up the social life of Shanghai. And brighten it up they did, if they were not first forcibly ejected from the more staid homes. "Rollo, old fellow!" Edward extended his hand. "Meet my fiancée, Countess Elena Oblimova, and her twin sister Countess Sophia Obli . . ."

"Ah, Sophia!" Rollo drawled, looking down into her intense face. "Maria's told me all about you."

Sophia smiled. "Good things, I hope."

"Of course." Rollo took Sophia's hand. "Let's go off together in search of adventure. These boats are so stuffy. Let's grab a bottle of champagne and explore the vessel. All right with you, Sir Ed?"

Edward did not object. "Don't get her into any trouble," he said.

"You have my word." Rollo grinned. "I'll be on my best behavior tonight."

Sophia was amused and slightly excited. Rollo gave her the feeling that she could never be quite sure what he would do. Shoulder-length red hair was something she had seen only on Russian peasants and in picture books illustrating the balls that used to take place in the old Russian palaces. Here it looked completely out of place, amid the Army and Navy uniforms and the black dinner-jackets of the few civilians. Several of the senior Triad leaders were on board with their long Manchu-style coats and round silk black hats. But Rollo, while appearing completely improbable in the setting, was also very much at home. In fact he walked around the boat as if it were his own personal yacht and the guests mere servants at his command. "Let's go down to the wardroom and put our feet up. All this standing about is most tiresome. Come along." As they made their way below deck, he grabbed a passing bottle of opened champagne, deftly lifting two glasses as well. "Huh. Not a bad year at all. No, indeed."

Once in the rather narrow wardroom, he poured Sophia a glass of champagne then sat with his feet on the mess table. "Now," he said in a business-like fashion, "tell me about the sad look in your eyes. Whom are we missing tonight? Don't blush. I saw you looking for someone in that awful crowd up there." He made a moue of disgust. "Don't tell me you're in love with some pipsqueak young officer? Don't tell me you've fallen for an airman? Above all, don't tell me he's an American? I don't think I could bear it." He put up a commanding hand. "Say nothing until I have fortified myself with a glass of bubbly."

Sophia shook her head and waited until he had emptied his glass. "Actually, I was looking for someone. I've only seen him once. And he's German." And the story came out in a flood.

Soon they had finished the bottle. Rollo wiped his hand across his brow. "Let's go on top and cool off. It's damned stifling in here." They climbed up onto the foredeck, and leaned companionably, elbow to elbow, on the railings.

The tender was pulling away. Looking down, Sophia felt her heart stop. There, in full uniform, the German eagle shining on his peaked cap, stood Elter. Looking back at the frigate, he saw Sophia leaning over the rail, her hand automatically outstretched as if to pull him back. He smiled, and Sophia knew that he had known all along she was on board and that he had not wished to speak to her. The thought tore her heart . . . But then he raised his hat to her and she quite distinctly saw his lips mouth the words, "I love you." Sophia stood there, a finger to her lips, and waved a shy little wave that returned the words to his mouth. They stared motionless at each other, until he disappeared into the night. Sophia felt robbed of him and his body, but she was satisfied: he loved her. Knowing that, she was content to wait.

"That's the man?" Rollo asked.

"Yes," she said. "That's the man. Oh, Rollo, he loves me!"

Rollo shook his head. "Elter Betzelheim. He has a terrible reputation for womanizing, and worse. He's a dark horse. I should be careful, if I were you."

"Rollo, don't you know that the love of a good woman can change any man? I can change him. Really I can."

Rollo smiled down at her beautiful flushed face. "I can see I'll have no luck in changing your mind but let's be friends anyway. Can I come and call on you?"

Sophia smiled. "I'd be delighted." They rejoined Edward and Elena.

Oh no, Sophia groaned inwardly when she heard what they were talking about. Now Elena has taken up good causes, we keep getting detailed descriptions of dreadful diseases. "Do shut up,

Elena. Since when have tapeworms been a subject of cocktail conversation?"

Edward smiled indulgently at Elena. "I suppose talk of serving one's community might offend some ears," he murmured.

"Dinner," Sophia said firmly. "I need dinner."

Elena smiled at Edward. "Do you think Rollo could take Sophia out to dine? I'm a little tired."

"Of course, darling." Edward was only too pleased to have Elena to himself. "We can go home and have a quiet meal together. Rollo, old man, would you like to take Sophia out to dinner?"

"Certainly, sir." Rollo grinned at Sophia. "How about we get up to some mischief together? We can go and find my disreputable friends and have a party."

"Not too disreputable," Edward said. "Remember, she has a reputation to keep."

Sophia giggled. "Come on, Rollo. Let's say our goodbyes and leave. I'll see you later, Elena." As Elena waved, Sophia noticed that Elena had two pale shadows under her eyes. She's working too hard, Sophia thought. And then she felt guilty because she herself wasn't working at all.

❦ CHAPTER 34 ❦

Rollo and his friends spent a riotous evening debunking the leading lights of Shanghai. Sophia, who normally would have relished the acid wit and the glasses of wine, could not bring herself even to smile. She was surprised to find herself eager to get back to Miss Trublood and talk. Sitting in Rollo's study, she could see the trees outside his house swaying in the night wind, and she wished the branches were Elter's arms and the wind his soft kisses. "Buck up, Sophia. Don't mope. You'll see the fellow again."

Sophia stretched. "I'd like to go home, Rollo. I'm tired and I need to rest."

Rollo snorted. "What spoilsports women are! If you moon about after him, you'll never catch his attention. Men like the hunt, the chase."

"I suppose you know all about that, don't you?" Sophia was feeling waspish and a little defensive.

"In a way. You might say those of us that follow the Beardsley fashion know all sorts of things." Rollo pointed to a lithograph on the wall of his study. It showed a woman, her back swathed in black silk.

Or, Sophia wondered, was it a woman? Could it be a plump man? She walked over to the piece and gazed at it carefully. She caught a faint smell of patchouli. A slim dark-haired person stood beside her. Long hair hung down like a curtain over a beak of a nose. The eyes were round and the mouth tight, like a clove of garlic. The figure giggled. "Very camp, our Aubrey!" the thin high voice fluted.

Sophia turned and stared at the crowd of revelers, whose presence she had mostly ignored in the hour she had been in the room. The creature next to her minced away on tiny high-heeled shoes to join a small figure swathed in colored silks and Jersey wool under the dim light of a chandelier that dripped melted wax onto a table below. They were talking about Sophia. She knew that because the one who had stood next to her jerked his head in her direction every so often, and the other's eyes followed the motion, then were cast down again as they talked. Rollo stood at the door waiting for her to leave.

As she brushed past him she said in a strained voice, "Some of these men look like women, and some of the women look like men. Who are they?"

Rollo sighed as he accompanied her downstairs. "I'm sorry, Sophia. I didn't realize you were *such* an innocent. I had no business inviting you here with this crowd."

"Tell me. Who are they?" Sophia felt sick. Her love for Elter was a pure passion. Was it possible these people dreamed of passion too? "They're freaks," she said loudly. "Freaks. Oh, Rollo, how could you know such people?"

By the door the houseboy was waiting to see Sophia out. Rollo frowned. "Sophia," he said, "you mustn't generalize about people like that. You've lived in a very protected world. You've always been rich. You've never known poverty or lack of food or clothing. You have known sorrow, I know—I heard about your family and I am truly sorry—but open your eyes and look around you."

Sophia cocked her head and looked up at Rollo. "Are you like them, Rollo? A man-woman?"

Rollo smiled. There was something tender in his smile and also sad. Sophia realized then that the tenderness was reserved not for women but for men. "I am who I am," he said and he put his hands to his breast. "I don't wear labels. I love whom I must love."

"You mean not exclusively women?"

"Yes," Rollo agreed. "Not exclusively women. I think that after the English establishment crucified one of our major playwrights and best poets, we all tend to go underground and only really come out when we are with each other." Rollo took Sophia's hand and said simply, "But I still want to be your friend."

Sophia smiled. Gently she drew herself up and kissed him on the cheek. "So do I," she said, noticing the softness of Rollo's cheek. Like a child's, she thought.

The houseboy rolled his eyes unseen. These foreigners, he thought. First one way and then the other. The young missie had better be careful in this house.

Rollo's driver deposited Sophia at her door. Edward was not in the study; he had evidently gone to bed. The light was out under Elena's door, but Miss Trublood was still awake. Sophia put her face around the door. "God answers prayer, dear!" Miss Trublood beamed. "You're home safe."

"He certainly does."

Miss Trublood saw a sparkle in Sophia's eyes. "Somehow I get the feeling we're not talking about the same prayers," she said warily.

"Oh, Miss Trublood. Don't be cross. Please. I saw him." Just to say the word *him* made Elter hers. "I saw him for just an instant but . . ."

"Sophia . . ." Miss Trublood's fleshy face wrinkled in concern.

"You've nothing to worry about, Miss Trublood. He said he loves me. And that makes everything all right, doesn't it?"

"Well . . ."

"I'm not sure, but he was waving and it looked as if he said that. Oh, Miss Trublood!" Sophia sat down on the wide comfortable bed. "I'm so happy tonight."

Miss Trublood put down her book on mission reliefwork in Peking and, wrapping her large hands around her knees, she leaned forward and said, "I think you'd better tell me just what you've been doing this evening."

Sophia flushed. She really did not want to talk about the evening at all. She wanted to wipe from her memory the hour spent at Rollo's and go back to the time when she had never contemplated the unnerving idea of men loving men, or women women. The image that came into her mind seemed depraved and downright disgusting. Miss Trublood, seeing a shadow cross Sophia's face, put a warm hand on Sophia's arm. "Listen, honey," she said. "Your mom isn't here to help you and you need someone to talk to. What's worrying you?"

"I don't think my mother would have known anything about this sort of subject," Sophia said firmly. "You see, after the party, Elena was looking tired. So instead of the three of us dining out, I met Rollo, whom Edward knows, so he said we could go off and have dinner together and Rollo promised to see I got home safely. Rollo has a fabulous house in the German concession, not far from here. Miss Trublood, is it true that women can love women?" She remembered the occasion when Maria had kissed her on the lips and thought of it now with an odd combination of fear and delight.

Miss Trublood frowned. "Who's been putting this kind of thing into your head? That man you've been chasing after?"

"Not him," Sophia replied truthfully. "It was the people at Rollo's house. For a long time I didn't take much notice of them, but then I did. Particularly one little man. Or maybe it was a woman. You couldn't tell." She shivered. "I felt awful. Rather as if I'd been made unclean."

Miss Trublood shook her head. "Sophia, I'll be straight with you. Shanghai is full of people who are on the run from something. Sometimes it's the police, sometimes it's their families, sometimes it's booze or debts. And most of all they're running away from themselves. And that's why you gotta be careful with a man you don't even know. Why, he might . . ."

"Rollo says that an English poet was ruined, and he actually died, because he loved another man."

"To tell you the truth"—she shook her head—

"we don't get much of it in Des Moines. But in the Bible it's called 'man lying with mankind as with womankind,' and it's a sin."

"I should think so, too," Sophia snorted.

Miss Trublood smiled. "But then remember. The bigger the sin, the bigger God's power to forgive." Recalling Maria's kiss, Sophia made a quick act of contrition. "Nonetheless, Sophia, I hope you don't get caught up in this kind of thing." She said this thinking wryly that it was just the sort of thing that Sophia would get caught up in. She realized that Sophia had an unbounded enthusiasm for the mysterious and an unsurpassed interest in the unconventional. "I think you'd better go to bed now, honey. Say your prayers and have a good night's sleep, OK?"

"OK." Sophia laughed.

"And about this man of yours . . ."

"Miss Trublood, *please*. A man loves me and I love him. What's wrong with that? There's no sin involved. And I won't hear a word said against him."

"You won't, will you?" Miss Trublood recognized that no further warnings would be of any use, at least not tonight. "Good night, then, Sophia. God bless."

"And you," said Sophia, shutting the door behind her.

Miss Trublood lay back on her pillows, picked up her book and put it down again; she was too worried to read. But at least Sophia trusted her as a friend. That was a start.

❧ CHAPTER 35 ❧

A week later nobody could avoid the fact that Elena was ill. Seriously ill. Not just with flu but something much more severe. The English doctor consulted the French doctor, who called upon the German specialist. They conferred day after day until a yellowish tinge to her skin and rosy spots on her chest made them realize that Elena had typhoid. Edward was aghast when he learned of the diagnosis. He stood by Elena's bed, her thin hand in his.

She smiled weakly at him. "Don't be cross, Edward. I had to nurse the children who were in quarantine. No one else would do it except for Elsie, Margaret, and myself."

"Oh, darling." Edward fell to his knees. He was exhausted after long sleepless hours at her bedside.

Sophia arrived carrying a bowl of chicken soup. "Here you are, Elena. Let's get some of this into you. Misha made it for you and he swears by it." Elena smiled and tried to sip the broth, her thin neck convulsing with effort.

"Sophia," Edward said. "Can you stay with her? I absolutely have to go now, but I'll be back this evening." Sophia nodded. "See that she's not left alone for an instant."

"I will," Sophia said. Her voice did not betray the terrible fear that Elena might die.

Sophia sat by her sister for the afternoon. Every so often Elena would stir and open her eyes, too weak to talk. "You'll be better soon," Sophia would say, as much to convince herself as to comfort her sister, and Elena would nod, too tired and wracked with pain to do more. Sophia realized that Elena's beautiful blonde hair had begun to fall out, and her eyelashes.

Miss Trublood came in at tea-time to relieve Sophia. As Sophia left she could hear Miss Trublood praying at Elena's bedside. Sophia could not sit alone. She took her cup of tea and wandered down to the kitchen, where she knew she would find Misha and Mei Mei. Katrina, who had planned to leave that week, postponed her journey willingly. They sat around the table in the kitchen with little to say to each other. "Mrs. Dinnison"—who had been nursing with Elena—"died this morning." Katrina broke the news after a dull silence.

"Elsie?"

Katrina nodded her head. "She's to be buried tomorrow because they don't want the contagion to spread. The only precaution the family took to ward off the disease was to wash their hands and faces with vinegar." Somehow even to admit that they too might catch the fever was to side with the fates against Elena. If they all stood firm, with their united wills pulling on this side of eternity, they might save Elena's life.

And no, they decided they would not send Elena in a fever ambulance to the local *Krankenhaus,* the big German hospital in Shanghai. They would keep her here in her own room.

The doctors visited the next day and left shaking their heads. The British. What could you do with them? "Mad dogs," the French doctor muttered as he climbed into his car. "No discipline," the German doctor sniffed. "Frogs and Huns," the English doctor snarled of his professional colleagues. And they left Sir Edward's household to tend its sick child.

Edward kept vigil at her bedside from ten o'clock until midnight, gazing into her beloved face. He watched her scalp gleam pink in the lamplight through her thinning hair and anxiously counted her breaths. "In and out," he whispered. "In and out." Occasionally the in happened and the out did not. Then he prayed. "God, let her breathe. Please, dear Lord."

Now he understood agony. In Edward's life there had been much sunshine interspersed with only rare shadows. The death of his mother years ago was the darkest moment of his life. Otherwise his memories really centered around Eton, and then Oxford and a brief stint in the Army, where he saw no combat. In his heart he had never left Oxford and when he had time to dream he dreamed of the great chapel organs on a Sunday morning filling the gentle Oxford sky with hallelujahs. Now, with this figure lying so quietly before him, he felt that should he lose her he too would die. For Edward emotions were tidy, disciplined things. A traditional English gentleman, he had always found that a *"How unfortunate"* was an adequate response to any unpleasant piece of news. Edward preferred the undertone of sympathy rather than a full-blown demonstration of emotion. Now he felt as if all the emotions he had ever suppressed were threatening to burst free, ripping at the hinges of the old battered suitcase in his mind in which he had contrived to pack them away.

He looked down at his hands, hands that had never really toiled in their lives, and began to make promises to his maker. "If she lives, I'll take her away from this place. I'll keep her safe. I'll never let her down. Oh please, God." He was down on his knees, his head in his hands. Tears leaked through his fingers, tears that had not run since boyhood. "Please don't let her die." He gasped like a wounded hare. "Please."

He felt a hand on his shoulder and looked up. Elena was smiling, a faint echo of a smile. "Oh thank you, thank you!" Edward took her hand and kissed it. Then he returned her hand to her side. He was breathing hard to calm himself, and then he began to talk. "First thing we'll do when I get you back to England is to go for dinner at the Savoy. You'll love it there, I know you will. We'll sit at our table by the window and watch the lights on the Embankment and the river and the bridges and far across on the South Bank. It's magical, Elena. Really it is. And if you want, I'll take you to a sweet shop in the daytime. Same one I used to go to when I visited London as a boy. You can still get a box of jujubes and toffee hanky-panky. Oh, and my favorite—sherbert dabs. Or, if you prefer, I'll buy you boxes and boxes of the finest chocolates from Switzerland. Whatever you want, darling. We have only two more years to do here, and then we can go home. You'll love London, darling, and even more you'll love the Monastery, our family country house."

He realized that he was rattling on, like an old tin can tied to a car, but he didn't care. Over the last few days he had not dared to think of the future, but now he took her smile as God's promise to spare her. And indeed she lay more calmly on the bed. Before her smile, she had seemed doomed to give up the frail clutch she held on life. The breath she drew now was expelled with the confidence that she would continue to be the major part of his life. Looking at her lying there helpless and wan, Edward knew that Elena had sealed a hole in his lonely heart. Women, he observed, lived for many things, but a man needed a woman in a way that made men so much more vulnerable. Elena filled his life as fresh water fills a vase, and only she could make his vase brim with happiness. How grateful he was to have found a woman who let him know the full satisfaction found in the brimming!

Misha came in and was surprised to find Edward smiling.

"She's pulling out of it," Edward said. "She's going to be all right."

"Good, good." Misha had a blanket with him. He sat down beside the bed, his head reaching the edge, and gazed at Elena. He nodded approvingly. "Yes, yes. Look, she has a little color in her cheeks. Katrina is coming with the soup. You go now. I'll take care of her. And sleep well. The worst is past."

Katrina was pleased when she found Elena able

to sip her soup more easily. "Good, little one, good. Try some more. An extra mouthful. Come." Katrina's large brown hands held the spoon to Elena's mouth, while Misha held the sick girl by the shoulders, and the two of them labored to get the nourishment into the starving body. Then they laid her back on the bed and she was able to open her eyes fully. "What a fright you gave us!" Katrina scolded. "No more heroics. Humph, I should be back in Georgia by now, and here I am still. But you need to get your rest. Good night, darling." She kissed Elena's forehead and left.

In the quiet of that early-summer night the lamp at Elena's head cast the only pool of yellow light in the darkened room. Misha groaned and grunted, wishing he could lie in Mei Mei's comforting arms. But for now he was on guard, as he had been on guard for his mistress, the Golden Salamander. He turned and twisted on his blanket until he found a comfortable position to lie in, and then he watched, his big eyes wide open and staring, remembering the days many years ago when Anna was the toast of St. Petersburg. Ah, those days before the wars that for ever changed the Russia he knew. Those fabulous lost days . . .

CHAPTER 36

The Kaiser's war was long ended, followed by treaties. Endless treaties. The words *Versailles, Saint-Germain, Trianon, Neuilly* and *Sèvres* cropped up with unfailing regularity in discussions among the men at parties held to celebrate peace in Europe. But China was still held in the grip of opposing forces. The Japanese were determined to overrun China and annex her as a Japanese colony. The Russian communists, victorious in their own revolution, were extending olive branches to the tiny Chinese People's Liberation Army, and the Kuomintang, adopting at least in theory Sun Yat-sen's principles of reform, had established a government of their own, based in Canton. But it was the leader of the Kuomintang army, Chiang Kai-shek, who gave a frightening and militaristic air to the tides of change moving ever northward on the Asian continent.

Edward was greatly worried. China's upheavals, he feared, were only just beginning. Now, with Elena well again, he very much wished he could simply pack his things and take both girls back to England. But Sophia had no intention of leaving Shanghai. For a while, during her sister's illness and the year it took for Elena to convalesce, Sophia had put aside her passion for Elter. During that year neither of the girls had attended parties. Elena needed the rest, and Sophia was the only person who could keep her occupied and bring a smile to her lips, except for Edward, but he was busy. Many of the nights the twins wished he could be at home, he was unavoidably detained elsewhere. His wedding to Elena was postponed so that she could fully recover her strength and health before assuming the responsibilities of being a wife.

Katrina left two months after the crisis was over, knowing Elena would be well. "Goodbye," Katrina sobbed into Sophia's neck. "Don't forget your old Katrina."

Both girls cried bitterly, but Miss Trublood was sanguine about the whole affair. "Katrina will be much happier once she gets home. The Bolshies are mostly heathen, but at least they aren't starving any more and Katrina won't go short of food. Just you wait, Katrina, until you get that first mouthful of real Russian tea you keep telling me about. Boy, oh boy. If I could only get my mouth around a bottle of Coca-Cola. Real Coke!"

Katrina laughed. Misha escorted her and all her bundles and bags to the train station. "Goodbye, Misha." Katrina stooped over the little man.

"Goodbye, Katrina," Misha said softly. "I'll take care of them both for you. Don't worry."

"How many times have you and I made those promises to each other?"

"Many times," Misha agreed. "Too many times to count. Now I feel as if the ghosts of their parents and my lady are listening to us." The great train hooted. Dramatic last-minute dashes were being made. Vendors yelled their final prices to arms waving out of windows, and then Katrina stood at the doorway, framed by the window, with tears streaming down her rough red face.

"Goodbye, Misha. Goodbye." Both of them were crying, she for the past and he for the future.

Slowly Misha turned away and made his way back to the car. Sitting next to the chauffeur, he wondered how on earth they had all managed so far.

A year after Elena's illness, the girls were about to re-enter the social life of Shanghai. Edward was hosting a great ball to celebrate their twenty-first birthday. Sophia had persuaded Edward to send Elter an invitation. For the many months of Elena's recuperation, Sophia had attended no social functions, nor did she make efforts to find Elter—her own form of self-imposed penance for the fact that Elena should have been stricken as a result of her good works, while Sophia, who did nothing, remained healthy. Instead, Sophia stayed in the house with Elena, the least she could do for her sister.

It was a day of preparations for the birthday ball and Sophia and Elena were studying the guest list. Ah Ling brought in the day's post and the girls marked off the acceptances. Sophia was tense. Half of those on the list had replied and most had accepted. Would the one acceptance she so passionately desired come?

Maria had called fairly regularly during the months of isolation. "I'm not afraid of a few germs," she would boast on her visits in those dark terrible days when Sophia thought she would go out of her mind with worry. "Tell me," Sophia always asked urgently. "Have you seen anything of Elter?"

Sometimes Maria had seen him. "Tell Sophia," he once announced, "that I am busy in Germany and in Amsterdam, but I do not forget her. And as soon as I have time I will be there. Tell her not to forget the last time we saw each other. Tell her I meant what I said." After these messages Sophia would be content for days. Silly, she scolded herself as she took each sentence apart, as she caressed the words in her mouth, as she dreamed and imagined their bodies locked together. Then her impatience would return, accompanied by an unbearable rising tide of lust, and Sophia would storm about the house, restless and disheveled . . .

Opening the acceptances, Sophia finally found what she sought. "Herr Elter Betzelheim takes pleasure in accepting the invitation to . . ." There it was. He was pleased to attend. "Elena!" Sophia jumped up and ran across the room to where Elena was sitting at her desk, ticking off names on the list. "Look! He *is* coming."

Elena looked up. "So is Rollo St. John," she said.

"Oh, good. But, Elena, don't you see? Elter is really going to come here for the whole evening. Can you imagine? After all these months, and it's been more than a year since I saw him, he's actually going to be here and we can talk. I can't believe it! Where's Miss Trublood? I must find her." Sophia dashed out of the room.

Elena, still a little pale, looked pensive. Oh dear,

she thought. Here we go again. Why couldn't Sophia fix her heart on Rollo instead? Rollo seemed such a nice boy, and on the few occasions she had met him, she had liked his quiet charm. Sophia was set on this Elter whoever-he-was. She glanced at her three diamonds. I'm so lucky, she thought, so very lucky. And then she went back to the list, a list so long that it reached from the table down to the floor. Three more days and the house would be filled with guests. Elena was pleased. This should be one of the best balls in Shanghai. She hoped she would be a good hostess. That, she felt, was the least she could do for Edward.

✤ CHAPTER 37 ✤

"Happy birthday, darling!" Sophia put her head around Elena's door.

Elena sat at her dressing-table, a cup of tea by her side, combing her long fair hair, which had mostly grown back. "And you." Elena turned toward Sophia and held her arms out. They kissed and stood looking at themselves in the mirror.

"Aren't we beautiful?" Sophia laughed. "Who would have thought two scrawny twin sisters could grow up and look like a pair of film stars."

Elena frowned. "Really, Sophia. I don't want to look like a film star. That's vulgar."

"Well, I *am* vulgar." Sophia stuck out her leg and put her hand on her hip. "There," she said, pouting and gazing at her reflection with smoldering eyes. "What does Madame Chiang Kai-shek have that I don't have? Age, dear. Age. She may be known as the sex kitten of China but she is no longer a kitten. It is I who will take the city by storm. Tonight is my night. Ahh, to be twenty-one in Shanghai and to have one's lover come dancing in attendance!" Sophia mimicked the slinky walk required of any woman encased in a cheong-sam.

"You are not going to embarrass us by wearing one of those native dresses are you?"

"Oh, no, no, no, no. That would be too silly, Elena. I'm not in a cheong-sam mood."

"Thank goodness for that," Elena muttered.

"I'm in more of a bewitching mood. I want Elter to think I'm a sweet young thing without a lascivious thought in my head. Virginal, for his eyes only. Men know how to fish, but only women know how to let themselves be caught. Elter's a clever fisherman, but I'm cleverer."

"How do you know?" Elena asked. "Really, Sophia. For a girl . . ."

"Please, *please,* Elena. We are *women* now. Today is the first day of our womanhood. Why don't you offer yourself to Edward?"

"Really!" Elena was pink with anger. "How can you talk like that?"

"Like what?"

"As though love and commitment were just something to do with sex."

"Well, aren't they?" Sophia strolled up and down the room swinging her hips.

"The two things don't necessarily go together. What I feel for Edward and he feels for me is not the same thing that happens in the houses of ill-repute in Shanghai. That's just a sordid transaction between two people where money is exchanged. It's a sin, anyway."

"Oh, Elena, you're such a prude."

"No, I'm not. Do let's stop this conversation. You're putting me off my tea."

"Well, I like this sort of conversation, and it makes me hungry. For everything. Hurry up. Let's go down and see what presents we have."

Both girls walked down the stairs arm in arm. Elena's dress was white with cascades of lace and a small Peter Pan collar. Sophia wore a deep blue button-through with small pearl buttons. Her sash pulled the dress close to her now full figure and her slanted eyes glittered with excitement. In only a few hours she would be in her lover's arms. Now that she knew he was coming she felt the waiting had passed as if in a dream. "He will be here," she whispered, seeing the front door ahead of her as she turned the corner to go to the dining-room. That door must open tonight, and he will be there on the threshold, and today will be the beginning and the end of my life. Time must inexorably bring Elter into her waiting arms. It was just a matter of surviving the day.

❦ *CHAPTER 38* ❦

"So, Elter is going to the ball." Maria was sitting on Rollo's bed. She was dressed in a flamingo pink ball-gown which oddly complemented her coloring. Her hair for this evening hung loose down her back. She had kicked her shoes off and now ran her fingers through her toes. "My goodness, I must be one of the few brave new women who don't wear corsets."

Rollo held up his hand to quiet her incessant chatter. The evening sun had set his auburn hair ablaze. He looked worried. "Are you sure this is the right thing, Maria? After all, Elter can have any girl he wants, you know. Sophia is high-spirited, but she's a good girl at heart. I'm very fond of her. I know I've been a bit neglectful over the last year, but I can't bear illness. People smell so awful when they're ill."

Maria laughed. "You're too fastidious, Rollo."

"I guess I am. But we see enough unpleasantness in our lives without having to seek it out. Wouldn't you agree, dearest? Sophia and Elena are like innocent flowers. I don't want to watch that bright light in Sophia extinguished. She looks like a purple rose bejeweled with shimmering dewdrops. How sad to see that rose bloom too early and then fall apart, the petals on the ground trampled underfoot by anyone hurrying through her life."

"You're also a chronic romantic."

Rollo sighed. "I am," he said quietly. "I also

know that before I succumbed to the indulgences of the flesh, I too had the beauty of innocence."

Maria shook out her mane of hair. "Everyone has to lose their innocence at some time or other. Anyway, Sophia's been lucky so far. None of life's unpleasantness has touched her, except for the death of her family. But most of us lost our families and our way of life. We all had to make adjustments. Now I'm a prostitute. No, don't make a face. That's what I am, so I might as well use the word. Simple fact. We can make up all sorts of euphemisms to excuse what I do or pretend I do it by choice. Sometimes I do, but when the Tongs issue orders, I do what I'm told. You and I serve one master. The same master guides Elter. Quite what Lau Tchi's plan is—and I don't expect he will tell us—none of us knows. But I do know that he never reveals the future, because we have free will, and if we knew what was in the future we would try to bend it."

Rollo stood by the window of his bedroom and looked out into the dying day. Morosely he imagined his former life in London. He remembered the joy of sitting with his friends at his club. Now they're all called buggers, he thought. I am too. Exiled from my country. Jeered at. Rollo was lonely for his friends. Some had gone to France, others were exiled even farther, but Rollo had decided to go to Shanghai so that his family would be kept safe from the scandal of his adventures. It's hard, he thought, to bear the company of heterosexuals. Just as they think we are unnatural, we find them so one-dimensional.

But he did love Sophia's company, and Maria's. Both girls shared another dimension, a perverse sense of humor so close to his own. "Still," he broke the silence in the room, "I do hope that Elter doesn't break her heart."

"Oh, he will," Maria prophesied. "He will. But how is she to grow up if her heart is never broken?"

"She could try getting married to a decent man like Edward."

Maria lay back on the bed. "That's not possible for her. Sophia was born with a curious itch. And even if she did opt for a life like Elena's, she would die of boredom or run away. Sophia wants to risk herself. And why not? Since that's all there is to life."

The fading sun left the two friends, fugitives in exile, and shone its beams into other windows all over Shanghai.

Sophia was on her knees in her bedroom, laying out the tarot cards for the fifteenth time that day. Miss Trublood barely tolerated this practice. It came under the heading "heathen" in her book, but Sophia was besotted with the cards. I feel, she thought, that I have control over these cards. They can tell me of the future. Put down the card of the Fool. That is all of us in this life. "Particularly me," Sophia muttered. Across me, above and below me, behind me, four cards ahead of me, and the answer to the question. Will he come?

Feverishly she turned those cards that lay face down on her future. The card that covered her was the card of Justice. Not bad. The card that crossed her was the King of Discs. Huh, she thought. A powerful male figure with money. That would be Edward. He's not going to approve at all. Well, maybe the only way around that is that he and Elena should not know. The card above her was the Hierophant. Guided by gods, thank goodness. And with Miss Trublood's fervent prayers, my soul should survive. So far so good. Nothing awful yet. Below me? She turned the card slowly. Oh dear. Sophia put her hand to her mouth. "Wow," she said in the American slang caught from Miss Trublood. It was the card of Corruption. Green slime hung from the branches of a decayed tree. Sophia shrugged. Everyone needs a little corruption now and then, thinking of Maria—*she* was doing quite well out of it.

The four promises came next. The first—this really was not going too well, but Sophia was caught up in the question. Maybe I should just stop now and get dressed. "No, no, no," the voice corrected her, the voice that had lived with her since the first day she visited the Gorgon. "You must meet your destiny. You must not run away. If you do not take the path with heart, you will live to regret your life. Pick up the card."

The first card was the Falling Tower. The second was Death. He grinned at her, his empty eye-sockets gleaming. He stood there, with his huge sickle swinging close to her face. "I am the sole arbiter of your fate," he sighed. In the stench of his mouth lay the bones of others who had not acknowledged his power, those who heeded not his warnings and then met Death unprepared. Sophia acknowledged Death as her superior and turned to the third card, the Aeon: the mystical union and communion between man and his universe, the figure of good or evil, the dominator of this subjective world. So, Sophia thought. The Tower falls and my life now changes. Death is here to scythe away the old and bring in the new. The Aeon is to rule my life. One more card, the fourth. The Circle, Sophia nodded. How accurate, she thought. The Circle of Completion.

Now for the question. "Please God," she begged. "Let it be *yes.*" Sophia felt her bones melt and her blood turn cold as she knew before she turned the card what it was. How do I know? she wondered. "You are learning," said the voice. "Sophia, you are learning to live in another dimension. You know this card before its time. Turn the card!" the voice demanded.

Sophia sighed with relief: the Knight of Cups. Not only had Elter sent his note of acceptance—which was at this moment lying under Sophia's pillow—he also intended to come tonight. "Thank you, God," she prayed and crossed herself carefully.

The cards at times made her afraid. They seemed to possess a supernatural power not of this world. But then, she reasoned with herself as she put them away, they are only cards.

Sitting on his mat in the empty room, the Gorgon raised his head. He sat on his heels on his wooden bed, his face pointing to the hole in the roof, his eyes unseeing. He sat like a dog sniffing the wind. The smells floating around his nostrils were his messengers, as were sounds—sounds now of the great city emptying for the night; the rustle of silks and taffetas; the chink of jewelry from the grand houses; the purr of the big cars. All waiting for this day that he, Lau Tchi had made. Lau Tchi was well pleased indeed.

He sneezed and then he relaxed.

The night was on its way like a thief with a swag-bag over his shoulder. In the bag were Elter and Sophia. Their time had come. The ending was yet in the future and known only to Lau Tchi, but he could wait. He sensed the centuries behind him pushing at his back. Lau Tchi waved them away. "Destiny cannot be hurried," he reminded the impatient ghosts. "You have had your time," he berated them, and they slunk off moaning and wailing. These were the souls chained for ever to this earth because they had failed to embrace their destinies. Because these specters had led unfilled lives they were doomed to roam eternity. "Be still and listen," the Gorgon said.

Sophia stood on Edward's left and Elena, as his fiancée, stood on his right. Sophia could hardly remember the dining-room as it had looked at breakfast. All day a team of decorators had been piling into the house with bamboos and tropical flowers. Now the summer was at its height, but this year a fortuitous amount of rain had made Shanghai green and luxuriant. Behind them the ballroom (for this was what the dining-room had become) was empty, and the first guests could be heard coming down the hall. All the presents for the girls were piled on a table. Sophia had to be reprimanded by Elena since she kept pulling off bits of wrapping-paper in an effort to see the contents. "This," Edward said, "should be a wonderful party. I've not invited too many of my old cronies, just enough for me to have a good chat while you young things dance."

"You'll dance with me, Edward, won't you?" Elena looked anxious. She was dressed in a white muslin gown that fell delicately over her breasts and had a small silk train. Her hair was a bright golden chignon tied with a pale pink scarf.

He squeezed her hand as an answer. Edward's heart lurched as he looked at her and thought, I have this beautiful creature beside me and she will be here for the rest of my life. Having almost lost her, he now found her doubly precious.

Sophia on his left yawned. "Here come the troops," she said.

"Lord and Lady Lacelles!" The announcer wore a bright yellow tailcoat which was at odds with his red face.

"How wonderful to see you both." Edward bent low over Lady Lacelles's hand.

"Jolly good birthday I hope for you girls." Lord Lacelles liked pretty young things and these two were surely the prettiest in Shanghai.

Sophia curtsied and tried out one of her long lascivious looks.

Goodness, Lord Lacelles snorted to himself and shot off into the ballroom. That young filly has a very game look in her eye. Some fellow had better look out.

The musicians at the far end of the room were tuning up, waiting for sufficient guests to arrive to begin the ball with the opening waltz. The noise caused confusion in Sophia's head. She did not want to be curtsying prettily on the end of a receiving line, but she did want to be the first to see Elter coming down the hall. I would resent it if Elena or Edward saw him first, she thought. He's mine. *Mine, mine, mine* . . . The word expanded in her head.

When enough guests were present, Edward bowed to Elena. "We must lead the waltz."

Rollo emerged out of the blur of the new guests. "Sophia," he said. "Let me partner you." He took the little booklet hanging from her wrist and entered his name for every dance. Then he smiled at her. "Of course," he said, "this is to keep you free. You don't have to dance them all with me."

Sophia smiled. "Oh, Rollo, you're so understanding. I'm dying of waiting. Can one die of waiting? Is it a certifiable condition? 'Here lies Sophia, dead of waiting.' "

Slowly the waltz disciplined the milling guests into couples. Chandeliers gleamed, dresses swished to and fro, like the sound of thousands of seas all over the world. Men and women moved in unison. *One* two three, *one* two three. And then came the turn that brought the women's bodies close to their partners and their small hands deeper into the hollow of the men's white gloved hands. Tonight everyone was a prince or princess. Tonight the stars shone especially over the house.

By the end of the third dance Sophia was desperate. "Do you think he's coming, Rollo?"

Rollo looked down at her intense anxious face. "Yes, my darling," he said with a fatal weariness in his voice. "He'll be here." Rollo saw Elter leaving the Gorgon's lair. And fully briefed he will be, Rollo thought. He looked at Sophia, so bright and hopeful. "Promise me one thing, Sophia," he said urgently. "Promise me that you will never do something that you will for ever regret. Too many of us in Shanghai are here because we have betrayed ourselves and other people too. Those who loved us." He looked at Edward who was dancing with Elena, their cheeks pressed close together, their bodies enraptured in the flow of the music. "Promise me, Sophia?" he said.

"Oh, I do, I do," she replied lightly. She turned her eyes once more toward the door. "Where *is* he?"

"One more dance and he will come."

"How do you know these things, Rollo?"

"I'm learning," he laughed. "I've decided to become a bit of a seer myself."

The music stopped and the guests fell into pockets of conversation. Then Sophia heard Elter's footsteps. They could only belong to a German with long years of training in the army. His feet rapped out the yards to where she stood, and then she was in his arms and they were moving onto the dance floor. Other couples stood and watched them swaying together—she lithe and dark, he blond and handsome. Their bodies, though unaccustomed to each other's forms, melted into each other in immediate recognition. When they turned, Sophia felt as if she were flying off the planet into a delicious dark space reserved for the two of them, an oblivion where they could live for the rest of their lives undisturbed.

Slowly other couples joined them until the whole room turned and circled. When the dance ended Elter took her hand. "Come," he said. "We'll go to a room where we can talk." Sophia followed him, aware that she was being watched by two pairs of eyes, Rollo's, looking mournful, and Edward's, looking anxious. I don't care, she thought defiantly. Elter won't harm me.

He hurried Sophia up the corridor to the drawing-room. Chairs were set out for those who wished to sit. Miss Trublood sat implacably silent in one of them, busy with her embroidery. She was there as the self-appointed guardian of the young girl's morals. So far she had little to do, but the evening was young and the champagne had only been circulating for an hour or so. Sophia realized there was no way of avoiding Miss Trublood. "Elter, this is my chaperone, Miss Trublood. Miss Trublood, this is Elter Betzelheim."

Miss Trublood rose from her chair and stared hard at Elter. "Mr. B. I've heard so much about you." Sophia glared at her. Miss Trublood subsided. "You two young things get on with your talking. Young things do like to talk so. Why, back in Des Moines, we did it for hours. We lay on the haystack and talked and talked and talked. None of this modern stuff. What we had were hoedowns, good old-fashioned dances. None of this holding on, clinging like vines to each other."

Elter was grinning when Miss Trublood finally left them. "Why are you smiling?" Sophia was mortified.

"She's a nice old thing," Elter said. "Here, let's sit down. We're far away from other people, yes?"

Sophia nodded. "We're as far away as we can get, unless we run away," she said.

Elter shook his head. "But we can't do that. Sir Edward would never let me visit you again. No, *liebchen*, first we must talk. Tell me all about yourself."

❧ CHAPTER 39 ❧

For the first time in her life, Sophia felt she was pouring out her soul to someone who understood what she was trying to say. "I know everybody loves Elena and thinks of her as a sort of saint. And because we're twins we're always compared with each other. Which is why I feel such a sinner."

Elter smiled. "You have little occasion to sin at twenty-one."

Sophia flushed. "Well, not really, I suppose. But there can still be sin in thought."

Elter smiled again and took Sophia's hand. "You worry too much," he said. "You plan too much and you think too much. Now you are twenty-one and can make decisions for yourself. You no longer need to be chaperoned by the good American lady, and legally Sir Edward has no control over you any more."

Sophia leaned her head to the side. "Is that why you waited so long before coming to see me?"

Elter tilted his head. "I did not want you to betray the wishes of your guardian, nor to deceive your chaperone. But from today onward, your life is in your own hands. And we are free to do whatever we choose."

How the word *we* thrilled Sophia! The only other *we* in her life had been herself and her twin sister, the *we* that bound two females together even *in utero*. At birth Sophia had struggled in her rush to get into the world, but in her struggles she had caused her mother pain and distress. She had a caul over her face when she was born, but Elena, emerging three minutes later, looked perfect. "It's funny, Elter." Sophia paused. "I was trouble even before I was born. I scared my mother with my impatience, and I have a defiant nature. Are you sure you can love me?"

Elter sat back in his chair. He felt afraid for a moment. Would this beautiful young girl take his heart, the heart that for forty years had beaten only for himself? He had many memories of many women, good and bad. They all climaxed the same way, with cries of rapturous ecstasy. Many of the so-called good women were not at all "good," and he often found the madonna in the whore, but he had never fallen in love. What on earth am I doing here? he wondered. A German mercenary in a foreign house seducing a twenty-one-year-old girl . . . "Yes, I know I can love you, Sophia. I have waited nearly two years for this moment."

It was the way Elter said the words *I know* with a deep resonant ring of certainty, with a promise of marriage. But that can wait, Sophia thought. "First we must get Edward to allow us to visit." Sophia smiled at Elter. "Let's go and find him."

The room was filling up with tired dancers. Dinner was announced. Elter and Sophia took their place at the top table. Sophia smiled when she saw the big heavy curtains stirring slightly in the breeze and remembered the occasions when she had inadvertently spied on her father's seductive sporting with his mistresses. Now the memory did not hurt quite so much. Opposite her Elter sat, his big chest waiting to protect her, his sinewy arms there to enfold her . . . She sat dreamily while plates swooped up and down before her. Distractedly she picked and sipped, and then picked some more.

Elter and Edward were deep in conversation over the future of Germany. Both men, with the war over, were now able to relax as past but not present adversaries. Edward had not enjoyed the knowledge that Sophia wanted to consort with an official enemy. At least Elter was no longer the enemy. "Do you golf?" Edward asked. Though wary of Elter, Edward adored golf and he was always on the lookout for partners at his level: a good game was a rarity.

"I love to play golf," Elter said.

Edward shook his hand. "Tomorrow at ten?"

Elter was pleased. Edward was going to be easier than he had thought. The weakness of an honest man is that he does not suspect dishonesty in another.

Edward smiled. "Sophia, it would appear I've found a golfing partner."

"How wonderful!" Sophia said and she too smiled. And *I* have just found a lover, she thought. But of course nobody would know that, except for Maria who was far down the table. Rollo was closer, and he caught the gleam of victory in Sophia's eye.

Well, what's done is done. Rollo took his glass of champagne and waited for Sophia to look his way. When she did so, he raised his glass, and his collar-length hair fell forward.

How like a girl he looks, Sophia thought. How very beautiful he is . . . But tonight was no time to be sorry for Rollo. Tonight was to be savored as much as possible with Elter. And tomorrow she would let Elter spend the morning playing golf. In return she would ask Edward if she could go alone to have dinner with Elter.

At four o'clock in the morning breakfast was served in the dining-room, buffet-style. A sleepy throng of dancers clustered around the tables. Scrambled eggs, kedgeree, deviled kidneys, kippers shipped from London, English bacon thinly cut, toast, marmalade, and Chinese porridge with garlic. "Try some," Elter said. "It's delicious."

Sophia grimaced at the idea. They sat on spindly

golden chairs that had been brought in for the revelers. Nevertheless, she tried the porridge and licked her lips. "It's good," she said.

"Yes, I first learned to eat that gruel when I was running for my life and living in kampongs in Malaya."

"Elter, how very exciting! Why were you running for your life?"

He laughed. "I needed the exercise, I suppose."

"Oh, don't tease! Tell me."

Elter shook his head but did not lose his smile. "Sophia, you must learn a first lesson from me: I don't explain. Much of my life you will not know about. Do not ask."

Sophia saw a look in his colorless eyes that spelled danger. Only sharks look like that, she thought, remembering the big sharks that followed her father's yacht. One in particular seemed to know the yacht and wait for it. Then he would roll his greasy belly, nudging the stern, and look up at the young Sophia as if to say, "One day I'm coming for you." She shuddered at the memory. "I won't ask," she said hurriedly.

"Good." Elter bowed slightly. "On that same journey, I learned to eat rats, and mice, and even snakes."

"What does snake taste like?" Sophia was interested.

He chuckled. "A little like chicken."

Dawn crept up and took the house by surprise. People began to leave until there was just a handful left. Maria and Rollo came over to the table and sat down. "Ah, Maria." Elter greeted her with an easy familiarity. "What have you been doing with yourself?"

"You know. A bit of this and a bit of that." Maria was tired but happy to see Sophia in love.

Rollo acknowledged Elter, and then clutched his head in his hands. "Too much champagne," he said. "I must go."

"I'll go with you," Maria said. "Sleep calls. Goodbye, Sophia. It was a wonderful party. And happy birthday again." She tipped her head to Elter, who bowed in return, and left the dining-room with Rollo.

Sophia and Elter were completely alone. The dining-room looked devastated. Everywhere were piles of food and plates and many glasses, some dropped, some spilled. But for Sophia the lace tablecloths and the gold tassled curtains gave the impression of a church and seemed to call for a vow to be made that would for ever bind her to this man and to her destiny. Now she believed that the Gorgon did have supernatural power. Since she had first been to see him, her mind had seesawed in debate. There was no longer any uncertainty. She stood up and turned to Elter, who was waiting to kiss her. His firm lips came down on hers and she felt the first stirring of shared lust and rapture. His tongue ran around the edges of her lips and then explored the inside of her mouth gently. She felt herself breathing hard and then sensed a throbbing between her legs. Her sexual longings had been unfulfilled for the last few years. Now her passion could and would be shared. They held each other gently and with an unfamiliar touch.

Later, when the sun was climbing the sky and the blue of a clear day filled her bedroom window, Sophia sat on the windowsill with her arms around her knees, as she had done so many years ago as a little girl, watching for her beloved father . . . No longer to be associated with the sorrow of his death, this image of her past self now took its place among her happier memories. Now she had a future. No longer was she alone. "Dear Lord," she prayed, "please let him love me." Then she blessed her family and she blessed Miss Trublood as well.

❧ CHAPTER 40 ❧

Edward was encouraged to discover that Elter could hold his own at golf. After the game Edward did the polite thing and invited Elter to a favorite restaurant. He wanted a chance to sound out this Betzelheim fellow without the distraction of Sophia, which would not have been possible had they lunched at home.

When they were seated in a private dining-room, Elter brought Sophia and Elena into the conversation, saying what an excellent ball Edward had thrown for them.

"The least I could do," Edward said. "They've suffered so dreadfully."

"Indeed. Will you remain here once you're married, then?" Elter sensed a confidence coming.

"We'll be going back to England in a year or so. I'm due a posting home."

Stop now, Elter thought. I have a goal set. A year. "I imagine it must be wonderful to begin to think of home again. I get nostalgic for Berlin and the museums and art galleries."

"So do I," said Edward. "I miss the silly things—fresh English sausages made by my butcher. Good wine—wine simply does not travel well. I have mine laid down in a cellar at Dover. Actually my grandfather laid down the first bottles and then my father added to those. I keep imagining myself opening a bottle of port . . . Ah, the taste of it!" Edward, Elter realized, was a very lonely man. In love with his bride but hungry for companionship. Good, so much the better. "What do you think of this one?"

Elter paused while Edward pushed the port toward him. Elter was glad that he had taken the time to learn the eccentric after-dinner drinking habits of the British upper classes. Smoothly Elter accepted the decanter and poured his own glass of port. Elter held the glass up to the light. "Nice color," he said and then tasted it slowly. What fun to drink another man's port and then to seduce his about-to-be sister-in-law! How could Edward be so silly? But then, Elter reminded himself, how could Edward not? Edward was born to a heritage shortly to become obsolete. The World War was over, and with it a whole generation of Edwardians, so steeped in tradition, were going to become as extinct as the dodo. Men like Edward—classically educated, willing to die for their King and country—would be swept away, and in place of the decency, courage and morality they represented would come the age of the common man. In a way Elter was sorry. Then again, he thought, now people like myself can operate freely. The time had come for the carpetbagger, as the Americans would say, to have his day, for the British lumpen proletariat to have theirs, and for the opium-suppliers, like himself, to reign unchecked.

"A little musty, don't you think?" Edward asked.

"No, no," Elter reassured him. "Excellent, excellent." He saw Edward relax. Good. He had passed two important tests: the golf and the port. Now Edward would accept Elter as the gentleman he was not. Or did Elter detect an edge still in Edward's voice, that English gentleman's way of appearing candid while revealing nothing, of being friendly and polite even to someone whom one dislikes? "May I call on Sophia, Edward?"

The question came suddenly but was not a surprise. Edward dreaded this question. He did not trust Elter, despite the man's practiced charm. But with Sophia now of age, could he really prevent her from seeing him? Perhaps it was wiser to play along for the moment . . . "For tea, do you mean?"

"Most certainly for tea." Elter inclined his head graciously. "How about tomorrow?"

"I'll tell Sophia this evening."

Elter pushed back his chair. "And now you will

pardon me. I must go to the office and catch up on a few things."

"By the way, Elter, just what exactly do you do?"

"A little of everything. Venture capitalism." He shrugged. "A bit of importing. I have some nice Havana cigars coming in tomorrow. I'll bring you a box?"

"That's jolly decent of you." Edward smiled.

The men shook hands. "Good afternoon," Elter said.

As the door closed behind him, Elter felt a sudden sense of freedom. A game of golf and a box of cigars in exchange for the seduction of a young virgin. Not a bad deal.

Elter was hungry, though he had just eaten. He always felt hungry when he was on to something. He stopped at a food stall near his office. "Fried ginger prawns. Twelve of them." Elter needed to feel he was back underground again. For the last twenty-four hours he had had to play-act the perfect German diplomat. Elter did indeed miss Berlin, but not his boyhood there when, as a small barefoot child, he had sold his body on the Kurfürstendamm to wealthy homosexuals. He remembered well the rich British buggers and he hated them for their money and their arrogance. In a twisted way, seducing Sophia under Edward's nose was also a way of taking his revenge for those awful years. But he had survived. Now, when he went back to Berlin, he went as a man of means. He stayed where he wanted to, he owned his own castle in the country, and the gold watch on his wrist told of his success.

Elter finished the prawns and looked about him for a woman. Sophia had excited him, her small warm body nestled against his own, and he remembered the innocence of her kiss. He spotted, standing against a post a little way off, a young girl in a tight-fitting green cheong-sam. He nodded and walked along the street. She followed him, ten paces behind. He went into a tall house with many windows. She went in after him and he shut the door. Here he had no servants. He preferred it that way. He walked up the stairs that led to his office bedroom. When on missions he slept next to his hidden wireless station. As he ascended the stairs he threw off pieces of clothing. The girl picked up his coat, then his shirt, a vest, and trousers last. Before reaching the door, she bent down and picked up his underpants. Walking naked and fully erect into the bedroom, Elter made a motion for the girl to undress. He flipped through yesterday's letters. Nothing that can't wait, he thought. And then, when the girl stood unclothed and submissive beside him, he pounced, bearing her down on the bed. He pumped her small body, ignoring her cries for mercy. Why give her mercy? She was only a Chinese whore. Finally he reached his climax and rolled over. "Go," he said. He picked up his trousers and handed her some notes.

The girl dressed quickly and was gone like a shadow.

Elter lay on his bed, the sheets soaked in sweat and semen. A feeling of disgust made the back of his throat contract. Why couldn't he overcome his lust? Why could he discipline every part of his life except that? Why, when he needed a woman, did he lose his iron self-control? He stared at the ceiling, searching in vain to find an answer.

Later that night, while all of Shanghai was sleeping, the girl in the green cheong-sam was sitting in a room thick with opium fumes. Faces loomed in and out of the gray mist. "So, the German made *chichi* with you?" The girl was nervous. The Enforcer looked greedily at her from the corner of the room. But the man to whom even the Enforcer was accountable had a soft spot for young prostitutes. This man put a reassuring hand on her shoulder. "Don't be frightened," he said. "You have taken the oath and you have done well. Did he say anything at all?"

"No," the girl stammered. "Nothing."

Chu Wing was hideous to look at. He was from the south of China. He was tall and had broad pendulous ears and round full cheeks. The flared flat nostrils of his nose were dense with hairs. He had five repulsive warts. "Did you notice anything?"

The girl nodded. "I saw letters with foreign stamps. And beside the bed he had a curious box. It was covered with a cloth."

"Good girl!" the giant beamed. "Well done! You have been well trained." Ah, ah, he was thinking. So. He called his assistant to his side. "Get a fix on the house and listen. He has a wireless, so we can now verify broadcasts." The assistant nodded and went out of the room.

"You may go now," said the fiercest man in Shanghai to the young girl. Chu Wing's name was hated and feared throughout China. His men were ruthless. But the fear only added to his legendary stature in the land, and his opium hongs were the largest in the East. His far-reaching influence extended not only over China but also to Europe and America. Opium went to America with the first Chinese who left their country. Many a pipeful filled an empty belly and made dreams a reality. The Americans took to the drug as readily as the Chinese had embraced it when the British first imported Indian opium into China a hundred years before. Chu Wing enjoyed the present irony. Now it was China that dangled opium before the glazed eyes of the West. Now the tiger had turned and its great fangs would tear at the throat of the barbarians.

The girl was gone and Chu Wing wished to play chess. His huge fingers picked up the chess pieces with surprising delicacy. He mused and pondered over the ivory-inlaid board. "We will have to move you here," he said to the knight. "Now for the rook. He must go." He looked up at the Enforcer, who was known as One-Eyed Charlie. "He will have to go. There is no other way."

The Enforcer nodded. These two had little need for words. Charlie had lost his right eye in a fight with a rival Tong. His face was sharp as a scimitar; he was so thin that, if he stood sideways, one had the impression that he did not exist. But exist he did. The Enforcer for Chu Wing's Blue Gang, he was well known within the city and without and his one-eyed face was dreaded even more than the sight of Chu Wing. He tortured those who needed to be taught a lesson and he was famous for his ability to strangle slowly. Charlie felt no scruples as he saw the life-force fade and the soul slip away. He had no religion except for his love of Chu Wing. Chu had rescued him from a lonely boyhood in a shack on the borders of northern China. Chu was riding by with his men when he heard a cry. Chu, wishing to relieve himself anyway, got off his Mongolian pony and walked up to the shack with his bayonet extended. Charlie was crouched over his mother's dead body, he himself dying of cold and starvation. Chu lifted Charlie onto his horse and motioned one of the men to bury Charlie's mother. For that one act of compassion years ago, Charlie loved Chu. So any foe of Chu's died with no sympathy from Charlie. One less enemy for the boss, was Charlie's attitude. He knew Chu slept better for his own shadowy presence, though he himself slept little. "Don't you ever sleep, Charlie?" Chu once asked. Charlie shook his head. "How can I, with the noise of you playing with your concubines, not to mention the chattering of the eunuchs they bring with them?" Treacherous lot, eunuchs. Charlie especially liked torturing eunuchs. They screamed with such a shrill voice, it made Charlie laugh.

Charlie hoped tonight Chu would go straight back to his jade palace and stay there. Charlie had to go and find the man Chu wished to have killed. A quick death, he thought, probably poison. The air would seem lighter without this particular disobedient Son of Satan. Charlie had attended a missionary school chosen by Chu so that he could learn the language and ways of the barbarian.

Chu made a sign and everybody stood up as he lumbered out of the door. "I'm going home, Charlie," he said. "You tend to the business. It's been a good day. Number One Wife wants me to have dinner with her. I'll see you tomorrow."

Charlie made off into the night, his long nose sniffing the air. He knew and had records of all that went on in Shanghai. The Silver Spoon Triad met and ate in several restaurants and tea houses. Quietly he went into the back of six restaurants along the riverfront until he saw his quarry sitting among friends. Now the prey was hunted down, it was time to strike. Charlie's enemy was just sending his plate back to the kitchen for more pork ribs. Good, thought Charlie. Pork ribs are spicy and the sauce will hide the few drops of poison.

Charlie glided into the busy kitchen. The room was hot and hectic, for out front the restaurant was very full and busy. Busier than usual, because tonight was a full-moon festival. Miniature boats made out of Chinese paper carrying candles were bobbing about the Whangpoo River in remembrance of the dead. Charlie's quarry and his friends had been drinking all evening. Among their own Triad they felt safe. So much better to die among friends, Charlie thought.

His presence was not noticed in the kitchen. He wore the same blue smock and trousers as the waiters. The plate was passed from hand to hand. He stood beside the cook, who ladled the ribs onto the dirty plate. Charlie stretched out a hand and took the plate, while the cook was busy gazing into the vast vat of food. A half-second later Charlie passed the plate to a young waiter. And then he left, having made a shadowy entry and an invisible exit. He paused to watch. Would the marked man ask his taster to try the ribs first, and thereby earn his place in heaven? Or would he, as Charlie hoped, forget this late at night and let his guard down? In which case, it was time for the head of the Silver Spoon Triad to die. Charlie grinned. Such good poison, he thought.

The man greedily sucked a rib which was dripping with sauce, and the poison took hold. His face crumpled first, then his hands grasped at his throat as if he would gladly tear open his neck if only to breathe again. "No, no, my friend." Charlie grinned. "You will never breathe again." The body bucked and swayed and finally fell with a satisfying crash.

The Triad members leapt to their feet and charged into the kitchen. "Poison! Poison!" they were shouting. It was time for Charlie to move on.

He walked quietly along the riverbank into the German concession. Tonight, he thought, the German will be broadcasting for us to hear. Good. The little paper-borne lights bobbed and swayed on the river. Next year the poisoned one will have a lamp of his own, Charlie observed. I must remind Chu Wing that we need to give money to the wife and the two children.

The job for the night done with, Charlie felt strangely at peace in the cool of the evening. Better than sex, he mused. Killing always satisfied him in a way sex could not.

CHAPTER 41

Miss Trublood was worried. She knew Sophia had every intention of pursuing Elter with or without her permission. Edward shared her concerns but stressed that the stronger the resistance they put up to Sophia's association with the man, the more determined Sophia would become. "Better for us to let her have her head," Edward confided to Miss Trublood, "but keep our eyes open." Three mornings a week Edward went off to play golf with Elter. By now Miss Trublood could recognize the sound of Elter's soft footfall in the corridor. *"Guten Tag,"* he would say as he pushed open the door of the dining-room.

Miss Trublood watched Sophia's face. Gone was the innocent rapturous smile of childhood. In its place she saw the face of a grown woman desirous of love. Elena began to feel that maybe Elter did not warrant suspicion after all. So far he had been content to come to dinner and after dinner to play cards with the family. He stayed until ten o'clock, when Sophia accompanied him to the door and kissed him a chaste goodnight. But the day would come—or rather the night—when Elter would demand time alone with Sophia. And much as Miss Trublood lamented that occasion with all her Christian soul, like Edward, she knew she was ultimately helpless should Sophia put her mind in earnest to the conquest of this dubious man. Still,

Miss Trublood could not help but admit, Sophia did seem happier when Elter was around.

The summer trailed to an end. Mornings turned into days less warm, but comfortable. Thin linens were abandoned in favor of light silk tweed. Sophia and Elena wore their cloche hats low over their brows. Stockings were thicker, and worn with sensible brogues. Winter fashion was less voluptuous. No longer could the beholder stare entranced at the curve of a breast beneath satin chemises covered coyly by silken dresses. Now, with winter breathing disapproval, one had to guess or perhaps remember from summer the sinuous shapes that made the summer months so sensually satisfying.

Edward and Elter were both in love. Or rather, one man was in love and the other walked like a predatory wolf on the edge of a canyon. Edward began to think that his marriage need be postponed no longer. Perhaps in the spring he would wed Elena, a lovely time for weddings. And the sooner he could get Elena to England, taking Sophia with them, the better. Meanwhile, Elter prowled, waiting for the best moment to strike.

Both twins were in love. Or perhaps one was in love; the other stalked her prey like the young snow leopard—untried, untrained, but the instinct there, born into the world to hunt.

In the first week of November Edward felt cornered into granting Elter permission to take Sophia to dinner unchaperoned. Miss Trublood could only shake her head. "Don't be so silly," Sophia chided her. "We're only going for dinner. Miss Trublood, *really.*" She laughed, her eyes bright and her face flushed with excitement. She kissed Miss Trublood on the cheek. "I must change. He'll be here in an hour and I've hardly begun to get ready. Please, *please,* don't worry. Really, there's nothing to worry about." And she pushed Miss Trublood's silent reproachful bulk out of the room and shut the door behind her. Oh dear, Sophia thought, I've upset her. But I do have the right to have dinner with Elter on my own.

Since their first kiss on the night of the ball, months had gone by and they had only been able to exchange moist but chaste kisses at the door. By now she felt she had known Elter all her life. She knew that Elter would fill the place in her heart her father had previously occupied. Only Elter had the charisma and the depth of character to match in any way her love for her father. Only Elter had the power to capture her body and soul. They had both waited patiently. Sophia trusted Elter absolutely and waited with resignation for the moment when he decreed they should seek a resolution to their desperate desire for each other.

On the days that he did not come to the house, she sat and gazed into space. Love, she thought, had made her a zombie, only awake and alive to his touch, or to the sight of his handsome face with lines etched deeply in the corners of his eyes. She sat on her window-ledge and imagined love, sexual love, and was glad that there was no one to observe her face. She thought of herself gloved by his body. Often when she put on her black leather

gloves to walk about the garden, she imagined
him. As she thrust her forefinger into the leather
pocket of the first finger of her glove, and then the
second, and the third, and the fourth, and the
fifth . . . The leather fitted tightly and she closed
her eyes in ecstasy. How does one imagine the unimaginable and the never-known? she wondered.
Maria could have told her, but Sophia did not want
to hear any details from Maria's lips. Somehow it
would spoil her love for Elter. For Maria, passion
was a commodity to be used for gain; for Sophia,
it was a private act of communion between herself
and the man she loved. The absolute privacy of the
act hallowed the moment. No, she would not talk
of it to Maria.

Sophia dressed slowly. Tonight would be the
first time they went out together without any other
interference. *Tonight,* Sophia breathed. She
stroked her cheeks with rouge and brushed her
lips with a touch of carmine. Maria had given her
a pot of black sooty kohl. "Just a little around the
eyes," Maria had advised. "It was used in ancient
Egypt. Just think, Cleopatra wore it to drive Cae-
sar to despair." Sophia grinned. Could I drive
Elter to despair? I certainly hope so . . .

She heard the bell ring at the front door. Elter.
She picked up her clutch-bag and her coat and ran
lightly down the stairs. Elter stood at the foot of
the staircase talking to Edward. Golf again, Sophia
thought with dismay. Really, Edward was so banal.
"How about a sherry?" Edward boomed. "That
hooked low iron shot on the third hole is a devil.
I can't wait to try again tomorrow."

"Edward, please don't drag Elter off for a drink. We must get going."

"Oh. I just thought he might want a drink. Well. I see. Sorry, old chap. You'd better get off. Take care of her, Elter. And Sophia, you be good."

Sophia made a face. Elter laughed. "She'll be good, Edward. Don't worry. I'll take care of her and return her here at ten o'clock."

"Ten o'clock, then, old man." Edward saw them out. One thing he believed he could trust Elter not to do was to keep a woman out past the designated hour. Besides, an evening alone with Elena was to be cherished, whatever else he had on his mind. They could pick up their wedding plans where they had left off, and there was much to arrange. He hurried into the drawing-room where Elena sat by the fire, her embroidery in her hands, the flames flickering on her serene face. "You do think Sophia will be safe with Elter, don't you?" Elena asked.

Edward opened his mouth to speak, then paused. Starting again, he said, "Darling, we've done all we can to protect Sophia. Now we must trust her, mustn't we?"

"That's all we can do," Elena sighed.

"Let's have a glass of champagne. I'll ring for Ah Ling and we can enjoy an evening by ourselves." As the bell pealed through the house, Edward and Elena sat in a comfortable silence, he gazing into the fire, thinking of his home in London, she thinking of the rose pattern she was embroidering for the dinner chairs in their marital home.

Downstairs Misha was also staring into a fire, thinking of Sophia. He worried about her, and he worried about Elter. Mei Mei, who knew much of what happened on the streets of Shanghai, warned Misha. "Chu Wing knows this German man."

"Who is Chu Wing?" Misha asked.

"He big man, biggest Tong. Much opium. Dangerous work."

Misha understood Mei Mei's advice. He knew from tea-room talk that Shanghai existed on two levels. On the surface, like formal lily-pools, were the great homes of the foreigners. But underneath seethed the real life of Shanghai, the city of brothels, of prostitutes, of opium. Way below the lily pads lurked the carp and the pike, the Triads and the Tongs. Misha feared everything that moved unseen in the depths. "Oh dear," he said, pulling Mei Mei's loyal little head to his chest. "I wish Katrina was here. She would know what to do."

"Katrina happy now."

"Yes," Misha said. "Katrina happy. And," he smiled at Mei Mei, brushing her lips with his, "so am I, Mei Mei. I'm very happy."

Mei Mei giggled and ran the tip of her tongue around his mouth. "Ummm," she sighed. "Lucky Mei Mei." For a time they forgot Sophia and lay content in each other's arms.

Sophia was pleased to find that Elter had booked a private dining-room at the Hong Kong Hotel. The room was elegant and intimate. A fire crackled in the grate. The small round table was covered in a pink tablecloth. In the middle of the table stood a pink art deco lamp. The plates were also pink with a gold rim and the napkins matched the tablecloth. The only other piece of furniture was a plush pink chaise-longue, overstuffed but inviting.

The waiter who led them to the room was a Russian. He recognized Sophia but said nothing. The Oblimov family were well known in Shanghai. What, he wondered, was this girl doing with Elter Betzelheim? Elter he knew extremely well. This was not the first time he had escorted Elter into a private room. Usually the women were high-class courtesans. The meetings were not for food, nor necessarily for sex, though usually by the end of the evening the chaise-longue in any of the private rooms bore the imprint of two bodies who had satiated more than their alimentary appetites. Poor girl, the waiter thought. I wonder if she knows what she's doing. He held his guiding arm out to the table. It was her life. At least she was rich. For him the world was a very changed place. From the university in St. Petersburg with the prospect of becoming a doctor to working as a waiter in the maw of the city of Shanghai . . . "I'll get your menu, sir." He bowed to Elter.

"And some champagne," Elter called.

"Of course, sir."

Elter was pleased. The first act of this particular drama was about to take place, and Elter was always happy when things went according to plan. "Make it a magnum of Perrier-Jouët *Fleur du Champagne.*" The door closed and they were alone at last.

"Let me take your coat." Elter held out his arms and Sophia came into them as if drawn by the strings of a puppeteer.

Maybe that's what she was, she thought. I'm a puppet that has waited for my master all my life. She felt her heart fluttering and she pressed herself close to Elter's chest. "How long we have waited!" she said, eagerly looking up at Elter's face.

"Yes," he said and he smiled down at her shining eyes. So innocent of guile, he thought. So very fresh. Almost he feared the weeks to come. Never before had Elter feared making love to a woman, or even to young girls. But somehow this girl caught at his heart. Could he go ahead with the plan? Must he recruit her? Did they really need this young countess? Yes, he knew they did. Sophia could go places and mix with people unsuspected, in a way that Maria and her ilk never could. There was something in the aristocratic upbringing that taught Sophia a poise from birth; a swing of the shoulders, an imperious nod of the head that could not be later acquired through instruction, and these were the very qualities that made her useful. She was at home in the streets of Shanghai as she was in the salons. She could watch and listen and report from anywhere. And the Gorgon had a purpose for her.

But then—and Elter inwardly shuddered—so did Chu Wing. There was no way out of that. Both the Gorgon and the Tong, though working toward seemingly disparate ends, often shared the same servants. Sophia would learn this fact later on. For now, Elter was determined to enjoy their evening together.

ᶜᐢᕲ CHAPTER 42 ᕲᶜᐢ

Elter handed Sophia a fluted glass of champagne. She watched the way his fingers curled sensuously around the stem and his broad hand engulfed the fragile glass. Soon, she thought, his hand will be on my breast. She felt her nipples tingle with desire. How would Anna have handled this? she wondered, wishing she had spent more years learning from the Golden Salamander.

Sophia envisioned sloughing off her skin as a young, inexperienced virgin; she would emerge as the Snow Leopard. She gazed across the table at Elter. She felt a heat in her veins. Her eyes were aflame. She sensed her many, many past lives urging her on. She looked down at the champagne glass and then lifted the glass before her face. Gazing at Elter through the bubbles, she said slowly and carefully, "To us, Elter. To us, always and for ever."

Elter was slightly astonished and apprehensive. He usually counted on toasting a nervous woman; he hardly expected to be toasted. "My dear," he said, raising his glass, "there is no such thing as for ever."

"In my world," she said with a silkiness in her voice, "I decide what is to be for ever or not."

Elter looked at Sophia. He felt drawn into her eyes like a man wound in a shroud. He sensed her small determined hands tugging at the binding around his heart. A light yet insistent pull that made his heart ache. He did not know why he should feel such pain. Certainly no other woman had ever affected him this way, except his mother, and she was long dead. Elter reminded himself that he had a job and a duty to fulfill. He was not here on innocent business. But he did admit, as he rang for the menu, that he was enjoying himself more than he had anticipated. While Sophia had been in the company of her family, she had a relatively subdued air, apart from the one passionate kiss at her birthday ball and the good-night kisses on the doorstep. Then, Elter had hoped for a flowering of this passion. But now, alone with her in her rather raffish mood, he wondered which of them was the pursuer and which the pursued. Was it possible that it was she who planned to seduce him? That would make an interesting change. "What would you like to eat, darling?" he said.

"Oysters," Sophia replied dreamily. "A big plate of oysters, followed by a huge lobster. Let's eat an enormous amount of seafood. I do love the sea, you know. What do you want to be when you come back again, Elter?"

"Come back again?"

"In your next life, I mean."

"I don't know. I haven't really thought about it." Elter was looking at the wine list.

The waiter smiled. Huh, he thought. He's going to have trouble with her. She's a wild one.

"Well, Elter, think."

"I think we'll have a bottle of the Chardonnay. It's a good year, no?"

"Yes, sir." The waiter bowed and left the room.

In the silence that fell, Sophia looked at Elter. "You know," she said, "you talk about things too much."

"What do you mean?" Elter was amused.

"I mean," she said, "you talk to Edward about golf and horses. You talk about Germany to Elena, and religion to Miss Trublood. And to me you talk about almost anything except feelings. Tell me, what do you want to be when you come back again?"

"*If* I come back again." Elter raised his eyebrows.

"Of course you'll come back again. Everybody does, except those who don't believe in it. It's like believing in God. I'll see God and heaven and everything God has promised me, because I believe in Him absolutely. But those who don't just don't see Him. Ever. Now, try again. Imagine you are going to come back to this earth after you die. Not for ages, of course," she added hurriedly with a smile.

Elter relaxed. "Let me see," he said slowly. "Maybe I'll be a seal."

"Oh no!" Sophia interrupted. "We can't be

seals. The water is too cold, far too cold. Let's be something tropical."

"Very well then." Elter folded his hands and studied his thumbs. "How about a dolphin?"

"Everybody wants to come back as a dolphin, and we're not everybody, are we?"

"Certainly not." Elter grinned. "Then why don't we return as eagles?"

"Perfect!" Sophia was entranced. "Can you imagine us flying high? We will be so fierce. We could spend the summers in Mexico where it is hot and then go to North America if we wish to cool down. You could be a bald-headed eagle," she giggled.

Sophia was still giggling when the waiter arrived with the oysters. Elter sat feeling mortified. He was not used to this sort of teasing. He didn't know quite what to say to this girl who was choking with mirth, sipping water to calm herself.

Sophia fell upon her plate of oysters and devoured them with relish. "More champagne, *Kopfchen?*" he asked.

"What does *Kopfchen* mean?"

"Little head. An expression of endearment."

"I see. Yes, I'd love another glass of champagne. There is nothing quite like the bubbles that get up your nose and then explode under your eyelids. So sensual, don't you think?"

Elter shook his head. "Really, darling," he said, "you must watch what you say."

"Why?" Sophia was astounded. "Why, Elter? We *are* on intimate terms, aren't we?"

Elter, to his horror, felt the warmth of a blush

rise in his cheeks. Good heavens, he thought, I am losing control of myself. This is absolutely ridiculous. He poured himself another glass of champagne and then, realizing the bottle was finished, up-ended it in the bucket and rang for the wine. "Darling, you must learn to be more tactful. People may misinterpret your behavior."

"And then?" Sophia inquired. "What would they think, Elter?"

"Well," he began, "they might think you were a little forward."

"But I am forward!" Sophia exclaimed. "If you asked Edward or Elena, or especially Miss Trublood, they would all tell you I am dreadfully forward. Do you want me to be backward?"

"No, of course not. But you could just be a little calmer."

Sophia threw herself back in her chair. "I could," she said, "if only the lobster would arrive. Those oysters were excellent. I love the feeling of a briny oyster slipping down the throat." Sophia stared at Elter and he shifted in his chair. Damn the chit, he thought. She is making me nervous.

The huge lobsters did arrive. "Just think," Sophia said, "a few hours ago they were looking about the restaurant at all the passersby. Neither of these two knew that their assassins were sitting in a small room in the hotel, plotting their murder."

"Sophia—don't let's discuss the gruesome details. I would just like to enjoy my lobster. I promised to take you out to dinner. Dinner is what you are having. And you shall be home by ten."

Sophia lowered her lashes and picked at the lobster. "I see," she said with fallen voice. She took a bite of lobster and her mood seemed to brighten slightly. "Well, thank you for the lobster. It's delicious. The roe is lovely."

"I'm glad you like it. You just eat and we shall savor it in *silence* for a while."

"All right, all right. Ten minutes' silence," Sophia agreed. Silence fell like an itchy blanket on both of them.

In the kitchen the Enforcer was paying his nightly visit. The Hong Kong Hotel was the biggest and best in town, and the gambling returns from the Casino brought Chu Wing enormous dividends. "Has number 316 what he needs for his pipe?" One-Eyed Charlie inquired.

The comprador nodded.

Charlie beckoned to the Russian waiter. "How are your clients coming along?"

The waiter smiled. "Very well. But," he shook his head, "she has a mind of her own, that girl. I have never seen the German so put out." He laughed.

And Charlie grinned. "Good," he said. "That's just what we need, a girl with spirit."

"Do you have to break her?" the waiter asked, remembering his initiation ceremony.

"No," Charlie replied. "Not if she behaves. After all"—and his one dead eye gazed at the waiter—"we are all one big family."

* * *

After dinner Elter drank more brandy than he intended to. He found himself rather bemusedly lying on the pink chaise, Sophia's head resting on his chest. He was content to lie still and digest, but Sophia turned her head upward to kiss him on the mouth. Giving in, he kissed her deeply. Then he pulled his mouth away. "Really, Sophia. We shouldn't be doing this."

"But it's marvelous. I never imagined kissing would be such fun."

"Do I kiss well?" Elter asked. *Really*, he scolded himself. To have to ask a mere girl such a question!

"Fabulously." She smiled. "Let's kiss again."

Slowly Elter was becoming less bemused. He felt a warm glow of lust growing in his belly and traveling outward to his arms and legs. As she kissed him, her small pink tongue ventured into his mouth. He moved his right hand into her dress and felt her smooth breast strain to fill his hand. "You have lovely breasts, Sophia."

"Do I?" Sophia stopped the kissing and lay on her side. They both looked down at the breast as it slipped out of the dress. Elter bent his head and took the nipple in his mouth. "What a heavenly feeling!" Sophia whispered. "Do it again."

"No," he said. "You must not give me orders. It is time to take you home."

Sophia was crestfallen. "Why?" she said. "What are you afraid of?"

"Afraid? I'm not afraid of anything." He looked at her defensively. "I'm merely taking care of you."

"But I'm tired of being taken care of!" she stormed. "Everybody is always taking care of me. I manage one evening alone with you, and now you can't wait to take me back home. Will you never want anything more?"

"In time, Sophia," Elter muttered. "Please, let's get our coats and go home." I have a headache, he thought.

As they crossed the great hall, Charlie grinned. He was leaning on the balcony watching the gamblers move in and out of the casino on the second floor. The German, he observed, has bitten off more than he can chew. He chuckled.

"Don't come in," Sophia commanded when Elter's red Bugatti pulled into the curb. "I'm cross with you and I don't know if I shall want to speak with you. Not for a long while, anyway."

Elter looked hard at her. "Life isn't a game, you know, Sophia. You think it is. Life's what happened to your parents."

His words cut deep. But Sophia did not believe she was playing a game. She was genuinely hurt. Elter, she felt, had rejected her. "I know," she said, "but they played by the rules. If they had left and not stayed to do their duty, as Mother said, they would be alive now." And, she thought, I would not be doing this. She furiously missed Anna at this moment. Anna would have known what to do. She leapt out of the car. "Goodbye," she said and ran up the path.

Edward was standing in the hall to greet her when Sophia entered the house and shut the door a little too loudly behind her. "Ten minutes to ten," he noted, looking at his watch. "I'm pleased. How was your evening?"

Sophia did not stop in her steps. "Elter was a perfect gentleman," she said over her shoulder. "You should be very happy."

"I am," he said to her back as she climbed the stairs. "Good night," he called after her but received no reply.

Elter drove home to his empty house. He realized, as he pushed open the door, that he felt as if a light had gone out and suddenly there was only blackness. "Hello?" he shouted into his dark hall, but he knew there would be no answer. There had never been any answer to his call; only living from day to day. Surviving. Never trusting any man, still less a woman. He wandered into his drawing-room and poured himself a Scotch. Standing by his empty grate, he gazed at a picture of a young woman, also standing. She had rough tumbled hair and a warm smile. I'll never get over your death, he thought. Never. Why did you leave me? I'm so alone and . . . He felt a sob threaten to burst from his throat; he pulled himself together. Good heavens, he thought, I am behaving like a child. Everybody's mother must die some time.

Sophia found Miss Trublood anxiously sitting in her winged armchair in her bedroom. Once the front door slammed, the house lost its air of anxious waiting. "Sophia's back," the wind sighed.

Misha glanced at Mei Mei. "Sophia's cross," he

remarked. "She always bangs the door like that when things haven't gone well."

Mei Mei took his hand. "Big temper, that girl," she said. "Maybe she needs to learn."

Misha nodded. "Maybe," he said, and they sat in a contemplative cocoon of silence.

In the library, Edward took a seat beside Elena. He rubbed his chin. "I don't often misread people," he said, "but there's a chance this Elter fellow might not be the bounder I took him for."

"I hope not," Elena smiled, "for Sophia's sake."

"Well, only time will tell." He kissed her lightly on the cheek. "We can go to bed, darling. She's home safe. I have a lot to do tomorrow."

"So have I." Elena leaned her cheek against his shoulder. "I have lists and lists and more lists. Getting married is rather like starting up your own country. Only a few more months and we will belong to each other." They held each other for many moments.

How calm she is, Edward thought. He did not know what to make of Sophia's evidently ill-tempered entry, but then Sophia always moved like a whirlwind.

Edward is such a safe harbor, thought Elena as she snuggled in his arms.

Upstairs Sophia flung herself into Miss Trublood's arms and blessed her for her comforting bulk. "I had a horrid time. Elter is awful. He's so stern. No fun at all."

Miss Trublood gazed owlishly at Sophia. "Really?" she said. "I've always thought of him as very jokey."

"Not tonight he wasn't."

Miss Trublood was tired. "Why don't you just sleep on it," she said. "Sometimes what seems awful at night looks quite different in the morning sun. We'll say a prayer together, then you beetle off to bed and sleep as snug as a bug in a rug."

Sophia had to smile. Honestly, Miss Trublood's American sayings were too funny. Here was she, having spent a night trying to get seduced, and Miss Trublood was talking about beetles and bugs. "OK, OK," she said, feeling very American.

Miss Trublood bowed her white head. "Please, dear Jesus, bless us tonight, and the whole house, and . . ."

Sophia knew they were about to do a religious round-up of the whole of Shanghai, so she added a prayer of her own. "This might not be quite what You had in mind, Lord," she prayed fervently in silence, "but could I love Elter, um, not just in the religious sense, but also in the other?" She hugged Miss Trublood when they each had finished their respective prayers and then went off to her own bedroom and bed which, to Sophia's displeasure, remained virginal.

CHAPTER 43

Edward was homesick. Often he found himself thinking of England. And recently he realized, with Elena in his arms, he could hardly wait to take her home. He longed for the wet rain and the dampness; he even missed the fog. He remembered the blue flowers that hung on the old mossy walls of his country house, empty now of his mother and father who slept in the vaults of the family chapel that stood in the gardens, cared for by a kindly sexton who doubled his income by burying the old and the poor at the local stone church. Edward missed his walks to that church, where a medieval knight lay huge and gaunt in an attitude of prayer, his hands folded sternly to his breast, while the small belligerent face of a griffin stared stonily at him. Edward missed his dogs, now long since buried, having died of old age. Only Boots, his very elderly nanny, and Turner the gardener ran the house. Edward wished to give Elena a chow-chow, his favorite breed of dog. He must wait until they returned to England, he knew, but his hand longed for the rough feel of a dog's coat.

And for the first time in his life, he did not own a horse. He played polo and used the club's horses. When life grew hectic, he would have liked to find consolation in the smell of a stable and in the sympathetic understanding of a mare's soft brown eyes.

Though the world had reorganized itself through the crucible of war, Edward sensed that no real order had been found. Many treaties had ended the war, but Edward did not see in them a reliable prescription for peace. All these troubles he was trained as a diplomat to deal with. Commotion at home, however, he found difficult to come to terms with. Thank God only serenity existed between Elena and himself. But Sophia seemed most unsettled and was therefore unsettling to Edward's orderly nature. Increasingly he hoped that carting Sophia off to England—even if he had to take her against her will—might be just the change needed to set her up in a life of some stability.

For the moment he was grateful that Miss Trublood bore the brunt of Sophia's passion for Elter. Elter himself seemed fairly sanguine when Edward and he played golf together. "Sophia all right?" Edward tried to make conversation as they teed off.

Elter smiled at Edward. "Good," he said. "Very good girl. Very strong."

Strong indeed, Edward thought. The idea of Sophia running amok at the Monastery back home made his blood turn to vinegar. What on earth would the locals say about a wild dark-haired Russian countess? Elena would fit in beautifully. Her fair hair and gentle eyes, he knew, would captivate his neighbor, old Lady Renshaw, and old Lady Renshaw's goodwill once assured, the rest would take care of itself . . .

Still, he must get over his melancholy; he was due home in eighteen months and would be married in six. Not too long now. It was an icy winter's late afternoon and Sophia was entertaining what

Miss Trublood considered to be her louche friends: Maria, Vassily and Rollo. Miss Trublood was not pleased. She did not want them in the house.

Maria, sensing Miss Trublood's disapproval, was awkward in her presence. "She looks at me as if I smell," Maria complained. Rollo and Vassily were—as was not unusual—late. Maria had had a trying day and she felt flustered and nervous. Really, this mountain of an American woman who was always carrying on about God was not what Maria needed. "I need some champagne, Sophia. I'm dead weary."

"What have you been doing to get so tired?" Sophia looked at her friend who, though only a few years older, already had cruel lines engraved across her forehead and around her green eyes. From the edge of her small nose a line threatened to appear that would run to the corner of her mouth.

"Nothing much," Maria replied.

Sophia rang the bell for Ah Ling. "Champagne, please," she ordered. "Oh, and, Ah Ling, how about some petits fours? Are you peckish, Maria?"

"Starving." The word came out of Maria's mouth with such vehemence that Sophia was astonished.

"Maria," she said, "how on earth can you be so hungry?"

"It's time you grew up, Sophia. Half the world— no, more like three-quarters—doesn't have enough to eat."

Sophia sat down and leaned close. "Do you have

money? If you don't, I'd be happy to give you some."

Maria felt her heart blacken and a feeling of pure dislike sprang up in her. "You're a very sheltered privileged girl, you know. You can't just give me money. I need to earn my own money. I didn't claw my way out of Russia to live off you or anybody else. I'll have money soon, but for the moment I'm content just to get a decent meal. I can make money. Not necessarily the way I would choose, but," she shook out her red hair, "beggars, as they say, can't be choosers. And there are worse ways of making a living." She wrinkled her snub nose. "Although for the moment I can't imagine one." Pleasing One-Eyed Charlie was one of her more onerous duties, and One-Eyed Charlie's idea of pleasure was to watch her lash his victim into tatters. Even though in some cases the victim was as masochistic as Charlie was sadistic, pain was no part of Maria's pleasure. Today had been tiring and odious. Maria was just glad to sit in a deep chair in this quiet harmonious house, to gaze at the screens, the paintings, and especially the drawings of flowers Elena had hung everywhere. The flowers in their Chinese green bamboo frames breathed tranquillity. Maria felt jangled and blown about in a world that seemed to be slowly going insane. If she could only return home refreshed and sleepy after a good dinner she would count herself lucky. Maybe she should even confess herself to Miss Trublood. Perhaps Miss Trublood's God had something to offer her.

She sat, her feet primly close together, and

waited until Sophia put the glass of champagne in her hand. She sighed. The sigh released many awful memories. She sipped and then smiled. "I'm sorry, Sophia. I didn't mean to be rude and cross. It's just been one of those days; it'll pass."

Sophia looked sympathetic. "I get those days too, but for different reasons. You're right, though, I am overprotected. Elter says so all the time." She grinned. "But I'm doing my best to get unprotected. You've no idea how hard it is to get Elter to seduce me. That man is built of stone."

Maria frowned. "Does it ever occur to you that Elter might know best?"

Sophia shook her head. "I don't care if he knows best. I don't want him to make an honest woman of me. I don't know very much about him, except that he has a comfortable bachelor-type house and an office he goes to, though I've never seen it. He's ridiculously secretive."

Inwardly Maria winced. She knew Elter's office all right. She helped to monitor the transmissions that flashed from Elter's office to Amsterdam and sometimes to Germany. Elter was moving merchandise around the world, a large amount of merchandise. No wonder he had so little to say to a young girl like Sophia. But Maria could see for herself that Elter was besotted. Occasionally their paths crossed. They found themselves in the same rooms, among the same faces: Maria, Elter, Vassily, Rollo, all moving in the underbelly of the big fish. One sitting on his pallet, another pulling the nails off a victim's fingers. All in conjunction with Chu Wing's plans, the ever-present Chu. Even now, as Maria waited for dinner, she was due to return to account for her evening.

And then she would get her handful of money, money to keep her body whole and her appetite satiated . . . Maria drank deeply from her champagne glass. It was but a short step to the communal graves that lay open in the cesspit that was the city of Shanghai. There were more brothels here than anywhere else in the world. Anything you wanted could be found somewhere in the foul guts of this place. Maria was grateful for the few hours of sanity that Sophia provided for her, but she was also aware that she would betray her friend. From this there was no escape. The Brotherhood craved fresh blood. Chu Wing needed Sophia. She was his catch and he wanted her as the old emperor had wanted his golden nightingale. In that tale, once he had caught the nightingale with the ruby eyes, the bird refused to sing. But with Chu the bird would have to sing. Maria only hoped that Sophia would survive Chu. Many songbirds hadn't. But then she remembered Sophia had a tough streak in her, unlike Elena . . .

"Good Lord!" Rollo's voice broke the silence. "Is this a wake, or do you just like sitting there like a pair of frightened ducks, saying nothing?" Rollo bustled in with Vassily behind him.

"Maria's had an awful day and we were just resting. Silence, dear Rollo, is against your nature."

Rollo nodded. "Talk, talk, talk keeps the glooms away. What's the matter, Maria, got a case of the glooms?"

Maria smiled. "Nothing that a glass of champagne can't get rid of."

Rollo helped himself to a glass and offered another to Vassily. Both men were in good spirits. Slowly Maria shook off the cobweb fingers that clutched at her mind. Maybe it won't happen, she thought. Maybe I'm just being paranoid. By the time the four of them were at the table eating imported steaks from Japan, Maria had forgotten her nagging fears. All four were talking about the theater and making plans.

Finally full of food and wine, Maria made a promise to herself: I'll take each day as it comes, and anticipate nothing.

Sophia was leaning forward, earnestly conversing with Vassily. Vassily, his blond curly hair a halo in the light of the candelabra, nodded. "You're right," he said. "The point of good theater is to keep the audience guessing right to the very end. But once the suspense is over, the audience must be made whole again before it's sent off into the night. That's why I don't like Chekov. You know that his characters are going to wait until the very end of the play and then *boom!* One of them is dead. And *bang!* That's the end. Very unsatisfactory. I need to know that life will go on."

Well, Maria thought, Edward and Elena will be returning to London in eighteen months. Sophia might go with them and be safe. Maybe she will have recovered herself, and Elter will just be a small chapter in her life. Maria hoped she was right.

*　　　*　　　*

Later that night as she lay in bed in her room she snuggled into Vassily's brotherly arms. "Vassily," she said. "I can't sleep. I'm worried about Sophia."

"Don't be," he said. "Sophia can take care of herself. You never knew the legend about her grandmother, did you?"

"No." Maria sat up. "What about her?"

"Sophia's grandmother was Anna Oblimova, the famous Golden Salamander. And she had many, many lovers. There's a line in a book of poetry, written by a poet who killed himself for love of her. *'If you seek to love me,/ If you can stand the pain,/ Then kiss me, touch me,/ Again and again and again.'*"

"That was Sophia's grandmother?"

"Yes. Now go to sleep and stop worrying. Sophia's just like her grandmother. She'll survive."

Maria lay back on her pillow and was comforted.

☙ CHAPTER 44 ❧

Spring had arrived, and Elena was worried about Sophia. For a while she tried to deny her fears and to concentrate on the arrangements for her wedding. Her talks with Miss Trublood failed to comfort her. "I really do hope Sophia is going to be sensible," was her usual approach.

"I do too, dear." Miss Trublood only shook her

gray head. "But Sophia never was one for being sensible, and sometimes I think deep down she's jealous of you."

"I've wondered about that myself. You see, it can be so difficult for twins. Separating, I mean. And when I marry Edward, then we really will be separated. Edward says he'd like a new house after we're married. I must talk to Sophia and see if she will come and live with us. I don't much like the idea of the two of you rattling about in this enormous place. We can take Misha and Mei Mei. Edward says there's a splendid house down on the Bund with room for us all. I know Ah Ling would love the house because he would have a proper wine cellar. It really bothers him that we have only a cupboard here. Edward has wine in his cellars in Dover and we could have some shipped out to us." She paused. "And then, of course, we're going to England next year. Sophia and I will be twenty-three by then. I don't know how Sophia will cope with England."

"Well, dear," Miss Trublood rose to her feet, "we shall have to pray, and see. Now I'd better run off and fetch Sophia. She's been on a buying spree lately and I promised to meet her for lunch. See you later."

How odd, Elena thought. I'm to be married within three months, and then I'll be able to make love whenever I want. And if I get pregnant, that would be wonderful. Sophia is also in love, but if she makes love and gets pregnant, it would be a tragedy. Rules, Elena reminded herself. Life is so full of rules. If a girl breaks any of them, the consequences are terrible. I do hope Sophia knows what she's doing . . . I must check the guest list again.

Recently checking the guest list for the wedding was one way that Elena dealt with her guilt at deserting Sophia. I'm *not* deserting her, Elena scolded herself fiercely. I'm getting married, just as Sophia in her turn will get married. Oh, I hope she doesn't do anything silly!

Elena pored over the guest list. This time it failed to comfort her.

For Sophia the last months had been months of torment. Would she sleep with Elter or would she not? So far Elter had been sweet and responsive, but pushed Sophia away when she pressed to go further. She often put his hand on her breasts and was gratified to see how she managed to make his eyes light up as his fingers trailed across her nipples. But then he was also able to draw back from these sensual caresses, saying, "No, Sophia, it's not right. You're too young."

"Too young?" she exploded. "I'm practically an old maid. Are you going to let me grow rusty with disuse? I'll be like an old rickshaw. Creak, creak."

Elter had to laugh. Sophia grew so pink and angry when he rejected her. Indeed Elter was well aware that he was not rejecting her; he was merely confused about his feelings. I'm not used to this sort of thing, he mused to himself alone in his quiet drawing-room, quiet only because Sophia had yet again stormed out to her waiting car. "Why not, Elter? Why ever not?" she had bawled at him. "What's the matter with you or me? Why can't we allow ourselves what everyone else enjoys? Maria does all the time, and Elena is about to. Why am I left out?"

"Feeling left out is no good reason to throw away your purity, *Puppchen*."

"I am not throwing it away, Elter. I'm offering it to you." By now Sophia's voice had a dangerous quiver.

That was when Elter most wanted to comfort her. "Wait, darling. Just wait and be patient."

"Patient? That's all I ever am, patient!"

The door slammed louder than usual, and Elter remembered all those days when she had nestled in his arms. He smiled. He was getting sentimental in his old age. Now he had to admit that he looked forward to Sophia's visits. He enjoyed squiring her to parties. He watched her at the balls they attended together. Even if he refused to dress up in fancy dress, he still delighted in watching all eyes focus on Sophia. All the men envied him and all the women wanted him, but he himself had eyes solely for Sophia. If he were to seduce her, he now knew, it would mean an offer of marriage. Under the circumstances he would have to get her out of Shanghai and safely back to his home in Germany. The Kaiser's war had not touched his country estate, purchased with money from opium-trading. His aunt was still alive and living in the castle. She would look after Sophia until he had made sufficient money to go home and retire. The thought of Sophia awaiting his arrival in his many-turreted German castle pleased him. He had never before imagined another woman living in his castle, or taking the place of his mother in his life, the mother he missed dreadfully since her death. Sophia—effortlessly, it seemed—had captured his heart, so much so that now he must plot against his employers. How to make a huge fortune quickly. How to fulfill the standing orders and to siphon off some of the precious drug in order to sell it for his own profit and his future with Sophia. And then one bright day for both of them, he would simply slip away from Shanghai and join for ever the girl for whom he felt an increasingly overwhelming love. Edward and Elena were going back to London. Later, when he could be sure he himself was no longer being hunted, the two women could meet, but for a while he would lie low with Sophia. This would all take some planning. But Elter was patient, even if Sophia was not.

Sophia watched Elena carefully. Recently she was aware of a barrier growing up between them. At one time Sophia discussed everything with Elena. Now there were things that she did not tell her sister. Sometimes when she visited Maria, her friend lay back in her bed with Vassily beside her, or maybe another man. Sophia would sit among rumpled sheets stained with food and littered with cigarettes, and smelling of sex. Sometimes she arrived just after Maria had made love and then she felt welcome. Maria, lying back with her arms over her head, her armpits thick with red hair and her breasts barely hidden by the sheet, would wave her in magnanimously. Other times, if Sophia arrived before Maria had made love, Sophia would feel the impatience in Maria's body for her to be gone. She would leave and then walk up the busy road feeling empty and forgotten.

These were the kinds of things she no longer felt she could share with Elena, any more than she could imagine Elena and Edward in bed together. Returning home was always alienating. What did their calm, measured, clean existence have to do with the room she had just left? How could their evenings sitting at dinner served by Ah Ling compare with the meals taken on the floor of Maria's room, consisting of wine by the bottleful and food brought from the restaurant next door. Sometimes Sophia reclined with her head in Rollo's lap while he crooned English lovesongs to the other bodies lying or sitting around the room talking and laughing in the cool night air . . . Sophia found it hard to live in both worlds. She was tired of the schizophrenic disparity between her two lives. There was the Sophia at home, the Countess Oblimova, the society hostess; and then there was the she-wolf inside her that wanted Elter to take her in his arms and make love to her for hours, for days, for ever.

Sophia found the days slow and unaccommodating. Finally she decided that the only way she was going to get Elter to make love to her was to make it impossible for him to refuse. If Elena was to be married on June 6 and spend the night in her husband's arms, then she, Sophia, would grant herself the right to spend the night in the arms of her lover. The idea of Elena effortlessly receiving what she had striven so hard to achieve infuriated Sophia. What Elena had, she wanted for herself. Now Sophia had a plan, and Sophia was always happiest when she had a plan.

"Yoohoo!" Miss Trublood tracked Sophia down at the emporium in the French concession. Sophia was just picking out some gold silk. The material was exquisite. "Gee, that's nice, Sophia. What's it for?"

Sophia smiled. "Oh, a nightdress, I think." She took the material and ran it through her fingers. Lovely, she thought. She felt the fabric cling to her hand and envisioned herself pressed naked to Elter's firm body. "Yes," she smiled at Miss Trublood, "a nightdress."

Miss Trublood looked into Sophia's curtained eyes. Not just for yourself, she thought. "Glad I ran into you. I'm just about to grab a bite to eat. Care to join me for lunch?"

Sophia trailed behind her, lost in thought. Now, she thought, the stage is set. I only have to make sure that he spends the night with me. All through lunch Sophia sat distracted while Miss Trublood tucked into her steak. Poor little thing, Miss Trublood thought. So long ago, but I can still remember feeling that way about Will . . .

Two ice-creams arrived, served with a large helping of chocolate sauce. "Go on, Sophia, eat your ice cream."

Sophia licked her spoon. The hot sweet chocolate lay on her tongue like a caress. Sophia had been learning about tongue kissing from Maria. "You do it like this," Maria had said. She had leaned forward in her bed and rested her lips on Sophia's, then parted her mouth with the tip of her sweet tongue and gently slid her tongue into Sophia's mouth.

"Umm, that feels nice." Sophia was amazed. Described in cold blood, it seemed ridiculous, but the actual sensation was glorious.

Maria laughed. "If a man is good at kissing, like the French, it's fantastic and sexy. But sometimes men are slobberers. Then it's disgusting."

Sophia shook her head. "Elter would never slobber."

Dreamily she played with her ice cream, mentally enacting the imagined moment of pleasure and of love.

"Let's get a move on." Miss Trublood was rather bored with the silent Sophia. Oh dear, she thought as they left the restaurant. My Christian friends made life so easy. You either married and made love, or you didn't, and became an old maid. An old maid like myself never made love. There were of course women who had made love but not married, but Miss Trublood was glad she had not stooped to this. It was sinful and she preferred having a clean record. Look at poor Sophia, she thought. Oh, I wonder how it will all end!

"We had a lovely day, dear, didn't we?"

"Yes, we did." Sophia was grateful. "Thank you for lunch."

And Sophia hugged Miss Trublood until Miss Trublood's blue eyes filled with tears. Really, the girl was so unpredictable. She prayed for Sophia as she went off to the privacy of her own room.

CHAPTER 45

While Elena was occupied with wedding preparations, Sophia thought back to her childhood days in St. Petersburg, that safe and happy period of the life she shared with Elena. She recalled the smells and sounds of the peasants singing and working in the grounds of the castle. She remembered Katrina's face, and was glad of the news of Katrina's return to her village. "I work in my cooperative," Katrina wrote in a curious formal handwriting. "Gone are the years when we worked for others. I miss you all, but am happy with my village and my friends. We are no longer too tired to talk in the evenings. It is a good thing that has happened in my country."

Sophia missed Katrina. Miss Trublood had proved herself a friend indeed, but she did not have Katrina's rough loving approach. Katrina's hands had known Sophia from the day she was born. There was an intimacy between herself and Katrina that could never be found with Miss Trublood. The facts of life, described by Katrina, had been plain, if a little gory. Conversations with Miss Trublood always managed to juxtapose sex with the notion of sin.

The days passed and then the weeks. Misha and Mei Mei seemed the only two people in the house who were not tense and strained. Misha tried to comfort Sophia. He knew how much she was going to miss her twin sister. "You have us, Sophia. We will always be here for you."

Sophia tried talking to Elena. She felt she would die if she had to share a house with Elena and Edward. "Please, Elena, understand," she pleaded one wet dismal day when the wind howled in the chimneys and the rain lashed the doors of the house. "I need to live my own life. I can't go and live with you and Edward. I must learn to run my own house and stand on my own two feet. I know we don't have all that much money left, but I can get some sort of a job. Don't make a face, Elena. I know Edward would provide for me, but I have my pride. And quite a few women work now. I could act as a hostess for some of the bachelors here in the community. Maybe I can give dancing lessons." Sophia rose on her toes and twirled around Elena's bedroom. "Look," she said. "Still light as a feather."

"Oh Sophia, you're always so dramatic. Of course you can find something you want to do. I worked as a nurse. Why not try that?"

Sophia wrinkled her nose. "It's the smell," she said. "I can't bear the smell of sickness. No, I want to find something exciting to do. I want to be mysterious, like Elter. You know, try as I might, I can't really pin Elter down. He told me he buys and sells, but buys and sells what? It's none of my business, he says. Maybe he'll know of something. Besides, I quite like the idea of having this house to myself. I'll hang the walls with green silk and put in statues. I'll make it all oriental and mysterious. Maybe I'll start a brothel."

Elena burst out laughing. "You do get carried away! Only three more weeks and I'll be married."

Elena flushed. "I'm so happy, Sophia. Are you happy for me?"

"Of course." Sophia put her arm around Elena's waist. "Yes, I'm happy for you. But both of us always knew the day would come when we would part."

"We'll always be as close as we are now."

Sophia hugged her. But one of us will always keep secrets, she thought to herself. She was envious of Elena. Elena had no secrets and no need to keep any. Sophia felt riddled with secrets. Elena reminded Sophia that the world was still a safe place for those who obeyed the rules. But those who did not, like the Chinese who defied the law and cut off their braids, immediately endangered their lives. To refuse to wear the mask of servitude and to risk death rather than shame was something Sophia understood. If she lived by her own rules, at least she would feel alive. Far too many girls who had grown up with her married as soon as possible and lived lives relatively untouched by passion or feeling. By the ages of twenty-three or twenty-five many of them had several drooling children and their talk was all of castor-oil and quinine. Sophia found them loathsome; Elena found them riveting. Elena, Sophia realized, would no doubt be one of those matronly ladies in the not too distant future.

Until now Sophia had said little about the prospect of traveling with Elena to England. Later, once she had ensnared Elter, she hoped to go back to Germany. The idea of England was not at all appealing. The English she had met from the Brit-

ish concession, apart from Edward, left her with
an unsavory impression of bad teeth and red faces.
They seemed emotionally constipated. No, Sophia
had no intention of going to England. She must
make it her business to get settled. When Elena
and Edward were in England she could always
visit . . .

The last three weeks skittered away and then the
day of the wedding dawned bright and clear. Elena
washed herself in her room. These were her last
hours as a single girl. Tonight Edward would take
her on his yacht to Hong Kong for their honeymoon.

Sophia, dressing in her own room, also sat contemplating her last day as a virgin. Tonight after
the wedding she was going to dine with Elter on
his junk that was moored in the village of Hang
Chow Nan. Sophia had never seen the junk, but
the idea intrigued her. Would Elter give in and
make love to her? Sophia grinned. She had her
dress of gold silk. She had made it herself because
the dress was not so much a dress as a slight veil
between her body and the rest of the world. The
anticipated look of amazement on Elter's face
made Sophia's mouth curl. He had never seen her
naked; tonight he would. Sophia giggled. She had
told no one about the dress, not even Maria. Sophia blessed Katrina for having taught her to
dressmake, but if Katrina could see this particular
fruit of Sophia's efforts, she would regret those
lessons.

The day marched on. There were late wedding

presents arriving. Edward, like any good groom, was not to be seen, but Elena knew he had relatives coming from England. Elderly, rheumatic and creaking, they were descending from boats and arriving in taxis. Poor Edward, she thought, smiling to herself.

By half past eleven both girls were ready. Six minute bridesmaids, the children of Elena's friends, had been deposited at the house with two matrons of honor in attendance. Sophia, as senior bridesmaid, wore a demure ivory-satin dress. Elena looked startlingly lovely in her long white embroidered gown, the train of which lay thick on the floor. As they left for the church, the girls gave each other a last kiss. "I do love you," Elena whispered to Sophia, standing in the doorway of the house. Her veil was drawn down over Elena's face and they kissed through the gauze.

"I know." Sophia smiled. "I love you, too. But this moment had to come. It's the fate of twins. Maybe we should never have anything to do with men who only separate us from each other. Maybe being a twin is a curse in itself."

Elena smiled. "Sophia, let's not go all Russian and fatalistic. Edward loves you and cares about you. Really he does. Once we're married and back from our honeymoon, you'll find nothing has changed."

"It already has." Sophia felt a leaden sadness steal over her. "*We* no longer means you and me; it means you and Edward. I have to get used to being an *I* on my own. Funny, you know, I feel as nervous as if I were about to have my right hand cut off."

"Come along, girls." Miss Trublood was herding children into cars and generally taking charge. It's a bit like rounding up cattle, she thought as she fitted children into empty spaces and counted the remaining cars. "Let's get a move on, Elena. I know the bride is entitled to be late, but not too late."

Elena sank into the cool gray interior of a Rolls-Royce. "I wish Mother and Father and Grandmother could see us now," she said, seeing the guests who were leaving from the house.

"So do I." Sophia's voice sounded hollow. This often imagined event was slowly coming into reality and the truth of what was about to happen hurt.

No amount of rehearsing mentally for the moment when Elena married Edward had prepared Sophia for the shock. "Do you, Edward, take this woman, Elena, to be your lawful wedded wife . . ." The words were flung into the air by the very patrician priest. Sophia had to put her hand across her mouth to stop a shout of *No! No, you can't do that! She's my twin. She's the part of me that's good. Without her I'm just a sad, bad, severed thing, a half-person . . .*

Behind her stood Elter and she turned and sought his face. He realized she was in pain, so much pain that he longed to hold her and comfort her. Tonight, he reminded himself, tonight we will be together. Tonight he had ordered her favorite dinner, lobster, to be followed by her favorite pudding, kumquat ice cream. Tonight I will make her feel wanted and loved, he promised himself.

Sophia saw Elter nod gently in her direction and was consoled. Tonight, she promised herself, she would give herself over to the shadowy side of her nature and abandon the young vulnerable girl called Sophia. She would leave the girl behind on the shores of time.

Maria also realized that Sophia was suffering. She sat in the back of the church with Vassily and Rollo. "Poor Sophia," she whispered. "It must be hard for her to lose her sister."

Rollo was made philosophical by the ecclesiastical surroundings. "I sometimes think it's better when you lose all the people who love you for what you're not."

Vassily agreed. "Maybe those of us who want to be free must cut the rope. Otherwise the pain of trying to be two different people is too great."

"Shh!" A behatted matron frowned on the unconventionally dressed little group. "Be quiet! What is the world coming to?" she remarked to her husband. "They must be Bolsheviks."

The husband looked across his wife's ample bosom. "I hardly think so, dear," he intoned. "Bolshies don't believe in God. Wouldn't be caught dead in a church. I rather think they're scum."

Maria grinned. She sat back and watched the ceremony to the end.

Finally Sophia lifted her sister's veil and Elena's face swam into Sophia's tear-filled eyes. "Goodbye, Elena," Sophia whispered inaudibly. "Goodbye, my sister and my friend. I've lost you to

Edward and the pain will never go away. But he'll take good care of you, I know."

Elena was now standing in front of Edward. Her hand, a thick gold band on her finger, was in Edward's hands and their mouths touched in a fleeting kiss. Sophia breathed very carefully in case the pain should cause her to faint. As the couple turned to leave the church, the bells pealed out wild clangs of joy. Sophia followed the little ones who gamboled and skipped down the aisle, their duties over. Organ music cascaded about the procession. A holiday mood seized the guests. Outside the wind whipped at the dresses of the ladies and insolently tweaked the tails of the stiff-suited gentlemen. Not long, Sophia thought, and I will be away from all these people.

She was now free to find her friends. A reception was to be held for the wedding party at the house. Maria had promised to attend with Rollo and Vassily. "You must come," Sophia had pleaded. "I'll die if I have to put up with Edward's relatives on my own." Somewhere in the crowd Maria was waiting and Sophia went to look for her.

❦ CHAPTER 46 ❧

"So, you're going to have dinner with Elter on his junk?" Maria was amused. "Not many of us have ever had the honor of seeing that fabulous contraption."

Sophia smiled. "Elter felt I would be lonely after Elena had gone away on her honeymoon, so he asked me to have dinner with him. I'm grateful. You know, Maria, when I first met Elter I thought he was going to be a hard man, sort of dangerous. But underneath he's really very kind."

Maria looked doubtful. "Perhaps you see something in him I don't. I find him frightening."

"Maybe. But he's not all bad. Like tonight. He doesn't have to take me out for dinner or go to such an effort. Anyway," Sophia smiled, "I intend to thank him."

"You do, do you?" Maria's smile became a wicked grin. "How best to thank a man who has had everything, eh, Sophia? Give him something no other man has ever had before."

Sophia shrugged her shoulders. "Well, if Elena can, why can't I?"

Maria looked across the room at Rollo who was deep in conversation with a beautiful Russian dancer. "Elena is entitled to do what she wants to do. You're breaking the rules again."

"I know, I know. But I want him, Maria. There's no other way. We've waited for more than two years now. Elena's married and if I'm not careful, I might end up having to go to England with them.

I can't stay here by myself, and I have no money. Most of the jewels are gone. If I go back to England, I suppose I can get a job. Though goodness knows what I can do."

There was a flurry and people crowded into the main hall to watch the couple descending the staircase in their going-away outfits. Elena looked so young, Sophia thought. Sophia felt old and jaded by comparison. Edward wore a gray three-piece suit with his father's watch tied securely on a gold chain. Sophia had often held the big watch in her hand and she envied Elena her security. That watch had been in the Gray family for a hundred years. Elena's brown eyes sought out Sophia's. She gave a half smile, a preoccupied smile of recognition, but also of abandonment. At this moment Sophia was not her prime concern. The coming night in her husband's arms, the great moment she had waited for—and now she was doubly glad she had waited—was floating in her vision. She carried her bridal bouquet of white roses and carnations. The carnations too were to have been white, but a mistake had been made and they were red. "Sophia!" Elena called. "Here, catch!" And she threw the bouquet high over the heads of the crowd into the waiting hands of her sister.

Sophia smiled. "Thank you," she said.

Rollo watched the two women and laughed. "Blood red carnations for the sister of the bride?" he said out of the side of his mouth. "Sort of makes you shiver, doesn't it?"

"Oh go on, Rollo! Don't read things into everything." Maria stood on tiptoe to watch the wedding couple. "But I guess this is Shanghai and we're used to seeing bad joss everywhere."

"Particularly at a wedding," Rollo interjected.

Vassily, swaying with champagne and sentiment, laughed. "Especially as you'll never have one, eh, Rollo?"

Rollo wrinkled his nose. "No, I don't expect I will. But I'll come and weep at yours. Weep for the poor bride, of course."

"Save your tears." Vassily swung his arm over Rollo's shoulder. "I'll never get married. I don't want to wake up to anybody else's face but my own. Imagine! Someone else's hairs in the bath! Another toothbrush on the washstand? No, no, no. Simply too undignified. Fuck them and leave them is my motto."

Maria raised her eyebrows. "Really, Vassily. I'll pretend I didn't hear that. You've had too much champagne and you've never been one to hold your drink. Thank God not all men are like you."

"Oh but they are, Maria. Edward over there is the exception, not I. Don't you think so, Rollo?"

"I do," Rollo said, suddenly serious. "And that's why everyone in Shanghai has turned out for this wedding. We all need to see real love in action. It gives us hope. It makes for a refreshing change. Otherwise it's always the same stained sheets and the grimy feeling of yet another night of disillusion. Whatever. I really hope they'll be happy. If two people can be happy together, then who knows? There may even be hope for me."

"Rollo, you *are* tired." Maria shook his hand. "Come on, Vassily, help me get Rollo home. You two are becoming useless. Let's say our goodbyes. Mei Mei says if we go by the kitchen she'll give us a big bag of food."

Maria enclosed Sophia in her arms. The newly-weds had gone, and the guests were preparing to leave. For a while everyone had been caught up by the happiness of the couple just married. Their shining faces and the obvious love they shared made the guests kinder and more attentive to each other. For a few hours the women did not primp and compete. They conversed in a friendly fashion. But now that light was gone and the sound of the couple's car driving off into the distance told the guests that real life was about to re-enter the arena, and they fell back into their more familiar ways. Coats were called for, cars summoned, and the Ambassador's wife saw to it that she left before anyone else, particularly the dreaded Marquise de Verdier Boudilly, who made it her business to upstage any of the English, as she was of French royal blood. The English, she was fond of hissing through tight lips, were, after all, of German descent.

"Have a wonderful evening, Sophia." Maria held her friend tightly.

"I will."

With the house full of people, no one noticed the presence of an uninvited guest. But then One-Eyed Charlie was careful. And it was not the happy couple he had come to see, or their champagne he had come to drink. It was information he wanted. And he did not need to mingle with the guests in order to obtain it. He dipped into the kitchen and, passing himself off as one of the guests' drivers, asked Misha for a glass of water. In no time they were chatting away like old friends.

"And what will happen to you when your mistress goes back to England?"

Misha wriggled his eyebrows and pursed his lips. "Mei Mei and I will go into the country and grow our own fruit and vegetables. Mei Mei comes from a village in the north. We hear that a woman can own land as well as a man. Mei Mei's mother tells us that we can live among the cave-dwellers."

Charlie smiled. He liked this odd little couple. He sensed no guile in either of them. They sat at the table answering his questions with the innocent look of two small birds, downy in their nest. "I wish you luck," he said. But he knew that it would be a long time before the two of them could realize their dreams. Sir Edward might leave with Elena, but Misha would stay to take care of the newest recruit to the cause. Sophia soon would be groomed for her part in the performance, and tonight, if all went well, the first step would be taken. Elter did not know of a presence on his junk, nor did he suspect that his every word and movement would be heard. Charlie smiled at the thought. Chu would be delighted. He loved to overhear the making of love nearly as much as he loved to watch the dying of the flame in the eyes of his victims. Both love and murder were each in their own way a form of dying. The only difference that he could see was that in the act of love death was only momentary, while the death of the body was permanent . . . But these were idle reflections on his part, especially with regard to Chu, for Chu would never know an act of true love, despite his multitude of wives and concubines. And what he didn't know, Charlie opined, he could never miss.

One-Eyed Charlie slipped out of the kitchen as unobtrusively as he had come in. Slowly he made his way to his car. The junk was moored in the fishing village of Hang Chow Nan. He wondered why Elter had chosen the junk. Nobody had ever been invited to the junk except for the crew that carried the cargo from Hong Kong to Hang Chow Nan and on to Shanghai. Charlie had never had reason before to check out the junk. He knew it was always moored there, but now he had a hunch and he always played his hunches. The itching of his empty eye-socket had often saved his life. If it itched, there was something afoot. *By the pricking of my thumbs, something wicked this way comes.* Charlie loved Shakespeare, particularly Shakespeare's witches. The witches were closer to Charlie's heart than any other characters. In them Charlie found his heroes. The mission school had taught Charlie English; the English writer and poet fired his imagination. Chu did not share Charlie's great love of the Bard, but he did enjoy some of Charlie's renditions. Chu especially liked the strangling and the stabbing. "That man Shakespeare," Chu remarked, "he had good joss. He knew how to kill, to poison. He was like us." Charlie smiled. I do hope the German is clean, he thought. Otherwise he'll have to go. A pity. He's worked for us for a long time, but then you never can tell when a woman is involved. If the little Russian is to be compromised, that is one thing. But if he attempts to do anything other than follow orders, he must be eliminated. Aye-eh! Women. They cause such problems.

❧ CHAPTER 47 ❧

The first sight of Edward's yacht, the *Elizabeth*, filled Elena with delight. She had always loved the sea. As a child she and Sophia sailed with their father and mother in the Baltic. Boris was a fine sailor and often Elena thought he would have preferred to live at sea with his crew than to return to St. Petersburg to worry about the royal family, who largely behaved like neurotic poodles. Now the car turned into the harbor and she could see Edward's yacht straining at her mooring. The *Elizabeth* was named after Edward's mother. She was a trawler refitted by Edward when he bought her several years before. In the two years that they were courting, Elena had often taken her meals on board. Tonight they were leaving for Hong Kong and then on to Bangkok. Elena was thrilled. She had always wanted to see the jade Buddha housed in a monastery in Bangkok. She looked forward to calling in at the little city of Macau on the way, and to buying pearls in Hong Kong. Most of all she would have Edward to herself.

The crew on the *Elizabeth* were discreet. She knew this from her previous visits on board. Lundy Chagwell, known as Jaggers, captained the *Elizabeth.* He was probably Edward's best friend in the world. They had met in the first year of Edward's posting to Shanghai. Once transferred out of Russia, Edward had arrived in Shanghai after a year spent up in the north of China. Immured, at the Foreign Office's request, with a Chinese family for the purpose of learning to speak fluent Mandarin, he had almost forgotten how to speak English to another Englishman. Eventually, on leave in Shanghai, Edward had decided that he could no longer bear the isolation. He found the *Elizabeth* moored at the Shanghai Yacht Club. She was listing to one side and taking in water. Edward, who loved the lines of a boat, could see that under the grime and the peeling paint she was a magnificent vessel. Lounging nearby he saw a tall man with burly shoulders. Something about the man attracted Edward's attention. "Do you know the owner of this tub?" he asked.

"He's gone back home. She's for sale, though." The voice was warm and deep. The man smiled and Edward felt less lonely.

"I'm Edward Gray, and I need a boat badly. I'm posted up in the North and I never see a soul."

The big man laughed. "One of those Foreign Office wallahs, I bet."

Edward laughed back. " 'Fraid so. I do miss a

good meal. All I get to eat is rice, rice and more rice."

The stranger took his hand. "My name is Lundy Chagwell. Call me Jaggers, like everybody else. I'll find you the best steak in Shanghai. Come along. And then we can drop by the club and find out about the boat. She could be a hell of a craft with just a little money and a lot of elbow grease." Months later Jaggers sailed the refitted boat up from Shanghai to north of Tientsin, where Edward was waiting for him. The *Elizabeth* was indeed magnificent. From that day on Jaggers took care of the *Elizabeth* as if she was the only woman in his life, which she was.

Tonight Jaggers watched the car nose along the harbor road and he was pleased for his friend. Elena would make Edward a wonderful wife, but Jaggers was glad he did not have a wife himself. He would not share his cabin on the *Elizabeth* with anyone, particularly not a woman. He cast a quick eye over the sailing charts. He was ready to up anchor. The master stateroom awaited the couple. There was champagne in the sitting-room and flowers everywhere perfumed the air. Jaggers was well pleased. "Good lad," he congratulated his cabin steward. "Now off with you and see they have a perfect evening."

For a moment Jaggers envied Edward the feel of a young woman's body close to his own. It had been a very long time since his young wife died, giving birth to his son. The memory of her dear face still haunted him, but the knowledge that his boy was now being raised by Jaggers's own father

cheered him. His father could give the lad perhaps
more security than Jaggers with his uncertain rov-
ing life.

Edward waved at Jaggers from the quayside.
Elena ran up the gangplank and breathed in
deeply. "Oh Edward! What a wonderful smell.
The smell of tar and salt water. Nothing else
comes close."

"Not even expensive French perfume?"

Elena laughed and shook her head. Edward had
ordered Elena's favorite scent, including a precious bottle of bath oil for the big many-hoofed
bath that stood in the center of the bathroom off
the master stateroom. The *Elizabeth* was built not
only to sail all the seas God made, but also to satisfy a man's senses. Here one saw a side of Edward
generally unknown to his friends and acquaintances in Shanghai. Gone was the model English
gentleman and in its place stood a man who felt
at home at sea. Once on deck Sir Edward meta-
morphosed into Edward the sailor. "Come on,
darling," he said, picking Elena up in his arms.
"Let me carry you over the threshold. *Our* threshold. Let's get changed and then take a turn around
the deck. I want to show you the whole boat."

"She's beautiful, Edward, really so beautiful."
Edward carried Elena through to the master stateroom. There the huge bed lay inviting the touch
of two bodies. All around the room stood baskets
of white flowers.

Edward put Elena down and drew her to him.
"We don't have to do anything tonight, just be-

cause we're married. I've waited for you for years, and a day or so extra makes no difference."

Elena looked up at Edward. A small shadow lifted from her eyes. "You're so understanding, darling," she said. "You know, I just need to get used to you. I mean, we know each other so well in so many ways but the one. Let's just see what happens."

Edward smiled and threw himself onto the bed. "See?" he said, bouncing up and down. "We have a fine mattress."

Elena laughed and jumped onto the bed beside him. "Gosh," she said, "we are going to have fun."

"Yes, indeed," Edward agreed. "Now, I'm just going to slip into my dressing-room and get changed. You put on something loose and comfortable. While we're on the *Elizabeth* we can just be ourselves. We don't have to change for dinner. We don't have to get up, and we can do just what we like. Hurry up. There's a bottle of champagne waiting to be drunk. I ordered a Perrier-Jouët to be put on ice. And a lovely year, at that."

Elter was among the last of the guests to leave. "I'll go ahead and see that everything is ready," Elter said.

"I'll just get changed," Sophia had said, "and then I'll drive myself out to Hang Chow Nan. Is it far?"

"Maybe an hour in the car. But I think you'll enjoy the trip, and you'll love the junk."

"I know I'm looking forward to this." Sophia took Elter's hand. They were standing at the front door. "I really don't want to be here alone to-night." Sophia realized how much she minded the absence of Elena. Try as she might, even with Elena's bouquet dangling from her hand, she felt betrayed and abandoned.

"Of course, my dear," Elter sympathized. "You'll take a little while to get on your own feet, but you will, *Kätzchen,* you will. Now, if you'll excuse me, I'll go and make arrangements."

"What arrangements?" Sophia smiled, her eyes brightening.

"Oh, just a few surprises for you."

Ummm, Sophia mused on her way upstairs. Maybe I have a few surprises for you too. Elter hurried off.

❧ *CHAPTER 48* ❧

The wind was gusting. Jaggers expertly weighed anchor; the *Elizabeth* threw up her prow joyfully and headed out to sea, her hull deep in the water. The moon shone through the porthole upon Elena who lay peacefully asleep in her husband's arms. Edward, awake, smiled down at her glossy bright head. He had his whole life ahead of him to make love to his young wife. Tonight Elena was tired and slightly groggy from the champagne. She had changed into her negligée in the bathroom and fallen into Edward's arms. "Good night, darling," she said. "I'm ready to drop."

"So am I," Edward whispered. Elena gave a huge sigh and snuggled up against him like a small kitten.

Edward was still smiling as he fell into a deep sleep beside his wife. The ship carrying the lovers forged resolutely out to sea.

Looking up at the back of the junk, Sophia was intimidated by the sheer size of it. She had seen junks in the harbor and on the river gliding about their business, but this junk was indeed special. The prow was adorned with the figure of a dragon lady. She hung over the front of the ship, her bosom bared and her black hair streaming back off her face, as if perpetually windswept. The line from the front of the boat to the high stern looked like a cardboard cut out, unreal in the night.

Midnight was near. Sophia shivered. She remembered that other midnight when the sleigh pulled out of the castle and she and Elena clutched Katrina; a night silent but for the hissing of the snow and the howling of the wolves. Tonight she also felt afraid. What was going to happen? Maybe nothing. She wished she was with Elena. She wished they were back in St. Petersburg going off to ride their horses through the forest.

Maybe she should go back to the house, to her safe warm room, and to Miss Trublood, who would be lying in bed worrying about her. No, it was too late for going back. Sophia felt she must go to meet the future, with no more looking back.

Clinging to what was safe and secure was just a bad habit. If you don't go looking for adventure, she reminded herself, then adventure will never come. Living means taking risks. Tonight Sophia felt this very keenly. Her hands trembled and the blood thudded in her temples. Underneath her cloak of black velvet she wore only her covering of soft gold silk. Once she took off her cloak, she would be nearly naked. Dressing—or rather, undressing—in order to come to dinner on the junk had seemed like fun in the sanctuary of her own bedroom. Imagining Elter's face when she dropped her cloak had also been a thrill; now, with the wind whipping through the cloak, the darkened village of Hang Chow Nan lying desolate before her, the only sign of life being the light that seeped under the door of a run-down restaurant nearby, and silence everywhere, she was not so sure. It was an eerie silence, the junk creaking in the wind and pulling restively at the mooring.

"Hello there."

Sophia relaxed. She looked up and saw Elter standing on the deck. "Are you coming up, *Kätzchen,*" he asked, "or are you going to spend the evening staring at my boat?"

Sophia laughed. "I could easily stare all night. She's beautiful."

Elter stretched out his hand and helped Sophia step down from the gangplank onto the deck. "Yes," he said. "And she's all mine. This is my home. This is where I feel most like myself." He gave a bleak smile. "You are the first woman ever to come on board this junk." Sophia believed him.

As they entered the main cabin she saw that the walls were lined with red leather. The armchairs looked as she imagined chairs in the men's clubs in Shanghai to look. These too were upholstered in red leather. The place smelled of tobacco and port. Or maybe brandy. It was certainly no place for women to sit and chat. "I gave the crew the evening off," Elter said. "Do go and leave your cloak in the bedroom over there." He extended his hand.

"Not for the moment," Sophia said, trying to sound equally at ease. "I'm a little cold. Let's have a drink. My mouth feels dry."

Elter chuckled. "I drank a little too much champagne as well. How about a brandy Alexander? That should put you on your feet."

"Lovely." Sophia sat down in one of the chairs and wished the leather had not been so hard. A light supper was laid out on the table: a side of smoked salmon, a small silver tray filled with caviar and a cold lobster salad. For the moment Sophia was not hungry. She waited for her drink and again wished that the surroundings were more congenial. Those curtains, she thought. They'll have to go. Someone had chosen those curtains a very long time ago and they were unfortunately made from a very loud and vulgar tartan. Must have been owned by an American, she thought . . .

"Here you are." Elter was at her side. "To your sister and Edward. May they have a long and happy life." He lifted his glass and knocked back the drink.

Sophia said "Amen" very loudly and threw the

brandy to the back of her throat. "Another one, please," she said. If she was going to get into the mood to seduce Elter, she would have to get drunk. Otherwise she would spend the rest of the evening wrapped tightly in her cloak.

Elter returned with another round and they both drank quickly. Elter did so, he realized, because he was rather nervous of the situation. What he said was true: he had never had or entertained a woman on board this junk. So far the junk had been his private domain. Here he was secure, lord of all he owned. Suddenly the presence of a woman threw him off balance. Here sat Sophia, demurely wrapped in her black cloak. The light fell on her long black hair, which streamed over her shoulders. Her moist red mouth trembled and Elter realized that she was as nervous as he was. "Darling," he said, taking her hand, "you're frightened." Sophia nodded tremulously. Elter pulled her to her feet and gently kissed her. Full of champagne, and now brandy, Sophia let herself go and responded to his kiss. "Perhaps we should wait . . ." Elter drew back.

"No, Elter. Don't push me away this time," Sophia pleaded. "I want to make love with you."

Elter removed the cloak from Sophia's shoulders. He urgently needed to feel her pressed against him and the bulky cloak obscured the beloved lines of her, her breast that he knew, and the swell of her thigh. A sigh escaped him. The cloak fell, leaving only the thin yellow gold silk between him and her nakedness. Within Elter something stirred. Electricity ran through his limbs. What was going to happen next was a matter of destiny and he felt a small voice whisper, *Take her. She waits.* Lifting Sophia up, he clutched her tight in his arms. "We will never regret this moment, darling," he said. "I promise you, you will never regret loving me." This oath he made as he strode out of the saloon and into his bedchamber.

His bed was stark and uninviting, but with Sophia's eyes upon him, he felt as if the world had been given to him anew. He took off his clothes and then lifted the silk until it slipped over Sophia's willing shoulders. She lay before him, her arms held up to him, awaiting his embrace. He gazed at her body so pure and so vulnerable. He saw the rosy folds of skin between her legs like a fresh blossom. He fell on top of her and buried himself in her body. He was an expert lover and he was patient. He waited, rocking her gently in his arms until he had fully penetrated her, and then began his slow ascent into explosion and oblivion. He could hear Sophia's cries reach the roof of the great hull. Finally he released her into the stratosphere. After moments that seemed to stretch into infinity, they both turned their heads and smiled into each other's faces. "Have I made you happy?" he asked tenderly.

"It was lovely, Elter. Absolutely sublime."

Elter smiled and reached for a cigarette. Usually when he reached for his post-coital cigarette, he was aware of a great sadness. *Post coitus tristum est* he had often reminded himself: he was not the only man to feel the sense of loss. Usually the woman beside him he never wanted to see again.

This time it was different. He drew the smoke deep down into his lungs, unaware that his love-making had not gone unobserved.

A thin shadow slipped into the restaurant on the dock. So, One-Eyed Charlie thought, the German is in love with the young Russian. Interesting. Charlie smiled a mean smile. My, my, he observed—he had been standing under the porthole looking into the bedroom on the junk—he can make her howl. I hope he has the good sense to keep her strictly for business.

Elter finished his cigarette and fell asleep beside Sophia. He put his hand on her warm thigh and sighed contentedly. Dawn was just starting to illuminate the harbor. The junk rocked and swayed, lulling its occupants.

Miles away the *Elizabeth* was making her way down the coast of China. All was well.

Almost all. Charlie was driving to Shanghai to see Chu.

✤ CHAPTER 49 ✤

Miss Trublood, after waiting all night for Sophia to return, realized that the worst had probably happened. She sat in her bedroom armchair, facing the open window, watching the sun rise over both her girls: one legitimately able to celebrate the act of love, and the other without the Church's blessing. Miss Trublood wiped her tired eyes with the palms of her hands. She had no recourse left to her. Edward was very far away on his yacht and he deserved his honeymoon. She could not try to contact him. He had borne the burden of Sophia's behavior for many years, and Miss Trublood promised herself that his honeymoon with Elena should be undisturbed. Having given up on sleep hours ago, she pushed the bell for Mei Mei and a hot cup of jasmine tea. "Mei Mei," she said when the small sweet face presented itself in her room, "Missie hasn't come back?"

"No." Mei Mei shook her head. "Misha very worried. He sit up all night long."

Miss Trublood lay back in her chair and felt less alone. At least both Mei Mei and Misha worried as much as she did. Miss Trublood really loved Mei Mei. If she had had a daughter, it was a Mei Mei she would love to have had. Tiny Mei Mei was delicate and feminine. She pattered after Misha and flitted about the house like a small radiant nightlight. Today she looked tired and there were blue shadows under her eyes. Miss Trublood shook her head. "No good can come of this," she said. "No good at all."

Mei Mei agreed. "He dangerous man. That man not good for Missie Sophia. But," Mei Mei shrugged, "if a man is good, Missie not want him. No different topside. No different here. Man good, bad. Chinese or foreigner. I get you hot cup of tea, Miss Trublood. You very tired? Not sleep?"

"No, I didn't sleep much. I was too worried."

Mei Mei padded off to the kitchen. "Missie Trublood really worried, Misha."

Misha sat at the kitchen table glumly. "She's right to be," he said. "Sophia can be a very silly girl at times."

Sophia felt far from silly. She awoke before Elter. She realized that they had both overslept. She lay naked beside his tall strong body and gazed at his penis, studying it close up. Strange, what last night had given her such pleasure now looked curiously flaccid, rather like a pickle lying on its side, flanked by two round testicles. Welcome to the world of women, Sophia thought. Her hand strayed between her legs, feeling the moisture still welling out from her body. The moisture made her smell different from the day before. Now she smelled like a mature woman, Elter's semen mingling with her womanly fragrance. She smiled a calm victorious smile. She moved her legs and felt the strain and the stress of the coupling in the muscles of her thighs. So this is what men and women die for! she marveled. And now I can do it whenever I want.

She put her hand on Elter's groin and softly stroked the end of his penis. Obediently it expanded in her hand. She smiled again, feeling very powerful and commanding. Elter's eyes began to flicker. Gently she licked the head of the penis with her tongue and was thrilled to see it blossom. Elter was awake now. "Go on," he said hoarsely. "Go on."

Sophia, delighted with the trace of desperation in Elter's normally calm voice, went on. She pulled herself on top of him and sucked and stroked and licked with her little pink tongue until he exploded into her mouth. "Umm." Sophia grinned, looking down at Elter. "That was lovely."

Elter laughed. "Well, it's certainly my favorite way to wake up," he agreed. "Goodness!" He looked out of the porthole. "We overslept. You must get back. What on earth will your chaperone say?"

"She won't say anything." Sophia rolled off Elter's still throbbing body. She lay wetly beside him, thinking, we can spend the rest of the day making love. She stretched her hands above her head and arched her back. "Let's spend the day in bed."

"I would love to." Elter leaned over her. "Nothing would please me more, Sophia, but I must get to work and you must go home. I'm afraid I've compromised you, and Miss Trublood will not like me for it. I really had no intention of seducing you." He flushed because he lied. But in truth, last night was not the night he had chosen.

Sophia laughed. "Oh? But my intentions were entirely fulfilled." She got up and walked to the porthole. The dock was still fairly deserted. The door of the restaurant gaped open. The place was empty. A few gulls sulked around the gray sky. "Oh why do we have to go back to the real world, Elter? Why can't we just lift up the anchor and sail away like Elena and Edward? They're so lucky. Off to Hong Kong and Bangkok. I should so love to go to Bangkok."

And so you will one day, Elter said to himself.

For now Bangkok lay in Sophia's future. For now, she could only dream. He walked up behind her and put his hand on her shoulder. "It's not for us to know the future," he whispered. "Let's get dressed. I'll make a pot of coffee and some toast. And then we must go."

Sophia turned in his arms and looked into his eyes. "I do love you, Elter."

To Elter's surprise he heard himself say, "And I love you, Sophia. Really I do." This shocked him so much that he smiled awkwardly and was quick to go off to the galley. Silly fool, he muttered to himself. You really are a stupid old idiot, saying such things at your age. Too late, he thought, as he poured the boiling water over the coffee grains. Words cannot be retracted.

Coffee was very important to Elter. When he was a little boy he would drink from a warm blue bowl of coffee much diluted with milk. That memory was always with him, as was the memory of his mother's warm smile . . . He recalled sitting in his little chair, his knees up to his chin; he sank his nose into the bowl and inhaled the smell. Then he looked up and returned his mother's smile . . .

The coffee he made for Sophia was imported from an island called the Brac, a small island in the Caymans. Connoisseurs might go to Jamaica for their coffee and boast after dinner of the effort of shipping Blue Mountain beans from the West Indies to Shanghai, but for Elter there was no problem.

He brought a pile of hot buttered toast to the

dining-table and then the pot of coffee. "What a gorgeous smell!" Sophia looked up.

"Isn't it?" He poured her a cup and filled his blue bowl. "A wonderful smell. When I was a little boy . . ." And then he felt a lump form in his throat. Until this day he had never said the words *when I was a little boy* to anyone. But he found he could say anything to this beautiful young woman who gazed at him with tenderness and love. He finished his story and then said gruffly, "Come along now. We must leave."

Sophia jumped. "Must we? This is all so perfect."

Elter smiled. "We can always come here again. This can be our hideaway. I won't tell anybody if you don't."

"I won't. We'll keep this place our secret. I won't even tell Elena." They kissed one last time and then walked down the gangplank to dry land.

Sophia sat at the wheel of her car and luxuriated in her sense of sin. Beat that, Elena, she thought in her best Americanese. Just you try and beat that.

Day one on the yacht *Elizabeth* was heaven for Elena. She woke up with a start and lay in bed wondering where she was. Of course, she remembered, I'm married. She looked up at Edward who was awake but not moving beside her. "Are you happy, darling?" she said, lifting up her left hand and gazing at the gold band that had so recently joined her engagement ring.

"Utterly," Edward replied. He put his arm under Elena's head and pulled her close. "I never thought I would be so happy. The idea of marriage always frightened me. But today I feel as if we've always been together. I almost can't remember life before I met you."

Elena smiled and softly kissed Edward on the lips. "Breakfast?"

Edward was up and bounding off to his dressing-room. "See you in a minute, poppet."

Elena rose from the bed and went to her cabin trunk. She pulled on a dark red swimming-suit and over it she wore a breakfast wrap. Feeling very elegant, she swished around the room until Edward reappeared in his dressing-gown.

"Just think," he said as he held the door open for her to lead the way into the dining-room. "No more formal clothes." He gave a huge boyish grin.

They sat down to a full English breakfast. "Kippers," Edward murmured. "I love kippers."

Jaggers joined them for breakfast. "Not just kippers, old boy," he said. "I asked Chung to get you thinkers as well."

"Thinkers?" Elena asked, and then she made a face. "Oh. I see," she said. "Brains."

"You have to be English to eat pigs' thinkers." Jaggers laughed.

"Well, I'm Russian," Elena replied. "I'll stick to kippers." The three of them sat contentedly as the ship continued to plow its way through the sea.

The gong sounded for lunch by the time Sophia had returned home and bathed herself. She felt she could not possibly sit with Miss Trublood with the smell of love in her nostrils. She lay in the warm scented bath-water wondering how she could arrange to meet Elter again at the junk: they could meet during the day and Maria would cover for her. Miss Trublood might suspect the worst, but Sophia did not have to confront her with the truth.

Refreshed but still aglow with last night's events, Sophia pulled on a modest sailor blouse and long black skirt. Demurely she gazed at herself in her mirror. Good heavens, she thought. I look far too young to be a lady of the night. Then, turning around and regarding herself over her shoulder, she reflected, I could get to like being a sinner or a scarlet woman. Making love is miraculous and exciting. Such rapture. Such pleasure.

The gong sounded for the second time and Sophia ran down the stairs. "Sorry I didn't come back last night," she excused herself as she slid into her seat.

Miss Trublood was sitting at the end of the table. She raised her eyebrows over her gold spectacles. "So am I. We were worried about you, dear."

"You needn't have been. I was perfectly all right. I was with Elter and the hour got so late I decided to stay overnight. But here I am." Sophia thought she sounded like an idiot.

Miss Trublood just stared at her quizzically. "Sophia," she said after a silence. "You do know what you're doing, don't you?"

"Of course." Sophia nodded. "After all, I'm twenty-three, not sixteen, Miss Trublood."

"Of course you are." Miss Trublood pursed her lips. "I mean, you will be careful, won't you?"

For an awful moment Sophia felt confused. "Careful about what?"

Ah Ling arrived carrying two bowls of soup. Sophia plunged her spoon into the liquid and then gasped. The soup was hot and burned her mouth. Even worse was the sudden thought that she could get pregnant. Why, oh why, did I not think of that before now? she asked herself.

Miss Trublood noticed Sophia burning herself. "Think before you act," she said, then bent her gray head and began to drink the soup, noisily blowing on it first.

CHAPTER 50

Love for Elena happened in the early morning of the second day at sea. She lay close to Edward and then, brushing her hand against an unaccustomed body, awoke with a start. Feeling her jump, Edward too opened his eyes and smiled at her sleepy dazed face. "It's only me," he said. Elena burrowed into Edward's side. He, holding her, gently kissed her. Slowly they came together in a glorious moment of communion. "Are you happy?" he asked softly.

"Wonderfully happy," Elena said.

Indeed, the act of making love, which Elena had

read about in her books, far from proving to be the ordeal she had imagined, seemed an almost supernatural experience. Elena, her breath quietening, lay against her pillow and floated into a dreamless sleep. Love had drained her limbs and stilled her mind. Beside her Edward also slept, but he dreamed of the sea and of shining coral strands and finally he dreamed of his home in Devon.

At breakfast on the boat's foredeck they were shy of each other. They knew each other now in a different way. Edward talked to Jaggers. "Now that I'm married, we must use the boat more often. I'll have to discipline myself to take more time off. This is a wonderful way to relax."

The wind was light and the prow of the boat carved her way through the sea that was light green in the early morning sun. The Formosa coast was visible on the port side. Way ahead to starboard was the city of Foochow. "Let's tie up at Foochow," Jaggers suggested. He too felt the slight uneasiness in the air. Privately he hoped that Edward would use the yacht more often, particularly if he would bring Sophia. Jaggers had met Sophia a few times and watched her in the company of Elter. Jaggers did not like Elter, but he was attracted to Sophia. Not—he thought as he bit down hard on his thick slice of wheatbread toast—that Sophia would be interested in me.

Elena smiled at Jaggers. He visibly enjoyed his food and he was a good-looking man. "Tell me, Jaggers," she said, relishing the sound of his name. Since she was married to Edward, she could call another man by his first name and not be thought forward. "How did you meet Edward?"

"It's not much of a story, really. This old tub brought us together and we've known each other for years. When you go back to England, I'll be skippering you there. And then I think I'll put down some roots. The farm back home's run by my father. I miss the old place sometimes. The earth's so black and rich there. I think those of us from Devon or Dorset, even Somerset, never really stay away for long. The soil calls us home, you know."

Edward grunted. "Quite right. Not just the soil; the smell of the apples. What I would do for a taste of a cox or a pippin!" He sighed. "Oh, they're types of English apple," he explained in answer to Elena's questioning glance. "Coxes are small and red. And when they're too ripe, their skins are like faces of very old ladies, all soft and wrinkled. A pippin, on the other hand, is sharp and sweet with a hearty crunch. I was an excellent scrumper when I was a lad. Did you scrump, Jaggers?"

"Of course." Jaggers grinned. His blue eyes lit up. "Remember, you climbed into a neighbor's orchard and grabbed as many apples as you could before the farmer saw you and chased you down the lane. I was the first boy in my area to make cider. We had an illicit still behind the barn. I got roaring drunk and my father found me. He leathered me until I could hardly walk. Worth it, though. I'll never forget that scrumpy. Never has a drink tasted better."

Elena smiled. Before her eyes both men had reverted to being boys again. "We had apple trees in our orchard," Elena ventured. And then the wintry vision of her dead parents soured the memory and shadows darkened her face.

"So you did, darling." Edward covered her hands with his. "And we shall again, when we get home. We'll plant as many apple trees as you like."

"That would be marvelous," she said. "One for Grandmother and one for my mother and father. They would like that."

Chung, the cabin boy, was signaling to Jaggers. "I must be off to get ready to dock. Edward, I'll give you a yell when I need a hand."

"I'll just finish my tea and I'll be along in a minute."

Jaggers took his last piece of toast and ran up the deck to the pilot house. Edward left the table and stood by the railing, gazing down at the swirling water.

"I wish we could live like this always," Elena observed. "Cut off from the rest of the world. Maybe we could even bring a piano on board and I could play and you could listen. We could spend our nights reading poetry under the stars, and drift about the ocean and stop whenever we felt like it. I don't see the point of the real world at all."

"Neither do I, to tell you the truth. When we get home we can move into the Monastery, pull up the drawbridge, and let the rest of the world get on by itself. When we're not in London, that is."

"Do you really have a drawbridge?"

"Yes, we do. The house was an old monastery. It came into our family during the time of Henry

VIII. He had the place sacked and gave it to an ancestor of mine, many great-grandfathers ago. I love it there, precisely because it's self-sufficient. We have a mill in working order, a cider press, and we make our own wine—I have a few grapevines. The Monastery is surrounded by a moat which I had cleaned and restored when I inherited the house from my father. There have been Grays living there for centuries. We've always been a hardworking busy family."

Elena smiled. "And now you're taking home a Russian wife brought back from the Orient. How do you think the servants will feel about me?"

"They'll love you as much as I do," Edward replied. He put his arm around Elena's slim waist. "I think you'll come to love the Monastery too. For a while we'll have to live in London, but we can spend the weekends there."

"Poor Edward. You're very homesick, aren't you?"

He laughed softly. "But now there are two of us, and the different parts of my life all seem to fit together—my life in Shanghai, my life on this boat with Jaggers, and the life I miss, far away in England. But with you at my side, I feel at home wherever I am." He fell silent, at peace with the world. "We must bring Sophia out sailing one of these days."

Elena sighed. "I know I should feel guilty, but I don't miss her as much as I thought I would. Still, I expect she's busy with Elter."

"I expect so." Edward heard a shout. "I must go and help Jaggers."

"I wish I knew why Sophia can't be interested in someone like him," said Elena. Edward kissed her forehead and was gone. Elena leaned over the railing and saw her own face reflected in the water. Maybe, Elena thought, Sophia is something of a Janus: "I laugh with one face; I weep with the other," she murmured, quoting the Kierkegaard she had read the other day. She walked up the deck and went down to the master stateroom. A coldness enveloped her. I must get a cardigan, she thought. It's cold up there.

The boat heaved and bucked as the men steadied her and pointed her into the mouth of the harbor of Foochow. Elena looked out of the porthole and relaxed. People were milling around everywhere. What a change from being alone at sea. She staggered with the thud of the boat as it docked. She could see Edward walking lightly along the harbor wall. This life suits him so well, she thought. Then she imagined a small boy looking just like Edward running beside him. I'll have children, she promised herself, lots of them. And dogs. "Elena!" Edward called into the wind.

"Coming!" she shouted back, and with that she began to run to him.

CHAPTER 51

"Do you think I could be pregnant?" Sophia was in Maria's room, finally alone with her. For over an hour she had to wait before Vassily and Rollo stopped gossiping and left.

Maria shook her head. "I don't think so. It's a lot more difficult to get pregnant than one would imagine." She grimaced, thinking of her own near misses and abortion. "Anyway, if you did get pregnant you could always get rid of it."

"I couldn't." Sophia shook her head. "I know I could never do that. I couldn't kill my baby."

Maria seemed to take offense. "There you go again, Sophia. How do you know you wouldn't get rid of it? How can you say what you would or wouldn't do before it happens to you? I had to." Bitter lines ran down her smooth face. "No, I didn't want to either, but I had no choice. I was alone, abandoned, and pregnant. I had to get rid of it. I had to. To tell you the truth, the memory still haunts me, and I always remember the anniversary of the day the baby should have been born. Sometimes I imagine my child running around . . . But I try not to think like that." She shook herself. It was all a horrible nightmare. "Besides, Elter can use a prophylactic."

"A what?"

"You know. It's made from the lining of a sheep's gut, and a man pulls it on and it stops the semen from getting inside you."

Sophia laughed. "How unappetizing!" she said.

"Maybe. But it's better than getting pregnant. Speaking of deterrents, how did Miss Trublood take your night out?"

"I was surprised. She took it very well. Just told me to be careful."

"At last they're letting you grow up! About time, too. Now, if you'll excuse me, I have to go off and do some work." She did not say that work meant delivering papers for the Gorgon, who would be meeting with Chu tonight. A big shipment was coming in from Amsterdam, en route to other parts of the world, and it had to be moved very quickly. The police had been paid off, having demanded more than what Chu considered reasonable. Nor did Maria tell Sophia that she would be seeing Elter, and that it was his shipment. There were some things Sophia did not need to know.

"All right. I'll go home and catch up on lost sleep." Sophia stretched. "Sex is wonderful, isn't it, Maria?"

"At times, I suppose." Maria looked at Sophia wryly. "It is if you have a choice."

"You don't seem to have much choice in your life."

"That's the difference between us. You have choices; I don't. Then again, because you have choices, I suppose you also have to make decisions. I didn't have any decisions to make. I was young, without family, homeless and penniless."

"Was that before you became an actress?"

Maria hesitated for a moment in confusion. Then her face regained its composure and she said, "Yes. But even my acting had to be put aside when I came here and found myself on my own again." She turned to leave. "Lock up when you go, Sophia, and leave the key under the mat."

Sophia stood alone in the little room, listening to Maria's light footfall on the stairs. The room was strewn with cigarette-ends and half-finished cups of tea. The bed, a mattress on the floor, was unmade. Four chairs were loosely grouped around a rickety table that stood lopsided by a stove. This was all that a twenty-five-year-old woman could call her own—precious little. Sophia felt a great need to be in her own home, to steep herself in the history of her own possessions, in the security of good furniture, paintings and carpets. Her bed was substantial and her bathroom white and palatial. Maria was like a small butterfly that could be blown out of Shanghai and out of China at any moment. She had no roots. She belonged nowhere. How terrifying, thought Sophia.

She imagined Elena and Edward on the boat, Katrina back in Russia, Misha and Mei Mei permanent in her life. Miss Trublood . . . Even now, Miss Trublood. She hurried out of the room and ran down the stairs. She hailed a taxi. "Take me home," she said urgently.

"Where is home?" the taxi driver asked the frightened-looking young woman.

"Rue Fleury, in the English concession. Please hurry," she said. All the way back Sophia said her prayers. *Please, Lord, let me not be pregnant.*

❦ CHAPTER 52 ❦

"Must you stare at me like that?" Elter was feeling irritable. It was a hot day. Sweat trickled down his naked belly and ran between his legs. Sophia lay beside him, evidently fascinated by his genitals. Elter did not enjoy the scrutiny.

"Don't be so touchy. I'm not staring," Sophia said. "I'm admiring. I don't get to see a live penis in broad daylight every day."

Elter could not get used to Sophia's directness. Sometimes she was seized with a playfulness that made her quite unpredictable. He did not know how to handle her in these moods. Elter crossed his legs defensively in an effort to hide his deflated penis.

Sophia laughed. "How are the mighty fallen in the midst of the battle!" she quoted.

"Perhaps we should leave the Bible out of this discussion," Elter said nervously.

"I shall have to give it a name," she said as if making a decision.

Elter snorted and turned over. He lay with his white buttocks tightly clenched. God knows what the girl would do next. If he put on a contraceptive it sent her into paroxysms of laughter.

"I think I'll call it Wilhelm."

"The Kaiser would be delighted, I'm sure," Elter grumbled.

"Then I'll call it Little Willie, for short."

"It's not short, nor is it little."

Sophia flung herself on top of Elter. "Don't

sulk, darling. I didn't mean it that way. Let's just make love."

Elter released a long sustained sigh. "Sophia," he said, "you give new meaning to the word lust."

She hugged him. "Are you objecting?"

"By no means," he said, gathering her in his arms and feeling new life return to his groin. The slight worry of a possible pregnancy vanished as her mouth found his. The junk rocked appreciatively and the gulls cried their sad cry.

Elena watched Hong Kong rise out of the sea. How different, she thought, from Shanghai. Shanghai, the city of brothels and night-clubs; the city of foreign concessions, where at night only the tall bearded Sikhs stood outside the embassies and legations. Rubble from the bombing—there was perennial conflict between countless factions— filled the streets. Hovels lined the roads of the main parts of the city. But Hong Kong was different. Built exclusively for trade and for the making of money, Hong Kong glittered and shone. Tall buildings graced the city and Elena was already a little in love with the place even before they docked.

"We're not staying at the Peninsula," Edward announced. "We're staying at the Repulse Bay Hotel. You'll love it. It's one of the most beautiful hotels in the world."

Elena was enchanted. She looked forward to being alone with Edward. Jaggers was to stay with friends in Macau and they would join him and the yacht in two weeks' time. "Think, darling." Elena put her hand on Edward's arm. "We have two weeks completely alone together. Just you and I." So far Elena had been unable to undress before Edward and he too was still using his dressing-room, but their love-making was gentle and satisfying.

Edward kissed Elena's hand. "I'm looking forward to the break," he said. "And wait till you see the beach!"

The Repulse Bay Hotel was long and low and stood on a lovely white beach. Elena had seen beaches on the Baltic Sea but never such a luxurious stretch of sand. She wore a new black bathing-suit and felt quite shy. Edward wore a bathing-suit that exposed his chest. Elena laughed as they walked down to the water's edge. "Goodness," she said, feeling strange and vulnerable, "we look like a pair of underdone kippers!"

"We do indeed. We'll have to be careful not to get burnt. Come on, Elena!" He started to run. "Last one in is a monkey." Edward hurled himself into the sea, then together they swam out to a raft. They lay quietly side by side, breathing hard from the exertion of the swim. Edward noticed a sudden lull in Elena's good mood. "You've something on your mind."

"It's nothing." Elena shook her head. "I couldn't be happier. Really." She frowned a little. "I just do worry about Sophia."

Edward turned over and ran his lips down Elena's arm. "I do too," he said. "But really there isn't much point in spoiling our honeymoon.

However much we worry, it won't make any difference to what Sophia is doing now."

"I know, but she's so impulsive, I just hope she doesn't do anything silly."

"You mean Elter?"

"That's what I am afraid of."

Edward lay back and stared at the sun. "We've done everything we can to keep her safe. Miss Trublood is in charge and if anyone can stop her, it's surely Miss Trublood."

Elena shook her head. "I don't think anybody can stop Sophia from doing what she wants to do. But part of me feels I should be there trying, and I'm not . . ."

"Nor should you be there, darling. You're entitled to a life of your own. She's your sister, not your child. And she's responsible for her own life."

"You're right, of course, but you don't know how it is with twins. I know Sophia is furiously jealous because I married you. I sense it in her all the time. It's as if she feels I've abandoned her."

"You haven't, Elena. You simply got married." They were silent for some minutes while the sun warmed them until they were eager to plunge themselves into the cooling sea. "Come on, let's go back and get changed. I'll take you to lunch at Jo Li Li's. You can see all the ex-pats making fools of themselves misordering Chinese food. These days they send the dregs from England out to the colonies. Most of them can't even speak the King's English."

Elena smiled. She never could help but smile when Edward was being so British.

CHAPTER 53

The honeymoon spun in Elena's mind like a fine glass Christmas hanging. The days forged out of the blue of the water and the white of the yacht an eternally remembered space in time. Very much she hoped that those first fragile days of married happiness would stay with them always.

Edward preferred Macau to Hong Kong. To him Hong Kong was ostentatious, whereas the quiet serenity of Macau reminded him of his youth, when he traveled the world and met with the mandarins. Jaggers too was relaxed, and happy to spend time with his old friend again. Elena missed the privacy she and Edward had enjoyed at the Repulse Bay Hotel, but she knew she had married a man's man and Edward would always have friends like Jaggers who would want to talk of politics and finance. She did not join in these conversations; she was quite content just to listen. In the evenings the three of them would sit out on the balcony of Macau's Pousada Inn and listen to Beethoven pieces played beautifully by a fellow guest on the small Steinway that must have been shipped here by some music-lover many years ago. Time had mellowed the strings and the notes fell softly into the darkness and drifted out over the harbor.

Tonight while the men talked Elena thought of Sophia.

*   *   *

Sophia was in Elter's arms, lying on his bed. "I really will have to tell Elena that I can't live with her any more. I feel bad about it, but I just can't live their life. Elena and Edward are a very conventional couple. I'm just not that conventional. The dinner parties make me want to scream. Do you like dinner parties?"

"No, but I don't know that many people do."

"Elena does. She loves organizing the damn things. As soon as one's over, she's making plans for the next. And when they're alone in the evenings they read poetry to each other."

"What's wrong with that?"

"Nothing, I suppose." Sophia sat up. "I mean, I can't bear the type of poetry they read. You know: *The boy stood on the burning deck.* Bloody fool, I say. Now, if they liked revolutionary poetry or jazz, I could listen. But then, I prefer people to antiquated verse and dead music." She flung herself back on the pillow. She would not dare tell even Elena her secret. She was four weeks late now. Three of those weeks had been spent anxiously waiting. The first week she reassured herself she was merely late. The second week she began praying in earnest. Now she was in a panic. "I'm going to ask if I can stay where I am with Miss Trublood and Misha and Mei Mei. And I'm sure Ah Ling will want to stay with me."

Elter had not told Sophia of his plans to take her from Shanghai and slip back to Germany with her. Telling Sophia of such a plan was dangerous. The more time they spent together, the more he fell in love with this enchanting child. She made him feel young. She made him laugh. She brightened up the room when she walked in. Her moods were tempestuous, but she played no complicated games. What she said she meant. Elter had become very disenchanted with women. So many of them relied on well-worn female ploys. From them Elter had taken what he wanted and then left. Sophia was different. She was warm and affectionate, and took the same joyous Rabelaisian pleasure in sex that she took in food. Few women, Elter thought, actually enjoyed making love. Most of them used sex as a bargaining counter and Elter did not bargain with women. He could see himself married to Sophia. He could imagine hours of laughter. He envisioned Sophia running down the long corridors of his very Gothic German house and out into the warm heavy summer nights. "You do whatever you want, *Kätzchen*. One day maybe I'll show you the castles that look as if they are going to fall down the steep mountains. I'll take you to the castle of the insane Bavarian King. German aristocrats were rather nice when they were mad. It is only the peasants who get dangerous."

"Will you go mad, Elter?"

Elter shook his head. "Never." He smiled at Sophia and ran his hands down the inside of her thighs. "So soft," he said and closed his eyes.

Sophia opened her legs slowly and pulled him to her. "Take a long, long time," she said. "We have hours before Miss Trublood expects me home."

*   *   *

One-Eyed Charlie, sitting in the back of the little restaurant on the dock at Hang Chow Nan, made a note. Whatever Elter was doing with his shipment of opium, some of it had been stored behind a bulkhead. The main order was all accounted for, but a relatively small amount was still stowed away on the junk. Would Elter try to make a deal of his own? If so, he would be guilty of treason against the Tong. All opium belonged to Chu. Charlie's missing eye prickled. He hoped Elter was playing straight. If not, he would die. And that would be a pity because Charlie rather liked Elter. He tutted to himself. "Such a shame a man has to risk his life for a mere girl." Still, judging by the amount of time they spent on the junk, Elter must be a very happy man indeed.

Sophia came dancing down the gangplank with Elter behind her. She flashed past the door of the restaurant and then they were in the car roaring off to Shanghai. Charlie watched them go and scratched the brow over his hollow eye-socket.

He walked out of the restaurant and slid into his car, pointing his razor sharp nose toward the city.

CHAPTER 54

As the weeks slipped by Sophia's suspicion that she was pregnant became a growing conviction that she was going to have to accept the worst. She found that she was completely unable to drink her morning cup of tea. The very smell of the milk made her feel as if her whole stomach was going to break loose from her body. The feeling of nausea persisted for much of the morning. She knew Miss Trublood watched her face at breakfast. On two occasions she had to leave the dining-room quickly.

There was no point in writing to Elena to tell her of all this, but Sophia did write to Elena to put the idea to her that when she and Edward moved into a place of their own in Shanghai, Sophia would like to stay where she was, and maybe Maria might move in to keep her company . . .

She waited for a reply. In the meantime, try as she might to keep her worries at bay, she could think of little else. She wore herself out with visits to the lavatory, all for no purpose. She felt certain that she was pregnant indeed.

At last a letter from Elena arrived, full of descriptions of what a good time they were having. And, Elena wrote, Edward and she would house-hunt when they got back, and Sophia could remain where she was with Miss Trublood and Misha and Mei Mei:

Edward is really homesick and looking forward to going back to London. What do you feel about leaving Shanghai? Yes, I think Maria is a good idea. The weather has been wonderful and I'm looking forward to spending time with you on the Elizabeth. *She's a lovely yacht . . .*

Sophia read the letter in the drawing-room. When the letter trailed off into details of sunsets and meals taken in Macau, a feeling of doom settled in Sophia's heart. Why, Lord, she thought, is it always me? Why do I have to be pregnant? Why isn't Elena pregnant? After all, they must have made love, too. I'll bet they took no precautions. And I was unsafe only that one time. "Oh God," she muttered, walking to the window, her shoulders sagging, "Why me?" She gazed up at the uncomprehending sky. "What on earth shall I do?"

"Have an abortion." Maria sat in her usual position on her bed. Rollo lay at her feet, smoking his pipe.

"No question. Have an abortion," he said. He sat up. His long hair fell over his collar. "Only problem is, you're not the sort to have an abortion," he remarked. "Is she, Vassily?"

Vassily shook his head.

"Oh I see," Maria retorted, stung. "And I am?"

Rollo put his hand on her shoulder. "Sorry, old dear," he said. "You had no choice and Sophia does. I've seen too many girls have abortions then take to drugs and to drink to forget."

Sophia had to admit she very much wanted Rollo's support. In an odd way over the weeks she had become attached to the idea of a baby in her stomach. When she was not worrying about the pregnancy, she imagined the little human being growing inside her womb. What an awful word, *womb*, she reflected. Almost as awful as *udders*. The English language was very terse about things of a sexual nature.

Maria sighed. "You're right, Rollo. I expect the happily marrieds will come back and then Sophia can shock them with the news."

"I'm more worried about telling Elter," said Sophia.

Maria smiled. "He can cope. I'd wonder more about Miss Trublood."

Sophia blushed. "Isn't it dreadful? She warned me to take care. Oh well, I suppose I'd better break the news to her and get it over with." She paused. "And by the way, Maria, Elena suggested that you move in with me. She wants her own house and so do I. What do you think?"

A look of delight came over Maria's face. The idea of living in a big, comfortable, warm home thrilled her, but there would be another time to have this discussion. Until she had drawn away the veil between Sophia and herself, she could not move into the house as a friend. Whether after the initiation they would still be friends remained to be seen. She knew she had to wait in this dingy little room for the Gorgon to make his move. "I promise to think about it, Sophia." Maria smiled. "It's a lovely thought. Give me a few months."

"All right. If you say so." Sophia was hurt. She went home feeling like a discarded jersey. She very much wanted her friend to share her house. It would be far too big and quiet by herself. Then again, she cheered herself up, she would have her baby and maybe a long, quiet, gentle pregnancy was just what her baby needed.

On the way home she made a firm vow. Now she was pregnant, there was no point in pretending she wasn't. She must keep her head up and defend the honor of her baby. True, the whole community would be shocked. She had shocked them before. This time she would really give them something to talk about. She marched into the drawing-room and rang for Miss Trublood.

"Miss Trublood," she said, her heart beating and her eyes shining, "I have something to tell you." She stood with her feet in the third ballet position and looked at Miss Trublood's large, jowled, concerned face. "Miss Trublood, I'm pregnant."

The hurricane that Sophia anticipated did not arrive. Instead a strained silence followed. A fly whined at the window. A chair creaked. Then Miss Trublood said, "Are you sure, honey?" She spoke with such honest concern in her voice and such affection that Sophia lost all her self-control and found herself enveloped, sobbing, in the woman's big arms.

"I'm sure. I know I'm pregnant. And I'm so frightened."

Miss Trublood carried Sophia to a soft armchair and sat down with her. "Here, take this hankie and wipe your eyes. Yours isn't the first pregnancy I've had to deal with. Have you told Elter?''

Sophia took the handkerchief, mopped her eyes, and shook her head. "I will, though. I'm seeing him tomorrow night. I'll have to tell him. Maybe he'll say, 'Wonderful, let's get married,' and that would make it all right, wouldn't it?"

Miss Trublood sighed. "Sophia, if you make love before you get married, then this is the risk you take. There's a lot of sense in staying away from sin, for good reasons just like this. I hope he will marry you, if that's really what you want."

"Oh it is, Miss Trublood! I swear it is. You see, Elter and I go together. He keeps me on the straight and narrow, and I knock him off his perch when he gets too pompous. Elena likes Edward to be pompous, but I don't let Elter . . ."

Miss Trublood put her hand over Sophia's quickly talking mouth. "But do you love him, Sophia? That's the whole point."

"I love him very, very much." She lay back like a small child, her head on Miss Trublood's breast. "Just imagine, a baby. I want a boy, to look just like Elter. The same blue eyes and fair hair. He will be tall as well. I hope . . . Gosh, I'm getting quite excited."

Miss Trublood smiled. "And very English with that *gosh.*"

Sophia grinned, the tears drying fast on her face. "I must go and tell Misha. He won't mind."

"No, but he and Mei Mei do plan to marry, you know."

"Really?"

"Yes." Miss Trublood flushed. "They're both attending my church and, well . . ." She paused. "Misha is thinking of becoming a Christian. Mei Mei's not sure, but I think we're going to have Misha as one of us."

"Fishing for Christians, Miss Trublood." Sophia laughed. "By the time you've finished, you will have evangelized the whole of Shanghai."

"So I will," she agreed. "So I will. Run along now, Sophia."

Sophia, calling for Misha, took off down the corridors and the long stairs. Miss Trublood bowed her head. "God, take care of her," was all she could find to say. How they were going to manage an illegitimate pregnancy, and how they would keep Sophia safe from the vicious gossips in this community, she did not know. But one thing was for sure: they would have to leave Shanghai and live quietly until after the baby's birth. Protocol would demand that as the price for illicit love-making. Rules were still rules, Miss Trublood reminded herself. Such a pity, because she was just beginning to love this city. But Sophia must come first. She got to her feet slowly and realized that she felt tired. Unusual, she thought. Must be the heat.

She walked to her room and lay down. All the cares of the world seemed to flatten her shoulders to her pillow. Another young girl pregnant. What could Elter have been thinking of? Certainly not of her honor. How things were changing. And for the worst. Miss Trublood felt guilty, but not surprised. She knew, and she hoped God knew, that she had tried to protect her charge, but the girl—no, the young woman now—had a life of her own. And God in His wisdom had given free will to mortals as a holy gift. Sophia was not using her gift prudently, but God still had His plan . . . Miss Trublood fell into a troubled sleep.

Misha and Mei Mei were dismayed when they heard the news. "Oh Sophia!" Misha breathed and snuffled, his eyes bulging greatly. "What would your mother and father have said? And my lady, your grandmother?"

There was such upset in his voice that Sophia bit her lip. Mei Mei's eyes filled with tears. "He must marry you!" Mei Mei declared in ringing tones. "He make honorable woman out of you!"

Misha grunted agreement.

"He will," Sophia said. "Of course he will. We can get married quietly and no one will ever know. Just a baby a bit prematurely. Happens all the time, doesn't it?"

"No." Misha frowned. "Girls from good families wait to get married, like Elena."

"Oh Misha! I'm going upstairs. It is too horrid of you to make a fuss!" Sophia flounced out, leaving Misha gazing mournfully at Mei Mei.

"I feel I've let Countess Anna down, and Sophia's parents. I think I haven't made enough of a fuss. Not early enough, anyway."

Mei Mei hugged him. "What can you do?" she said simply. "Missie Sophia determined girl. You had no choice."

"But we have a choice." Misha took her hand. "You will marry me, won't you, Mei Mei?"

"Of course, silly." Mei Mei grinned. "I don't want twelve little children and no husband."

"Twelve?" squeaked Misha. "What about one? Just one. A little girl."

"We see." Mei Mei tweaked Misha's nose and ran off down the hall into the garden.

Sophia heard the laughter on her way to her room. She passed Miss Trublood's door but the light was out. Elena's room was empty, of course. In her own room she looked out of the window. She hadn't felt hungry so she did not have dinner. Now she felt faintly sick. She looked out at the street below. She heard bells ringing and gongs thumping. Priests and beggars still thronged the highway. Here she was, towering over them in this big house protected by unusual amounts of glass. And she was carrying a child. Thank God she was privileged and pregnant, and not just pregnant. How awful to be one of the many young girls pregnant in the bamboo hovels. At least her baby would be born safely in the German hospital. She knew the hospital. It had tall barrack-like walls. It looked more of a prison than a hospital, but it was clean and safe. And then she would walk up these stairs with a bundle of a baby in her arms. A baby of her own to kiss and to dress in lovely outfits.

She began to smile. Though she had lost her twin, she would have something of her own. Someone to love, a child she could watch grow up and flower into something spectacular. Maybe she was not destined after all to be the Snow Leopard but a simple wife and mother instead. Maybe her baby would take her place. A Snow Leopard could be either a boy or a girl . . . She opened the window and leaned far out into the Shanghai scented night. I'll send Ah Ling out to buy a bowl of stir-fried peas. Or perhaps he has a jar of pickles. She laughed. I must be pregnant, she thought. I would kill for a dill pickle.

❦ *CHAPTER 55* ❦

Sophia lay in Elter's arms, her face pressed close to his flat stomach. She breathed in the warm familiar smell of him, half his own spicy body-smell and half his cologne, which he ordered from Hamburg in heavy thick crystal bottles that stood on his night-table beside his dressing-case and his silver-backed hair-brushes. Why she was thinking about these items she did not know, but she was struggling to tell the man she loved that she was pregnant by him and feared his disapproval. "I think, Elter . . ." she said, closing her eyes. "I am dreadfully sorry, but I think I'm pregnant."

She felt his body stiffen, the muscles of his stomach grow taut. He put his hand under her chin and turned her face to his. "Are you sure?" His voice was soft and concerned.

She nodded. "Sure."

Elter flopped against the bed and stared blankly at the ceiling. Damn, he thought, and unprotected only that one time. What awful luck. "Never mind, *Puppchen.*" He stroked her smooth dark hair. "I'll just have to plan a little faster."

"Plan what?"

"Never you mind. Don't worry your lovely head about it. Do you want me to be with you when you tell Edward?"

"No, I can tell them. I've told Miss Trublood and Misha and Mei Mei." Sophia sighed. "Edward already thinks of me as a rebel. I doubt he'll be very surprised."

Elter smiled. "Don't worry," he said again. "I will have to make an honest woman of you. When the time comes, I will tell you of my plan. But until then," he put his finger to his lips, "don't say anything to anyone else."

More than ever, Sophia felt an intense love for this man. "I won't. Edward and Elena will be back by the weekend. They're the only other people who need know about the baby."

Charlie knew. So did Chu Wing. Charlie paid the undercook in Edward's house to listen at doors. He overheard Mei Mei and Misha talking. It was his job to report what he heard. He did very well out of the transaction and spent all the profit in a whore-house in Shanghai.

This was not the first time Elter had fathered a child, but it was the first time he wanted to make the child legitimate. He drove Sophia back to her house and opened the door to let her out of the car. "Take care, darling," he said as he kissed her goodbye. The kiss was long and loving.

It rather startled Sophia. She hugged the tall figure and then she patted her stomach. "I'll take care of him for you," she said.

Elter smiled. "I hope it's a her. I would like a little girl who looked just like you."

Sophia laughed. "Well, I want a boy. Maybe we can have twins, one for me and one for you."

"Off you go now." Elter patted Sophia's bottom playfully. "I'll telephone you tonight. I have some arrangements to make."

Sophia waved from the doorstep and watched as his long gleaming Bugatti roared off into the night. "Goodbye, my darling." She wandered happily into the house. Maybe getting pregnant wasn't such an awful fate after all. Maybe everything would turn out all right and she could be, at last, Frau Betzelheim.

Edward, returned from the honeymoon, was very shocked when, at dinner, Sophia announced she was pregnant. Before marrying Elena, Edward had had several love-affairs, but they were with women known to be loose. Ladies from the Russian ballet. Women who were experienced and therefore had methods of protecting themselves. He had never considered making love to Elena until she was his bride. He had grown used to his role as guardian of both girls and here he was, faced with a beaming Sophia obviously very proud of her new condition. Indeed he felt a little outraged that both he and

Elena had exercised self-restraint and Christian abstinence until after their marriage, and Sophia had exercised no control at all. Elena would have had every right to be pregnant in her married state, but Sophia was the pregnant one and showed no sign of remorse. "I really don't know what to say." Edward stared at Sophia. Why must the infernal girl always ruin a perfectly good meal with such bad news?

Elena, knowing how Edward felt about his dinner, tried a delaying tactic. "Shall we discuss this matter after dinner in the drawing-room over a nice cup of coffee? Edward, I've ordered a simply marvelous brandy for you."

"I think I'd prefer a shot of whisky." He would not let the matter drop that easily. "Well, Sophia, since you are determined to ruin my dinner, we might as well discuss the matter now and then I can at least have my coffee in peace. I suppose the chap is going to insist on discussing it with me?"

"He's not a chap, Edward; he's Elter. And we're going to get married."

"I should think so, too. Good heavens! What on earth do you expect the rest of Shanghai will say?"

"Truthfully, it doesn't concern me. I'm happy to be pregnant with Elter's child."

"Couldn't you have been married first, like everybody else?"

"I'm not everybody else, Edward. I'm . . ."

"I know, I know," Edward said mournfully. "You don't have to remind me. And where, by the way, is the fellow now?"

"He's gone on a trip down the coast. He'll be back next week and then he'll come to pay a call."

"Fine." Edward turned away. "In that case, we don't have to talk about this any more for the time being, do we?"

"No, of course not, darling," Elena soothed him. "Sophia and I can talk later. It's women's talk."

"Quite," he grumbled. "Quite." He missed Jaggers dreadfully. How women could spend hours discussing unsavory gynecological details always baffled him. Now take Jaggers. You could discuss the finer points of shooting with him for hours. Edward wished he was still out at sea. He wished he was in the saloon drinking champagne with his wife. He wished he was anywhere except in this house with Sophia. At least, Edward consoled himself, if the cad marries Sophia he can take her back to Germany. The thought comforted him enough to keep him in fairly good spirits until bedtime.

In bed Elena looked dolefully at him from under her cloud of fair hair. "Why is it Sophia's pregnant and I'm not?" she asked.

Edward did not like the question. "It isn't for want of trying, my dear," he reminded her.

"It's not fair." She slid down the bed. "Sophia breaks all the rules and gets pregnant; I obey them all and I don't."

"Life isn't fair," said Edward ruefully. He stretched out his arms and pulled Elena close to him. "We can have the most glorious time trying."

Elena smiled.

CHAPTER 56

The junk was tacking upwind, having left Wen Chow on her final journey back toward Shanghai. She was loaded down with opium, but the right port authorities had been paid sufficient money to let her pass unapprehended. Elter prowled nervously on the deck. So far so good, he calmed himself with a cliché. He had fulfilled his quota, and the rest he had hidden in the false bulkheads. As far as he knew no one had any reason to suspect him of withholding any of the drug. Now that Sophia was carrying his child he needed to accelerate his plans and take her to safety, and safety must mean out of China and home to Germany. He wanted his child born on German soil. Who knows what could happen in China? Elter knew of the increasing insurrection in the north of China already nudging its way southward, aided by the Russian communists. It was time to go home, taking his bride with him.

He gazed into the dense fog that surrounded the junk, his ears straining for the sound of pirates or of a boat creeping up on him. He felt so near to his objective but so far from Sophia. At midnight he went to his cabin. "Take over," he motioned to his small crew. "You," he said to a newcomer with the slashed face of a man used to violence and to drink, "you navigate."

The man smiled, his crooked teeth visible in the light of the lantern that hung beside the chart table. "I sail," the man said.

Elter felt uneasy. He had picked the man up two trips before. He was a competent seaman and an excellent navigator. Good navigators were getting rare . . . Still he unsettled Elter.

Elter lay down and closed his eyes, only to open them a few hours later. To his horror he was staring into One-Eyed Charlie's face. Elter lay still. A shard of ice seemed to stab his heart. He thought quickly. Charlie must know about the stash. My God, he thought, the new navigator. Of course. A plant. Why had he not suspected? Too late, far too late. Elter knew, without a word exchanged, that he was to die. "Well well," he said as pleasantly as he could. "Can you tell me, Charlie, old friend, why I have the honor of this visit so late at night?"

Charlie chuckled. "Maybe you tell me, Elter, old friend."

Elter got up.

Charlie stepped back and bowed. "At least," he said, "you haven't betrayed us by short-changing us."

"No. Nor would I," Elter said. "I took my vows and I am a man of honor."

"But you have been running your own business on the side." He shook his head as if grieved. "What I have to do," said Charlie, "is not what I would wish to do."

"I know. Charlie, I have one request to make."

"Ask."

"May I send a letter?"

Charlie nodded. "We have plans for her, as you know."

Elter breathed deeply. "I know. Mine were better."

"She will be taken care of well," he said with a shrug. "Go and write your letter. I will wait for you on deck."

Elter went to his writing-desk. There, as usual, lay his own writing-paper, the heavy gray sheets beside the wide thick envelopes. He dipped his pen into the ink and began to write.

> *Darling,*
> *A man will give you this letter. Do as he tells you. By the time you read this I will be dead. I tried to get us out and to take you with me to Germany. It is not to be. When you get this letter tell no one. Let them think I have disappeared. It is important for you to know that I planned to marry you. Take care of our child.*

Death, which for him had been a matter of indifference, was now an awful reality. Having found love after all these years, he was about to lose his life.

Elter straightened his shoulders. Death, he reminded himself, must be faced with honor.

He trailed his signature across the bottom, slipped the letter into the envelope, and walked out onto the deck of his junk. Charlie was waiting. Behind him sat Chu Wing. Chu looked impassively into the night. Elter approached Charlie and put the letter in his hand. "See she gets it," he said.

Charlie tilted his head in affirmation. Elter took off his coat and unbuttoned his collar. He looked about the ship and felt the wind lift his hair. On the deck stood a lone wooden block. Elter bent his knees and leaned his head forward. Charlie was mercifully swift.

Elter's head hit the deck with a whump. Chu spat. Charlie looked down at Elter's body. "He could have had her, and his life too. What a fool." He walked away and motioned the navigator to tidy up. "Throw him over," he said. "The sharks will do the rest." The navigator grinned.

Charlie escorted Chu off the junk and onto the launch that had brought them from shore. "She will get the letter?"

"She will," Charlie said.

"Good. She is ready to be initiated. Let her get over the shock first."

"OK."

Chu was going home. He had a new concubine to play with. Charlie saw him to the shore and then returned to the junk to see to the unloading of the stashed opium. On the way back he watched the last of the blood being mopped from the deck. Such a pity, he thought. I liked the fellow. I need a drink.

He walked to the junk's dining-room and poured himself a shot of whisky. Good stuff, he thought, swallowing. The man had admirable taste, both in women and in whisky. Well, he was dead now, all his troubles over. Charlie poured a second. His own weren't over, he thought. Not by a long way.

❦ CHAPTER 57 ❦

"I feel guilty about involving Sophia." Maria sat on the floor beside the Gorgon's pallet. The last of the summer sun cast shadows across her face.

The Gorgon, his cowl hanging loosely down his back, raised his palms. The palms were flat, the color of dust. They reminded Maria of two deserts thirsting for water. "The man brought it upon himself. He took his oaths and he broke them. No one did anything to him that he did not invite upon himself. This is the law of karma. Now he returns to another revolution on the endless wheel of death and birth." The Gorgon shook his head. He was at times very tired of the human condition.

"But," Maria pleaded, "what about Sophia?"

Lau Tchi paused. "She must know the way of suffering."

"She already does," Maria reminded him. "She lost her parents and her grandmother."

"No." The Gorgon shook his head like a very old tortoise. "You see things with a Western mind. We have no parents. We are born alone and we die alone. You were created in a void. The Western mind is still very young. It fears the void. The Eastern mind is very, very old. The Eastern mind, like the African, can accept the idea of nothingness. This is too simple, and yet too complicated, for the Western mind that wants to think of eternity in a material sense: God as man. You want to think of Sophia as a person who is going to suffer because her lover is dead. I don't think of her that way."

"How do you think of her then? She's lost her lover, and she's carrying his baby . . ."

"Not *his* baby," the Gorgon corrected patiently. "A baby. A new being."

Maria straightened her back. "Oh dear," she said, "it's all so difficult. When I am here with you I can understand what you're saying. But then I get out there and other thoughts crowd into my mind."

"I know, but you must find Sophia and bring her to me."

"Will you tell her?"

"I will. I have a letter for her."

"I hope she can forgive me." Maria looked anxiously at Lau Tchi.

Lau answered with an upward movement of his chin. "To understand is to forgive. There is much change coming. A huge upheaval. Do you want to see?"

"You mean we are going to do a reading?"

"For you it is good to catch a glimpse of the future. Come. Sit straight and I will sit beside you." The old man climbed off his cot and settled himself beside Maria. Just sitting next to him, she felt the brittleness of his form, yet also the enormous power and vibrant energy in him. Lau Tchi closed his eyes. Maria for a moment gazed sideways at the stony-featured face. His eyelids were so thin it was as if the eyeballs radiated through them. His nose beaked over a small wispy moustache and the firm lips were sealed. She could hear him draw air through his flared nostrils. Maria too now felt ready to concentrate. She loved looking forward. "To the song of the turtle," he said, just as he had when they first met. "Listen to the song of the turtle and hear what she says." Maria drew in the breath of the moment. "You are only the air that you breathe through your nose. Your body is an unwieldy envelope filled only with breath. Cut off the breath, and you are a sack ready to rot." Sitting beside this man who had so changed her life, Maria breathed in, out. Slowly their inhalations synchronized. In, out. The silence increased around them. The sounds outside the house died away. Far, far away. The two of them became weightless and left the floor.

The hermit put his hand in Maria's. His touch was firm, and she pulsated with him. Both rose higher and higher until they cleared the roof of the house. Maria could see the tiles as they flew upward and then on into the future. There, ahead, Maria saw fighting. Chinese against Chinese. She saw one face shining above all others. Maria gasped. This face she realized was one that she would come to love in the future. It was a broad face with brown laughing eyes, shining with intelligence. The mouth was generous. This was the face of the future of China. She half-recognized the face . . .

And then, abruptly, the turtle ceased to sing and they were back sitting on the floor, breathing together. Slowly the hermit opened his eyes. "Much trouble to come," he said simply, "but good trouble. Much much change."

"Will we be safe?" Maria opened her eyes.

Lau Tchi smiled. "No one is ever safe," he said. "Safety is an illusion. Some will try to live safe, but we are not born to be safe. We are born to our destiny."

"Who was that man I saw?"

Lau Tchi grinned. "What man?"

Maria said, "You won't tell me, will you?"

"I do not interfere with your karma," he said. "Now you must go and get Sophia and I will talk to her."

"And break her heart?"

"No. Sophia is a strong woman and she has much ahead of her. She will survive. I have faith in her."

"I'm dreading this visit."

"You have nothing to dread. Simply go and get her. I will tell her."

Maria got stiffly off the floor and stretched. She walked out of the house and climbed into her car.

She drove reluctantly to Sophia's house and rang the bell. She heard footsteps coming down the hall.

"Oh, it's you." Miss Trublood smiled at Maria. "I'm just on my way out to the mission. I guess you've come to visit Sophia?"

Maria nodded dumbly.

"You all right, honey? You don't look too good."

"I'm all right. Just a cold. Maybe a touch of flu."

Miss Trublood hurried off down the road. These young people, she thought as she walked the long road to the mission. They don't take care of themselves nowadays.

CHAPTER 58

"Maria, you look awful. What's the matter?"

"I've been sent to get you by Lau Tchi. He wants to see you."

"Maybe he might be able to tell me where Elter is. I've been leaving messages for him all over the place. He seems to have disappeared again. I don't know where he goes, but he's gone. He's probably back in Germany on business." Sophia smiled at Maria. "Cheer up," she said.

"I'm just not feeling well. Hurry up. Let's get going."

All through the city Maria was silent. Inwardly she was as worried for Sophia as she was sad. She had grown very fond of Sophia in the years that she had known her. She desperately wanted Sophia to remain her friend. She felt enormously guilty that she had kept secrets from her, but of course she had to think about herself. Shanghai, and the future of Shanghai, was her destiny. If nothing else, she had to make a living. At least working for the Gorgon and for Chu Wing she could retain a measure of dignity.

If she must betray Sophia, she could rationalize that it was for a good cause. China was in the throes of an upheaval. The Japanese, since the end of the Great War, controlled the German concession in Shanghai, and the Japanese army clearly had intentions for Manchuria, if not for all of China. If the Americans ever managed to drive the

Japanese out, the next fear was that China would then become Westernized and adopt the ways of the foreign barbarians. More and more, the Chinese wanted China for themselves, as their current efforts to be a republic demonstrated. They were tired of the hordes of invaders who for centuries had overrun the country and made slaves of its people and plundered its treasures. Boat after boat left Shanghai loaded to the gunnels with the inheritance of the Chinese people. Chinese laborers had been massacred in the American West. Thousands of Chinese looking for a better life had been burned, strangled, maimed and killed by the indignant inhabitants of America. The Chinese were willing to work long hours for low pay, and the other immigrants hated them for it.

Slowly the stream out of China reversed and they flooded back again, returning to the land of their ancestors, to their old ways, to their spiritual heritage. But in the fight against the overwhelming influence of foreigners—an influence and an interference welcomed and encouraged by the Empress Dowager herself—the young republic now could be bloody and brutal in pursuit of its vision of a China for the Chinese. Maria knew all this and she was willing to fight for her new homeland in any way she could. But what of Sophia?

"I'll just drop you off," she said to Sophia. "He wants to talk to you on your own. But I'll be waiting outside." As they drew up, she leaned over and kissed Sophia on her cheek. "Darling," she said, "listen carefully to what he has to say. He's centuries old, you know."

"Do you honestly believe that?"

"Yes, I do. He's an ancient soul."

Sophia grinned. "And I am a very new soul," she said. "He told me that last time."

"Yes, that's true. I think Rollo is the only old soul among the rest of us."

Sophia smiled. "See you later," she said and Maria watched her as she walked confidently toward the front door.

"I haven't seen you for several years now." Lau Tchi was still sitting cross-legged on the floor. Hours had elapsed since he had sat with Maria, but those hours counted for nothing with the hermit. His time was not linear, nor did he wish it to be. "Come and sit." He patted the floor. Sophia sat down and crossed her legs. "Are you comfortable?"

"Yes." Sophia smiled. "Thank you." She wondered if the hermit knew she was pregnant.

"Of course I do," he answered her thought. "After a while one does not need words. You see," he observed, addressing Sophia's sense of surprise. "I notice you are surprised, not because you look surprised," he answered, "but you feel surprised. I can feel the baby within you. But we have more important things to talk about. I need you to go on a journey of understanding. It is a long journey and not the first in your life. You will go back in time and meet . . . Well," he said, "you will see for yourself. For now, all feeling is to be suspended."

As he said those words, Sophia felt a great lightness lift her heart. "Look at me." The Gorgon had moved position and now sat in front of her. Face to face, they gazed at each other. His eyes stared straight into hers. "Watch my right hand," he said. Slowly his third finger curled over to meet his thumb and, the moment they met, Sophia slid through the crack in time and was hurled again into the past.

Back she flew, disembodied but aware. Layers of humanity peeled away and then there was a wide desert, endless miles of thick white sand. Camels and a baggage caravan lolloped through the dunes . . . Out of the sand rose the edifice, the pyramid with the black open doorway. Then she stood again before the eagle with the emerald eyes. "What do you see?" the hollow voice asked.

Sophia looked into the depths of the eagle's eyes. "I see something moving," she said breathlessly. "It's . . . It's . . ." She caught a glimpse of a face. "Elter," she said at last. "It's not him. Not his body, but it is Elter. Where is he?"

"He is beyond the world," the voice said. "He is an essence now, awaiting his next life."

A sadness crept upon Sophia. "You mean I will never see him again?" She felt the sorrow at a great distance.

"You will always see him again," the voice answered. "We are all eternal."

"Why has this happened to him?"

"He disobeyed his destiny." The voice returned into her thoughts. "He took human steps to protect you. He loved you more than his destiny. We are not born to love each other but to serve. To love is acceptable, but only after service. He forgot his lesson. He is an old soul, but he forgot. If we make errors we must bear the consequences."

Sophia nodded.

"You must go back now. You will feel human pain when you reach the other side, but you will have inhuman understanding. That will protect you. And, my child, one thing more."

"What is that?" Sophia felt very weary.

"Cling to your faith. Never let faith fall from your heart."

A feeling of cold dread surrounded her. She did not look forward to her return journey.

She re-entered the room and her body slowly. For a while she sat before the hermit trying to wrestle with the fact that she was going to have to accept that something awful had happened to Elter. She battled with an overpowering desire to disappear into a dark void rather than hear details of the events of the last few days. When Elter did not telephone, she had held an icy fear in abeyance. Her mind had refused to consider the possibility of anything horrible that would separate her from the only man she loved. Before meeting Elter, Sophia had remained a virgin not because she wanted to or because she felt she should remain a virgin. She had never met a man she loved enough to want to share his bed and his body, and to have his child. Even now, carrying his illegitimate offspring, she felt no shame.

Sitting in this room, she realized that she was to be cheated of her chance of happiness. "Is he really dead?" she heard herself ask.

Lau Tchi leaned forward. "Yes. But death is only another condition. Another illusion, as life is an illusion."

"Is all life an illusion?"

"It is. But it is an illusion we must take seriously." Sophia began to feel the pressure of long-held-back tears. "Let your human self cry now," Lau Tchi commanded. He put a hand on her knee. "Your eyes are rivers of sorrow and your body a cracked ravine. Feel my energy draw over you the tide, the waters of death and lamentation. Now, breathe in and out, as a tide."

Sophia felt the sobs blocked inside her chest dissolve. Indeed, she felt as if she had melted into sand and sea on the floor. She saw only gray now, with foam and flecks curling over her. "Breathe in time to the heartbeat of the ocean." His voice trickled into her mind like sand through fingers. Sophia experienced a booming sound inside her. She felt herself pushing, pushing, then she was dragged back, then forward. Soon her body found a rhythm and she grieved in harmony with the universe. Elter was dead. Elter had gone away. To where, she did not know. But he existed now without her, although she carried inside her a living reminder of what they shared together. All the tears of the world were reflected in the whirlpools of her eyes. After a while she could see reefs and shallows along the fringes of her eyelashes and then she heard the dry sobbing of her own voice.

She blinked and was back in the room sitting with Lau Tchi. He had pulled his hood over his face. He bowed toward her and placed an envelope beside Sophia's knee. "Take this and go," he said. "For three months you will be in much pain. Then the memory will fade." He looked at Sophia. "On this earth," he said, "we pay a high price for attachment. A very high price. Some say too high a price, and that nonattachment is the only way."

"Do you think it is?" Sophia asked.

The hermit gave a wintry smile. He jutted his chin. "You answer. Do you regret your love for the German?"

Sophia was silent for a moment. "No," she said, placing her hands protectively over her stomach. "No, I don't regret." She sighed a hiccoughing kind of sigh. "I feel as if I had known him for a thousand years."

"Indeed, you have, and you will know him for many lifetimes more. The wheel goes round, the wheel goes round."

Sophia folded her hands and bowed to Lau Tchi.

Once outside the door she put her head in her hands. She felt Maria's arms around her. "I'll read the letter when I get home," she said. "Oh Maria! Did you know?"

"Lau Tchi wanted to tell you himself."

"Do you know what happened? Why Elter died?"

"I do." Maria could no longer lie. "But let's go back to your house, where you can feel safe, and I will tell you the whole story." She looked down at the letter in Sophia's hand.

"Lau Tchi said to take it."

"Let's get you home and then we can talk."

The women drove away, leaving behind the Gorgon. He rose from the floor and walked to his bed. Lying down he crossed his hands over his chest and breathed deeply. His eyes rolled back, white in his head. The Gorgon was in the fabulous future of his beloved China. All was proceeding as it should. For a moment his attention focused upon the small figure of Sophia. She is doing well, he observed. She is a strong woman. And he smiled a benediction.

❧ CHAPTER 59 ❧

Miss Trublood, sitting in the drawing-room with her feet up on a foot-stool, heard the door open. "Yoo hoo, girls! I'm in here!" she called.

Sophia went straight up to her room but Maria ran into the drawing-room. "I've just brought Sophia home," she explained. "Elter's dead. Sophia's in an awful state . . ." Maria winced as she saw the shocked look on the older woman's face.

"Is there anything I can do?" Miss Trublood asked, caught off guard by such sudden news of death.

"I'm sure Sophia would be grateful if you organized a pot of tea for us. I expect Sophia will talk to you later. She's in a state of shock."

"I don't wonder," Miss Trublood muttered.

"God have mercy . . . Get along, Maria. You take care of her and I'll see to the tea."

"What on earth can have happened?" cried an incredulous Misha when Miss Trublood told him the news.

"Poor missie," Mei Mei wailed. "And she have a baby."

Misha's eyes filled with tears. "Poor Sophia."

"I take tea," Mei Mei answered. "Plenty sugar for shock. Misha, help me."

Miss Trublood bent her head in prayer for Elter's immortal soul.

The contents of Elter's letter wrung Sophia's heart. When Maria told her that Elter worked for Chu Wing, and one of Chu's plans was to employ Sophia, she was not hurt nor did she feel betrayed. "He may have believed that he was going to seduce me," Sophia said, "but I'm sure he didn't plan to fall in love with me." She sighed. "And if we hadn't fallen in love, he would still be alive. I feel so guilty. I loved him so much." She was again shaken with sobs, but without Lau Tchi to help her. She had never felt a pain so sharp. Her chest ached. She struggled to breathe. "I didn't know how much love can hurt," she said breathlessly.

Mei Mei arrived on soft feet and put the tray of tea down silently. She left the room, casting a horrified glance at Sophia's contorted face.

Maria was confused. Here she sat, partly confessing her guilt in knowing a great deal about Elter that she had never shared with Sophia. She felt treacherous. If she had told Sophia earlier, perhaps Sophia would have ignored Elter, and then this tragedy need never have happened. At the same time she realized that Sophia was in no fit condition to make sense of the day's events. Only time would give her an opportunity to fit the pieces of the jigsaw into place. "I think I should go now," Maria said, desperate for some time alone to think. "Do you want to see Miss Trublood? She's waiting."

"In a minute."

Maria put her arms around Sophia. "I know how awful you must feel," she said, remembering the moment after her abortion and the feeling that something in her had died, and then the death of a lover. Gravestones marking the years of her life. "I'm so sorry, Sophia."

Sophia clung to her. "Come and see me tomorrow," she said. "Although at the moment, I don't feel there'll ever be a tomorrow, just a long desolate night."

"Remember what you've been taught," Maria said firmly. "There will be a tomorrow. There will be your baby, and there will be an ever-after. I promise you that."

"Do you really?" Sophia stared with teary eyes.

"I do."

As Maria drove back to her little room in her car, she wondered why she could have been so sure. I don't feel I know anything about anything, she thought.

"Poor Sophia."

Rollo was silent. He and Vassily were sitting on

Maria's bed. "Poor woman. Poor Elter," Vassily said uneasily.

Rollo's face was gray. "Those men really mean business. We forget that. Do you still think Sophia will join?"

Maria brushed hair from her face with her hand. "I don't know. She's in absolute despair. We'll have to see."

"She can always go to England with Edward and Elena."

"Yes, I know she can. But somehow I don't think she will, any more than I can see you ever living in England again."

Rollo stretched. "I don't fit in there at all. If we get chucked out of here, I'm going to America. What would you do, Maria?"

"Oh, I have no idea. I think, having got Sophia into so much trouble without warning her, I'd probably stay with her, whatever she decides. Off you two go now. I'm worn out after today. I want to sleep everything away."

Sleep did not come easily, but finally Maria drifted off into a black hole.

Sophia sat alone in the dark, feeling an implacable loneliness. "Yes," Miss Trublood had comforted her, "we are all eternal. We are all potentially divine. It says so in the Bible." But, at the end of the day, theology failed to stop the pain of Elter's death and Miss Trublood found herself at a loss to ease Sophia's grief.

Sophia sat and reflected. It is the body, not the mind, that causes pain. Her mind accepted death as inevitable, but her body yearned for Elter, yearned for his touch, his hands, his chest pressed against her breasts; the amused look in his gray eyes when he was privately delighted by her; his fingers inside her; his mouth on her body. No amount of philosophizing was going to take that longing away. No dissertation on East and West could change the fact that the most important part of herself, her Elter self, was gone.

The image of Elter dead made her cover her face with her hands. She had taken in some of the explanations given by Maria. Elter had been trying to get her out, to save her and the baby, and to get out himself. He knew the risks he was taking. She was already at risk before they met. Chu Wing had decided on her role in his operation. It was just a matter of time before she was drawn in. She in her own way had made herself vulnerable. Unlike Elena, who stuck rigidly to her class and her caste, Sophia had been out and about in Shanghai. Her friendship with Rollo, Vassily, and Maria, and her love for Elter made her an obvious target. Edward and Elena toed the line with good reason: by keeping themselves on a straight course they steered away from unknown dangers. But Sophia had let herself slip into the dark side of Shanghai. She had fallen through the crack. Chu Wing had seen the looks exchanged between Elter and Sophia, and, with sure instinct for a fly trapped in a web, had begun weaving his own web, then waited. Certainly he had not banked on Elter falling in love. Then Chu misunderstood their Western way of love. An Eastern attitude to love was quite dif-

ferent and not all-enveloping. In an odd way, Sophia felt she understood Lau Tchi's philosophy.
The Gorgon had taught her, as had her parents,
the concept of living for a higher self. Her parents
and her grandmother were prepared to die for the
Tsar and his family; more, for the Russia they
loved. Elter made the decision to die for her, and
now she had to make a decision about herself and
his baby. Tonight was not the night for such a decision. Tonight was a night to take a large
sleeping-draught and then to rest.

Drowsy from the drug, Sophia said her prayers.
Her eyes filled with tears as she prayed for Elter.
Even while she slept she wept. The night surrounded and held Sophia until morning broke. A
clean new day.

❧ CHAPTER 60 ❧

For three months Sophia was hardly human. She
felt in the grip of some tremendous force that paralyzed her mind and racked her body. Most of the
time she was in a dark fog which responded to
nothing at all. Very occasionally she caught a
glimpse of the world—a tree or a blade of grass—
but mostly she felt a blinding agony that seized her
throat and her lungs, and made her gasp. She saw
people talking to her, but their mouths made
empty sounds and meaningless grimaces. She pre-

tended to listen. She nodded politely in an attempt to convince them she was not mad. Food was a gritty substance she forced down her throat. Misha's face occasionally swam into view and Edward's concerned, uncomprehending blue eyes.

Elena felt restive and helpless. Edward was worried, as were Misha and Mei Mei. Together they would sit in a family conclave to discuss the woman who lay for hours on her bed upstairs. None of them was able to come up with any fruitful idea of how to help Sophia through her sorrow. If Sophia was not in a trance on the bed, she was staring out of her window. What they did not know was the sexual agony she suffered. To have known such love, such physical enchantment, and then to have this pleasure snatched away by death was itself a kind of dying. Sometimes Sophia felt her body throbbing and panting in a frenzy of loss. Walking was the only thing that helped. Often she let herself out of the house and walked for hours, for miles, until she was exhausted. Her only reality was the baby that slumbered in her womb, and when the baby did not sleep it kicked and moved. She talked to her baby. "It's all right," she said. "You'll be fine. I'm going to see that you have everything you want."

When she did surface for a few moments during those demented days, she planned for the child. Miss Trublood once made contact with Sophia by waving a small knitted jacket in her face. "Sophia," she said. "See? I made this for the baby."

Sophia smiled and nodded as Miss Trublood's face receded into the darkness.

The thing that finally saved her and brought her unwillingly back to life was Mozart's *Requiem*. She played that exalting hymn to life endlessly on the gramophone in her room. She would sit at the open window, breathing in the autumn air of Shanghai, and listen, her head bowed and her eyes filled with tears, to those angelic voices. The great composer knew he was to die and in this music he said his goodbye to the world that rebuffed him. He was lucky, she thought. Elter had no time for goodbyes, or celebration. He went into the boundless night alone but unafraid. Sophia was sure he had been unafraid.

Whatever she had seen or not seen when she had sat with the Gorgon, now she was unsure of what had taken place. A puzzling thought kept gnawing at her: why did Lau Tchi have a letter from Elter? Little burrs of worry floated past her eyes. What was Elter's death about? Who was the Gorgon and why had he come into her life? What connection did he have with Elter or Chu Wing so that he ended up with the letter? The more she thought about it, the more the mystery deepened. She knew Maria must have the answer, but for a long while Maria was absent. She was out of the city, away somewhere. Sophia felt a great nostalgia for Russia, for St. Petersburg, for any place but where she was now.

Elter's presence filled the house. She saw him in the drawing-room, his handsome face at the dining-table, his back in the corridor. Finally Edward and Elena decided that, instead of searching for a new home themselves, they should take a small place outside the city for Sophia. "The country air will do you good," they said. Sophia nodded a weary agreement. Misha and Mei Mei were only too happy to move with her, and Miss Trublood, who from the start had believed it best for her to spend her pregnancy at some distance from Shanghai, concurred wholeheartedly with the idea, and offered to oversee the running of the house.

The day Sophia moved into the country house was the day she recognized that there was no way of not living. She had no choice but to live: she was carrying Elter's baby. Without the baby she could have done away with herself and joined Elter on the other side. Surely she knew it was a sin even to contemplate suicide, but a large part of Sophia was greedy for the absence of pain. This experience, the death of Elter, had plunged her back into the pit of desolation, the hell of the death of her parents and her grandmother. Because she was young when they died and relatively untried, she had not mourned as she might have. The long journey and the new life in Shanghai had mitigated some of the agony, but the pain had lurked in the periphery of her life. Upon Elter's death, it pounced like a wild animal, claws and yellow fangs bared.

The day the car pulled away from the tall house in Shanghai, she breathed a sigh of relief. Now, she told herself and her baby, I must put the past behind me and live for my child. She put her hand on her stomach, still just a small mound under her blouse. The baby, feeling its mother's touch,

kicked lazily in affectionate response. Miss Trublood looked at Sophia. "You will be OK, won't
you?"

Sophia nodded. "I have to be all right."

"I guess so," Miss Trublood said. "You don't
have much choice."

Sophia looked up sharply. "What an odd thing
to say."

"Odd? No, it isn't. The Good Lord called your
name before you were born, Sophia, and He has
a plan for you."

"That's funny." Sophia frowned. "I know a Chinese monk who says just that."

"Sure you do. All religions spring from the
same source. The Good Lord, when He walked on
earth, would have read Buddhist literature, and
the Tao. Have you ever read the Tao?"

"No, I don't think so." She looked sideways at
the American woman. "Anyway, why would you
have read Chinese philosophy?"

"You think I'd come all the way to China without finding out what I was up against?" Miss Trublood smiled. "Here. Think about this," she said.
"What is the most important part of a wheel? The
spokes themselves or the spaces between the
spokes?"

Sophia considered the question. "I suppose the
spaces between the spokes."

"OK. How about a clay pitcher? The clay,
or . . ."

"Or the empty space in the middle of the
pitcher?" Sophia interrupted, catching on. "I'd
have to say, again, the empty space."

"Good," Miss Trublood laughed, watching the color return to Sophia's face. "That's the Tao. There's not such a difference as you'd think between East and West. Those Eastern paradoxes have their counterpart in Western doctrine—like when Jesus said, 'Blessed are the meek, for they shall inherit the earth.' And what's the Tao anyway? *Tao* means 'the way.' And what does Jesus call himself? 'I am the way, the truth, and the life.' Everybody has to follow the way, or they end up going nowhere. The problem is, lots of people are too dim and impatient to realize just how subtle their own Bible really is. Let an Eastern heathen chew on that!"

Outside the city the fields were beginning to settle down again, having been shorn of their crops. The land, still hedged with dense thickets, looked bald and browned. The summer had been unusually hot, but the late-autumn weather was agreeably warm. Chinese peasants raised their hands as the car went by. Misha and Mei Mei were waiting at the new house for Sophia to arrive.

So far Sophia had not seen the house. She had relied on Elena to sing the house's virtues, to describe the gardens and the waterfall that splashed in the courtyard. Elena told her that there was a tree in the garden, the famous *Prunus mume*, the Chinese plum-blossom tree. Elena promised how beautiful the tree would be when it bloomed in the spring. Sophia knew all about such trees. For centuries, poets and painters revered the five-petaled blooms, symbolizing purity, feminine beauty, solitude and endurance. Trying to give Sophia at least something to look forward to, Elena assured her that spring would follow the on-coming winter and the tree would flower.

Sophia found it hard to be enthusiastic about anything. Elter's death had robbed her of the man she loved and of the future she had hoped to share with him. All she had now was the promise of a rebirth in the baby she carried, and she knew for its sake she must pull herself together. Sometimes she remembered with a cold shiver that a summons would come, as implied in the letter she kept in her Bible. She would be called to do she knew not what. Maria had the answer, but Maria was nowhere to be found . . .

They turned the corner of a long lane and there was the house. The gates hung open and Mei Mei stood nervously in the doorway, wringing her hands. "Here she is, Misha!" she called. "I hope she like."

Misha laughed. "Of course she will, Mei Mei. It's as beautiful as a jewel."

"But she is city girl."

Misha put his arm around Mei Mei. "Don't worry. Sophia will soon make a life of her own." His eyes darkened as he watched the car pull up. "I do wish Miss Trublood didn't look so tired. Perhaps a rest in the country will do her good." The chauffeur hooted and Misha ran out to take the luggage.

Sophia stepped down from the car and looked about her. Elter would have loved this house, she thought. A catch in her throat made her cough. "How pretty it is here," she said.

Mei Mei nodded. "I show you round." Mei Mei led the way through the square hall and on into a courtyard.

There, as Elena had described, was the waterfall. Sophia stood, mesmerized by the sight of it. For a moment she could see each droplet separated from its like, each falling individually into the big stone basin. Every drop had a life of its own, she realized. But, together they also had an order. As she watched, she saw the Gorgon's face come through the glistening veil of water. He knows where I am, she thought. Strangely she felt comforted by this thought. Even if she had her doubts about this man, she found him central to her life. In the universe she inhabited, he seemed to be the only force with a wisdom that gave her confidence in a world where nothing was certain. Now she believed without question that always there would be the man who sat in his room with the bamboo growing in his garden, thinking about the world. Thought creates matter, he told her. Well, her thoughts did not seem to create matter. However hard she tried, she could not re-create Elter. He was gone for ever.

Before the blackness could engulf her, she wrenched her eyes away from the fountain and followed Mei Mei, who chattered cheerfully. Sophia's room was at the back of the villa. It was large and white. She had a big bathroom and a small sitting-room. Good, she thought, my own private suite. The room had French windows that opened onto another courtyard. This little courtyard had a sundial. A bed of white roses perfumed the air and tobacco plants and night-stock released their twilight fragrance. "Dinner served at eight o'clock," Mei Mei added as she closed the door, leaving Sophia alone.

"Well, my baby," Sophia said, her hands on her stomach, "if we must continue to live, this is certainly a lovely place to have as a home." She wandered out into the courtyard. Standing in the evening shadows, she breathed in the scent of the flowers. "We will be happy again," she said. "It'll take time, but soon you'll be with me and when I hold you in my arms you'll remind me of him." She looked up to the sky, wishing she could see Elter as a star. Maybe he's up there with Mother and Father and Grandmother, she thought.

The first star of evening looked down on the young woman who stood in the garden, her belly a small moon on her slim figure, and twinkled sympathetically. Sophia blinked and turned to change for dinner. One day she would understand more about this business; until then she must look after her child.

❧ CHAPTER 61 ❧

The birth was long and hard. Sophia heard herself pant and scream. "Nobody told me how awful this was going to be!" she cried.

Miss Trublood brushed away the hair that stuck

to her forehead. "You'll get through this," she said. "Here, sip some water."

The Chinese midwife hissed through her teeth. The doctor had been and gone. "She has a small pelvis," he had said, "but she is a fine, healthy young girl. I have no worries. Telephone me if she hasn't given birth by six this evening. The midwife is my best."

Elena walked with the doctor to the door. "Oh Edward," she said when she had seen the doctor out, "Sophia's having a hard time."

Edward sat glumly in a chair in the sitting-room. "My horses don't make this fuss. They just get on with it." He winced as he heard another ear-splitting shriek. "I can't sit here and listen to this. I'm going for a walk."

Elena patted his shoulder. "You go back to town. I'll telephone you when it's all over." She knew Misha was huddled in the kitchen. "Take Misha with you. He can go to the market and get me some fresh chicken and raspberry tea."

Edward called Misha and the two men shot out of the house. Elena smiled as she saw Edward grinning with relief. This weekend, she thought, we'll go away on the *Elizabeth*. Miss Trublood would look after Sophia. She hurried back into the fray.

She was relieved to find Sophia resting quietly on her pillows. "Not long now," the midwife comforted her. "You have a good big baby."

Sophia was weary. She felt the tiredness stealing over her, but above all she was lonely as only a woman can be, a woman who gives birth and bears the agony of delivery without her man at her side.

Not that Elter would have been with her. He was not the sort of man to brave a birthing chamber. Like Edward, he would have been happier to wait elsewhere until it was over. But she would have had him beside her once the baby was born; she would have seen his face light up and heard him exclaim with delight. All those joys should have been hers, but she had been denied them by whatever gods of fate were leering over her.

Two hours later the baby arrived. "A girl!" Elena cried out. "Oh Sophia! You have a beautiful little girl."

For a moment Sophia felt a stab of disappointment. She had so much wanted a son for Elter. But then she remembered Elter's face close to hers. He had wanted a daughter. "You have a daughter, Elter," she whispered, holding the child in her arms. She smiled at the three women at the end of her bed and Elena realized that Sophia was back in the world of the living. Miss Trublood wiped away a tear on her own cheek and the midwife grinned. The four women communed in celebration of this new wrinkled life that was crying lustily.

"Thank you, Lord!" Miss Trublood said loudly.

"Amen," Sophia replied, feeling bruised and sore all over. The pain of the birth faded beside the exhilaration she now felt. The baby rooted happily for a nipple and Sophia laughed.

"Come on, Elena," Miss Trublood said. "Let mother and baby have a rest. Anything I can get you, honey?"

"No." Sophia smiled. "I just need to lie still for

a while." Sliding down into the soft pillows, she held the baby in the crook of her arm. She's so perfect, she thought as the room emptied. Every bit of her is perfect. She held a small foot in her hand and gazed at the toes. Little mother of pearl nails gleamed and the leg kicked rapturously. What a miracle, she breathed. An absolute miracle.

❧ CHAPTER 62 ❧

The news of Sun Yat-sen's death in 1925 hardly touched the little community living quietly outside Shanghai. Sophia woke up one sunny spring morning and realized that she no longer grieved for Elter with the same aching sense of loss. He might be gone in body, but he still stared at Sophia through the eyes of the baby, whom she had named Maria. Even now at two years old, Maria had a fierce gaze. She looked as if she understood everything Sophia said. She seemed to reach out and grasp life in her small chubby hands. Sophia never thought she could love any living thing with such passion.

The christening had been a quiet affair. Rollo, Vassily, and Maria were the only guests, apart from the family, to attend. Maria was touched to find the child named after her and slowly the two women renewed their friendship.

Now Sophia found she enjoyed sailing on the *Elizabeth*. For Maria's second birthday a small tea-party was organized by Jaggers on board the ship. Jaggers had come to recognize that he was in love with Sophia, though his fears of clumsily imposing himself on her grief had made him hesitant to say anything. Baby Maria looked upon Jaggers as a constant companion when she was on the boat. They were inseparable. Something in the child's trusting innocence enchanted Jaggers, who missed his own boy.

However, a cloud hung over the whole party on that otherwise sunny day. Edward was more than ready to go home, but he and Elena had delayed their departure for England until Sophia was back on her feet again, before moving with the child to a completely new way of life.

Elena, in preparation for the trip, was reading the new writer E. F. Benson. "Is England really like this?" she asked Edward.

Edward stared over the bow of the ship. "For some," he said. "For us it will be. But there are many desperately poor people."

Sophia relaxed. She stretched out in a long deck-chair. "I do hope we can settle in England," she said. "I'm sure the climate won't be awfully good for Maria."

Elena laughed. "We'll settle and Maria will grow up to be a well-behaved little English girl."

Later on, as tea was cleared away, Jaggers found Sophia leaning over the stern of the boat. "Thank you, Jaggers," she said simply. "That was a lovely party. Maria really enjoyed herself."

Jaggers stood dumbly beside Sophia. "Sophia," he began, feeling suddenly very shy and awkward. He looked into those dark eyes that watched him steadily. "Sophia, now that Maria is, well . . . I mean, now that you have been on your own for quite a while, actually, what I am trying to say, Sophia, is will you . . . would you consider marrying me?" The last phrase came out in an explosive rush.

Sophia looked stunned. "I'm sorry, Jaggers. I didn't realize you felt this way about me." She reached out and took his hand, a rough seaman's hand, well used to manual work. It lay in Sophia's slim grasp. She turned his hand over and then she shook her head. "It's no good pretending, Jaggers. I'd make you a horrible wife. I honestly don't think I am marriageable. I like my own company too much. I've grown selfish over these last few years. I have my baby and my friends." She shrugged. "I'm just not ready to settle down. Besides"—she stared into the water—"I'm afraid of happiness. Once you've had it, and it's taken away from you, you don't trust it any more. My job is to take care of my baby, to bring her up, even in England. I don't much relish the thought of going there, but then I have to think of Maria."

Jaggers remained quiet. He felt deeply disappointed, but he also understood that, if she had agreed to marry him, he could never have made her happy. His farm in Hartland Point was as dear as his country to him. He thought of the long low farmhouse and the cow-barn at the back. He thought of the soft-nosed cows he raised. He knew that the idea of marrying Sophia and taking little Maria out to feed the ducks and the chickens must for ever be only a dream for him. He simply could not see Sophia as a farmer's wife. He could not envision her wearing a pinafore and sitting by the stream that ran outside the farm door, cutting vegetables. He could not afford the army of servants that she was accustomed to . . . No, she would have to live with Edward at the Monastery. There she could have one of the cottages on the estate and no doubt Edward's old Nanny Boots would be on hand to tend to Maria. She would have a gardener and a maid. Her lovely hands would stay for ever soft and clean. He looked out to sea. "Forgive me for asking," he finally said. "I can't believe you're unmarriageable, but honestly I'll never be able to offer you the sort of life that would make you happy."

"I don't think anybody can," Sophia interrupted. "There was only one Elter, and he's dead. Look." Sophia pointed to the sun. "The sun's over the yardarm. Let's get a drink."

Jaggers laughed a soft embarrassed laugh. "I'll be along for whisky in a minute. I must go below."

Sophia walked quietly back to the saloon, where Elena was playing with the baby. "Jaggers just proposed to me."

"Did he? What did you say?"

Sophia grimaced. "There's nothing to say. I could never make him happy, could I?"

"I don't know." Elena picked up Maria and sat her on her lap. "He would love you. You could be sure of that."

"Yes, but I . . . I still miss Elter. And truthfully I don't think I'll ever meet anyone I can love as much as I loved him." The baby stretched out her arms and Sophia reached forward and hugged her. She walked to the window holding the warm body close. "I'm so lucky," she said, "so very lucky to have you." Maria smiled at her mother. Her eyes beamed with pleasure. "You're just like him," Sophia said.

Later that night, alone in her own room at home, Sophia watched Maria asleep in her cot. How wonderful to be a baby, Sophia thought. To lie sprawled in sleep, little fists curled over thumbs. Maria was breathing fast and lightly, her tiny flared nostrils moving in and out.

For a long time Sophia had stayed away from her tarot cards. Now they sat in her top drawer among her scarves and gloves. She felt the irresistible urge to read them, but still she hesitated.

Don't be so silly, she told herself. They're just a pack of cards.

You're afraid of them, her other voice said.

When Rollo or Vassily visited with Maria—who was now called Aunt Maria—Sophia avoided all talk of the Gorgon. She even refrained from asking about her letter from Elter. How did the Gorgon come to have it? Why did he have it? No, those things were better left in the past. Sometimes she fancied Maria looked at her with a question on her face, but Sophia shrugged off that impression. She was not going to allow the past to interfere with her future. From now on, for the sake of Elter's child, Sophia was going to be a respectable matron. When she got to England she would wear a wedding-ring on her finger and put out the story that her husband had been killed by the Japanese in an attack on a Manchurian outpost. Her child must not know of her illegitimacy . . .

Do the cards, the voice commanded.

Oh very well, Sophia agreed. The night was warm and Sophia opened the French windows onto the courtyard. It was a night filled with the hootings of owls. She could hear their feathery flight. Sophia loved owls. There was a white owl that frequently visited her courtyard and sat self-importantly on the back wall and stared at Sophia with his big round eyes above a small imperious beak. Tonight he was there as usual. "Hoot," he said conversationally.

"Hoot, yourself," Sophia replied. She moved back into her room and sat down on the floor. "To cover and to cross," she recited, laying out the cards. "Above and below. Four more cards. And then an answer to the question. All right. Let's see what the future has in store for me . . . Damn!" she gasped. The Tower, the Hanged Man, and . . . Sure enough she looked down at the card that was to answer her question. Staring up at her was the Hermit. The card in her hand dissolved and she was once again sitting in the hermit Lau Tchi's room, staring into the shadows of a face hidden by a cowl. This time, though, he was very far away. His eyes were rolled back and his body perfectly still. The room was dank and clammy. Sophia felt an absolutely terrifying moment of panic. I must get out of here, she thought. I must get back to my home and my baby. She felt lost, as if locked in this room with a man holding her against her will. She pinched herself hard and then relaxed. She was back in her own room.

Quickly she looked at Maria and then she saw that the cards lay scattered on the floor around her. "I'm such a fool," she said aloud. "It's only a game." She gathered up the cards and put them tidily back into their box. Still she felt uneasy. If I can be drawn into a card, then I am better off without them, she thought. She found a box of matches and put the cards in the grate in her fireplace. She set light to the box and watched the cards curl and twitch in the bright flames. For a moment she was transfixed as the Hanged Man seemed to loom out of the fireplace. The flames swirled around his head as he hung, his long beak nose pointing accusingly at her, one glazed eye staring at her. "I'm coming for you," he said. Sophia shivered and went to close the French windows. She pulled the doors shut and drew the curtains, holding them together tightly.

"Don't be so damn silly, Sophia," she scolded. "They're only cards."

Maybe I should marry Jaggers and be a Dorset housewife, she thought as she climbed into bed. Wherever Dorset is. She lay for a while, her arms behind her head. Then she yawned. No, she knew she could never marry Jaggers. Elter's face hung over hers. "Good night, darling," she whispered and her eyes filled with tears. She wondered if the pain would ever go away.

The vigilant owl outside, aware there was another watching nearby, hooted a warning.

But Sophia misheard him. "Good night, owl," she murmured wearily.

❦ CHAPTER 63 ❦

Chu Wing was angry. "How much longer must we wait for this woman?" he said in his native Chinese.

Charlie was nervous. "It depends how you want to play it. I mean, if we seize her now, Sir Edward will have time to take action here. In fact he will have weeks to negotiate her release and he's very powerful among the foreign community. I would prefer to wait until they board the yacht, then ambush them. With the threat that they will all die if they do not give her up."

Chu circled his finger around a wart on his cheek. "We can leave an armed skeleton crew to sail with them to Hong Kong, or maybe even further. By that time it will be too late. They will have the baby. We will have the mother." Chu pinched his pendulous bottom lip. "Hum," he said. He sat back in his chair and contemplated his belly. "You know, Charlie, things are going to get a lot worse for those of us who have worked so hard for our empires. The bald-headed peasants in the north are out to get rid of the likes of you and me." He shook his head. "I know many of the warlords are fighting with them, but I don't give a pig's fart about war. Or about the Japanese. I just want to keep what I have. Maybe we should start thinking about getting some of our money out of China and bury it in America or Taiwan.

"You see"—he leaned forward—"this is why we need that woman. We need a high-class woman who can get the ear of that new American general. If she can become his mistress, then she can hear pillow-talk. The trouble with the women we already employ is that they have reputations and the police can check them out. Take Maria, she has a police record as long as your arm for prostitution, here and back in Russia, which is why she had to leave in the first place. And if this American general is at all careful—and the Americans are—he would refuse her. Sophia has no such reputation. She will have no family, and she will have taken the oath under your direction. With her help we can keep our ear to the ground and know when the time is right to move. It may be ten years or even twenty years ahead of us. But one day we will have to move, and move fast if we are to escape with our lives.

"In the meantime, there's good business to be done, with the American's help. That rebel Mao Tse-tung threatens to reduce this country to a land of peasants. He intends to do away with opium, with prostitution, and with privilege. Where would we be then? Answer me that!" Chu's voice rose. "I would lose everything I own. Can you imagine Chu Wing having to work with his hands?'' He gazed at his left hand. The little finger had a full two inches of carefully tended nail. The fact that he could allow his nail to grow so long denoted that Chu thought of himself as a scholar, like an old-style mandarin. "Oh no, no, no, we must be out by then. If the communists ever win, Chiang Kai-shek will go into exile and I'll go with him. What would you do, Charlie?''

Charlie shrugged uneasily. He was not looking forward to grabbing Sophia and taking her off the yacht. He had been following her for some time. Stalking was usually a great pleasure for Charlie. He found something akin to sexual satisfaction in bearing down on a prey. The prey, not realizing that he or she was being followed and watched, usually did something intimate, like lifting a skirt. If a man, maybe he would put his hand down his trousers and scratch his scrotum. Charlie enjoyed those moments that should have been private. Following Sophia, he got none of this satisfaction. Indeed, when he watched her from the back of the courtyard, she had raised her eyes from the deck of cards she had dealt out on the floor, and for a moment he thought she could see him. Her big dark eyes held not only pain but also anger, a fierce hot anger that he knew was directed against the person who had taken her lover's life. That person, he further knew, must fear her revenge. Charlie was an expert in human instincts, and at that moment he had felt a stab of fear. Sophia was capable of killing, he could tell from her eyes. That was one of the reasons Chu wanted her so badly. But she would not kill to order. Oh no. Sophia

would kill only those who hurt her or hurt someone she loved. Charlie was already guilty. And
when he took her from the yacht, that would be
his second crime. Twice guilty, he had no choice
but to look behind him and to sleep with his eye
open and add her to the list of the people who
wanted him dead. He sighed. "Maybe I'll go to
Japan and sit in a little bamboo house and put my
feet in the water and catch carp. At least it would
be a quiet life."

Chu laughed. "Yes," he said, "perhaps some
day you will sit by your pond and fret over your
next line of haiku. But now let's get on with the
plan to board the *Elizabeth*. I like it. It'll work."

"You can smile," Charlie said, "you don't have
to do it yourself."

"I know," Chu said gleefully. "That's what's so
nice about being the boss. Mind you"—he gazed
at Charlie—"I remember some boarding-parties
in my time as an Enforcer."

"I bet you do." Charlie grinned.

"They used to be fun. Dead bodies everywhere.
Now everything is so much more *civilized*." He
raised his nostrils as if sniffing something distaste-
ful. "I must practice my English accent. *I say, old
stick, we come for your ward.*"

Charlie laughed. "Not bad for a scrimshank."

"But hurry, Charlie. I must go. My wife and
daughters are waiting to go to the opera. Oh, that
opera. I say women go only to show off their new
clothes."

Charlie heard Chu's powerful car drive away. A
cold fear entered his soul. I wish I did not have

to tackle this woman, he thought. In Charlie's life men were no problem. Men lived and died according to rules. But women? He shook his head. You never knew where you were with women. They made their own rules, most of which men never came close to understanding. Charlie shuddered. A man who was the nearest thing he ever had to a friend had been killed by his own wife, of all people. She told the court that he beat her and abused her. She was let off and the truth of the matter never came to light: she killed him because he was going to leave her for another woman. Charlie remembered his young dying face. The knife wound in the neck was patched. But he remembered the blood that hit the ceiling, and remembered his friend on the floor. "Why did she do it?" his friend whispered as the light drained away from his eyes.

"I wish I knew," Charlie answered . . .

He shook himself. You're getting morbid in your old age, he scolded himself. What you need is a long night with a tall bottle.

❧ CHAPTER 64 ❧

Misha, upset and worried, stared at Sophia. Now he was a married man. It had been a small family ceremony overseen by a pastor at Miss Trublood's mission and Miss Trublood was delighted to see two new Christian souls united before the God they had vowed to serve. Edward, acting as best man, had towered over the bride and groom. Now happily bound to Mei Mei, Misha more than ever wanted to move out of Shanghai and begin his married life in the north of China. Mei Mei had a big family in Shintu, high in the mountains. The climate there was temperate and the soil good. Misha longed to be close to the earth, to grow his own produce. And now that Sophia and Elena were going to England, he felt he could let them go and enjoy life on his own. Still he loved them, and he treasured the little toddler Maria as well. How fierce the child was and how like her mother! Sophia, during these years of child-rearing, had softened. He could see curves in her body that had not been there before and her face was relaxed.

She stood before him holding the child in her arms. He watched her as she gently kissed the top of Maria's head. The baby, laughing, put her hands around her mother's neck. "I do hope we like England," Sophia sighed. "I can't help feeling it's nothing but a land of mists and rain."

Misha laughed. "But you will have London and you will be near Europe."

"It's for the best, I suppose. And of course Maria will be able to go to good schools, but I still wonder." Sophia shook her head. "China is in my blood. I love it here. England seems the other side of the world, so far away, I just can't imagine being there."

All around her were boxes. A virtual army of coolies had invaded the house. They squatted conscientiously over their task: each plate and each glass was wrapped in straw and reverently put into packing-cases. These packing-cases were a symbol of the European invasion of China. The most precious objects of art, priceless linen, gold, silver, and paintings had found their way into tea-chests which then traveled by rail or by mule across the country to the great seaports and from there were shipped to distant parts. In New York, London, Paris, and Amsterdam these chests were unpacked and the straw, redolent with the smell of China, was thrown away. In drawing-rooms and tea-rooms in the West a new China was re-created, in which repatriated foreigners would sit and talk of their life in the sun, and their eyes, creased from the years of living in the sun, would water as they recalled those days through a haze of nostalgic fondness. "Oh China!" they sighed. "Those were the days!" Those were the days indeed.

All this Sophia knew from reading E. F. Benson's books, borrowed from Elena. While Elena chuckled at the tongue-in-cheek humor, Sophia found nothing to laugh about. "Boring. Boring little people," she said.

Today she just wanted to curl up with her daughter and ignore all the packing. She hated the sight of her belongings disappearing into these boxes. They stood like coffins, she thought, in every room of the house. "Come along, Maria," she said, taking the child by the hand. "Let's go out for a walk."

She put the child into the high stately pram and pushed her down the long dusty road that ran alongside a stream. The autumn sun was melancholy. The fields and the trees were painted an orange-brown ochre. Everything seemed to hang limply. The fallen leaves rasped against each other as the pram's four big wheels ran over them. Maria sat up bright-eyed and talkative. "Mum mum mum," she recited.

"Who's my little girl?" Sophia cooed back. But inwardly Sophia felt a great sadness. How wrong it seemed that fate should have deprived this child of a father. And now, with Maria fatherless and her mother manless, they were leaving to start a new life in a country that Sophia regarded as more imaginary than real. It is for the best, she reminded herself. Once she was in England, nobody would have to know of her past.

She pushed on, and the road, empty of any human being, appeared an outward manifestation of Sophia's inner landscape, bleak and barren.

❧ CHAPTER 65 ❧

Jaggers and the cabin boy, Chung, stood waiting on the yacht, watching the shore. Jaggers was in a hurry to catch the night tide and Edward was late, which was unlike him. He knew the importance of going out on the tide. The river was shallow and if they did not leave within the hour a whole day would be wasted. Jaggers glanced impatiently at his watch.

Behind the yacht a sleek black junk was moored. One-Eyed Charlie had ten men crouched out of sight, the high walls of the junk hiding them from view. Chu, too, waited for Edward and his family to arrive.

Mentally Jaggers double-checked the bill of lading: one hundred and fifty boxes stored in the hull. In his head he visualized the course they would follow: south to Hong Kong, around the coast of Singapore, and then to Colombo, up the Red Sea, through the Suez Canal, west across the Mediterranean, and home. If the wind and weather were favorable, they might even make it there a few weeks before Christmas. Jaggers was eager, not just to get home, but to spend time with Sophia. Perhaps she would change her mind.

He relaxed. He saw in the distance the two cars bringing Edward, Elena, Sophia and the child. Good, they would get off in time.

Behind him Charlie hissed a hoarse order. "Ready!" he said. The men turned to their leader and grinned. Several of them carried knives in their teeth, pistols in their hands. The cars drew nearer and pulled up on the dock. The second car contained Miss Trublood—who was to remain with her mission in Shanghai—and Misha and Mei Mei, both very tearful. Misha bustled to help the chauffeur unload the car. Sophia knelt to embrace Mei Mei warmly. "Take care of yourselves," she said, "and I will write to you both." Mei Mei hugged the baby.

Miss Trublood kissed Sophia on the forehead and said, "Don't forget that the Lord is with you, and so are my thoughts. I'll come and visit you when I'm on leave."

"You must, Miss Trublood. And please look after yourself and don't work too hard. You're looking awfully tired." Sophia did not think she would be so upset at leaving this kindly woman.

"I'm just a foot-soldier in God's army." Miss Trublood laughed. "Just following orders."

"Hurry up!" Jaggers shouted. "We must be leaving." Sophia ran up the gangplank and Jaggers pushed the switch to raise it to the side of the vessel. Elena had been holding baby Maria while Sophia said her farewells.

It was Miss Trublood who saw the men first. From where she was standing, she saw what looked like a horde of bandits surge over the deck. "Look out!" she screamed. "Look out!"

Charlie tore through the commotion and grabbed Sophia. "Stand back!" he yelled. Both Jaggers and Edward were too stunned to move. Elena tried to run forward to Sophia, but Edward held her back.

"Don't move!" Charlie shouted. "If you do, I will kill her."

The baby in Elena's arms began to scream. Sophia stood still, her heart pounding with fear. The men took their positions on deck, their weapons drawn, the muzzles of their guns pointing at the hearts of their prisoners. From the dock Misha watched helplessly, the chauffeur beside him. Mei Mei had her hands over her eyes. She was weeping; she knew who these people were. "Chu's men!" she said hopelessly. "What they want with Missie Sophia?"

"Shh," Misha cautioned. "Shh." He knew how expendable they all were.

For a moment nobody moved and then Charlie dragged Sophia past Jaggers and pushed the button to let down the gangplank. "You're coming with me," he said to Sophia. "Don't shout, don't scream, or you will never see your family again." He turned to Edward and Elena. "Do I need to explain, Sir Edward?"

Edward said nothing.

"It's very simple," Charlie said without loosening his grip on Sophia. "You will go and the young lady will stay. I would advise you against making any efforts to return. If we learn you are back in China, the young lady dies. If you try to send anyone—*anyone*—to get her, she dies. We watch every port and we have people in every city. We are like a giant spider. If anyone so much as touches our web, the whole web shakes and we know who and where you are. Our web is sticky, and intruders die. Do you understand?"

"Perfectly," Edward said evenly.

"And as for you," Charlie said to Sophia with a jerk of his arm. "You are now in our family. If you try to leave, your baby will die. Yes, our network extends all the way to London. And to Paris, New York, and San Francisco; the whole world is within our reach. We will always know where your baby is; she will never be beyond our grasp. Your baby will remain safe in England, as long as you don't try to leave before we *let* you go. Does everybody understand?"

Grim sighs and suppressed cries were the acknowledgments of understanding.

Charlie turned his single eye to Edward. "These men," he motioned with his chin, "will stay with the boat until it's sailed far beyond Hong Kong. Don't do anything to upset them. You have the baby. Just remember, we have long memories and our people are everywhere. I say again, any attempt to get this woman back, and the child will die. In London, or wherever else you go. Do I make myself clear, Sir Edward?"

A cold fear seized Edward's heart. Keeping his eyes fixed on Charlie's single eye, he nodded slowly. He, too, knew of Chu's men. Murderous psychopaths, ruthless killers, the lot of them. Now his life would be shadowed with their presence. He pulled Elena and the baby close to his side. For a moment he was angry with Sophia. Damn her! he thought. Why did she have to encourage her raffish friends? Why did she bring the shame of an illegitimate child on them? And now this. Then he felt guilty. Poor, poor Sophia. Even worse—poor Elena. How would she manage without her twin? He met Charlie's one-eyed gaze with a look as cold and hard as marble, but inside, he recognized with despair the hopelessness of the situation.

Jaggers stood there rigid, his hands frozen in fists at his side. How much he wanted to rescue Sophia! But he knew they were defeated. He blamed himself for not watching more carefully. He had anticipated the possibility of bandits in the China

Seas, but he had been caught off guard: the *Elizabeth* had not even left harbor.

Charlie picked up Sophia and slung her over his shoulder. He walked down the gangplank to where Misha stood. "Don't worry, little fellow," he said cheerfully, pleased with the success of the abduction. "You can have your charge back. Your house is still waiting for you—with a few extra servants to see that you all behave." He smiled at Miss Trublood. "You too, fat lady. You say prayers to your Jesus. And *you*," he shouted at Sophia, whom he still held, kicking and screaming, over his shoulder, "be quiet."

Sophia was wild with horror. Her baby, she was going to lose her baby. The shock and the pain were too much to bear. Her screams quieten to incoherent sobs. Charlie dropped her into Miss Trublood's waiting arms. "Here. Take her," he said. He pushed the chauffeur into the car. "Drive back to the house. I'll stay here and see that the yacht leaves safely."

On board the yacht the uninvited crew had taken over the running of the ship. Flags were hoisted and the yacht hooted a farewell. Though Jaggers now moved about the deck with a man and a gun at his back, Edward and Elena continued to stand motionless. The only sound was that of the child's sobbing; tired heart-rending sobs, as if she knew she was losing her mother. Jaggers, his shoulders slumped in defeat, cast off. Slowly the *Elizabeth* nosed her way from the dock and made for the open sea.

"Let's get you home," said Miss Trublood in a

worried voice to the trembling Sophia. She looked at Misha. "We must get her to bed. And she needs a warm drink. There's nothing we can do here." She ignored Charlie who was still watching the yacht.

Misha took Mei Mei's hand. "Darling," he said, "we must go."

Mei Mei quivered. "We not go to Shintu," she said. "We stay. Look after Missie."

"I know." Disappointment showed briefly on Misha's face. He squeezed Mei Mei's hand. "I promised her grandmother I would always look after her, and we will." He shook his head as he climbed into Edward's old car. "I can't believe what's happened," he said. He turned his head and looked out of the back window.

Charlie stood, lean and tall, gazing at the ship as she left the harbor. He watched keenly as the harbor-master, oblivious to what had transpired, gave the yacht permission to leave. Charlie curled his lip. "Well done," he said to himself. I must find Chu. He'll be pleased. Our little bird is in her cage. Now will she sing? That is the question.

CHAPTER 66

Sophia lay in Miss Trublood's lap, deep in shock. "We must get her home," Miss Trublood murmured.

No one said anything. The surprise and the horror had been so great. No one knew what to expect when they returned to the house which they had all left, they'd believed, for good. Misha and Mei Mei's luggage was waiting at the railway station in Shanghai. Miss Trublood's big broken suitcase filled with her few belongings had already been sent on to a mission on the other side of the city, to which she had been planning to move. Misha sat beside the chauffeur, his head bowed in misery. Though only three feet tall, he felt a Herculean rage. He wished he were a giant. He felt he had let Sophia down. Why had they not taken precautions? Hadn't the deaths in Russia been enough to propitiate the gods? Must this family continually suffer? And when they returned to the house, were they to be tormented and killed?

Mei Mei wept quietly. She had so much wanted to start her new life with Misha, all she could do now was cry. She did not resent Sophia; indeed her tears were also for the young woman who had been parted from her child, but she knew that she and Misha must now postpone their plans indefinitely.

Miss Trublood felt the relief at least of being some place familiar when they pulled into the driveway leading to the house. No one came out to open the car door, but a figure could be seen moving inside. The chauffeur came around to Miss Trublood's door and gently lifted Sophia from her arms. "Where are we?" Sophia muttered.

"Hush, honey." Miss Trublood's voice was deep

and comforting. "We're home now. Let's get you inside, and I'll fetch you something to help you sleep."

Tears welled up again in Sophia's eyes. "They've taken my baby," she whispered. Pain ripped ragged edges around her heart. She felt as if she had been torn in half.

The chauffeur carried her into the house. The unknown person inside opened the door as the chauffeur's feet scrunched up the pathway. The door closed behind them. Miss Trublood looked puzzled. Misha and Mei Mei stared. "Well," said Misha, shrugging his shoulders, "whoever is in there doesn't seem to want to come out. You two stay here until I call you." He marched determinedly up to the house and again the door opened. The door closed behind him and Mei Mei held her breath in terror.

"Who are you?" Misha demanded, looking fiercely at the man in front of him.

"I Mordecai." The man looked very like Charlie, gaunt and tall, except he had both his eyes and wore a large pair of spectacles. Behind the glittering lenses his eyes were obscured by blue milky cataracts, making them look like the eyes of a drowned man. His seemed a face fished out of the river, the mouth bloated and the neck as though wrinkled by water. Hands like fins hung loosely at his side. "I am the major-domo," he said, extending a fin.

Misha reluctantly took the limp cold hand in his. He winced at the idea of squeezing it, fearing water would run to the ground.

"You, funny little man, are Misha," said Mordecai.

"I must call in the others."

"Miss Trublood and Mei Mei?" Mordecai grinned. His face did look frighteningly like a fish when he smiled, the lips pulled tight across the protruding teeth. "You see? I done my homework well."

Misha looked around the hall. The furniture had been replaced. Instead of the English spinet and the beveled rococo gold mirror above it, there was now a large pale vase, and Chinese tapestries on the wall. Against the other walls stood massive chairs with squat legs and wide seats, the backs inlaid with lapis lazuli. In front of the chairs was a red rosewood table upon which sat a small tea-urn. Misha walked to the front door and beckoned the two women who waited white-faced in the garden. "Come in," he said. "We have company."

Miss Trublood stormed the door first. "Who the hell are you?" she asked, belligerent and angry.

Mordecai grinned his fish grin. "I appointed by Chu Wing to take care of you."

Miss Trublood snorted. "And to report all the dirt you can dig up to those damned thieves and brigands?" she bellowed.

Mordecai stepped back. He had done his homework, but he had been led to believe that Miss Trublood was a Christian lady, and in his book Christian ladies didn't swear, they were kind and submissive. Mordecai was a little afraid of this lady. "No, no, no," he huffed. "Chu just want make sure you all right. These days," he said, rubbing his spongy hands together, "the world dangerous place. Can't be too careful." He decided to try again.

"My name Mordecai, madam," he said, bowing his head. "At your service."

"Mordecai!" Miss Trublood cried, staring in disbelief at his Oriental face. "You don't look like a Mordecai to me."

"My parents," he explained, "influenced by missionaries."

"Even missionaries make mistakes," Miss Trublood declared, not trusting this man who was, after all, in the pay of Sophia's abductors. "And I can't spend all my time talking to the likes of you," she snapped. "I must see to Sophia. Get a doctor right away." And she sprinted off down the hall.

She was furious. How dare these no-goods kidnap Sophia? How dare they? Who did they think they were? As for that dreadful little man Mordecai who had been wished upon them, she would make it her business to see that he ended up wishing he had never agreed to take the post. She pushed open the door to Sophia's bedroom.

Gone were her four-poster bed, and the English Axminster carpet, and the Honiton pottery so lovingly collected from the junk-shops in Shanghai. Sophia lay on a wide carved bed. Her eyes were closed and she was breathing unevenly. On the floor stretched a blue-green Chinese carpet and by the window stood a long table softly gleaming. Miss Trublood stood stock-still, her hand on the door knob. She shook her head. This was all a bad nightmare and in a moment she would wake up. A bird began to sing in the courtyard and her eyes traveled to the waterfall. The water splashed into the basin and the bird, hot and dusty after a long day's foraging for food, took the opportunity to flutter its wings in the water. No, this was not a nightmare, not even a daymare. What had happened a few hours ago was all too real. Miss Trublood was not given to drinking, but for once she felt she would welcome a huge shot of brandy, or maybe whisky, or whatever it was that people drank to steady their nerves.

She took a deep breath and then went back to find Misha and Mei Mei. "Any more of the bastards in the house?" she bellowed.

Mordecai cringed. Misha shook his head, saying, "No. I've had a quick look around."

Mei Mei stood silently beside Misha.

"Misha," Miss Trublood took charge, "we need to get some soup for Miss Sophia. She's still in a state of shock. Is the doctor coming? Have you telephoned him?" She glowered at Mordecai.

Mordecai quivered inside. "I send for best doctor in Shanghai."

"He'd better be. If anything happens to Sophia, I'll hold you personally responsible."

Mordecai was so overcome by the prospect of Miss Trublood's laying those big murderous-looking hands on him, he ran off into the kitchen.

Misha followed. For all his fury and sorrow, he found an element of humor in what was happening. "She always like this?" Mordecai shivered.

"Wait until the full moon," Misha replied, putting as much mystery and menace into his voice as he could muster.

The cupboards were now stocked with Chinese food. Fortunately Sophia liked Chinese food, but Misha felt he must get to the market soon with Mei Mei. Mordecai, reading his thoughts, nodded placatingly. "I have plenty money for you," he said. "You buy what you want. I good man. Just do my job. I kind to you, little fellow."

"You'd better be," Misha grunted, echoing Miss Trublood's belligerent tone.

"Give me list." Mordecai was desperate to get out of the house. "Give me list and I go shopping."

Misha sat at the new kitchen table. Life was going to be very different from now on. He sighed. He was too old for change. He put the list into Mordecai's hand. "Go," he said.

CHAPTER 67

"May I take the child to my cabin?" Elena's voice was weak and plaintive.

The filthy bearded individual who was screaming the orders—the man she took to be the leader of this villainous crew—nodded. "You," he said to Edward, "go with her."

They were herded down the steps by one of the men holding a rifle. He ushered them into the cabin and then stood outside against the door. Elena laid the sleeping child on the bed and sat down beside her. Maria's eyelashes were still wet with tears. "Poor Maria." Elena looked defeated. Edward paced the room. "Edward," she said, "they can't get away with this, can they? Surely the British . . ."

"The British," said Edward, "might rule a great empire, but we're still visitors in other countries. I'm afraid people get away with this sort of thing all the time."

Up on deck Jaggers was swearing under his breath. "Dirty buggers," he said, glaring at the man who now took his place at the helm. "Fucking yellow-eyed bastard sons of filthy bitches." He knew he was outnumbered. Sophia was not the first woman to be kidnapped and spirited away. Jaggers just hoped that, if there was a God watching over them all, he would see to it that Sophia was protected from the evil lust of her abductors. He did not want to think of her relegated to one of the thousands of brothels that gave Shanghai its deserved reputation as the most debauched city in China. He knew he must keep himself tightly under control. These men thought nothing of killing. Human life meant nothing to them . . . He stood by the bridge, his hands clenching and unclenching, his heart raging.

The wind was light and blustery, and came from behind. Good, Jaggers thought, we'll make good time. I wonder when we lose the bastards. A silence descended on the ship, broken only by the sound of the engines grumbling and the occasional hissed command from the ruffian piloting the *Elizabeth*. Jaggers understood how the Ancient Mariner must have felt. When this is over, he thought, nobody will believe me when I tell the story. Things like this just didn't happen in England, and certainly not at Harland Point. The biggest thing that had ever happened there was when the doctor's wife ran naked down the streets, and nobody talked about it because they were all too embarrassed and felt sorry for the doctor. He desperately wished he was back in England. He thought furiously of the moors and sparkling waters of his trout stream. Anything to take his mind off Sophia.

Elena was worn out, too tired to think, but she somehow still found the energy to keep the child amused. With the remarkable resilience of the young, Maria was often full of life. She would sit on the bed, and play with baubles of Elena's jewelry. She would run to Edward, wanting to be caught in his arms and thrown up into the air and caught again—a favorite game. She would sit on Jaggers's foot and cling to his leg, like a koala bear to a eucalyptus tree, so that when he tried to walk he had to swing her with every step. But there were moments when Maria would revert to crawling instead of running about, and peek her head around doors and quietly stare. Elena felt sure she was looking for her mother. Elena did not know what to do. How could one explain to a child so young? Instead, Elena invented games to distract her niece, and hugged her especially tightly when, having stumbled, Maria would cry for her mother. Elena believed her own arms an inadequate replacement, but with each hug she tried to convey how very much she loved the child. At night, when Maria was wakeful and stared at the ceiling, Elena lay beside her until her eyes closed and her breathing became deep and even in slumber. Elena slept with Maria, while Edward lay sleepless in another cabin.

The tension among the three captives was great. Jaggers, unlike Edward, was young and untrained in diplomacy. Edward, his face a mask, sat at meals, making elegant conversation with Elena on the few occasions she was able to put Maria down and sit with them at the table. Privately, he would hold her in his arms when, overwhelmed, she wept. But Jaggers felt such consuming rage that he feared for his own life, and he kept his blue eyes on the deck when the pirates were around him. More and more he withdrew into daydreams, all those dreams centered on Sophia. His future seemed bleak without her. Never had he been so consumed with passion for a woman. Only a few years older than Sophia, Jaggers had known many women, some as companions and others as lovers—but none before had ever taken possession of his heart in this way. Even if Sophia had not asked for his love, it was hers nonetheless. "Captain says he get shop in Singapore," Chung the cabin boy told him with a jaunty smile that lifted Jaggers's spirits.

"Oh, he does, does he? With our money, I suppose. When do we get rid of these bastards then?"

"Captain and bastards go Colombo."

"Thank God for that." Jaggers went off to find Edward. "They'll leave us when we dock in Colombo. The captain's going to get provisions when we tie up in Singapore."

Edward sighed. "At least we know we only have another week or two more of their malodorous company. It'll take several days to clear up after them. Still, at least so far the weather's been good. I'll try to get permission to go ashore in Singapore and get some fresh food as well. I can't go on eating this Chinese muck. I'd feel a lot better for a good chicken and some fruit."

Jaggers and Chung secured the *Elizabeth* to the quayside in Singapore. Elena stood on the deck with Maria in her arms. The little girl was quiet now, her intense gray eyes taking in the beautiful white buildings and the tall palm trees that lined the docks. Elena managed to smile at Maria. "Look, darling," she said. "Horses."

Maria waved her fat fists and Elena felt yet another pang of grief. She and Sophia should be standing side by side, seeing this together. Elena felt the loss of Sophia keenly. On her honeymoon she had been happy away from her sister, but now the enforced and unexpected separation left her feeling bereft. How was Sophia coping? Where was she? Where were Misha and Mei Mei and Miss Trublood? She hoped and prayed they were all together. There were no answers to her questions here, just the hustle and bustle of a major port.

Elena stayed with Maria on the boat, with Jaggers to keep her company. Edward went off in a taxi to buy fresh food. Elena waved as the car drove away and wished she did not feel so afraid that he might never come back.

❧ CHAPTER 68 ❧

Sophia lay inert on her bed. "For the moment," said the European doctor called by Mordecai, holding Sophia's limp hand days later, "she's not responding to anything. What's happening here is a sort of crisis. The mind refuses to accept the events that have taken place." He coughed discreetly. He knew very well that the events he alluded to amounted to nothing less than kidnapping, but to call things by their true name was not always wise. "I'll give you some pills. If you can get her to swallow them, so much the better. For the moment I suggest you let her rest and see that she gets plenty of liquid."

Sophia became conscious of Miss Trublood's face looming over her. She wanted to reach out and hug the woman, but then the tide pulled back again and she was left alone on the edge of darkness.

One night she could have sworn that the Gorgon, Lau Tchi, was in the room sitting on his heels, his hands clasped around his knees. "You know your life is an illusion," he said, his voice a papery whisper in the moon-filled room. "An illusion that must be treated with intelligent respect. What you feel you have lost is also an illusion."

Sophia struggled to reply but could not.

"You must remember, it is only to a Western mind that human life and human relationships are important. We in the East see things differently," he said.

Still she could not speak.

"Your feelings are useless. Sorrow cannot bring change. Sorrow, regret, guilt—these are all Western notions. Your child does not belong to you. She was yours for a while. Now, no longer. Life continues outside this room but you lie here in the dark. This is the behavior of a coward," he said. "You are frightened of life." He vanished before Sophia could decide whether he was real, or whether she had been dreaming.

For the first time since she was wrenched away from her sister and her child, Sophia felt a small stirring in her body. A flame burnt brightly for a moment. Her blood, no longer sluggish, ran freely through her veins.

Miss Trublood came running. "What is it? What is it?" she cried. Sophia was sitting up in bed, her head thrown back, and her mouth wide open. The screams bounced off the walls and shattered the calm of the house.

Mordecai stood in the kitchen, his hands over his ears. Mei Mei clutched Misha and they listened in terror. A passerby, hearing the screaming, shuddered and made the sign to ward off the evil eye.

Miss Trublood simply bowed her head and prayed. Finally—after what seemed an interminable length of time—Sophia was spent. She lay back on the bed, her eyes closed. "Good night, Miss Trublood," she whispered. Her ragged words made Miss Trublood's blue eyes fill with tears.

"God bless you, child," Miss Trublood said, and she kissed Sophia on her jade-cold forehead. There was no answer as Miss Trublood made for the door.

"Is she all right?" Misha asked.

"Surviving," Miss Trublood sighed. "The worst is over. Sophia is back with us."

✌ CHAPTER 69 ✌

Edward realized that he was going to miss the yacht. Even though they had been held virtual prisoners on board, the *Elizabeth* seemed a safe refuge in a world that had apparently gone mad.

He watched the sea-swell. The wind was blowing and it looked as if they faced a storm in the Bay of Biscay. Chu's men had disembarked in Colombo. The boat seemed to relax to its very beams, though the passengers, for some reason, felt almost more empty without a visible enemy on deck to hate. Instead they were left with a child and no mother to take on the lonely journey to England.

Still, Edward reminded himself, we will be back in the Monastery for Christmas. In spite of all that happened he felt his heart quicken. Nanny Boots would be there to greet them, and Turner, the head gardener. Edward imagined Elena's face when he showed her his home, the home that now would be hers. And the child's, he added mentally.

"It's going to blow," Jaggers remarked.

"We could do with a storm," Edward said, throwing back his head and gazing at the sky.

Jaggers let out a small laugh. "She's solidly built and can ride out almost anything."

The *Elizabeth* bucked and rocked. The engine in her bowels roared and strained. Briny spray came up over the side and hit Edward's face. He could taste the salt on his lips. For the first time in months he felt fully alive, anticipating the exhilaration of a storm at sea.

Jaggers watched Edward and smiled. After dropping anchor in Plymouth, he would take the boat around the coast and up to the north of Devon and there she would wait, tied to her buoy, until Edward was ready to sail again. It gave Jaggers great satisfaction to know that both men would for ever be united in their love of the *Elizabeth*.

Jaggers checked the chart. They were making for Bordeaux. Edward wanted to pick up some cases of wine to take with him to England.

Down below in the main saloon, Elena sat with Maria on her knee. The child played with a new teddy-bear Elena had made for her, and did not seem to notice the lurching of the ship. Elena comforted herself with the thought that maybe one day they would see Sophia again. Her twin had always been resourceful and with any luck she would get away . . . Elena wished she could feel more certain of this.

"Not long now," she told Maria, "and we'll be in England. You must write a letter to Santa Claus and tell him what you want for Christmas. Shall we do that now, darling?"

Maria, half-understanding that presents were being discussed, nodded her curly hair and demanded, "Dolly." She said, "Big dolly."

Elena laughed. "Here," she said when she had finished a list for the child. "We'll take it over there to the fire and burn it and the ashes will fly all the way to the North Pole." She took the child by the hand and together they walked across the saloon. Elena opened the iron door of the heating stove and tossed the list into the furnace. Maria gazed at the flames. The fire flickered in the child's face and Elena saw how like her mother Maria was: the same mouth, the same shape of the eyes, but Maria's were gray like her father's, and she had Elter's nose and chin. The piece of paper burned and curled. Tragedy had visited this child twice in as many years: her father murdered and her mother kidnapped. Elena felt a pang of fear for the girl. She picked her up and hugged her. "We're going to have a storm," she said, rocking Maria in her arms.

Maria clung contentedly to her aunt's neck.

Elena walked across to gaze out of the porthole. She did not like the idea of a storm.

That night Edward spent the hours from dusk to dawn negotiating the storm with Jaggers. Chung was ordered to get some sleep, if he could, and Elena clung to Maria while they rolled about the bunk in the main stateroom. The waves were huge. They crashed over the boat, breaking on the deck. "Force ten gale!" Jaggers bellowed at Edward.

He caught the gleam of Edward's white teeth as Edward yelled back, "Steady! Keep her steady!" The *Elizabeth* turned and for a moment the top deck threatened to touch the water. But she righted herself. Edward felt triumphant. "Good girl!" he congratulated her.

By dawn the worst of the storm was over and Bordeaux was in sight. Both men were tired but elated. "Good show." Edward shook Jaggers's hand.

"Not bad, old man, not bad."

"For someone my age, you mean?"

Jaggers laughed.

"After last night, I feel a hundred," said Edward. "We'd better turn in and let Chung take over." He made his way down to the stateroom.

Elena was sitting up in bed. "Tea, Edward?" she asked. Maria was playing on the floor quite unperturbed by the rough night.

Edward smiled at his pretty young wife. "I'd love a cup of tea," he said.

"I made some toast for you too. I thought you'd be hungry."

Edward sat on the bed and gave Elena a long gentle kiss. For him the storm had been cathartic, helping him to shed the past, along with his guilt and remorse over Sophia's kidnapping. Such emotions would do no one any good. He had the future to think of. He must protect his wife and give the child the best upbringing possible. As an Englishman, Edward faced life with a pragmatism that the world's non-British might have found frightening. But he had taken to heart the lessons learned on the playing-fields of his schoolboy days: if knocked to the ground, a fellow didn't quit; he picked himself up and got back in the game. Edward sipped his tea and crunched his toast. The butter foamed on his tongue.

"You know," he said, motioning to Maria's fair head, "she could easily pass for your child."

Elena followed his eyes but said nothing.

"We'll be docking shortly," Edward said. "We can go ashore to buy wine and hams."

"Once we're settled," said Elena, "I'll learn to cook hams for you. I want to be the best wife in the world."

"You are that already." He took her hand and kissed her palm. "I really must catch up on some sleep. But after lunch we can leave Maria with Jaggers and celebrate making it through the storm."

Elena smiled.

She realized that she must not dwell on her own sorrow, so much more intensely felt than Edward's. He could not know anything of the mystical bond between twins. Sophia would always be in her blood and in her mind. And if God had decided to take Sophia away from her, at least he had given her the child. By caring for Maria, she would be fulfilling a vow to Sophia that whatever happened the child would be loved and protected until Sophia returned. But what if she never saw her sister again? Elena chased the thought away. Of course she was going to see her again. Sophia would get out of this, one way or another.

❦ CHAPTER 70 ❦

Sophia stood before Chu Wing, who was shoveling food into his mouth. She could not decide which disgusted her more: the flat leathery suction pads of the dead octopus he was eating, or Chu Wing's shapeless blob of a countenance. Two small pig-like eyes sunk deep in his fat face were fixed upon her. "I not take you off boat to make your life misery." Chu's voice was querulous. Who was this upstart who stared at the great Chu without respect? Who did she think she was? Why did she not shake or tremble? But, he remembered with a sigh, these were precisely the qualities he needed her for. But why did she have to be so troublesome?

Sophia had ignored Chu's orders to visit him for several weeks. Finally Charlie had been detailed to fetch the girl. At ten o'clock one brisk sunny

Shanghai morning, he had deposited her before his master. "You just behave yourself," he hissed at her. He was rewarded with a withering look of hatred from Sophia's brown eyes—a look that gave new meaning to the old cliché If looks could kill.

"We not wish to hurt you," Chu started again.

"Then why did you take away my baby?"

"Because," Chu looked offended, "we thought she safer in England. Work you will do very dangerous. In China children often go live with relatives. This not unusual. We not selfish people. Child's welfare come first. Now we need you. Who knows? You do well, one day maybe you travel to England see your child."

Sophia felt a surge of hope. "You mean you'll let me go if I do what you ask?"

"We reasonable people," he said, trying to look honest and sincere.

Sophia looked down at the red tile floor and then across the room to the mullioned window. Outside she could see a dragon on the corner of the roof. The gold leaf glittered against the pale-blue sky. The dragon was intended to guarantee good joss for the house and its inhabitants. I need all the good joss I can get, she thought.

This was the first time Sophia had been out of the house since her abduction. She had lost a good deal of weight. Her shoulders felt bony under the thin silk of her black cheong-sam. She had no clothes except what was in the small suitcase she had taken to the boat with her. These she had burned, then she had ordered Mordecai to find her a dressmaker. Within a week she had her cupboards filled with black cheong-sams. She could not bring herself to wear any other color but black, the color of mourning in the Western world, white being the color of mourning for the Chinese. But she was not Chinese. And these atrocities that had been visited upon her by Chinese people, she would never forgive. She was going to think in a Western way, even if she understood the arguments of Eastern philosophy. It was one thing to sit at the Gorgon's knee and listen to him talk about illusion, and to be told of the total unimportance of individual human life; it was quite another to have given birth to a child. Before, she had been free to philosophize all she wanted. But now she knew the reality of having had a baby. Her baby was not an illusion. Her baby's life was not something to be so casually dismissed.

Now she stood defiantly before Chu. She would submit to whatever they wanted from her, as long as some day she could get away and return to her sister and child. She bowed her head again. "What am I to do?"

Chu lowered his head. His chin buried itself in a deep roll of flesh. "Good," he said. "You speak prudently. Tomorrow night celebration of winter solstice."

Sophia had a vision of Elter's face, as she had seen it for the first time at the winter solstice. She knew she stood now in the company of his murderers. She held Chu's eyes until he uncomfortably shifted his stare. Damn the girl! he thought. She's hard.

"Tomorrow night," he continued, "you take the oath. Charlie come for you eleven o'clock."

"I'll be ready." She turned and walked away without a backward glance. The heavy doors slammed shut behind her.

"Sshhaayy." Chu let out a whistling sigh.

Charlie smiled bleakly. "Until tomorrow," he said and slipped out of the room through a door behind Chu's chair.

Chu gazed out of the window and he noticed a small cloud shaped like a man's hand cross the sky. The hand was largely white, but there was a small patch of black. Chu pinched his lip and thought of his ancestors. Good joss, he pleaded. Good joss.

CHAPTER 71

The room was hot and smoky. Chu Wing sat in a large chair that looked as if it once had served as a throne. The back arched above Chu's head and the arms were covered in gold cloth. The room's walls were lacquered red. On a side table stood an urn filled with scented tea. Chu was drinking whisky from a bottle close at hand. His bright eyes scanned the people in the room. He enjoyed this ceremony, especially the garrotting that would crown tonight's oath-taking.

There were two new recruits, Sophia and a man

named Stanislaus. Stanislaus was part-Russian and part-Chinese. He stood beside Sophia. Both he and she were naked. Sophia stood absolutely still, but inside she was trembling. Maria had advised her to go along with the ceremony. No, she could not give Sophia details. It was forbidden even to talk about it. But if Sophia did as she was instructed, she would not be hurt.

Sophia's long hair covered her breasts. Behind her Charlie drew a ceremonial sword from its sheath. The cold blade rested against her skin. On a bench behind Chu three people sat with their heads bowed. The first shuffled forward at a word from Charlie. "Turn," Charlie ordered. "You." He pointed to another minion who stiffened to attention beside Chu's throne. "Take off his shirt." Quaking, the man did as he was told. Two ugly purple scars marked his back across the tops of his shoulders. "Lift your hands."

"You know I can't," the man whined. Then, fearing his words might ring of disrespect, he added, "sir."

"First stripe earned by disobedience," Chu began addressing the initiates. "The Enforcer," he nodded at One-Eyed Charlie, who grinned back, "slash tendons of shoulders and you never raise your arms again. Go!" he ordered and the limp-armed man slunk back to the bench.

"You!" Charlie called. The woman sitting beside the man who had just returned to the bench crept forward, cowering. "Stand up!" Charlie barked harshly. "Open your mouth!" A good job, he congratulated himself once again. Very neat.

The stump of her tongue horrified Sophia. Good Lord, Sophia prayed, keep me safe. And my baby. She tried to go off into a trance. She conjured up a vision of her friend Maria's face. "No," said Maria, shaking her head. "I didn't know they were going to kidnap you and threaten your baby. I'm not told anything by Chu, except on a need-to-know basis." Sophia realized now that had Maria told her about the ceremony, she would have lost her tongue. These people were entirely ruthless.

"If you break oath by giving information without permission," said Chu in schoolmasterly tones, "second stripe."

"And of course," Charlie added, "there are other stripes: burning, whipping, isolation in deep holes in the ground. Some people, however, are still slow to learn loyalty." He pointed to the last man on the bench. "You." Charlie resheathed the sword and pulled a long thin thong of leather from his pocket. The man drew back, his body shaking convulsively. "This is one of the final solutions," Charlie explained.

Chu took a sip of whisky. "Get on with it!" he commanded.

Charlie jumped out and caught the man by the shoulder. Expertly he wrapped the leather thong around the man's neck. The man let out a sharp high wail and thrashed his limbs. Charlie pulled hard.

Sophia gasped and looked sideways at Stanislaus. The young Eurasian clenched his teeth. He had a straight nose, a wide brow, and his eyes were deep and brown. He focused ahead as if nothing was happening but Sophia could sense him trembling, just as she trembled. The only way she could deal with this situation was to pretend it was not really happening.

The man's tongue, grossly swollen and extended, protruded from his mouth. His body jerked and writhed. Chu grunted and groaned excitedly. Charlie thought, I wish the old man would hurry up and come, then I can get the job finished. Charlie knew Chu so well, he could time the orgasm. These days it took longer and longer before he could finish off his victims. His wrists hurt. Charlie sighed. What a way to make a living. He looked at Chu. Good, he was beginning. Chu groaned loudly. A big wet stain marked his blue silk trousers. Charlie pulled tightly and twisted the leather, audibly breaking the neck. The man slumped to the floor.

Charlie kicked him. "He's dead." He smiled at Sophia. "You don't want this around your pretty little neck, do you?" He laughed. "Eh, Chu?"

Chu rubbed his hands and nodded. "Good, good," he slobbered. "Continue."

Phrase by phrase, Sophia and Stanislaus repeated the oath, which Charlie translated into English as he read aloud from a very ancient parchment. Sophia's voice was firm. She held her head high and pretended she was her grandmother. *Noblesse oblige,* she thought, her mother's words ringing in her ears.

Charlie approached both naked figures with a bowl. In the bowl was blood, fresh blood. Sophia felt her gorge rise. "Drink," Charlie ordered. She lifted the bowl to her lips and felt the hot, sweet-smelling liquid trickle down her throat. Stanislaus beside her did the same. "Have sex," Charlie ordered.

Sophia lay on the bare floor staring at the ceiling. Stanislaus lay on top of her and mechanically pumped at her inert body. He said nothing. Sophia closed her eyes and thought, if this is what it takes to get my child back, then I'll do it. Finally Stanislaus reached an emotionless climax and rolled off.

Chu was bored by this part of the ceremony, but it was necessary to see that the man could perform under pressure and that the woman would obey. She would be called upon to lie on her back on many occasions. Chu grunted. Overall he was satisfied. "Go now," he said.

Sophia followed Stanislaus into an outer vestibule. She felt sick and degraded. Silently they put on their clothes. "I'm sorry," Stanislaus mumbled.

"Don't be," Sophia said. "You had no choice."

He gave a shy smile. "My name is Stanislaus. We haven't been properly introduced."

Sophia nodded indifferently. "Sophia," she said. She wanted to leave. Real life lay outside the massive door of this temple: everyday things, like rickshaws and happy smiling faces, Mei Mei's love for Misha, the moon looking down, peaceful and bright, on all God's sleeping creatures. Now she felt very much like something that had crawled out of a dark dank hell, ugly and defiled, trapped by these people who had eyes and ears everywhere.

Still, Chu had promised her freedom if she kept her end of the bargain. But for how long? How long must she live this nightmare?

Charlie walked behind her to the outside doors. "Go," he said, pushing open the door. "We'll call you when we need you. There's a car over there."

Sophia walked across the tiled courtyard to the long black car. She sank into the pillowy back seat, not even bothering to look at the chauffeur. She gave the address and the car pulled away. Behind the tinted glass windows she watched the lights of Shanghai, the city that had once given her freedom and happiness, now become her prison. Her reason to live was thousands of miles away. In the privacy of the car, Sophia let herself silently weep.

✑ CHAPTER 72 ☙

Elena was thrilled with England. They were in the restaurant of a comfortable hotel overlooking Plymouth harbor. "Just look at those waves, Maria!" said Elena, pointing out to sea. It was a brisk December day. The trees were bare and their branches crashed and lashed. Down far below the balcony miniature human figures jostled. Up the hill Elena could hear the hooting of trains. The noise of many people was everywhere—sailors in uniform, soldiers, everyone busy.

Elena and Maria met Jaggers and Edward in the downstairs dining-room.

"I've waited for this meal a very long time," Edward announced, fastening his generous-sized napkin under this chin. "Proper English food," he said, watching the chef roll a silver carver to the table.

"Roast beef?" the chef asked the diners. Receiving enthusiastic nods all around, he threw back the cover of his trolley, and Elena smelled the smell of English roast beef cooked to a turn, as the chef promised.

"Oh yes," she said. "And a little piece for Maria?"

Edward finished his meal with a suet pudding. Elena sat and glowed. The weak winter sun traced patterns on the thick carpet. She watched the flames in the fire burn orange. How safe she felt here in England! An England where nothing ever happened. She knew there had been a war, but there was no visible evidence of that war. The city of Plymouth seemed solid and prosperous. The streets were clean and beggarless. "How happy everybody in England must be," she commented.

Edward smiled sadly. "Would that they were. No, we have many people with reason for discontent. I see in today's *Times* that there are strikes in London. Even talk of a general strike." He shook his head. "Times are not what they once were."

Jaggers laughed. "Well, I'm off to North Devon tonight, where everyone's too contented to strike. Or too busy. Couldn't say which. Your boxes will be unloaded and sent down to you from there.

Then it's home to Hartland Point for me. It'll be good to get back to the farm and see my boy, if he still knows who I am. He'll be eight by now."

"You'll bring him down for a visit, won't you?" said Edward.

Jaggers nodded. "And you'll come up for a sail?"

"Without fail. We'll get the little one set up with Nanny Boots and then we'll soon be along for a visit. You know I can't stay away from the *Elizabeth* for long. Shall we get ready to catch that train, darling?"

"I'm ready." Despite the sadness that was always with her since Sophia's abduction, Elena could not help but feel a tingling exhilaration at the thought of seeing her new English home. "Just let me get Maria's coat."

Edward stood up and stretched. "Still have my sea legs," he remarked. He remained standing while Elena took Maria off to get ready. He shook Jagger's hand. "Goodbye, old man."

Jaggers's grin turned quickly to a frown. "I can't get Sophia's face out of my mind."

"Nor I," Edward agreed. "A very bad business. But there's nothing we can do. If I contact Scotland Yard, or indeed anybody, Chu will get to hear of it, and both Sophia and Maria's lives will be in danger." Edward shook his head. The two men walked out of the dining-room into the hotel lobby, where Jaggers's grip stood beside the mound of luggage of which most belonged to Elena.

In what seemed like no time, Edward, Elena,

and the child were at the railway station, settling into a first-class compartment. Elena sat with her back cushioned by the green cloth, resting her head upon a white square of cotton. A moment later the train whistled, and they were off.

As the countryside flashed past, Elena marveled at the greens and the browns of the landscape . . . But her thoughts soon turned to Sophia. She missed her sister's high spirits. Wherever Sophia was, there the world fizzed and crackled. By herself, Elena felt pale and uninteresting.

"A penny for your thoughts?" Edward said, knowing what must be on her mind.

"They're not worth a penny," Elena said softly. Maria was asleep, the child's little head lying trustingly in her lap. Elena bent over and kissed her. "But I'm looking forward to arriving," she said.

"I know you'll be happy there." They sat in companionable silence as the train made its way toward the Monastery.

CHAPTER 73

Sophia was back in touch with Maria and Rollo. Vassily had been sent away from Shanghai. No one knew where he was, or even if he was alive. Maria did not seem to miss him. There was a tension between the three friends, partly because Rollo and Maria felt guilty. Moreover, now that Sophia had grasped the full implications of her position, she realized there were things that could not be discussed, on pain of death. Gone was the artless Sophia who chattered cheerfully about anything. Now she guarded her tongue and censored her words.

She was angry with the Gorgon and refused to visit him, believing he had played some dishonorable part in all this. Maria, upon hearing of yet another refusal, said, "Sophia will come around in the end."

Rollo was pensive. "But I can understand how angry she must feel. Sometimes I feel utterly suicidal. We're so trapped here."

Maria disagreed. "People are trapped everywhere in the world. You can only be trapped inside your head. Look at me. Here I live well, in only one room, but that's all I need. In an odd way I'm free. Sometimes I like my work." She wrinkled her nose. "Sometimes I don't. But how many women lead wretched existences? At least the men I go with are intelligent and clean. Well, most of them." She thought about the chief of police, an obese greasy man who smelled. He was her latest assignment. "I have to run, Rollo. I'm off to see Sophia at her house." Maria climbed into her little car and drove to the outskirts of Shanghai.

"What do you actually have to do?" Sophia was sitting on her bed.

Maria lay stretched out on the floor. She wore a baggy pair of silk trousers and a green silk shirt. Sophia wore her usual tight black cheong-sam.

Her long legs swung from the bed and her bare feet lightly brushed the carpet. Maria made a face. "Anything they ask for," she said. "You see, most of these men are married. Once you've made love to them, they're going to feel guilty because their wives might find out. Sometimes Chu just blackmails them. Other times he takes pictures just in case he ever decides to use them."

Sophia groaned bleakly.

"I don't think you'll be asked to do any of the rough stuff."

"Rough stuff?" Sophia said with a rising note of anxiety in her voice. "What on earth's that?"

"Oh, whipping. The sado-masochistic routine. An awful lot of the Chinese like to play about what they call the jade gate."

"I don't follow you."

"Anal intercourse."

Sophia went white. "I feel sick," she said.

"You will to begin with. Then it becomes a job just like any other job. After a while you get numb to it."

Sophia jumped from the bed. "I won't," she said. "I've only ever made love with Elter, and it was nothing like any of this." She remembered Stanislaus at their initiation, but that didn't count. That was not love-making.

"Well, with Elter you were making *love*. That's the difference. Now you're going to be doing a job." Maria knew that she was sleeping with the chief of police for a reason. But this information she must keep to herself.

Sophia walked around the room. "I'm doing this only as long as I know that Chu will let me go."

Maria's eyes followed her. "The best way to live now, Sophia, is to live for the moment. Take every day as it comes. I've worked for Chu for a long time. Ever since I came to China actually. He's a man of whim. Please him and he might let you go. Annoy him and he will punish you. And if you betray him . . . You saw what happened in that room."

"Yes." Sophia shivered. "I did. I haven't been able to get that man's face out of my mind."

"It was intended that you never should. At my initiation—I guess I can tell you now, because you've been through it yourself—Charlie gouged a woman's eyes out before he killed her. I wish I could forget the holes where her eyes had been, the blood . . ."

"What had she done?"

"She tried to run away. They caught her, of course."

The matter-of-fact tone of Maria's voice threatened to deal a death-blow to Sophia's confidence that she would endure this ordeal and eventually leave China to be reunited with her child and her twin. "I have to believe that I can get away," she said breathlessly. "I have to believe it. If I thought I had no chance of ever seeing Elena and little Maria again, I might as well kill myself."

Maria shook her head. "We all feel like that from time to time. But you must understand: if you live one day at a time, it won't be so frightful. You can't spend your whole time looking to the future.

You'll go mad. After all, Sophia, you don't know what's going to happen."

"I don't, but the Gorgon does."

"Yes, he does. But you mustn't blame him. He did nothing but refuse to interfere with your karma. What Chu did is his own responsibility."

"And Charlie's," Sophia said with bitterness. "He murdered Elter."

"But Elter chose to put himself in that position."

The pain of Elter's death threatened to engulf Sophia afresh, but she fought to regain control of herself. "I don't care any longer. I just want to work hard and get out of here. If I have to fuck my way out, I'll do it." Sophia's voice was intense. "If I have to work for these people, then I'll work my way to the top. If Charlie can be the most feared man in Shanghai, then I can match him as a woman." Sophia's eyes were fierce and animal-like. "But I tell you, I will get out."

❧ CHAPTER 74 ❧

Elena immediately felt at home in the Monastery. They crossed the drawbridge, just as Edward had promised. She loved the big moated house that sat securely surrounded by the park full of ancient Domesday trees. Nanny Boots was waiting behind the heavy front door as the car pulled up with a welcome screech. Tom, the chauffeur, grinned with pleasure. An elderly, stooped man, he well remembered the day Edward had set off for Russia. "A long time ago. You were still a lad then."

Edward laughed and patted his stomach. "I'm a happily married man now," he said. "My wife feeds me too well."

"Ah," said Tom, turning toward Maria. "This is the angel you wrote about."

"Yes." Edward beamed.

"Such a pretty little thing."

The door opened and Nanny Boots bustled out. She wore her long gray dress and a white pinafore. She greeted Edward and was introduced to Elena, the new Lady Gray. Seeing Maria, she cried, "For 'eaven's sake, child!" She reached out and hugged her. "You must be tired after such a long journey. Dear, dear, dear. What about a nice biscuit and a drink of fresh milk?"

Maria looked at this round pink lady and smiled. She was going to like Nanny Boots, she decided. She took Nanny Boots's wrinkled hand, crabbed with age and thickened slightly around the knuckles with arthritis.

"Really, Edward," said Nanny Boots, standing on tiptoe to kiss his cheek, "what ever took you so long? I've been expecting you for weeks."

"It's a long story, Nanny. I'll tell you later, but for now why don't you take Maria off to the nursery. I'll show Elena around. Tom, would you take the suitcases to the master bedroom?"

"Yes, sir." Tom puffed up the front stairs and

disappeared into the house, followed by Nanny Boots and Maria.

"I have all Sir Edward's toys, just as 'e left them," Nanny informed Maria. "And a great big rocking-horse for you to ride."

The house was now quiet. Edward lifted Elena into his arms and carried her up the front steps. "You have no idea how many times I've imagined this moment."

Elena rested her head on his shoulder and smiled. She looked around the main hall. "I feel as if I've lived here before. Have you ever had that feeling? As if you've already lived in a place, or seen it, or even heard people say something when you couldn't possibly have done?"

"*Déjà vu*, the French call it. And it feels to me as if you've always been here."

He put her down tenderly and they walked up the main staircase hand in hand. Hunting pictures hung on the walls. The floor was polished to a proud shine. It smelled of cherry wood. The carpet on the stairs was thick, muffling their footsteps. "I can imagine monks gliding up and down these stairs," Elena said.

"Quite. There was once a thriving community here. Now there are only ourselves and the child. Let's hope Sophia gets here. She'll make the place hum." Elena caught the bleak tone that Edward tried to hide. She knew not to continue. "Here we are." Edward opened the double doors to their bedroom.

"How lovely!" Elena clasped her hands like a child before a basket of sweets. The room was large and square, the bed a high regency double, and the fireplace of black marble. Elena wandered over to the wide sashed windows. Green brocade curtains were caught back by gold ropes with heavy tassels on the ends. Outside the great trees spread twisted mantles of leafless branches over the cold hard ground. Away over the tract of land Elena could see an old deer, his head raised and his antlers brushing his back. She stood there for a moment and found herself waiting, just waiting. For what? she wondered. For the sound of Sophia's foot behind her, for the touch of her hand on her shoulder. Suddenly Elena was profoundly lonely . . . But this was Edward's day and she must not spoil it. Turning, she smiled. "Show me around, Edward." She took his hand and they both left the room.

✤ CHAPTER 75 ✤

Slowly Sophia reorganized her life. She called in her dressmaker and ordered more clothes. She curtained off her past in her mind. She refused to think about her child, or about Edward and Elena in England. She must live for the present. That was the only way to survive.

Miss Trublood watched her but said little. All she could do was to stay with Sophia and be there when she needed her. She watched Sophia's face change from one that betrayed a wild and rebellious nature to a mask of self-control and discretion. If Sophia was taking steps to cover herself with the armor of reserve, Miss Trublood would not be the one to pierce the shell with too much prodding. She regretted the hardening of Sophia's face, but she knew the person behind the face, and trusted that any hardness Sophia assumed was only to protect herself. She felt certain that Sophia was going to survive this ordeal.

Sophia did not tell Miss Trublood or Mei Mei or Misha about the ceremony or about her new role. They knew not to ask. Mei Mei in particular was frightened by One-Eyed Charlie and Mordecai. Better, she said, to say nothing but take care of Missie. Misha fully agreed.

Miss Trublood was busy with her mission and tired when she came home at night, but at least Sophia was coming back to life. She was ordering clothes in colors other than black. She went out and socialized with Maria and Rollo. Maybe she was getting back on her feet . . .

When the call came, Mordecai—who spent most of his life crouched in a corner of the kitchen—was the one to deliver the message. "Chu," he said, accosting Sophia in the hallway, "want see you. Chop chop."

"Well, I don't want to see him chop chop," Sophia replied icily.

"Must go, Missie. Must go." The idea of not arriving on time with his charge terrified Mordecai.

"Otherwise Chu hurt me." Mordecai made a gesture of slitting his throat.

"Good thing, too." Sophia disappeared into her bedroom. "OK! I'll go!" she yelled after a few seconds had passed with Mordecai waiting outside the door. "Have the car ready."

On the way there she looked at the back of Mordecai's stringy neck. She felt frightened but furious. Who the hell was that great fat ogre Chu to run her life? As the car pulled up, her fury abated. I am the Snow Leopard, she murmured silently. I am afraid of nothing.

Charlie was leaning against the wall of Chu's now familiar temple-like rooms. No one else but Chu and Charlie was present. Chu pointed at Sophia with his chin. "You," he said, expertly spitting the shell of a sunflower seed onto the floor, "have a job."

Sophia remained impassive. I hope it's not some awful sleazy man, she thought.

"You go to American General's party next week. I send you invitation. You make jigjig with him. Your partner photograph documents from safe in library. You keep him busy. You understand?"

Sophia lowered her eyes. "I understand."

"You listen pillow-talk. Big shipment come in and now must go America side. Our people in New York, Boston, Washington."

Ah, Sophia thought. A shipment of opium to America to keep the millions of Chinese there hooked and comforted. Edward had often talked to her about the attempts to stop the opium finding its way on American tankers to be then secretly unloaded in American ports. "Which general, may I ask?" Sophia looked at Chu.

He grinned, exposing the rotten stumps of his teeth, spittle running down his chin. "General Wayland," he said. "Good-looking man for you jigjig."

Sophia looked away. At least he's American, she thought. There's a good chance he's clean. "All right," she said. "Send me the invitation, and I'll be there."

"You meet your partner at party."

Sophia wondered who this partner would be. Well, she had learned this much: you did not ask questions. You waited. You obeyed orders and then . . . But no. She was not going to think of the future. Maria was right.

On the way back in the car Mordecai chattered to the driver. Sophia listened with half an ear, but she was already planning what to wear for the party.

Now Sophia had a different routine. No longer did she spend the evenings gazing out of the window or trying to listen to the BBC news. She spent her days buying clothes, shoes, jewelry—Chu was generous to his staff. At night she changed into a pair of loose blue trousers and an even looser blouse. A hat hid her hair, the brim was pulled down over her face. On her feet she wore a pair of little black rubber-soled shoes. In this guise she slipped out of her courtyard into the dark night.

In daylight she appeared a beautiful, successful, rich young woman in Shanghai society. Here and there she bumped into people she had known in the safe old days. "Still here?" they asked. "Yes," she answered pleasantly. "I sent little Maria abroad with my sister for a while. I'll be joining them later."

"Jolly good!" the pink-faced gin-steeped matrons of England replied.

Sophia smiled. If only they knew. Imagine their faces.

In the blue light of the night, however, Sophia transformed herself into an inconspicuous Chinese peasant on the streets of Shanghai. If I am going to survive at all, she thought, I must know Shanghai like the back of a tortoise—every corner of it, and every way out of it. I must know the city as Charlie knows it. No one ever paused to watch the little figure scurrying about its business. She rode into the city by bicycle, then walked the pavements for hours. Sometimes Sophia sat in a restaurant, a bowl of jasmine tea in her hands, and just watched. These were early days yet, but she was listening and she was learning.

Now the summons had arrived and she was ready.

For the next week she changed after dark, then pedaled until the country lanes became city streets. She haunted the area around the General's house. Guards patroled his gate. From across the road she watched him step in and out of his shiny American chauffeur-driven car. He was a man of about fifty, she guessed. He had a graying crew cut. His profile was stern, but there was a softness about his mouth that suggested a disposition toward weakness. He was tall, not slim, and broad shouldered. He had the paunch of a senior military official no longer required to maintain a soldier's trim. Sophia sat by a stall that sold succulent meat on sticks. People came and went. Secretaries, probably. A housekeeper, but no wife and no children to be seen. General Wayland seemed an easy target.

❧ *CHAPTER 76* ❧

Late one afternoon Mordecai stood in the shadows, waiting for Sophia to return. His moist loose mouth fell in folds of contentment. In his hands he held not only the invitation promised by Chu but also a parcel. "Tell her she can reply. But you must censor all she writes," Charlie said when he handed the parcel over. Very boring letter, Mordecai decided after reading the note enclosed.

The door in the courtyard creaked and he withdrew, making his slithering way to the kitchen. "Boo!" Miss Trublood screamed in his ear. He jumped, then tittered, placing his transparent hand over his protruding teeth. "Spying again!" Miss Trublood shouted.

Mordecai shook his head. "No, no," he said hurriedly. "I have parcel for Missie from England."

Miss Trublood beamed. "Good," she said. "Good." And she hurried off to her room to read her Bible and offer prayers of thanks that God had sent word from Elena and Edward.

That evening, the parcel lay on the kitchen table, with a separate envelope under it. Sophia had changed into her dressing-gown and a night-dress. "Miss Trublood's late going to bed, Misha," she commented. Then she looked down at the parcel and recognized Elena's writing. Her heart began to flutter. She tried not to shake.

Misha raised his shaggy head. "She's been doing so much for her mission. You know she works too hard."

Sophia nodded absently. She looked around the kitchen. Mei Mei had gone to bed and Mordecai stood near the kitchen window, leaning against the wall. "What is this?" Sophia asked, her eyebrows raised, afraid that it was a trick or a cruel joke played by Chu and Charlie.

Mordecai's eyes squinted gleefully behind his thick glasses. "Good news," he said. "Very good news."

"You've read it, I suppose." Sophia opened the parcel and held Elena's letter in her hand.

"Yes, yes. Must read all letters."

"And shall I be permitted to write back?" Sophia's voice assumed a hardened tone that tried to conceal her genuine excitement and joy.

"Yes, yes. Charlie say you write."

Sophia grabbed the parcel and the other letter that sat beneath it on the table. This letter was sheathed in a stiff white envelope with an embossed seal on it. She fled to her room.

Once in bed with the lamplight shining on her

dark hair, she opened the official-looking letter first. Ah yes, she thought, the invitation. She put this aside on her night-table and picked up the letter from Elena.

Elena explained that the letter was sent via the British Chancellery in the hope that it would reach Sophia, though it probably would not get to her until well after Christmas, if at all. England was as beautiful as she had imagined, and little Maria was settling well, but everyone missed Sophia more than words could convey. Maria seemed to have struck up an immediate rapport with Nanny Boots, who was looking after her well. Edward had bought her a Shetland pony which, with Nanny Boots walking alongside, she was learning to ride.

Elena went on to report that, as Edward had predicted, they would need to spend a fair amount of time in London, but Sophia was not to worry: Maria would remain in the safety of the country in Nanny Boots's capable hands, and Elena and Edward would be down for the weekends. There was much talk of strikes spreading throughout England, but Elena loved the Monastery and the village, and had already started pickling her own preserves and making jams.

Reading the letter, Sophia laughed. Pickles! Elena hadn't changed.

The letter concluded with the news that Jaggers would be joining them for Christmas, and that as they sat around the Christmas table, all their thoughts would be with her. And here was a box of Christmas crackers to include her in the festivities. The last line of the letter read, "I love you, darling."

And then Sophia saw the dear neat signature and felt the tears roll down her face. She grabbed her pillow and pressed it hard over her mouth so that no one in the house would hear the sob that erupted from her throat. She shut her eyes and cried in a mute pantomime of agony.

But then her tears became tears of hope, not of despair. Christmas had passed, a lonely uninspiring day for Sophia. Miss Trublood and Misha had tried to bring the yuletide spirit into the house, but their efforts proved futile. Sophia's initiation on the winter solstice was all too recent. But tonight, though it was weeks after the holiday, Sophia felt that this was her true Christmas. Until the parcel arrived, the thought of being reunited with her family had receded into the dim and distant future. With the familiar crackers in front of her and a letter from her twin giving her news of Maria, she did not feel so abandoned. They were safe and well. Now it was up to Sophia to work hard and, if Chu was prepared to allow her to write and communicate with her family, then he must be willing to let her go eventually—perhaps even quite soon.

Sophia held a Christmas cracker in her hand. The round barrel of the toy—remembered from the days she as a child first met Edward—was a connection, a stretching link in a long chain that took her from her home in Russia with Katrina to care for her and thence to Shanghai. She recalled the crackers in her life that exploded on Christmas Day every year, first pulled by the whole family.

She pictured her father sitting happily with his funny hat on his princely head. Sophia could see her mother and her grandmother and Edward all seated around the table with Elena and herself. She saw both of them tonight sitting in St. Petersburg and laughing . . . She wiped her eyes. Only a few more days and she was to attend the General's party, not the sort of event she would choose to attend. Never mind, she thought, if I have to do it I will do it well. Tomorrow I'll visit Maria.

She climbed into bed and her thoughts drifted. Maria was taking her to a brothel the next day. "One of the better ones," she had said. A place that might prove useful.

⊷ CHAPTER 77 ⊷

"You see, Maria? I *can* write back." Sophia's face was suffused with joy.

"I'm glad for you." Maria hugged her friend. She felt a great weight of guilt slide from her shoulders: Sophia had news of her sister and her child. Thank goodness. Chu had relented, Maria thought. But then a dark suspicion filled her mind. Maria knew Chu very well and understood that he never did a kind action unless there was a pay-off. Perhaps, she thought, Chu thinks Sophia will try harder if she feels less cut off from her family. Maria pulled away. "I wish I had a family to write to." She loosened her grip around Sophia's neck. They both sat down on the mattress on Maria's floor.

"Maria," Sophia lay back on the mattress, her head propped up on a pillow, "would you reconsider coming to live with us? With me, and Misha and Mei Mei, and Miss Trublood, I mean. I have lots of spare rooms with their own courtyards, so you could be as private as you want."

Maria was touched by Sophia's offer. "Are you sure you'd want a stray cat like me? And what about Miss Trublood? What would she say? After all, I'm a prostitute."

Sophia grinned. "Miss Trublood would be delighted. She says that Jesus' best friends were prostitutes and publicans, and with you on the premises she could redouble her efforts to save you."

"All right. Thanks." Maria paused, then said, "Are you really sure?"

"Positive," Sophia said. "Sometimes I'm so lonely . . . for company of my own age. And I get so fed up with that damned Mordecai slithering about all over the place. Listen, one thing I've been doing is going out at night to scout. I feel if I am to work for Chu I must make sure I know Shanghai—really know it. It's an amazing city. There are people living on so many levels, from the night-soil carriers to the white colonialists, the Tongs and Triads, the brotherhoods, the secret societies. All these people in one city. The brothels, the gambling dens, the tea-houses. Let me tell you, I've been out at night, watching. The only places where everyone in the city mingles are the gambling-houses. And the brothels, though I've never actually been inside one."

"Exactly," Maria said. "And that's why I'm taking you to the Golden Dragon. It's a European brothel."

"Yes, but don't you see? The Europeans think they have everything under control. The English think they run Shanghai. The Americans think they are going to keep Japan out of China. The French and the Germans make enormous profits trading in Shanghai. But the Chinese, like Chu, just sit back and let them think what they want. At the end of the day it's Chu who runs Shanghai with his immense network of connections, like a giant octopus."

Maria tilted her head to the side. They were on dangerous territory. "Shh," she said suddenly. She rose. "Let's go."

The women left the flat and Maria smiled brightly. "I don't like to talk of octopuses," she said. "I don't even like to eat them. Ugh! Those awful suckers. Anyway, thank you for the invitation to live with you. I'd like that."

Outside they hailed a cab. "The Golden Dragon," Maria ordered.

The driver grinned. Two prostitutes on their way to work. He wished he had the money, but these two looked expensive. He had to make do with Teng's Tricky-Tricky on Penang Road. The girls there were fat and dirty, but he got what he wanted. He drove through the streets honking his horn in frustration. One day, he promised himself,

I'll have some European pussy. For now he banged his foot on the accelerator and tore, tires screaming, around corners, swearing and cursing under his breath. Bloody foreigners, he snorted. Wait until the Northerners reach Shanghai. Then the barbarians will all have their throats cut. A man like himself, a decent hard-working man of the people, would be the first to do it.

CHAPTER 78

Sophia admitted to herself that she was nervous as they climbed the stairs of the house called the Golden Dragon. Certainly it was an unmistakable building. She had imagined that houses of ill-repute skulked in hidden gardens or lanes that ran nowhere, but this great house stood proudly in the middle of a square of other houses. The roof supported a huge golden dragon whose head arched over the door, the great jaws gaping widely. "This must be a very rich house," Sophia said, glancing sideways at her friend.

"Don't be nervous, darling," Maria said, taking Sophia by the hand. "It's also very civilized."

They walked through the door into a large waiting-room. All around the room women sat on banquettes. Sophia, who had been holding her breath, was surprised. These women were no long-in-the-tooth harridans driven to prostitution by hardship. They were beautiful—some young, some middle-aged, but all lavishly dressed and perfumed. It was three o'clock in the afternoon and Sophia felt as if she were visiting a finishing school.

"Come," a large-bosomed lady sitting at a desk in the middle of the room called to Maria, "and bring your lovely friend. We're all about to have a cup of tea and some cakes. Do you like chocolate cake, my dear?"

Sophia realized that this woman must be the owner of the Golden Dragon, she spoke with such authority. Sophia said, "I love chocolate."

"Excellent. Moira," she nodded her head at a slightly older woman in a black dress who looked like some kind of an administrator, "go and organize tea. Maria, bring your friend, and come and sit down. We will talk. Ahhh," she said. "I remember Vienna! How we would talk in those happy days! Sitting in those wonderful cafés . . . Oh, the coffee! There is no coffee like Viennese coffee. I won't drink it anywhere else."

She leaned forward and Sophia saw her big breasts part softly in the middle. For a moment, lonely weary Sophia wished she could fall onto those large-nippled breasts and suck contentedly as she had as a child in Katrina's arms. Sophia shook her head.

"I am Madame Kotalinski," the woman said, taking Sophia's hand in hers. She had large but soft hands. She turned Sophia's hand over and studied her palm. Her eyes opened wide. "Dear, dear," she said. "You must definitely learn to think before you act. Look at those lines between your thumb and first finger. Ah, you have a long life! An unusually long life."

Sophia smiled. "That's good to know."

"And for your lovers . . . Let me see. Yes. Many men. But only two more lovers. Ahh, I see." Madame's face softened. "One lover dead, *nein?*"

"Yes." Sophia was impressed by the significance of the German interrogative.

"And see here." She rolled Sophia's hand over and closed her unprotesting fingers. "See? One child. No more children for you, eh? But never mind. Look at your head line. Good, very good." And then, taking her strong middle finger, Madame traced a line running from Sophia's wrist straight up across the palm. "That, my dear, is your line of destiny. Here." Madame took Sophia's left hand. "Compare. See? The left hand is how you are born. The line of destiny is there, but cut up. Now look at the right. Here is what yourself achieve. You're doing well. That is a fine line."

Maria sat quietly watching. Perfect, she thought. Sophia needs Madame. She needs someone older to school her in the art of love.

Madame put her arm around Sophia's shoulder. "I will take you for a little tour around my house. The girls are resting. The men, and sometimes other women, will not come for pleasure until dinner. I'm very strict with my girls and my clients. I run a very orderly house, you know."

Sophia looked about her. She felt quite comfortable in the ornate décor. The girls were laughing and giggling. Madame's presence was a kindly one, and there was much affection in the way Madame and the women looked at each other. Women walked by, their arms entwined about their companions' waists. Really, Sophia thought, a brothel is not in the least what I expected.

Several women poured out cups of tea. The room resounded with talk and many of the women smoked herbal cigarettes. A haze of smoke settled over the crowd of flower-like creatures. Madame chatted to Maria. Sophia sat and observed. She contrasted Elena's letter with the conversations around her. She could almost hear Elena's voice. She imagined her sister in an English kitchen, with jars of brandied plums on the shelf turned a luminous red by the sunlight streaming through the window. A big room with a table in the center. Elena with her fair hair hanging loose down her back. No, no, Elena would never cook with her hair down. She was much too fastidious to risk a stray hair finding its way into food. Her hair would be tied up in a French roll and she would be wearing a white pinafore. Sophia pictured her walking contentedly around the kitchen, her hands covered in flour, baking a cake for Edward . . . "Sophia." Madame's voice cut through her daydreams, making Sophia jump. Madame smiled. "Live in the present," she said. "I gather you have a rather special invitation."

Sophia nodded.

"Well then," Madame said, "we have some homework to do. Come along. Let's go to my office." She stood up and put out her hand. "We'll be back soon, Maria. Do have another cup of tea."

Maria smiled. Madame was going to consult her notorious black book. Each woman was debriefed in Madame's office after her partner had left. Everything, every intimate detail, was inscribed on a page under the client's name, including the food the client enjoyed, which wine, which aperitif. And, of course, every sexual particular. Madame not only had blackmail material for Chu, but she also knew which woman would be willing to perform which acts. She had a nearly blank page reserved for Sophia, a sole instruction from Chu written on it: *High class only. No perversion.* "Lucky girl," Madame had murmured as she wrote the instruction down just the day before.

With Sophia following behind her, Madame walked the long corridor to the back of the brothel. How very lovely and innocent she looks, thought Madame. She pushed opened the black lacquered door to her office. Sophia followed her in and sat on a wide carved chair, her feet dangling like a child's. On all the walls hung nostalgic sepia prints of Madame's home town. The room was furnished with heavy Viennese sideboards and tables. Madame's commodious desk sat in the middle of the room. "Let's see now," Madame said, reaching to the bottom left-hand drawer. "What do we have here? General Wayland: recently arrived, no wife with him, two children back in America. He's taken house calls, but no visits here yet. Serious man, straight sex."

Sophia exhaled loudly. "Thank the Lord," she said.

Madame laughed lightly at Sophia's evident relief, then continued to read. "Likes claret. What do you know about claret?" She looked up at Sophia.

"Not much. Only what Edward taught me. But I'll learn."

"That's a good girl." Madame smiled approvingly. "Well, he likes French food, doesn't like Chinese food. Is typically American, does not chew gum, though. Prefers the woman-on-top position."

Sophia felt herself relax. "I think I can manage that."

Madame nodded. "Take your time to get to know him. Don't rush things. This is not to be a one-off fling. I understand that you are to make him fall in love with you? You're to be his woman. Now, let's go and see your room."

Sophia followed Madame, reflecting on the last few hours. She remembered Maria's words: *You grow numb after a while and it just seems like business.*

"Here we are." Sophia beheld a sumptuous little room, the principal feature of which was a double bed swathed in golden sheets. The walls were lined with silk and the floor covered in a thick carpet the color of clotted cream. Madame walked across the room and pushed open another door. There was a dressing-room, with cupboards lining two walls, and a door leading to the bathroom with a generous swan-shaped bath, the head pointing to a dressing-table loaded with crystal jars.

"It's lovely!" Sophia gasped.

"Yes, this is one of my favorite suites. And through there is the private dining-room. There's a separate entrance to the suite at the back of the house. It's all very discreet, you will find."

Sophia smiled. Perhaps things weren't going to be so bad after all.

CHAPTER 79

Two days before the party Sophia became jittery. Until then she had put off thinking about the actual event. Thoughts about which dress to wear, and which shoes and which perfume, had largely occupied her—when she wasn't thinking of her family.

"I am so glad to have heard from you," she wrote to her sister. "Now I can face life knowing you are all well and happy. I'm very busy." Here Sophia made a wry face. If only they knew what she was doing. She imagined the consternation in Elena's eyes and the frown on Edward's brow. She continued the letter with news about Misha and Mei Mei and how well marriage continued to suit them both. "Miss Trublood now has her redemptive sights set on Maria, who is moving in today." She finished her letter with impassioned inquiries into the welfare of her daughter.

Maria's moving in meant lots of trips and lots

of chaos. Mordecai wrung his hands at the idea of Maria joining the already recalcitrant Sophia. Why did these two young women not dread him? After all he was Charlie's second cousin and everybody dreaded Charlie. As for Miss Trublood . . . Mordecai moaned to himself as he carried Maria's suitcases to her room. Why am I doing this? he wondered. Am I not the major-domo? "Misha should be doing this," he whined as Miss Trublood passed him in the corridor.

"Do it with a glad heart, you heathen," Miss Trublood growled. "Do it or I'll tear the head off your shoulders." Mordecai fled.

Later, in the silence of the night, Sophia realized that she needed some spiritual comfort. Tomorrow, she resolved, I will go and see Lau Tchi. She was now able to admit that he had not harmed her in any way. For the first weeks after her kidnapping she felt bitter and betrayed. Subsequently, as the events of the following months unfolded, she saw that Lau Tchi lived in his own time and space continuum. It was not his way to take action in order to hurt people.

After breakfast, her first with Maria, Sophia took the car and drove herself into the city. First stop: the shoe shop to collect her new shoes. These were high-heeled, made from warm brown crocodile skin. Then on to the dressmaker. Here she picked up her dress, another cheong-sam, again in silk, only this dress was brown instead of her more usual black. She intended to wear a thick gold necklace with matching earrings. She had a large jade ring, the jade stone supported by two gold dolphins. She hoped the effect of the outfit would be that of a gorgeous box of chocolates—edible, of course.

With a room already assigned to her at the Golden Dragon, she intended to lure the General away from his house while her unknown partner got on with his business of photographing the contents of the General's safe. Sophia realized that anything that happened in the room at the brothel would no doubt also be photographed, to be used for possible blackmail later on . . . She turned the car into the Gorgon's courtyard.

He showed no sign of surprise at seeing her when she walked into the room, his servant bowing his way out behind her. Sophia sat on the floor and gazed at Lau Tchi. He was not present in the room. His eyes were rolled back and he seemed not to breathe. Slowly, as Sophia sat there with her legs crossed, she began to breathe in a more steady even rhythm and a serenity stole over her body. She concentrated on the air that passed through her nostrils and flooded her lungs. Uncountable moments later she opened her eyes and saw that Lau Tchi was smiling at her. "Do you know what you are doing?" he said.

Sophia shook her head. "No. I felt as if I was breathing up the city," she said, not sure she could believe her own words.

"You were," he said, "and then you returned the event to its essential purity. Remember what I taught you: life is an illusion, but you must be responsible for the illusion. You, by your actions, are responsible for what is now happening."

"Yes." Sophia began to see. "If I hadn't made friends with Maria, against Katrina's warnings, I might be in England with Elena and my child."

"You might," he said after a pause, "but you might well have side-stepped your destiny. Does your destiny make you happy?"

"Not always."

"Look at your Christian God. He came down for his people and they crucified him. But that was his destiny."

Sophia was afraid. Was this the plan for her, too?

"Now watch me," Lau ordered.

He breathed in harshly. The sound startled Sophia. His chest caved in to his backbone and then, when Sophia thought he could breathe in no more, he took another breath. His face turned purple and the veins in his temples bulged. In the frightful silence that followed Sophia realized that Lau Tchi was holding up time. There was no time; the world stood still. Sophia felt spaceless and weightless and beyond time. Her brain reeled. In the silence she heard something. *Thought creates matter. In the beginning was the word.* Intelligence. In the beginning was the Divine Intelligence and the word was blown upon the void and the void was filled with Divine Intelligence . . .

She was interrupted by a loud scream. "Paaaaaa!" Lau Tchi was exhaling.

And Sophia lost the words. Lau Tchi's body

sagged and wilted until he lay back exhausted on his mat. "You felt time stand still?"

"I did."

"Good." The Gorgon sat up. "You practice. It can save your life and hold your enemy back from you."

"I heard the words *Thought creates matter.*"

"Hum!" Lau seemed pleased. "Very good, very good. Everything from the universe is interrelated. Lifting your hand shifts the balance of the earth. A grain of sand sets the world spinning. You see? All is balance, all is balance."

"About tomorrow . . ." Sophia began.

Lau Tchi shook his head. "There is no tomorrow. Tomorrow is an illusion. You take illusion seriously. That is all. Go now. I am tired." He did look deathly. He lay still and white.

As she left she said a prayer for him. He appeared so alone and vulnerable. How much easier it was, she thought, for Miss Trublood and herself. Their God had a human face. But perhaps the Creator could be manifestly human or unmanifestly a void. The void she faced a few minutes ago was filled with light. Strangely she felt comforted by her visit to Lau Tchi.

Later she went to Maria's room clutching a bottle of Taittinger. They sat comfortably in Maria's small drawing-room. "What a blessing to know my family are safe and that I can keep in touch with them. You know, Maria, it makes all the difference to how I think about myself. Knowing that little Maria is being well looked after and growing up in England, I have something to live for. Now I don't ever need to think of suicide again. I have a goal."

"Then you got what you wanted for Christmas."

"Only a taste of it. I can't have what I want. Not yet, anyway. I guess I'll just have to make jigjig, as Chu Wing says, and sit on top of this man and think all life is illusion."

Maria grinned. "You can get to like it. Sometimes it's not too bad." Then she thought of the chief of police. "And sometimes," she added, "it's awful."

"I've asked Mei Mei to bring us a tray for supper. Is that all right with you?"

Maria smiled her answer. Everything was very all right. She had never experienced so much luxury as during the past twenty-four hours spent in her exquisite suite in Sophia's house. Her small voluptuous body basked in happiness. She was pink and clean from her long bath. Her red hair hung down her back glistening with drops of water. Under her thin silk peignoir she was naked.

Sophia sipped the cold liquid and leaned back in her chair. "Do you think you'll ever lead a different kind of life? As soon as Chu lets me leave, I'm going to head for England and my child. Even if I end up bored to death there and live the life of a spinster, I want my child more than anything else in the world."

Maria swallowed a fizzling mouthful of champagne. "I really don't know, Sophia. Sometimes I think I might give it all up and settle down with some man who will love and take care of me. But then," she wrinkled her nose, "I've tried to settle down a few times, but it just didn't work. It's funny. People always feel sorry for prostitutes, but they believe we have to do what we do. In a way I have to, in another way I don't. I could just as easily get married. I could get a job, nine to five, in an office. I can type and file—but it would kill me. This way I get to live an endless party. I never get bored, because as I lie there, and the client heaves and strains, I know that I'm going to be paid for it, and then I get a sexual rush that I never get making love with someone I care about."

"Are you serious?" Sophia was half-interested, half-shocked.

"Absolutely." Maria stretched her legs and then her whole body.

Sophia watched her. She looked like a beautiful Stradivarius violin, her arms the neck and the scroll, her body the sound-box and her breasts the bridge. Sophia felt a very strange urge to take this body, and to play music upon it. She restrained herself and thought, It must be the champagne.

Sophia stood up rather carefully. "I'll leave you the bottle," she said. "I'd better get to bed early tonight. See you tomorrow." She kissed Maria gently on her champagne-moist lips.

"Umm," Maria said, her arm around Sophia's neck. "You have such soft lips."

Sophia pulled away. "Really, Maria . . ."

Maria laughed, a small tinkling wind-chime of a sound. "I take my pleasure where I find it. I'll never change." She lay back, looking through her lashes at Sophia and smiling. "There's such a power in perversity. That's why I don't think I'll ever settle down. I'm like Rollo. We're hooked on the dark side of life. The strongest drug there is. As much as we weep and cry and complain, we get an undeniable thrill from it."

Sophia stared, a little befuddled by drink. She saw another face swim up in front of Maria's face, the face of a very old crone. It was Maria's face, aged but ageless. The cheeks were sunken, the eyes hollow: and one tooth stood in the rotten gums. Sophia shuddered. It was the face of evil. "Good night, Maria." Sophia left the room quickly.

"Must you sneak about the place?" she snapped at Mordecai in the hallway.

"Yes, Missie. My job." Mordecai grimaced and twisted his hands.

"Well, do it better!" And she marched off into her room.

Life is all an illusion, Sophia reminded herself as she entered her moonlit room. Tomorrow's dress hung in the darkness of her cupboard and the pair of shoes stood guard.

CHAPTER 80

Mordecai tapped nervously on Sophia's door. Sophia was dressed to leave. She could hear the car revving up outside. "What is it?" she asked.

"Instructions for you from Charlie," Mordecai said, his eyes watering. "You read and return paper to me."

"Why don't you just tell me what it says, since you've read it already?"

Mordecai shook his head. "No, you must read. Charlie say so."

Sophia opened the door and snatched the envelope from Mordecai's hand.

"You will know your partner when you see him. Do not attempt to communicate with him. He will know when you are ready to leave."

"*Ready to leave . . .*" So, Charlie knew she was going to try and lure her victim to the Golden Dragon. He doesn't miss a trick, she thought, amused. She was not amused at the idea of Charlie staring at her naked with his camera. Dirty pervert, she thought as she handed back the piece of paper. "Eat it," she said.

Mordecai jumped and put the paper in his mouth. Damn, he thought. Why did I do that? Why do I listen to her? He spat it out as Sophia walked off down the corridor. He watched her retreating back and wiped his thick lips. She was a good choice, he thought. As she went to meet her destiny, her stiletto-heeled shoes rapped out a message: *I am the Snow Leopard. And tonight I am going to take Shanghai.*

❦ CHAPTER 81 ❦

Sophia blessed the work she had done at night, for this evening it gave her confidence. A week ago she was sitting on the corner of the street eating hot peppers from a street-vendor's stall, bundled up in her blue padded peasant clothes. Now she stepped from her car and walked up the wide steps that led to the front door. She knew the house and its occupants so well that she had to remind herself to register surprise when the door was opened by the butler, whose face she had become familiar with over the past weeks. He nodded and bowed as Sophia held out her invitation. He took her chocolate mink-coat, then a valet led her across the hall into the drawing-room.

People drew back to let her through. By now it was well known in Shanghai society that Sir Edward and Lady Gray were in England with Sophia's child. "So much wiser that the little girl should be brought up there instead of in this heathen country," the women agreed. "Besides," they tittered to each other behind fans, "Sophia does have a reputation." Sophia knew what they were whispering. She stiffened her spine and swung her hips. The women's husbands could not take their eyes off her. This made her smile.

She could see the General across the room talking with a group of people. He was taller than his guests and he stooped to listen to what a small Chinese dressed in ceremonial attire was saying. The General's head bobbed with interest after each phrase. "The Countess Sophia Oblimova!" the valet announced. Sophia was amused. She strolled up to the man whom she had watched from the shadows and waited for his eyes to meet hers. When he raised his head, she was even more amused. This is going to be easy, she thought. She waited.

The General remained motionless for an instant and then took her hand. "Charmed, my dear," he said.

Ah, a Boston Brahmin. She could tell by the way he said *charmed*. What could be better?

"Do let me get you a drink. Boy!" he shouted. "Over here! A champagne cocktail, my dear?"

"Lovely." Sophia was enjoying herself. And there was no denying the old goat had fallen for her. She was ahead of the game.

"Stay close," he said. He patted Sophia's small hand that had found itself firmly clasping the General's arm. She gazed sweetly up at his hard-boiled blue eyes, the whites tinged with yellow as were the eyes of so many of the barbarians who lived too long in alien countries around the world.

She gazed about the room curiously. And then she saw Stanislaus. He was wearing the black trousers and white jacket of a drinks waiter. Strangely she felt comforted, not only that it was Stanislaus, but also that he was her ally, her companion and partner in this dangerous game.

"Stick with me," the General said tenderly. "Let's go and find some food."

"Certainly."

The General and the Snow Leopard strolled

among the guests. "The bitch!" a pink-faced Belgian woman snorted to her elaborately coiffured French friend. "Look at her!"

The French woman sniffed. "Well," she said, "he's only an American. *Tant pis.* As far as I'm concerned, she can keep him all to herself."

People moved in and out of Sophia's vision. She was busy, furiously thinking about her role as a spy. How very strange, she thought while she mechanically grinned at yet another young man's face that swam in front of her. All my life I dreamed and fantasized that a moment like this would exist, when I would make illicit love to some man in order to find out some huge secret.

There stood the man she had dreamed about except, of course, the man of her dreams had been dark and dashing. Never mind. I'll have to occupy him somehow, and not here. I must try and get him back to the Golden Dragon.

The room was thinning out. It was late for the cocktail hour, but some people stayed, for the Americans gave the best parties in Shanghai. Generally speaking, they were the wealthiest of the foreign communities. They looked taller and better fed than everyone else. They were also louder. Their voices bounced off the ceiling. "Well, *sure,*" "Aw, come *on,*" accompanied by the meaty crack of a friendly slap on a pal's back.

The English sniffed and minced. Sir Edward had always been an exception. But he, like most of the old guard, had retired back to England. Those left were the New English. These were a different breed, harder than their predecessors and humorless.

Sophia realized that beneath the apparent sophistication of the cocktail set, what lay at the root of most of the conversations in the room was the desire to sneak away to make love—married men with unmarried women, married women with anyone desperate enough for an assignation. Her affair with Elter had been so straightforward. From the day they met they knew with absolute certainty that they were to become lovers. Even the two years the tryst took to arrange were years of exhilaration. This evening she felt not exhilarated but resigned. This was something she had to do.

Now part of the sensuous web of intrigue herself, she recognized the dozen or so men and women who were the late hangers-on as people with sex on their minds and little else. She watched the French attaché lecherously ogle the young woman beside him. Sophia knew the girl vaguely. Emmanuelle was her name. She had very large breasts and thick black hair. Emmanuelle smiled at Sophia. Over her thick fleshy lips she had a slight moustache. Sophia remembered Maria saying that some men found hair around a woman's mouth erotic. The French attaché was evidently one such man.

But enough of this, Sophia thought. I have a job to do. She sidled up to General Wayland. He was talking to yet another Chinese businessman. Sophia leaned close to the General's side. Unthinkingly, the General draped his arm around Sophia's slim form. Sophia leaned a little harder. The General glanced down and appeared surprised. "Why, Sophia!" he said. "Have you had a good time?"

"Wonderful." And she held his eyes with her own.

The General cleared his throat. "Glad to hear it," he said. "If you'll excuse me, Mr. Tan, that was a very interesting talk and one I would like to continue first chance we get."

Mr. Tan nodded his head and tucked his hands into his robe. Damn the European whores, he thought. Damn the foreign men. All they want is to chase women. Mr. Tan walked off.

"Well, now." General Wayland was definitely interested. He had been in Shanghai for over a year and, apart from several unsatisfactory visits to a couple of brothels, and a few women whom he coaxed into coming back to his house, he had been a lonely man. Here standing in front of him was a beautiful young woman who seemed to want him as much as he wanted her. His arm was still around Sophia's shoulder. His hot hand touched her breast. Feeling the firm globe, he squeezed. "Nice?" he asked softly. There were still people in the room.

"Very," Sophia breathed, and rubbed her thigh against his.

The General's eyes changed. Suddenly he was a man with a mission. He looked around wildly. "Here, Lieutenant Ford. Take over. I have some business to attend to. Call the car."

Lieutenant Ford made a face. Hope I get that sort of pussy when I'm his age, he thought as he hurried across the room.

"Meet me at my car." The General pushed Sophia away. "It's the big gray Cadillac."

Sophia knew his car very well. She smiled to herself and walked slowly out of the room. She collected her coat and as she left she saw Stanislaus. He was grinning on the stairs. He had all night to do what had to be done. The General was leaving the house with Sophia. I'll keep him busy, Sophia silently promised her accomplice.

❧ CHAPTER 82 ❧

The car was luxurious. American cars smell different, she thought, ensconced in the back seat. English cars smell of old leaves and leather and polished wood. American cars smell modern, hygienic and new. The seats in English cars kept one sitting upright. In American cars one sprawled, the seats being padded like soft feather-beds. Good for making love, I suppose, she thought idly. The General slipped in beside her. "Tell me where you'd like to go." His voice was hoarse and throaty.

Sophia snuggled her shoulder under his arm. "Let's see," she said as if she didn't already know the answer. "We could go to dinner at the Hong Kong Hotel, or maybe dinner and dancing at Jimmy's. Or if you like," she put her small hand on his thigh and ran her fingers up and down, "we could go to the Golden Dragon, where I have a private suite. You choose." Good heavens, Sophia congratulated herself. I never thought I'd be so good at it.

The General stared at her. The Golden Dragon? A question hung in the air. The Golden Dragon, Sophia answered with a nod. "The Golden Dragon," General Wayland ordered his driver.

General Wayland pulled Sophia into his arms and began to kiss her. Sophia let herself be kissed, feeling very little at all. Finally the General came up for air. "You don't know how lonely I've been," he began.

Sophia looked sympathetically into his eyes, though inwardly she reminded herself that this was the bit Maria described as the most boring of all. "I can imagine." She took his hand. "I am on my own too in this big city, and it's so wretchedly lonely."

"Where's your family?" What could a beautiful young woman be doing on her own in a city like Shanghai?

Sophia lowered her eyes. "I'm a widow. I was married to a German businessman, but he died."

The General pressed her hand in his. "Gee, that's awful. I'm sorry."

Sophia inclined her head. "So now I look after his business. Import/export, you know. Not much fun. But I've only just come out of mourning and life must go on, mustn't it?" How useful clichés are, she thought.

"How true. You're right. Absolutely right. Life must go on." The General thought he might have a vague memory of the Golden Dragon but he couldn't be sure whether he had been there or not, or what kind of place it was. Maybe just a boarding-house for helpless single girls.

Sophia directed the chauffeur to the private entrance to her suite at the Golden Dragon. The car pulled up outside the apparently respectable building. "Wait for me here," the General ordered the chauffeur.

The chauffeur nodded. He had a pornographic book in his pocket. Some people have all the luck, he thought bitterly. I could really make her dance.

"Hey, Sophia! Nice place!" General Wayland stood in the small dining-room. The table was laid: dinner for two.

Sophia smiled. "You like it?"

"Hell, yes." The General sat down gingerly on a gold cane chair. "It feels like being inside a doll's house," he said.

"Well, it's all ours for tonight. We can do anything we like here," Sophia promised him. "Shall we order dinner, General?"

The General stood up. "I wish you'd call me Wayne." He blushed. "To tell the truth, it's my middle name, but I prefer it. My mother called me John Wayne Wayland. Mom thought it would be a good name. She never wanted me to be a boring old two-star general. She wanted to see her son in the footlights on stage."

"It's a fine name for an actor. It's also a fine name for a two-star general."

The General's blush deepened. "Maybe I should've listened to Mom after all. Being an actor would've been a hell of a lot less sweat than worrying about the Japs. Still, let's not give them a second thought tonight. The world can wait." A desperately eager look took possession of his face.

"What would you like to drink? Some wine perhaps? I have a nice claret . . ."

"Claret?" The General raised a questioning eyebrow. "I'm a great claret-drinker myself. But tonight I think I might stick to bourbon."

"Or I have a lovely bottle of champagne on ice."

"Why not?" the General laughed. "Champagne sounds like a good idea."

"It makes one so happy," Sophia said with an inviting smile.

"OK, if you say so." He reached for Sophia and she allowed herself to be folded in his arms, thinking, This might not be as bad as I expected. Poor man. He really is lonely.

"You see, my boy is twenty-one and in the army, but his mother doesn't want him there. No, sir. She wanted him to go to college. Ivy League, of course. And become a writer. Then there's our girl, Wilhelmina, who scrapes away at the cello." Wayne shook his head. "Say, this is good steak, Sophia. Very good steak. Haven't had anything like this since I left Boston." He emptied his glass of champagne. "Great choice, Sophia. I like your taste in wine. In fact," he said, looking about him, "I like everything. I like this room, I like the steak, and the champagne, and I like you."

Sophia sat back amused. Before her was a two-star general, his tie askew, the top button of his dress-suit undone. His face was flushed with champagne, his eyes shining, and he was having a marvelous time. True, his stories of his family life were boring, but rather endearing, she decided. She could do worse. "Would you like pudding?" she asked.

Wayne's face lit up. "You mean dessert?"

"Dessert." Sophia laughed.

"Do you think they have any ice cream?" he demanded. "I mean, *real* ice cream, like we have in America. I get so homesick for ice cream and apple-pie. Cold, thick, vanilla ice cream on a thick buttery crust, and steaming hot apples, and lots and lots of cinnamon."

"You can have anything you want, Wayne."

"You mean that, honestly?" Wayne was incredulous.

"John Wayne Wayland can have anything he wants."

"Then I'll have apple-pie and vanilla ice cream."

"Certainly." She rang the bell.

Wayne finished the last spoonful of ice cream and released a languorous sigh.

Sophia decided that enough of the evening had been spent on food. "Wayne," she said, "it's getting late. Would you like to come to bed?"

Wayne looked surprised. He was used to the fumble-in-the-dark approach, to backing into some room or other, too drunk to undress, and then the heaving and moaning, hoping he was in the right place at the right time, but glad for the moment of release, and even gladder for the short sleep that came after. Then he would stumble out of bed, and out into the early-morning air to his waiting car. "Huh?" he said.

Sophia walked around the table and held out her hand. "Come," she said. "I have a lovely bedroom. We can have some fun."

Wayne trailed after the small figure as she led him to another room. "Wow! This is even prettier!" Wayne sat heavily on the bed, a little dizzy from the champagne.

Sophia squatted down and began to unlace his shoes.

"I can do that." Wayne pushed Sophia away.

"But you must let me," she replied. "Look at me, Wayne."

She pulled at the neck of her cheong-sam and unfastened a few buttons at the waist, and the cheong-sam fell to the ground. Sophia stood there naked but for a suspender-belt of ruche silk and her sheer stockings. Sophia laughed as she saw Wayne's mounting excitement. She realized she was rather enjoying herself. She crouched down again and removed Wayne's shoes. Off came his socks, and then his belt. Finally Wayne, twitching and panting, lay naked in front of her.

Really, this is rather like horse-riding, she thought irreverently as she straddled him. He began to thrash and moan and she felt his hugeness inside her. Lying on top of this man, who gripped her like a bear, she realized to her shame and guilt that she too was starting to become excited. It was so long since she had made love to

Elter on the junk. Now she felt a man inside her and, she recognized as she arched to meet his thrust, she was just a woman in need of sex. Wayne came with huge cries and she too climaxed.

She slumped on top of his body. She could tell from the snore that Wayne was asleep. She rolled off and stared at the ceiling of the bedroom. "Oh dear," she whispered, confused feelings washing over her. One feeling was certainly a feeling of physical satisfaction, for the first time since Elter had loved her. Her orgasm had left her body very much at peace. And her head felt clearer. There was just a small nagging worry at the back of her mind. I know, she told herself impatiently, I shouldn't be doing this . . . She sat up and drew her knees under her chin. I'm going to have a bath and then I'd better see that he gets back to his house.

She looked down at General Wayland, a big man from a big country, and a very long way from home. He lay there defenseless, snoring evenly. "You sleep," she said and quietly padded off to the bathroom.

Once in the perfumed water she lay dreaming of nothing in particular. It helps, she thought as she drifted about, to have a place like this: suspended in time, hollowed out and secret. Not that secret, she remembered. Not that secret.

Miss Trublood was up when Sophia got back at daybreak. "Couldn't sleep," Miss Trublood said lamely. "I'll make you a glass of hot milk. Sophia, you look tired."

"I am a little," Sophia replied, her heart sinking. Whatever happens, she thought, I can't tell her.

Miss Trublood led the way to the kitchen. The door to Mordecai's room was, as usual, open. He lay on his bed, listening. Walking past, Miss Trublood slammed it shut. "Go to sleep, you heathen!" she shouted. "Humph. I'm almost beginning to get used to the little louse," she grumbled. "Sophia, I'm worried about you. You come and you go. Sometimes you look as if you're carrying the whole world on your shoulders, and other times you seem pretty happy. Please, let me help you. Is anything happening that I should know about?"

Sophia shook her head. "No, Miss Trublood. Nothing I can't handle." Sophia ached to tell Miss Trublood about the night's events. She yearned to confide in someone who would listen sympathetically. She wanted absolution, and oblivion. She wanted to wake up after a long sleep and to feel she had never given herself in prostitution. These were the feelings she had battled with on the drive home. General Wayland had put on his uniform and reassumed his rank. He kissed her stiffly before he left the suite and said, "Can I see you again?"

"Any time you like," Sophia had said lightly.

She took her cup of steaming milk and followed Miss Trublood into the sitting-room. Sophia sat cross-legged on the floor. The comforting smell of hot milk transported her back to her childhood in Russia. Tears welled in her eyes as she remembered her mother and father. But her grandmother was the only one who understood her. And now Anna Oblimova seemed to speak to her. "My child, you did well."

Miss Trublood sat quietly, sensing Sophia's confusion but powerless to help. "God will forgive you, whatever it is," she said, placing her square hand on Sophia's shoulder.

"Oh, I hope so!" Sophia finished her milk. "I must get some sleep," she said with a sad smile. She put her arms around Miss Trublood's neck and hugged her. "I'll see you this evening," she said.

"God bless you, child." She kissed Sophia and they both left the sitting-room where the cups sat empty, except for a trace of milk skin. Outside a bird clung to a creeper and began to instruct the new day of its duties.

❧ CHAPTER 83 ❧

Chu Wing sat in the weak early-morning sunlight. Stanislaus stood beside him, watching the man endlessly spit sunflower seeds onto the floor. They were waiting for Charlie. The plans on the table before them were taken from General Wayland's informative safe. Stanislaus, now one of the houseboys on the General's household staff, moved with impunity about the house. Tuesday evenings and Friday evenings the General, he knew, was with

Sophia. Those were the nights when he was safe to photograph. Before him lay the fruits of weeks of work. He heaved a sigh of weariness.

"Good." Chu grinned.

Stanislaus looked at the obese mountain of flesh, wishing that Chu would do something about his teeth. Chu's foul breath caused the young man to gag, but he stifled the urge to be sick and managed a smile. "Thank you," he said.

They heard a car pull up outside the window. Charlie came in. His eye was bright and his step light. "Ah, I see we have the plans."

Chu nodded. "This fellow do well."

Charlie rubbed his hands. "Chu, I need food."

Stanislaus rang the bell.

Shuffling and giggling, several young women padded in carrying trays of food. The three men moved to a table at the back of the room and sat down. For a moment the three were silent as they watched the girls lift the lids off the silver salvers. The mixed aromas of tiger shrimp and egg fu yong covered in a thick golden-brown sauce that smelled of oysters wafted before their nostrils— dinner at breakfast-time after a long night's work. Charlie licked his lips. "I'm so hungry. What a night!"

Chu grunted, "What happen?"

"The Tongs who run the red-light district fell out. One of the best fights I've seen in a long time. They used beheading swords." He leaned over and helped himself with his chopsticks to more food. Then he put two large prawns on Stanislaus's plate.

Stanislaus looked down at the prawns and wished Charlie could keep his nocturnal adventures to himself. Chu laughed. "That keep all quiet for while. But now to business. Ship from Kagoshima has gold from South Africa shipped by Germans to Japan. Now loaded in Japan to bring to Shanghai." He turned to Stanislaus. "Get plans."

Wearily Stanislaus retrieved the plans from Chu's desk and brought them to the table. He smoothed out the sheets and pointed to a fortified room in the stern of the boat. "There it is," he said. "Two hundred gold bars. All packed on flats ready to be taken off the boat. The corridor outside the strong room has its own exit giving access to the narrow-gauge railway on the Shanghai docks. The Japanese will be there to receive it. But the Americans have other plans for it."

"What?" Chu and Charlie said almost in unison. Charlie rocked on his chair, his one eye staring at Stanislaus with interest. He poked single-mindedly with a toothpick at his long yellow teeth.

"As far as I can understand, the Japanese intend to run the flats onto a small railway, as I have said. Then, as usual, they'll escort the cargo into a hong and guard it until it can be taken by rail to the Japanese quarter and distributed to all their various outposts: Manchuria . . ."

"But the Americans?"

"According to the information I've obtained from General Wayland's house, the Americans intend to intercept the cargo while the gold is on its way to Nanking. Just before the train reaches the city, they'll blow up the railway and attack the train, but the soldiers carrying out the raid will not be in uniform, in order to make it look like a gangland robbery. The Americans want to prevent the Japanese from being able to buy any more food from the peasants."

"Umm." Chu pulled at his lip, his eyes veiled. "We could do with two hundred gold bars," he said to Charlie in Chinese. "These next years are going to be difficult. How are our plans going on this?"

Charlie spoke in English, for Stanislaus's sake. "I have arrangements in hand to take the ship to a different destination. By the time the Americans and the Japanese find that she is not unloading in Shanghai, it will be too late, and we will be gone—with the gold." He grinned. "It's a nice plan. There's a dock in Ningpo with the narrow-gauge railway we need. By now two armored trucks should be making their way there. In two weeks' time nobody in the village near the docks will be thinking about the appearance of the two trucks. They will just be parked there, and part of the scenery." He shrugged. "The plan requires four of our men to take over the running of the ship and four passengers to lure the guards." He lifted his chin and made a cutting motion. "But only after the guards have opened the vault with the gold in it. It's the only way to get the vault open."

Stanislaus frowned. More killing, he thought. He looked down at his sensitive hands that used to play Chopin and Mozart, hands that must now kill. He wondered who his accomplices would be—

for he knew he would be part of the operation. He had killed before but with no pleasure, just the knowledge that he did a job that had to be done and that the men and women he killed would have killed him had he failed. Stanislaus did not fail. He was calm and steady. He rarely smiled these days, but there was not much to smile about.

"You leave now," Chu said.

"The *Nagasaki* will be ready to sail in ten days." Charlie spoke to Chu in Chinese, now that Stanislaus had gone. "The *Nagasaki* is due to dock in Shanghai at one in the morning. The captain will be on deck with his crew—a small crew. Our men need to overpower him, kill whoever is on deck, and then steer the ship away from Shanghai and take it on to Ningpo. Very quiet, very few people there. The important thing is that the four passengers must get the guards to show them the gold so that they are all in the hold when the boat fails to dock in Shanghai. The guards, too, must be killed. Not a difficult plan, but it depends on our people getting past the locked vault and the boat's other passengers continuing to lie undisturbed in their bunks."

Chu nodded.

"But don't worry," Charlie continued. "My men are experts. Very quiet. They can use strangling leathers."

"Yes, yes. And our passengers?"

"The Russians, probably. That dark-headed woman, Sophia, is excellent." His eye shone as he remembered the pictures he had in his room. Charlie looked forward to Tuesdays and Fridays.

They didn't need the photographs of General Wayland any longer. Once the gold was hijacked, Wayland's usefulness was at an end. Charlie grinned. "The American will never know how he was duped, will he?"

Chu threw his head back. His cavernous jaw gaped open. "He won't. Those Americans can be so stupid. Well, most of them anyway," he reminded himself. So far the Japanese hadn't managed to drive them out of China. "Good day's work, Charlie," Chu congratulated him. "Let's go and get a real drink."

So far so good, Charlie thought with satisfaction. Now to give the orders. He, Charlie, was going to mastermind this raid himself.

CHAPTER 84

Sophia found herself made very welcome at the Golden Dragon. Madame Kotalinski was unfailingly helpful and full of fun. The girls of the house sat about and gossiped when they were not "working." Mostly the talk was of the men they had pleasured, or of the boyfriends they loved and wanted to marry. The only women Sophia found unapproachable were the lesbians. They had a part of the house to themselves. They shared the same entrance hall and dining-room as the others, but they sat by themselves. The other women feared them. Sophia watched fascinated. The queen of this hive seemed to be a woman called Clarice. She was tall, like a poplar tree. She had fierce blue eyes and very blonde silvery hair. Her skin was like polished jade, with a slight green cast to it. Her lips were rose-petal pink. She had no eyelashes, so her eyes never seemed to blink. "Who on earth is she?" Sophia asked Maria. They were in the dining-room eating a late breakfast.

Maria made a face. "That's Clarice Carruthers. Her mother was Russian, but her father was an English lord. He lives in grand style in England, and she lives even more grandly here in Shanghai. She did go back to England, but she hated it there. You know, the English don't think women do it to each other."

Sophia laughed. "I suppose she's a friend of Rollo's?" she asked.

"No. Clarice and her women have nothing to do with men. Men, they say, are the enemy. At least, that's what she *says*." Maria sipped her tea. *"Chacun à son goût,* I guess."

"Where do you suppose we're going?" Sophia asked. Chu had unexpectedly announced that she was to be allowed a holiday, as a reward for her good work. She had been delighted to learn that Maria would be joining her.

"I don't know. I expect Mordecai will have some details when we get back. God, that police chief is an awful bore! He comes like a train, sleeps, and then demands sex again. And he's so very bad at it. The dreadful thing is that he thinks he's a marvelous lover. And I have to talk baby-talk to him.

Diddums, indeed!" She bit savagely into her toast. "I wish I could bite off his prick," she said crossly.

Sophia smiled. "I've actually grown rather fond of my General," she said. "When I told him I would be away for three weeks on holiday, he looked genuinely sad. Said he'd miss me. I think he probably will." She wiped her lips with the corner of her napkin. "He treats me very well. We make love, he rests, and then I wake him up and he goes home. He sits on the bed sometimes and talks about his life in America. Really, you know, Maria, I couldn't live like the Americans. It's all so clean, so hygienic, so boring. That's his problem: he has everything he wants in life, but he's bored. He has a neat American housewife, two neat American children, two matching cars in the garage, one for her and one for him, and a big ice-box which he says is full of ice cream and 'cookies,' as he calls them. On Saturdays he mows the lawn, and on Sunday afternoons, after church, he listens to football. Really, it's too dreadful."

"At least while he's in Shanghai he gets you twice a week and Stanislaus . . ."

"I know." Sophia frowned. "Stanislaus can take all the pictures he wants. I don't feel too happy about that. But I tell myself it's none of my business."

She looked up to find Clarice's eyes upon her. Failing to receive the response they sought, Clarice shifted her gaze to Maria. She obviously liked what she saw. Oh no, thought Sophia. Not Maria. I'm not losing her to the likes of you.

Clarice was famous for reducing her female lovers to abject adoration of her. Some said it was witchcraft, others drugs. Whatever the hold Clarice had on her chosen womenfriends, Sophia was not going to let it happen to Maria. "Come along, Maria." She rose from the table. "We'd better head for home."

Maria looked up. "Why so jumpy?"

Sophia indicated with her head the table full of women.

"Oh. I see." Maria smiled amiably. "Clarice has been after me for some time now." She stared at Sophia and stretched, the long line of her body uncurling in her chair. She tilted her head back until her smooth white throat hung over the chair and her hair fell loose and reached almost to the floor.

"Come on, Maria. Don't be such a fool."

"Why?" A wicked smile stole across her face. "Are you jealous?"

"Don't be absurd." Sophia grabbed Maria's hand and pulled her out of the dining-room, but not before Maria turned and gave Clarice a knowing wink and flashed her small red tongue at her.

Clarice looked away, smiling. They all thought they were so clever these young women, but really they were so naïve. The truly perverse always won. Evil was so much more fun than good. Clarice did not dislike men; she was merely bored by them. Even sexually decadent Rollo had a conscience. That was why she had nothing to do with men, either homosexual or straight: their consciences always got in the way. One simply could not rely on them to be completely and utterly amoral. *Immoral,* yes. Rollo knew when he sinned and often sinned anyway. But he did know, and he felt guilty. Clarice did not even begin to understand the concept of sin. If she wanted something, she just took it. She wanted Maria and in the end she would have her.

A sliver of smoked salmon lay on her plate. She picked up her chopsticks, speared the pink morsel and popped it in her mouth. "Mmm," she breathed. Yes, she would have Maria, sooner or later.

✇ CHAPTER 85 ✇

Sophia was pleased to find out that Stanislaus and Rollo were to be their companions on the mysterious holiday.

Mordecai handed both women their instructions with an air of great gravity. "Nobody to know," he said.

"Stop being ridiculous, Mordecai," Sophia snapped. "If you continue to sneak about, looking so self-important, everybody will know."

Mordecai sighed and retired to his bedroom, while the girls took themselves off to Maria's room.

"So, tomorrow we leave for Japan. Chu has one of his private boats all laid on. And look, it says here we're to take nothing with us. We'll be provided with everything we need."

Sophia could not help but feel a thrill at the prospect of going some place new. "This sounds like fun."

Maria looked at her sideways. "Could be," she said. "Or it maybe not, if you see what I mean."

Sophia caught the edge in Maria's words and felt afraid. She remembered the raid on the *Elizabeth*.

"Yes," Maria said. "Exactly. Someone always gets hurt. We can only hope it's someone who wants to hurt us. That way you feel better about what happens."

"You mean I might have to kill someone?"

"You may well have to kill or be killed," Maria said matter-of-factly.

"I can't be killed." Sophia's voice was definite. "I can't get killed. I have to get back to little Maria. Every day goes by, I miss seeing her grow. I've missed her baby teeth. I have missed her talking in sentences. I've missed her third Christmas. She's a child now. Do you know what I mean? A child. She's no longer a baby now. She's a growing child and I'm missing all of it." She looked out of the window. "When will this end? When will he let us go?"

Maria shook her head. "I wish I knew. But let's not worry about that now. I'm going to telephone Rollo, and make plans to get to the port."

"I'd better go and say goodbye to Miss Trublood. We're due to leave at a disgustingly early hour."

*   *   *

"Just a holiday, you say?" Miss Trublood looked doubtful.

"I promise." Sophia hated lying, particularly to such a kindly woman. "Maria and I need to get away and have some fun. We'll be back in three weeks."

"A bit of fun wouldn't do you any harm," said Miss Trublood, not sure whether or not to believe Sophia. "Well, take care, honey, and God bless."

Misha stared up at Sophia through his bushy eyebrows. "Look after yourself."

"And you look after Mei Mei." Sophia smiled.

"Goodbye, Mordecai," she said, repenting for her earlier outburst. "I'll bring you back a present, if I get a chance."

Mordecai blushed. Really, sometimes Missie Sophia could be quite nice.

The trip across the sea to Japan was unremarkable. The days on board were spent mostly in silence, each traveler mentally preparing themselves for the events that lay ahead. It was not until they reached the Japanese port that they began to feel a little excited by the prospect of adventure, and even danger.

Sophia was quite amazed to find so many Chinese in Japan. "Who are they?" she asked Stanislaus as they walked through the busy port.

"A strange mixture. Some are communist extremist revolutionaries hiding over here in Japan, hatching plots and hiding from the nationalists. Others are exiles from the communist settlements in northern China. Some are rich Manchus who have decided to throw in their lot with the Japanese, believing that the Japanese will finally conquer China and hand it back to a Manchu emperor."

Rollo walked through the human throng looking very odd, almost laughable in Sophia's eyes. He seemed completely out of place here, taken from the Shanghai that he had made his home. And, to make him less conspicuous, his long red hair was dyed black and cut short. "I feel stupid," he said, walking through the crowd of travelers.

Sophia watched the Chinese arriving and leaving. The back of the Chinese heads looked like smooth seals bobbing in waves on a beach. The Japanese by contrast had sharper heads and harsh necks. They were a thinner and brisker people. Their voices barked like dogs.

The long drive into Kagoshima surprised Sophia. Unlike Shanghai, Japan seemed untouched by war. Nowhere were there signs of bombing. The streets were spotlessly clean, the crowds disciplined. Not so the cars that careered around corners and screeched and hooted. This was a country and a people that had been isolated for centuries, shrouded in mystery. Then the Emperor had opened the ports to foreigners, and lived to regret the folly of trading with the West. For Japan opened itself like a beautiful woman and was promptly raped. But before long the abused mistress turned master and now Japan was sending out thousands of Japanese to fight for the motherland. The Japanese concept of the samurai was neither dead nor forgotten. New warriors were now eager to conquer as much of the Chinese mainland as they could. Sophia sensed the excitement in the air.

Their limousine stopped in front of an inn. They got out and followed Maria into the foyer. "This house for you." The manager beamed, delighted to have four rich visitors taking the rooms for a week.

"Thank you," said Maria. She led the way down a small white corridor. The walls were made from thin rice paper. Maria slid open a partition. "Here's the bathroom."

On the thick-planked wooden floor stood a large round steaming tub. Around the room were plush piles of towels. Sophia laughed. "You could wash an army in that tub."

"All four of us, anyway," Maria answered.

"You mean . . ."

"Well, this is Japan, after all."

Sophia felt crushed. She had never bathed naked with anyone but Elena and Katrina, and that had been long ago in childhood. Even General Wayland respected her privacy when it came to bathing. I'll get used to it, she promised herself.

They moved on. Sophia's room was next to Maria's. Her bed was a thick white goose-down pallet. She examined the wooden neck rest. She lay down on the pallet and listened to the other three acquainting themselves with their rooms. Maria has done so much more than I have with her life, Sophia thought. She probably knows what she's doing here . . . Then Sophia caught sight of the boxes standing against the wall beside a full-length mirror. "Maria," she called, "our clothes!"

Maria changed into a loose-fitting red silk robe bound at the waist with a matching sash. Sophia selected a black velvet high-necked dress.

They dined in a covered courtyard. Two young geisha girls served them. Sophia marveled at how different everything was. With Japanese food, the tastes were so separate, so distinct. Unlike the Chinese tendency to blend tastes.

"Well, whatever happens," Stanislaus said, "I shall certainly remember this meal." A silence fell. "I'm sorry, that was a silly remark. Nothing's going to happen. We'll just do as we're told and all go home. I'm tired." He took a final sip of saki.

Maria stretched. "Let's all go to bed. We can explore the city in the morning."

That night Sophia dreamed that Maria was making love to Stanislaus and she was watching with tears in her eyes. Don't be such a fool, her sleeping self said. Don't be such a bloody fool.

CHAPTER 86

The four days before boarding the *Nagasaki* passed quickly. Sophia felt as if she and her colleagues were children let loose on Kagoshima, an unsuspecting city. Rollo spent most of his time wandering about the shops looking at clothes.

"You can't buy anything, you idiot," Sophia reminded him. "We have to take our uniforms with us and throw out what we're wearing when we leave the boat."

Rollo pursed his lips. "Do I look as though I care, darling?" he said, scrutinizing his reflection in yet another mirror.

Stanislaus was bored. "I'd rather go to a temple," he said.

Maria, too, was admiring herself in a long mirror. "Fine then. You two go off and bother the Buddha. Rollo and I will tend to more worldly matters. Meet you back at the hotel for dinner." She grinned at Sophia. "And for a nice long hot bath. We have to make plans, you know. We can't avoid the issue for ever."

"I know." Stanislaus frowned. "I just don't like having to kill people."

Sophia looked apprehensive. "Have you killed many?"

"Too many," he said shortly. "I had no choice."

Rollo agreed. "Sometimes there are no alternatives. Anyway, let's leave it all until tonight. For now I want to find an impossibly tight pair of tennis shorts. Come on, Maria. Help me choose."

Sophia was left with Stanislaus. He looked somber and unhappy. Sophia took his hand. She said, "I know I shouldn't risk saying this to you, but I'm going to trust you." She smiled at the man and watched his eyes carefully. He stared back at her: there was no treachery in his eyes, no wish to hurt her, rather a soft acceptance of what life had to offer, a feeling of resignation, as if he put all he had into the world and it had turned him down. "One day," Sophia said, walking beside Stanislaus on the crowded but orderly pavement, "one day I'm just going to walk away from this life and escape. I don't know how I'm going to do it, but I will. They can't keep me enslaved for ever. Sometimes," she walked a little faster, "I feel as if Chu will never free us." She felt Stanislaus's hand tighten on hers.

"Let's make a pact," he said. "Just you and I. And talk of this to no one, you understand." Sophia nodded. "When the time comes we'll leave together. I don't want to live this way any more than you do."

"What about Maria and Rollo? Don't you think we should include them?"

Stanislaus shook his head. "For all their carry-on, they don't want to leave. The pay-offs are too great for people like them."

Sophia began to protest, but then she remembered the look on Clarice Carruthers's face and the correspondent flash of delight in Maria's eyes. "I think I see what you mean," she said slowly.

Stanislaus hailed a taxi. "Take us to the Yellow Moon Temple," he said. The car passed through different districts, all clean and orderly. Sophia missed the busy streets of Shanghai, but as she sat in silence she thought of Elena and little Maria. She wondered if they were enjoying the English countryside that soon would blossom into spring. She tried not to cry.

The taxi pulled up at the big gates. Sophia and

Stanislaus stepped through into a very different world.

Around them were monks, bald-headed and smiling. "They look so much happier than Roman Catholic priests, don't they?" Sophia remarked.

Stanislaus laughed. "They can have sex," he said. "Many of them didn't intend to be monks, but the families who are too poor to educate their boys put them with the monks from the age of seven or eight. And they in turn become monks themselves and serve the temples."

"Maria told me you were a priest once."

"Maria's exaggerating. Actually, I did study at a Russian Orthodox seminary for a while, on the Russian side of the Chinese border, where I was raised. I loved it. I love the Eastern religions as well."

"Why didn't you stay?"

"Because," Stanislaus said, "I had this strange notion that it wasn't good enough to live a religious life within the safety of a cloister away from the world. Surely it must be possible to live well even within the world." He laughed sadly. "Looks as if I was wrong. I'm in the world, all right, but my life falls far short of sacredness."

"How did you get involved with all this?"

"Does it matter? By necessity, like the rest of us. Everyone has their own story. The particulars don't matter. Let's just say this is very far from the kind of life I want to live."

Unselfconsciously Sophia held Stanislaus's hand and they wandered up and down long courtyards lined with sculptures of the Buddha. Sophia felt a faint tugging in her shoulder. She ignored the feeling for a while but it began to bother her. She jerked her shoulder irritably. "What's the matter?" Stanislaus asked. "You look jumpy."

"I don't know." Sophia twitched. "I feel as if I ought to be going somewhere, but I don't know where, if that makes sense."

Stanislaus looked at her. "It does make sense. You're being called here for a reason. Nothing happens without a reason. Everything interconnects, you know. I interconnect with you, don't I?"

"Yes, you do." She smiled. "I feel completely at home with you."

Stanislaus returned the affectionate glance. "I feel I've known you for a very, very long time," he said. "Relax. Take a deep breath and listen with your inner ear."

Sophia stood still. The crowds pushed by. Then a tall pleasant monk moved toward her. "Everybody out now," he said. "You," pointing to Sophia and Stanislaus, "go to end temple and sit inside."

Bells and gongs thundered and pealed as the worshippers rose from where they knelt in front of their favorite images. Bowing and backing out of the temples, the faithful left their piles of paper money, their joss sticks, their incense, and pictures of their ancestors, and prepared to leave. Pushing against a human tide of Japanese, Sophia and Stanislaus hurried to the end temple.

The door was open on a large empty room that lay in the shadows of a Japanese evening. The carpet, a familiar Buddhist orange, was the only furnishing. Stanislaus looked around and began to move backward and forward. "What are you doing?" Sophia asked.

"Finding where I feel safe," he said.

Sophia laughed. "Is there really a place where you can feel safe?"

"Yes, there is. For instance, I never sit with my back to a door. Never." He moved to the side of the room. "I'm always ready to leave a situation." He sat down on the floor and crossed his legs. "Watch this," he said. He shuffled about and grunted. "Huh!" Suddenly he shot back onto his feet.

"Good heavens!" Sophia was amazed. "How on earth do you do that?"

"Practice." Stanislaus was laconic. "And it may save your life. You have a lot to learn."

Sophia felt humbled. "An awful lot."

The hall was filling with monks, rows and rows of them. The first were the most senior monks and the last to enter were the small boys, their cheerful rubber-ball faces beaming. The senior monks began to chant. *Om-mahd-na-pahd-meh-Ommm.* The sound of the Om became round and enveloping until Sophia felt her self absorbed into the sound. She felt the boundaries of her body start to dissolve. And then she was the sound. *Om.* The first sound that disturbed the waters at the beginning of all time. Slowly she found her mind began to clear. She was all time for all time. There was no beginning or end, only now.

And being among the monks, hearing the chanting, a memory from long ago filled Sophia's mind, a memory that had buried itself deep within her—

the temple at Urga where she had found peace after . . . Yes, after the Russian deserter had awakened her and threatened her in her bed at the inn. Looking back, she realized what a child she had been. And the guardsman had wanted . . . She now knew what he had wanted. The same thing that so many men seemed to want from her. Was this her fate? Could it be that she had been called in life to do nothing but give herself to men? No. Some day, Sophia vowed, she would forge for herself a greater destiny. But first she must survive the moment.

Suddenly, without surprise, she saw the Gorgon's face of the present float in front of the memory of the past. The Gorgon smiled. Then his face became that of a warrior. He raised both his hands and with them he made slashing movements. The hands changed into knives. They flashed and blood dripped from them. He nodded at Sophia. "Do this for me," he commanded and then the vision faded.

Sophia blinked her way back from beyond, as if waking. She stared at Stanislaus. "Do you have your orders?" she asked him.

"I do," he said.

"From the same person?"

Stanislaus sat quietly for a moment, then said, "Probably." He pushed his hands against his knees and stood up. "Let's go." They crept out of the temple, the monks' voices surrounding them as they walked down the winding alleyways.

"About tonight," Stanislaus said. "Don't worry about it. I'll see that Maria behaves."

"Thank you." Sophia was genuinely grateful. "Sometimes Maria frightens me," she said.

"Sometimes Maria frightens herself," Stanislaus replied.

CHAPTER 87

Dinner progressed pleasantly enough. After two bottles of saki, discussion turned to the subject of the gold hijacking. Sophia found it hard to participate. "I'm really not laughing," she said a little flushed with the wine, "but it does all seem rather like a story-book adventure. I mean, here we are in the middle of a Japanese city deciding how to assassinate four Japanese guards."

Stanislaus looked serious. "Sophia, this is how it's done. All over the world there are people sitting at tables over wine and food discussing murder. Where else should such plans be made? Why not at the dinner table?"

"I don't know why not." Sophia paused. "It's just that I'm used to discussing music or literature over dinner, not murder."

"You're in a different world now," said Rollo. "We have to get the gold, and we have to kill all four guards or else they'll identify us later."

"OK then"—Sophia tried to sound tough, but her voice trembled—"how do you propose to do it?"

Rollo nodded at Maria. "You tell her."

"The oldest trick in the world," Maria said. "Their Achilles' heel, like so many men's, is just below their belts. We do whatever it takes to get what we want out of them."

"How do we know what they want?" Sophia asked.

"We find out and we improvise." Maria smiled, as if she was relishing the thrill of the unknown.

"And if that doesn't work?" Sophia looked nervous.

Rollo spoke. "Don't worry. Get them in the right mood, and they'll want to show off the gold. You and Maria occupy two of them and we'll keep the other two outside. As soon as the first two come out, we'll strangle them and then the other two after that. Then we quick-change into our uniforms, we dock, and we leave while the flats are being loaded onto the waiting armored cars. Four of Chu's men will be on board as crew to see the ship never makes it to Shanghai; should we see them, we're not to acknowledge them. They'll be down in the hold. By the time Shanghai port authorities have caught up with the ship, we'll be well away."

Maria's eyes were shining with excitement. "Think," she said, "of all that gold."

Sophia hung her head. She was thinking of the soon-to-be-dead men. She hoped none of them had families.

"Let's all go and have a very hot soak in the tub," said Maria.

Stanislaus took Sophia's hand. "Once you've

had a bath, you'll feel quite all right about your-self.''

Sophia smiled at him. She remembered the day she gave her virginity to Elter. Once it was gone, she wondered why she had ever made such a fuss. Anyway, sitting with Stanislaus would be like shar-ing a bath with a brother. She nodded and wan-dered off to undress.

The water was hot. Sophia stood on the edge of the big round bath gazing into the steam. Rollo and Stanislaus were already in, their bodies stretched out, floating. Several giant lily flowers drifted lazily on the top of the water. The moon streamed behind Stanislaus's shoulder, shadows hiding his face. A patter of bare feet announced Maria's arrival. She stood opposite Sophia. Maria, smiling and sexy, had the type of body that would rapidly cease to be attractive as she got older. Al-ready Stanislaus could see the thin veins that would become more prominent as the years went by, a certain heaviness of the shoulders and the top of the thighs. In his early twenties Stanislaus had bred horses. This had left him with a keen eye for good form. Maria, he could tell, was not bred to age well.

He gazed at Sophia. Her body was perfect. It re-minded him of a white iris, the stem fresh and sup-ple, the smooth white head shaken slightly in the wind. Stanislaus wished this was one of those mo-ments that could last for ever. He wished he could suspend time, merely to savor the utter beauty of this night.

Sophia stepped into the water. Slowly her thighs sank from sight, then her pubic hair covered, and finally her breasts, their upturned tips touched by moonlight. She sighed with pleasure. "Well," she said, "whatever happens, I'm going to sleep well tonight."

Maria grunted. "Spoil-sport," she said. "I want to play."

"Not your games, Maria," Stanislaus said severely. "Certainly not."

"Thanks," Sophia whispered. Stanislaus bowed his head. Sophia looked at him, radiating in the moonlight, and wondered. Is he, she thought, could he possibly be the Gorgon in a different form?

❧ CHAPTER 88 ❧

In the privacy of her cabin aboard the *Nagasaki* Sophia decided the only way she could go through with the plan was to remain slightly drunk. She had only felt this way once before: the night she decided to allow herself to be seduced by Elter. She sat on the edge of her bunk and looked out at the expanse of gray water that seemed to fill her porthole. The wind was blowing from Kagoshima. Soon she must go up on deck to meet the others. When boarding the ship, she had caught a glimpse of Charlie in the guise of a deckhand. He was on the under-deck leaning against the grease-stained engine plant. He was picking his teeth and staring out at nothing in particular but she knew that he had seen her—nothing escaped him, ever. They pretended to ignore each other.

The others had independently made their way to the ship. Now it was time to meet up. Sophia went over to the dressing-table. "From now on," she told her reflection in the mirror, watching her lips moving as she spoke, "you will have to become a completely different person." She imagined Anna's face at her shoulder gazing back at her from the mirror. Sophia knew that her grandmother had killed in her time. Poison mostly. Sophia winced.

She squared her shoulders. I must be more like Maria, she thought. If I don't think about tomorrow or the next day, but just concentrate on the present, I'll be all right. She heard the first call for lunch. Here goes. She stood up and ran her hands through her long hair, flicked it back over her shoulders. She smoothed the fabric of her dress over her thighs: no wrinkles. She checked her stockings. The long black seams were straight. She was ready.

Rollo was sitting at the first-class bar on the top deck. He sat nonchalantly gazing out to sea. Sophia slipped into the chair beside him, aware that she was being watched by a variety of men. Some of the men were very obviously married, sitting next to their fat little wives. Others were alone, scanning the room for a companion for as long as the journey lasted. Stanislaus walked into the bar and raised a hand in greeting. Unhurriedly he walked over and sat down. "Maria will be up in a minute," Stanislaus said. "How's the weather?" They talked casually of hurricanes and water-spouts and the possibility of seeing flying fish or sharks.

Rollo wore a white silk suit, a blue shirt, and a long full tie. Sophia noted that his hand fidgeted. Stanislaus wore a light brown suit that made him look inconspicuous and mole-like. He kept his eyes on the entrance to the bar, watching the arrivals. "Ah!" she heard him exclaim and looked around curiously. There in the doorway stood a group of four Japanese men in military uniform: the guards. In the middle of the group stood Maria, rocking with mirth. "She didn't waste any time, did she?" Rollo remarked under his breath.

Stanislaus made a face. "She was waiting for them. She knew they would make for the bar sooner or later. They must have come on board in the early hours of the morning with the goods. So by now they must be ready for a drink."

Maria guided her entourage up to the bar. "I'd like you to meet my friend. Sophia."

Sophia smiled.

"Sophia," Maria introduced, "these are my new friends, Osiku, Kaido, Ikai and Risherti. There. Aren't I clever? I never forget a name."

Sophia inclined her head to the four. She could see that Kaido very much wanted to know her. The number of stripes on his collar told Sophia that Kaido was second in command to Osiku, the group's leader. Osiku had taken an unmistakable liking to Maria. Ikai and Risherti, with no stripes on their collars, were clearly the underlings. Kaido, she could see, was to be her quarry. He bowed to her. She shuddered. Kaido had a small weasel face and ferret eyes. He was not a man she would wish to know, given the choice. But she had no choice any more. For a moment she wished she and Stanislaus were wandering down paths in temple gardens. What were they doing here? No good thinking like that, she scolded herself.

Maria introduced Rollo and Stanislaus as friends, subtly making clear to the Japanese that neither girl was romantically attached to either man. Fortunately, Sophia thought as she sucked on the straw in her cocktail, gazing at the four guards through hooded eyes, they're an awful crowd of men. Fortunately, because if she had liked any of them her job would have been that much harder.

Kaido bowed to Stanislaus and Rollo and politely asked the reason for their trip from Kagoshima to Shanghai. "Business." Rollo smiled. An unextraordinary answer.

"And you two lovely ladies?" Osiku turned to Sophia and Maria. "You don't live in Kagoshima. I'm sure I would have met you before now if you did . . ."

"We're just two working girls from Shanghai going home after a holiday," said Maria with a delightful laugh. She smiled meaningfully at Osiku, the expression in her eyes unambiguously inviting. The look that Osiku returned was equally unequivocal. Sophia noticed it. It was the look that men saved for prostitutes. A man might look at a nonworking woman furtively, questioningly, out of the corner of his eye; a prostitute, a woman who made herself available, attracted a direct look, a look that hid none of his intentions. *Working girls.* Maria had made it quite clear what was on offer. Osiku's look finalized the deal. Turning to Kaido, Sophia could see there was a new and confident look in his eye. Sophia sipped her drink.

"Ah," said Kaido to Sophia, following up on Maria's declaration. "I have been to Shanghai many times. We go back and forth. Kagoshima to Shanghai, Shanghai to Kagoshima. I like Shanghai. I like Shanghai working girls."

Sophia smiled as if flattered.

"You like Chinese-style?" Kaido asked, getting immediately to the point. "Golden Lotus?"

"I beg your pardon?" said Sophia, not understanding.

"Of course," Maria answered for her. "Of course she does. Now, shall we move to the dining-room? I hear the second call for lunch." As they left the bar, Maria whispered in Sophia's ear. "I'll explain later," she said.

Half-way through the meal—a meal to which a distracted Sophia paid little attention—the two ladies excused themselves from the table on the pretext of going to powder their noses. When they were safely within the sanctum of the powder-room, Maria explained. "He wants to make love to your feet."

"He wants to do *what?*" Sophia was not sure she had heard correctly.

"Chinese-style. That's what the customers call it. It's an old brothel trick. The Golden Lotus. That's the name for a woman's bound feet. Without the Golden Lotus for Chinese men to make love to, half the brothels in Shanghai would be bankrupt."

"But he's Japanese."

"It sounds to me as if he's spent enough time in Shanghai to have acquired a taste for some of the Chinese ways."

"But I don't have Golden Lotuses," Sophia protested. "My feet aren't bound. Why would he want to have anything to do with them?"

"Don't you see?" Maria shook her head, as if frustrated in her efforts to explain arithmetic to a recalcitrant young pupil. "Because you're different. He could have as many Golden Lotuses and all the Chinese girls he wants. But you're probably the first European white girl ever to let him touch her. You're different. Why do you think so many men go to prostitutes anyway? I mean, whatever they get up to, it can't be so different from what they do with their wives. There are only so many ways to have sex, however you look at it. But if they do it with a different girl, the whole thing becomes exciting. The excitement's in the difference. And because you're different from all the girls he's had before, Kaido's obviously keen on you. That'll make our job a hell of a lot easier. You're in luck."

"Lucky me," Sophia said. I need another drink, she told herself. It's the only way to get through this.

After a lot of drunken questioning during the

long liquid luncheon that followed, the men loosened up and began to boast of their eventual conquest of China. "Not long now," Osiku said, "we will own all of China. And then Africa, and finally the world."

Sophia grinned. Not these four. She watched Stanislaus. His eyes burned.

After lunch Sophia made her way boozily to her cabin and fell down on her bed. She awoke in the dark, her mouth feeling full of sawdust. The pain behind her eyes caused her to groan, but she knew she must get up and return to the fray. Three more nights like this and then they were away. She cleaned herself up, changed her clothes, and went up. Sure enough, the indefatigable Maria was dressed in a white flutter of clothing, revealing much breast. She was surrounded by the four men. Sophia took her place at the bar and Kaido joined her. He put his thick hand possessively on her neck; she willed herself not to flinch. She turned to look at him. His rodent-like brown eyes rolled in anticipation. So this is jigjig for real, Sophia told herself. "A Singapore gin sling," she said and Kaido nodded. As easy as that. He asked, and I agreed. Now I get drunk. The rest of the evening passed in a gin-soaked blur. Might as well be gin, she thought. It's as good a blur as any.

There was no taste to the food she ate. They all sat at the same table, Rollo joking with Ikai, who tried to stroke his leg. Rollo took it all in his stride. Kaido sat close to Sophia, so close she could feel the heat from his odious body. She watched Maria.

Maria was draped over Osiku, taunting him with her breasts.

When dinner was over Sophia decided not to postpone her ordeal any longer. "Your room or mine?" she asked Kaido with a world-weary lack of enthusiasm.

"Mine." He beamed. "Mine. I have saki. Very good saki."

Sophia rose from the table. " 'Night, everybody." Her eyes found Stanislaus's.

He appeared very sad. "Good night," he said and then winked. In that split second, Sophia found herself in outer space again. How very convenient, she thought. I can go through all this from up here. I can leave my body with Kaido and the real me can just float free and watch.

Maybe it's the gin, she thought as she watched Kaido lay her on his bed, undress her, remove her stockings, and huddle over a bowl of almonds that he kept in a bowl beside his bed. "Chinese-style?" he asked, making sure.

"Golden Lotus," Sophia assured him, coming back to her present situation for a moment, trying to make her voice sound as interested as possible. Then she elevated her mind out of her body, absenting herself again from the scene.

With trembling hands Kaido placed an almond between each of her toes, then went on to suck the almonds into his mouth, mumbling "White feet" all the while. He licked and slobbered long enough to excite himself thoroughly, then suddenly stood up at the end of the bed, pressed her feet together, and thrust himself between the soles.

The sensation, Sophia admitted to herself, less absent for the proceedings than she would have wished, wasn't unpleasant. She could even imagine deriving pleasure from such a practice. If only the man at her feet was someone other than Kaido. Anyone else.

Kaido began to groan and grunt his way to a climax. She looked at his ecstatic face. She saw herself lying passively on the bunk waiting. "You like?" he panted. "Good sex, yes?"

"Yes." Sophia nodded. He came and collapsed face forward on the bed. "Very good," she congratulated and patted him on his sweaty back in an attempt to show enthusiasm. She was fully restored to her body and sensed the onset of a terrible hangover. "I must go," she whispered. She need not have bothered to whisper. Kaido was out cold.

She collected her clothes, dressed hurriedly, and slipped down the quiet corridor to her cabin. There she found Maria sitting on her bunk. "I must have a bath," she said. "Immediately. Kaido is disgusting."

Maria laughed. "Well, they can't all be like your general. You have to take the good with the bad."

"I know, but he's not just bad. He's terrible."

Maria shrugged. "Just as well. He's a goner anyway."

Sophia pushed past Maria and climbed into her bathtub. "Hot water," she muttered. "Lots and lots of hot water." She poured handfuls of bath salts into the bath until it had turned a deep purple.

"Can I jump in too?" Maria asked.

"Why not? Feel free." Sophia, beginning to relax, smiled. Funny, she thought. After the other night she had lost her essential modesty. Before then she would have died if Maria had asked to share her bath. Maybe I'm becoming harder, she thought. The only person with whom she had ever shared a bath before had been her sister. An image of Elena, standing cool and quiet with little Maria by her side, came into her mind. Then her eyes focused on Maria's flushed face staring back at her out of the water. "I'm doing all this for my child, you know. One day I'll see her again."

"I hope you do," said Maria. But the steam of the bath seemed to deaden her words.

᭪᪉ CHAPTER 89 ᭪᪉

The days on the ship passed in a fog of drink and lechery. Sophia found herself positively relieved that Kaido preferred her feet to the rest of her anatomy. Many hours passed with him perched on his bunk, drooling and dribbling over her toes. It could be worse, she told herself. Osiku, according to Maria, favored the jade gate. "The back door," Maria explained. "At least you get to lie back without him bouncing up and down on top of you.

Osiku's insatiable. He thinks he's a sexual athlete."

Apart from appeasing Kaido and Osiku's sexual appetites, the women, along with Stanislaus and Rollo (who was less than delighted by his acquaintance with Ikai), swam in the pool with the four Japanese guards and played shuffleboard.

The *Nagasaki* was a day out of Shanghai when the captain announced to his crew and passengers, exactly according to plan, that the ship would be making an unscheduled landing along the Chinese coast. No cause for alarm, the captain explained. Just a minor repair. And we'll be taking on extra provisions. The passengers would please remain on board during the night the boat was docked.

As the boat approached the harbor at Ningpo, Maria teased Osiku about their mission. "I bet," she said, "you have something special down there that you have to guard. Why don't you let us go down and take a look?"

Osiku shook his head. "No," he said, glancing at Kaido, who sat beside Sophia at the bar. Only Stanislaus and Rollo were absent from the group. "Not possible."

"Oh, please." Maria put her head on one side and pouted provocatively. All four guards looked at her.

"Please," said Sophia, following Maria's lead. "Show us what you're guarding. Unless of course it's not really anything important . . ."

The four guards began to talk quickly in Japanese. Finally Osiku nodded. "OK," he said. "We'll show you something that will really impress you.

But all four of us go to show you. Just to be careful."

"Careful?" Maria laughed. "Careful of two little
girls like us?"

Osiku laughed as if he had said something silly.
But all four guards went anyway with Sophia and
Maria into the hold of the ship. Sophia could feel
the adrenalin pumping through her veins as they
made their way down. They passed Charlie with
one of his men, still dressed as deck hands. Good
luck, his one eye seemed to say.

Piece of cake, said Maria's smile.

Deep in the bowels of the ship, they rounded a
corner into yet another long corridor. At the end
of this one was a massive steel door covered in
knobs and wheels. By the main wheel was a combination lock. When they reached the door to the
vault, Maria and Sophia talked to the three men
while Osiku worked the lock. "Do we really need
everybody here?" said Maria. "I mean, I think
we'll get stuffy and crowded all going in together."
She winked at Osiku and Kaido. "Why don't Ikai
and Risherti wait outside? They can come in
later," she said suggestively.

"We all go in," Kaido said emphatically.

"Well, fine then," Maria said. "The more the
merrier." She heard the lock of the vault click
open. As of that moment, the guards had outlived
their purpose. Now here they all were and the
door was open. But the guards were too many.
How, Maria wondered, would Stanislaus and
Rollo manage to overpower all four at once? This

part of the plan left room for improvisation. Maria knew she would have to think fast.

They walked into the room. On the floor were flats loaded with gold bars. Even Maria and Sophia were surprised by the sheer volume of gold, never having seen so much at any one time. "You see?" Osiku said with a boastful pride in his voice. "This is what we guard."

"Impressed?" said Kaido.

"Very," answered Sophia.

Ikai and Risherti remained near the door while Osiku and Kaido strolled with the ladies among the gold. Osiku pointed to a bar. "If you can lift it, you can keep it," he dared Maria.

Maria walked forward with a confident smile. She put her hands around the gold. She heaved and strained and the men laughed. Then a footstep was heard in the corridor outside. The guards stopped laughing. "Go see!" Osiku ordered. Ikai and Risherti ran out and disappeared down the corridor. Perfect, Maria thought. Two at a time.

Sophia did not know what to think.

"Come!" Osiku barked to the women. He was alarmed and flustered. "You should not be here. We must go!"

"Wait!" said Maria. "We're impressed. We want to show you just how impressed." The two men looked at each other. "Ooh!" Maria cried seductively. "All this gold!" She ran her fingers lightly over the bars. "It's so exciting! Isn't it, Sophia?"

"Oh yes," Sophia said, unsure of what was happening. "Very exciting."

"And it was awfully good of you to show us."

Maria smiled to the men, running her tongue over her lips. "In return we'll give you a show. You like a good girlie show?"

The men stood there speechless.

She turned to Sophia. "Come here." She held her arms open. Sophia walked into her embrace. Maria ran her hands over Sophia's body.

"Our lives depend on it," Maria whispered in her ear. "Play along." She held Sophia's face in her hands and kissed her deeply on the mouth.

"But . . ." Kaido spluttered.

"But nothing," Maria said, turning to him. Then she pressed her mouth to Sophia's ear again and breathed, "This is for Kaido." She put her hands on Sophia's shoulders and sat her down on the gold. She knelt before her and slipped off a shoe. Kaido could be heard to exhale deeply. She slid her hands up Sophia's thigh, undid the suspenders, and rolled down her stocking. She raised Sophia's naked foot to her face and slowly licked from heel to toe, then took the toes in her mouth.

Playing along, as Maria had instructed, Sophia gave a theatrical moan. She glanced sideways at Kaido's face. His eyes were wide open and he was breathing hard. Maria had certainly caught his attention.

In the corridor around the corner, Stanislaus held Risherti from behind, as Rollo held Ikai, tightly pulling the ends of their strangling leathers. "Dirty bugger," Rollo hissed, giving the garrotte a final lethal pull.

Over Kaido's shoulder Sophia could see Stanislaus's head peering around the door. She looked at Maria. Maria had seen him too. The task now was to occupy Osiku and Kaido so that neither man would hear a footstep or turn around.

Maria sat down on a crate in front of Sophia and removed her underpants.

"Lick me," she said. The two men were transfixed. "Fake it, if you must," she said beneath her breath to Sophia.

Sexual exhilaration was the single most distant emotion from Sophia's mind. But she knew she had no choice. I'm saving my life, she told herself. And I'm doing this for my child. Trying to appear excited, she crouched before Maria's parted legs. I can't. I simply can't. For an instant that seemed to last for hours, she thought of the times Maria had kissed her in friendship, of the bath they had shared together, of the latent sexual attraction between herself and this other woman. Now, faced with the reality of making love with Maria, she realized it took all her will and self-control not to recoil in instinctive revulsion. She could not go through with this. This might be what Maria wants, she thought, and it might be what she's looking for with Clarice, but it's not for me. Not at all.

Sophia pressed the palm of her hand against the mound of hair in front of her and lowered her face between Maria's thighs. But it was the back of her own hand that her mouth touched.

The pantomime, nevertheless, achieved the desired effect. Kaido and Osiku started to shuffle toward the women.

Maria pushed Sophia's head away. Raising her

eyes, Sophia could see Stanislaus and Rollo looking in from just outside the door. "Care to join us?" Maria invited the guards.

No sooner had the two guards reached for the buckles of their belts than Stanislaus and Rollo were upon them. The guards twitched in hideous convulsive jerks, their legs kicking and their hands trying vainly to free their necks from the taut thongs of the garrottes. Sophia felt profoundly relieved—the relief of self-preservation—when she saw the bodies hang limp at last. The smell of urine and excrement, released in death, rose to confirm the sentence.

Stanislaus frowned as he let go of Osiku's form. "We'd better get moving. We dock any minute." He popped out into the hallway and returned holding a small duffel bag, which he tossed toward the women. "You two get changed." Quickly Sophia and Maria did as they were told, changing into the anonymous uniforms of dock workers, tucking their hair inside their collars and covering their heads with floppy caps.

"It all happened so fast," Sophia whispered to Stanislaus.

He nodded. "That's the secret of success."

"Are you sorry they're dead?" Sophia felt as if she was still running a very fast race and couldn't slow down.

Stanislaus shook his head. "Are you?"

Sophia would have said "No," but did not have time to answer. The boat shuddered.

"We're docked," Stanislaus said. He shoved the women's civilian clothes into the duffel bag. "Take this with you," he said. "No trace must be left behind." Then he looked at the two bodies on the floor and recognized the irony of his own words. "But they won't give us away." Up the corridor the big loading hatch could be heard to open. "You and Maria go on ahead. Rollo and I will help unload the gold. We'll catch up with you later."

From the dock Charlie's group of hired men entered the ship and began to shift the flats of gold. "Ho ho," the head man greeted Stanislaus with a happy smile on his face. "Good, good."

The men rolled the flats up the corridor, through the hatch, down the gangplank, and onto the cars of the narrow-gauge railway that would take them to the armored cars.

The moon was high as Sophia and Maria slipped out to the dock. Had any curious passenger looked out of a porthole, that passenger would have seen only uniformed figures apparently loading and unloading supplies and boarding to carry out some minor repair. Sophia and Maria, climbing into a car on the far side of the dock, were effectively invisible. When the boat docked in Shanghai bereft of its gold, the Japanese would surely notice the loss, but would be unable to connect the theft with Sophia, Maria, Charlie, Chu Wing, or anyone.

How perfect, Sophia thought, sitting exhausted in the car. Behind her four men lay dead. But the plan had worked. Sophia felt surprisingly pleased that they had carried it off. She could not deny a small feeling of triumph. This must be, she considered, how a general feels when he has won a very important battle. I hope Chu is pleased with us.

She began to worry she might find herself grow too accustomed, in time, to this life of adventure if Chu did not let her go home now.

Beside her Maria patted the driver's shoulder. "Let's go," she said. "We'll meet up with Rollo and Stanislaus at the mouth of the river. Chu's people are waiting there."

"Whatever you say," Sophia sighed. "I'm so glad it's over."

Maria said very little on the drive and Sophia was content to just sober up. The last five days were like a kaleidoscope in her head. She wanted to forget the events of the last few hours. She slept until the heavy vehicle came to a halt. Maria put a hand on her shoulder. "We've arrived."

Neither woman had said anything about what happened between them on the boat. Sophia decided it was best to leave it that way.

Stiffly Sophia got out of the car and walked over to the big cavernous house that Chu had provided for their debriefing, to find a room to change.

The sun was rising by the time Sophia, Maria, Rollo, and Stanislaus all stood dressed in their own clothes in the courtyard. "I'm truly knackered," Rollo said.

"We'll hole up here for a few days," Stanislaus said. "And then, when the Japs have got over the shock, we can filter back to Shanghai." He smiled at Sophia, who felt genuinely comforted by his presence.

She shook her head. "If Miss Trublood could see me now," she said.

Maria grinned, her eyes alight with mischief. "If

she could have seen you on the boat," she said, boldly raising a sensitive subject. "Your performance was magnificent."

Sophia laughed awkwardly. "Well, I always did want to be an actress," she lied.

❧ CHAPTER 90 ❧

Sophia lay beside General Wayland. In guilty silence she listened to his weeping. "I'm ruined," he cried. "Someone caught me with my pants down. God knows who! And they stole all that gold—all that *gold*—from right under our noses. The top brass have blamed the whole fiasco on me." For the first time Sophia realized that Stanislaus's forays into the General's study must have included obtaining information about the gold. Damn! she cursed herself. Why the hell am I mixed up in this at all? She knew she had betrayed—albeit unwittingly—this man lying beside her. She did not enjoy the feeling.

"Wayne," she said, taking his hand away from his eyes, "things will work out. At least that's what Miss Trublood always says when life looks black."

Wayne half-smiled and swung his feet to the floor. He made a face. Sophia gazed at the powerful man brought so low by a few photos, a couple of maps. "It *was* my fault," he said. "I should have checked my house-staff more carefully. One of the houseboys is missing. American Intelligence is looking to pick him up for questioning. We had to stop that shipment. We simply can't afford to let the Japs overrun mainland China."

Sophia held her breath. The houseboy was Stanislaus. He was still in hiding somewhere in the city. She must tell Charlie to warn him to lie low. Sophia raised her arms above her head. "Come here, Wayne," she said. "Let's make love now and forget the world for a while."

Wayne turned toward her. A smile hovered on his lips. "Oh Sophia," he said, "I'll miss you. That's what gets me most about being sent back home." He took her in his arms and she opened her legs for him, welcoming his body with kisses. She smiled as they made love and he grinned when he entered her, beginning a long slow ascent into pleasure. He liked to take his time, which suited Sophia. By now she had learned to enjoy Wayne and his love-making, particularly after her horrible experience with Kaido. As Wayne shuddered and cried out, she held him tenderly, surprised to realize that she would miss this man in her life.

Later they both lay propped up in the bed with the big satin pillows behind their heads. Wayne was sad. "I'm going back to nothing," he said.

"How can you say that?" Sophia demanded. "You're going back to America. The good old US of A. Land of the rich and the free. All the things you've been fighting for here."

Wayne shook his head. "No, it isn't like that for me. I go back to my white Caddy, parked in the garage next to my wife's white Caddy. My big white house in Chestnut Hill outside Boston. My four acres of landscaped gardens. My country club—no Jews or blacks, of course, not that anyone would ever admit to that publicly; we just fill our membership lists in such a way that the "unwanteds" can't get in. And if they did, they'd be made very unwelcome." He shook his head. "If I want a bit of ethnicity I can go down to the Italian North End, or to Chinatown, but it won't be the same for me any more. I've lost my white Anglo-Saxon Protestant self here in Shanghai. I can't go back to my wife. I know I must for a while, but I'll hardly ever see her. She flits from tennis to bridge parties, from bridge to lunch, from lunch to cocktails, and then to dinner, with or without me. She's busy twenty-four hours of the day, doing nothing as far as I can see. But I'm the guy who's considered dull by her and her friends. Maybe she's having affairs. But I honestly don't give a damn any more."

"Do you feel guilty for making love to me?"

Wayne pressed her hand in his. "You've made me realize that there are some women who actually enjoy making love. For you it's not a chore. And you don't make me feel guilty every time I come. My wife has a way of closing her legs after the ordeal is over that reminds me of the way she closes the china cabinet after she's had a dinner party. Every so often I get a little sex doled out as a reward for good behavior . . . And I am tired of it." He looked at the ceiling. "I've had time to think during the last few days. I've been relieved of my command here, but not dishonorably discharged. From now on I'm going to think about my life. And the change in me is thanks to you." He turned his head and he smiled at her. "Ever thought of being a missionary?" he said.

Sophia laughed. "I leave all that to Miss Tru-blood."

"Well, you have changed my life. See, I got caught in an awful trap. I made money to acquire things and relationships that ended up owning me. I was completely chained down with mort-gages, with a wife and children who don't need me any more, cars, clothes . . . Oh, the list is endless. But since I've known you, I know I don't need those things. I can sell up, give my wife a divorce, and get a job somewhere in the Far East. I hear Singapore is opening up. I like the idea of Singa-pore. Or maybe even Africa. A small import/export business. A little house, a few ser-vants. And peace. I never thought about peace until I found this room. All a man needs is to know where his next meal is coming from and a woman to love him. You know, we men are pretty simple at heart."

"I know." Sophia grinned. "Elena, my twin, al-ways says that. But not when her husband is around."

Wayne shrugged. "Well, I don't mind admitting it. I'm all for leaving cleverness to women. Just give me peace." He hugged Sophia tightly. "What's for dinner?" he murmured.

"Beef Wellington," she whispered, licking his ear gently. "Fillet steak wrapped in bacon on a bed of pâté, a sauce with red wine and herbs, all covered in a light pastry."

"Ohh," Wayne sighed. "You see?" he said gazing down at his rapidly expanding penis. "See how simple I am?"

Sophia laughed and took the tip of his penis into her mouth. Then she moved over him, her long hair covering his groin. "And," she said between kisses, "sautéed potatoes, fresh peas, and a bottle of *Les Amoureuses.*"

"Perfect," sighed Wayne. "Just perfect."

❧ CHAPTER 91 ❧

The Kuomintang—the National People's Party, the movement that years ago Sun Yat-sen had tried to establish as a healthy alternative to the overthrown Ch'ing dynasty—was now under the command of Chiang Kai-shek. Widely hated, Chiang had the potential to be a merciless dictator. The husband of a shrill tyrannical wife, he harbored none of the warmth or compassion for the people of China that had distinguished Sun Yat-sen. Silencing all dissenting voices, the Kuomintang, under Chiang's orders, marched through China, strengthening their military control of the country throughout the late 1920s. Meanwhile in the communist strongholds in the North there emerged a new vision for a united China. But for the time being, however, the communists and the Kuomintang shared a common objective that demanded their cooperation: to keep the Japanese at bay. By 1930 the Kuomintang had established a diplomatically recognized government in Nanking, all of China, save only those northern positions held by the communists, within its power. The Japanese, having tried and failed near the end of the previous century to dominate China, were now poised to try again. The question of which Chinese faction would ultimately control China must wait. First the Japanese, already making their intentions known in Manchuria, had to be dealt with. And the great foreign Leviathan, America, trying to find a secure foothold in the quicksands of Chinese politics, struggled to ensure that somehow the whole complicated business turned out for the best.

All this engaged Chu and Charlie in many hours of discussion. Their network of spies, including Sophia and Maria, worked hard, gathering and reporting the information needed to enable the great Tong warlord Chu to continue to run his domain. Ultimately, it was all a question of power, with men like Chu Wing and Lau Tchi working each in his own way, together or apart, to further his own ambitions, personal or political, religious or secular. And whoever won this power game would determine the future of China.

The years passed, and Sophia felt no closer to being able to join her daughter. She had missed all but the earliest months of Maria's infancy. The child was hardly more than the memory of a dream to Sophia, a cherished yet distant image in the shrine of her imagination. Her desire to be with Maria did not diminish with time, but her hopes for ever realizing her purpose faded subtly every year. The twenties became the thirties and Sophia's life—she too was now in her thirties—had become a tedium of hopeless obedience to Chu's orders.

Sometimes Sophia was too tired even to think when she returned home at night. She fell into bed and mechanically said her prayers. But now she wondered if God could hear her through the thick murk of her sins of commission and omission. her friend Maria flourished and became even more beautiful. For the first time, Maria was eating well and had an organized life, thanks to Misha and Mei Mei. Misha worried for his "family."

"You know," he said to Mei Mei in the spring of 1931, "Miss Trublood is not looking good."

Mei Mei nodded. "Mordecai concerned about her," she agreed.

Mordecai groaned. He was squatting against the kitchen wall, his face buried in his hands. "Missie God-lover no listen to Mordecai," he said. "She works too hard for them unbelievers. Heathens all of them." And he spat.

Mei Mei rushed over to him. "Don't spit on my floor," she scolded.

Mordecai grinned. Mei Mei looked fierce, but over the years Mordecai came to enjoy living in this family. He and Miss Trublood had a sparring but honest relationship. Mordecai had no time at all for her Western god but he had grown to love Miss Trublood and felt protective toward her.

Tonight she came in, trumpeting as usual. "Mordecai!" she bellowed. "Where were you? You promised to pick me up."

Mordecai shook his head. "Sorry, Missie," he said, bowing low and wringing his hands. "I forgot."

"Forgot! And I had to take a taxi all the way from the hospital!" Misha looked at Mei Mei. Miss Trublood had been spending a lot of time at the hospital lately. "Mei Mei!" Miss Trublood called. "Come to my room."

When Mei Mei nervously poked her head around the door she found Miss Trublood packing. "Where you going?" Mei Mei asked.

"To hospital, Mei Mei." Miss Trublood sat heavily on the end of her bed. "I'm afraid I have to have an operation. When Sophia comes back, ask her to visit me, will you?"

Mei Mei assured her she would. "You want me go with you?"

"No." Miss Trublood smiled a sweet but tired smile. "Ask Mordecai. He can stay at the hospital with me and you two stay here and look after Sophia and Maria for me." Mei Mei bowed and went off to tell Mordecai, who immediately began to pack his bedroll and the few things he needed.

Miss Trublood stood up and sighed. She had known things had not been right for a long time but she had done nothing about it. She knew she had lumps in her breasts, but she preferred to let things take their course. If God wanted her home, then she was happy to go. She did not wish to end up like the mutilated figures she had visited in the cancer wards. Too many times she had witnessed virtual corpses kept alive by new medicines that seemed to cause more pain than they relieved. No, that wasn't for her. Her only worry was that she would be leaving Sophia alone. In her last letter to Edward she had warned him that she was not well. Still, Sophia was a grown woman now. Miss Trublood was aware that at times Sophia suffered quite horribly, but always there was that fire in Sophia's eyes, a fire kept alive by the memory of her daughter, now at boarding school in the English countryside. Edward wrote back wishing Miss Trublood better health. He added news of the unrest in England and the strikes that had swept the country. Miss Trublood couldn't believe it. "Really," she said once to Sophia. "It quite spoils my idea of England, full of farmers chewing straw and tending sheep." She was pleased to see Sophia smile. "One day," Sophia had said, "I'll be able to write and tell you what it's really like."

Now Miss Trublood knew that the chances of Sophia writing to her were slim. Earlier today the doctor had told her she might well have cancer. He wanted to do an immediate biopsy. "But," he said sternly, as if she was a naughty child, "why did you not come in before?"

"Because," she said, "if the good Lord wants me, I want to go in one piece. We all have to die. I'm not afraid of dying." Her voice wobbled a little. "I suppose I'm sad," she said, fighting back the tears, "because I'll miss my little family and my mission." She saw the doctor's face through a mist of tears. She drew a deep breath and regained her self-control. "I have my faith," she said with dignity. "So I will take my chances. If there's no hope, please just close me up and let me die naturally." The surgeon nodded. In spite of himself he was impressed by this woman. Maybe she's wise, he thought.

Miss Trublood finished packing and Mordecai drove her to the hospital. "I find kitchen," Mordecai offered, when she was installed in her private room. "I get you Chinese tea?"

"Thanks, but I can't drink or eat until after the operation. But I'll tell you what: when I come to, will you have a lovely cup of tea ready for me? I've actually got used to the stuff, and I don't think I'd be up to coffee."

Mordecai smiled reassuringly. "I get you English tea. Or Chinese?" he said playfully.

"English, I think," Miss Trublood said. "How about Earl Gray with a slice of lemon?"

"Ho ho ho! I go now. See you soon."

As dusk was falling, Sophia and Maria made their way to the hospital. "I should have known," Sophia said, walking up the white-tiled hallway. "I've been so worn out lately I just haven't taken the time to be with Miss Trublood."

Maria said, "Well, let's hope the news is good."

"Mei Mei didn't seem to think that likely."

Maria tried to comfort her. "Mei Mei doesn't know much."

Miss Trublood was back in bed when the two

friends reached her room. "Hi," she said weakly. "I'm still a bit woozy after the anaesthetic."

Mordecai was hovering around the room. He knew the answer and he could hardly bring himself to smile at Sophia as she came through the door. But he looked miserable so often, Sophia could not read much into his face.

"Have you seen the surgeon?" Sophia asked.

Miss Trublood nodded. "He just popped in a few seconds ago."

"What did he say?" Sophia watched Miss Trublood's eyes.

"Sit down, Sophia, and let Mordecai get you a cup of tea. How about you, Maria? You're looking very pretty today."

"Thank you, Miss Trublood." Maria pulled up a chair.

Sophia remained standing. "What did he say?"

Miss Trublood smiled. "Well," she said, "in one way the news is not good. I have cancer. Both breasts. And it's metastasized, so I only have a few weeks left, if that." She paused. "And the good news is that I'm going home."

"Oh no, Miss Trublood!" Sophia gasped. "You can't die! Can't they operate? Can't they do anything?"

"There's no point. They can't. And, Sophia, I'm honestly glad. I don't want to die a slow agonizing death. I've lived a full life. I'm ready to go."

"But what about me?" Sophia threw herself into Miss Trublood's arms. "What about me? Oh, don't go! Please don't go!"

Sophia's cries could be heard down the corridor. The surgeon stopped beside a bed and raised his head. Poor woman, he thought, she's been told. He knew of Sophia by reputation. And he also knew that Miss Trublood was possibly her last link with all that was safe and good and holy. Poor young woman, he thought. He told his head nurse to take a sedative to Miss Trublood's room. The nun slipped away and collected from the pharmacy a cup with a slip of paper over it. She glided up the corridor and entered the room to be met with the sight of Sophia racked with sobs. Maria cried quietly into a handkerchief. Mordecai stood helplessly by.

Miss Trublood was also crying. Big tears slid down her cheeks and gathered in the crevices around her mouth. She hugged Sophia. "Please, honey," she said. "Don't cry. It's better this way. Believe me. Just watch. You have faith in me, and I'll show you. Dying can be a great adventure. After all, it's what we were born for. Every person has a race to run, and I've run my race. I'm tired now and I want my reward."

The nun gently pulled at Sophia's elbow. "Come, child," she said. "Take this." She put a cup of steaming tea in Sophia's hands. Sophia huddled onto her chair and clutched the bowl in both hands, feeling the sedative begin to work almost at once. In the new-found quiet of her room Miss Trublood, tired by her operation and by the emotional upset of breaking the news to Sophia, soon fell asleep.

Sophia watched her as her head fell to one side. Miss Trublood was far away, somewhere in the light, with the God she so much loved. Sophia sat until the room was dark.

Then she stood up stiffly. Maria, a shadow, followed her out of the hospital. They climbed into the car and drove back to the house. Wordlessly, they hugged each other good night and Sophia made for the safety of her bedroom.

Without Miss Trublood Sophia felt she had no reason to stay in Shanghai. She had been too long away from her daughter and from Elena and Edward. While she had Miss Trublood she felt she had a psychic link with the past that stretched into the future. Miss Trublood was a good woman; Sophia was not. Yet she knew her love for Miss Trublood brought out the best in her, and the fact that Miss Trublood could and did love her in return gave Sophia an enormous sense of self-respect. Now, with Miss Trublood dying, Sophia felt she was just a common prostitute. She climbed into bed and sobbed desperately. She lay there, feeling dirty and used. She too had used and defiled others in her turn. Her dream of going to England and being with her daughter seemed more distant now than ever. No, she could never besmirch her daughter or her family with her reputation as a prostitute. News traveled fast these days, and, should she upset Chu, he would see to it that she would never be able to hold her head up again. He had sufficient photographs of her in compromising positions. True, when she entered a room all eyes focused on her, some in lust, others in respect, and a few in fear. If Sophia was on the prowl, then there was a deal to be done or a death to finalize. Everywhere she went she was followed by Charlie. You saw one, then you saw the other—if you did not, then it was time to start worrying. Sophia had been riding high in Shanghai until now.

Sophia could not bear the thought of losing Miss Trublood, who loved and accepted her; who had seen her through the pregnancy and held little Maria in her arms. Soon Sophia would no longer be able to find comfort in those arms. The house resounded with her sobs.

Maria lay in her own bed crying, not for Miss Trublood but for her friend. She knew what this death would mean to Sophia. She also knew that it would not be long now before Sophia tried to escape from Chu and Charlie. Maria cried for Sophia's safety.

In the bamboo house where Gorgon never slept, Lau Tchi stirred on his pallet. All was well. A soul would leave this earth, and in its wake, like the tail of a comet, would follow a disturbance on the surface of Shanghai. A boil would burst, but in the erupting a soul would fly free. First the pain, then the prize. No pain, he thought, nodding sagely to himself, no change.

CHAPTER 92

Two days passed and Sophia tossed in her bed at night, swollen-eyed with grief. During the day she was at the hospital, sitting by Miss Trublood's high white bed. Miss Trublood lay on her heaped pillows and stirred little. She was not in much pain and a smile played around her lips as she talked to Sophia of the old days. "It's all so different now," she said yet again.

"I know," Sophia agreed, looking with shame at her own evil hands that clasped her knees. Miss Trublood's hands had never experienced the places, the orifices, the bodies of strangers. Miss Trublood's hands had been laid in love upon the shoulders of the people she strove to save in this world for the eternal joy of the next. Many shoulders no doubt shrugged off Miss Trublood's tender touch; Sophia's hands had been received with lust. Sophia folded her hands, leaned back in her chair, and listened.

At noon Mordecai crept in carrying a bowl of his special chicken soup. Gently he took a blue dragon spoon and put it to Miss Trublood's lips. During the last forty-eight hours Miss Trublood's condition had deteriorated fast. It was as if a great ship had run before the storm of life for so long that now, moored and anchored, she prepared to scuttle herself in order to rest her weary timbers on the bottom of the sea. Sophia could not bear for Miss Trublood to leave. She put her small strong hand in Miss Trublood's frail palm and wished she could pump life back into the body of her beloved friend. Miss Trublood finished the soup and nodded. "That was delicious, Mordecai," she whispered. "How many chickens did you have to murder?"

Mordecai smiled. "Many heathen chickens, Missie," he answered.

"Well, I said grace over them," Miss Trublood said with some asperity. "So they will all go to heaven."

"Chickens?" Mordecai squawked. "Chickens go to heaven? Oh, I think not. No, no, no." And he trotted out of the room thrilled that he had routed Miss Trublood.

Miss Trublood hurrumphed and stretched her back. "I'll get that heathen professing the Truth, if it's the last thing I do before I die." She paused, realizing that she had referred to her own death for the first time that day. She looked at Sophia whose head hung eloquently low. "Sophia," she said, "honey. I have to die some time, you know. I'm not afraid at all. In fact, I'm rather looking forward to it. Lying here is getting tough. I hate being in bed. You know that."

"Yes, but what am I to do without you? I know that sounds so selfish, but you're all the family I have."

"What about Maria?"

She shook her head. "Maria's a friend. I can love her, but I can never trust her." She saw Miss Trublood's eyes begin to close in sleep. She crept out of the room and found Mordecai. "I'm going to the Golden Dragon," she said, guilt clawing at her heart. She had to get away. She had to leave this stifling building full of death. Miss Trublood could meet her God in all good conscience, but not Sophia. She still found even the thought of death unnerving. She dreaded the moment when the last breath would leave Miss Trublood's body and she would be reclaimed by eternity. Would it be an eternity full of bright angels and the holy seraphim? Or would it be the eternity she had seen in the eye of the eagle perched in the dark room at the end of the long corridor inside the pyramid?

Sophia knew that she had none of the answers. She ran out of the hospital. Even Mordecai's devotion to Miss Trublood made her feel guilty. She jumped into her car and sped off to the Golden Dragon with a deafening screech of tires. "How is she?" Maria looked concerned.

"As well as can be expected," Sophia sighed. She very much did not want to discuss Miss Trublood's condition. She just wanted to lie back and lose herself on the tide of human activity in the Golden Dragon.

Today Clarice and her crowd of Sapphic ladies were particularly in evidence. Sophia could hear their voices from the drawing-room. Clarice had a distinctive, hoarse, tremulous voice. Her words hung disjointed and broken in the air. Maria and Sophia sat in two basket chairs. "Sun's over the yardarm, Maria. I'm thirsty. Do you want a drink?"

"Sure," came the answer. Maria had been drinking all day. Miss Trublood's impending death affected Maria profoundly, and her way of dealing with it was to find peace in a tumbler of alcohol.

Just the slight grating of Clarice's voice kept her marginally on edge, a voice that so bullied women . . . Maria liked the idea of having that voice at her feet, begging.

"Maria," Sophia said crossly. "What on earth are you thinking? You look quite manic!"

Maria's eyes were brimming with laughter. "I was imagining Clarice at my mercy."

"Oh, Maria! You're no lesbian."

Maria grinned. "But neither is she. Clarice is sexually perverse, like me. At the end of the day, it's not sex that's the turn-on, it's the power. And I tell you, it's power Clarice is after. So many people make that mistake with her. Just watch those two idiots, Moira and Velvet. They follow her around slavishly. Yes, Clarice. No, Clarice. Huh! It's time I dealt with that woman."

"Not now," Sophia said wearily. This conversation seemed hardly decent while Miss Trublood lay dying in the hospital. The drinks appeared and Sophia immediately ordered another. "Bring us a pitcher of martinis. We're both very thirsty," she said, feeling guilty.

The amah made a face as she walked back to the kitchen. She passed by Clarice and watched the three women with their arms around each other's shoulders. They call themselves women, she thought, disgusted. Moira's thick lips were bubbling with brandy. Velvet looked as if she was about to cry. But Clarice was laughing, her lashless eyes dancing. "Let's have a party tonight," she purred. "Let's make it a French party. The last trip to Paris was fun, wasn't it? New York was a disappointment and London was too cold. But Paris . . . Ahhh!" She raised her long arms above her head and rolled her eyes at her friends. "What fun, eh?" The three women sat for a moment in silence.

Her two companions, Moira and Velvet, exchanged a worried look. Paris, for them, had been the furthest thing from fun. Watching Clarice with as many females as she could find was no source of pleasure. But neither woman could face the thought of life without this magnetic woman, whether being involved with her made them ecstatic or wretched. Clarice had the ability to make people fatally addicted to her. Moira and Velvet both were hooked.

"Maria's around the corner drinking with the Countess Sophia," said Clarice. "Why don't we go over and invite them to our little do tonight? I'll tell Madame Kotalinski that we need a room. French bread, frogs' legs, *un peu de fromage* and *beaucoup de vin. N'est-ce pas?*"

Moira understood. So, Clarice was going to recruit Maria into her harem. With any luck, Moira thought jealously, Clarice's infatuation with Maria would be short-lived.

"Feel like joining us tonight for a little party?" Clarice's long shadow fell over the table.

Maria looked up, amused.

Sophia shook her head. "Sorry," she said. "I'm busy."

"Perhaps you could look in later."

Maria smiled. "I *might* be free," she said. "I'll see." And she giggled.

Clarice's eyes lingered for a moment on Maria's

breasts. She arched her eyebrows and then smiled a conspiratorial smile. "Of course," she said. "We'll both see, shan't we?" And she walked off into the rest of the afternoon, Moira and Velvet trailing after her like feather dusters rushing to catch up with cobwebs.

ᑭ CHAPTER 93 ᑭ

Miss Trublood, hearing the bell ring from the mission nearby, knew it must be eleven o'clock. For many years she had been at the church to watch the deacon pull the bell-rope with his strong hands. This bell had a harsh flat tone of command. Today Miss Trublood would not be there. Her usual place on the second bench on the left would be empty. She always sat next to the window. When she was bored by the sermon, she played with the pullstring of the blue chick rolled above the window. Outside was a bush of wild jasmine and a glorious pink hibiscus.

Miss Trublood knew she was dying. How odd, she thought, I'm not afraid.

The doctor had made his rounds. She had been virtually unconscious when he came in to see how she was. But now she had returned to her body and could see everything around her very clearly. She remembered the doctor's sonorous voice drifting on the edge of her consciousness. "I don't think this patient will make the night." There was a swell of sympathy among the group of students following him. She felt the surge of emotion. They were all young and to them life was signally precious. They knew nothing of the longing for death or the feeling of being so alone on this earth that a time could come when one wanted to die; when one wanted to claim one's reward for a life given in service to God and know that the disbelievers and the mockers were wrong: there was life after death. But first Miss Trublood had to speak to Mordecai.

She opened her eyes again. There Mordecai stood, silent and still. She whispered his name and he put his ear to her mouth. "Yes, Missie?"

"Misha has Mei Mei. They'll go off and make a life together at some point." She panted slightly. Talking was an effort. "They want to have a family. But that leaves Sophia. Mordecai, you have no one." Her voice faltered. Mordecai took her hand in his. "Will you take care of her? Please, Mordecai. She has no one else."

Mordecai gazed at this woman he had come to love. "Yes, Missie," he said. "You don't worry. You sleep, Missie. I never leave Miss Sophia. Sleep, Missie," he said as the light faded in Miss Trublood's face. He stood quietly beside her and he watched a gray shadow steal over her features and the corners of her mouth turn blue. Finally she drew a deep, deep breath, then breathed no more.

Tears rolled down his face and he felt a sharp

cutting pain in his chest. Miss Trublood was dead. He placed his two hands over her eyelids, and shut them. He took her hands and placed them on her chest, joined as he had so often seen them when she prayed. He looked around the room. There was a cross on the wall. Beside the bed was the Bible he knew she read daily. He took the small book with its missionary zipper and he slipped it under her hands. Where was her God when she died? he thought. He looked at her and shook his head. She lay there, almost smiling. A strange peace invaded Mordecai's soul. He was comforted to see no sign of suffering on Miss Trublood's face. I must telephone Miss Sophia, he thought.

Sophia drove to the hospital, guilty that she had not been with Miss Trublood at the last. But, if she had to make an honest admission, she was also a little relieved. She had been dreading the thought of witnessing Miss Trublood's death. Now that it had occurred, she was able to mourn. She cried as she drove. She wept for the catalog of sadness in her life. Miss Trublood, her last link with her family and her childhood, was gone. Sophia felt as if a great sea-change was coming into her life. The uncertainty of that change frightened her.

She stood beside Miss Trublood's bed, looking down. Mordecai stood beside her. She felt his sympathy. "At least she's not suffering any more," Sophia said. Her voice sounded hollow against the white walls.

"No," he said. "She die happy woman, Miss Sophia."

"I'm glad." Sophia caught Mordecai's eye. He

knows I feel guilty, she thought. How strange. Miss Trublood is no longer here. Instead there is an envelope lying inert on the bed. "Have you made the necessary arrangements, Mordecai?"

"Yes."

"I have a lot to do." Sophia wandered about the room touching Miss Trublood's belongings. "I must cable her relations, and I must go to the florist's. Then I'll go and see the hospital administrator. I'd better let Misha know and then . . ." She realized that the one place she wanted to be was with Stanislaus, in his warm embrace, with her head on his shoulder, his dark hair against her own. But that was the one place she was not allowed to find comfort. She and he were strictly forbidden ever to acknowledge each other when not officially working together. I'll go back to the Golden Dragon, she told herself, and find Maria. She'll be awfully upset.

By the time Sophia had checked Mordecai's arrangements for the funeral, by the time the telegraph lines from Iowa had sent messages informing her there would be no relatives coming in for the interment, it was getting dark. Sophia drove into the Shanghai night. Shanghai, whose daily death toll kept hundreds of family-run funeral parlours busy carving coffins and designing flags. The chink chink chink of the nails sinking into the pine . . . Sophia sped along, taking corners on two wheels. She was impatient to get to Maria. She had wired Elena, but Edward and Elena would not be coming back. During the reading of the death-notification, which had sounded so cold and unsympathetic, Sophia felt a strong resurgence of the need to break away from Chu Wing and the Tongs, dangerous though it was even to think of it. Don't be silly, she scolded herself as she dictated her telegram. "Miss Trublood died today. Funeral on Wednesday. Love to you all. Sophia." Elena would not be surprised because Sophia had written earlier to say that Miss Trublood had inoperable cancer. Elena and Edward would be sad because they could not be with her. And little Maria would probably not even remember Miss Trublood.

Running away, she thought, was the only solution. Miss Trublood had managed to run away by dying, but Sophia did not intend to die. She gunned the accelerator and screeched to a stop.

Inside the Golden Dragon, all was quiet. She could hear the hubbub of women's voices in a far room. The hall and dining-room were dark and empty. Tonight was one of the rare nights when the house was closed to clients. By the sound of things, Clarice was having her party.

Sophia moved quickly through the hall, past the dining-room, and into the ball-room. She stood transfixed, stunned by what she saw. Maria was dancing with Clarice, or rather dancing around Clarice. Maria's face was as flushed as Clarice's was congested. Behind Clarice, Moira hovered, rubbing her hands like a fieldmouse. To the left, Velvet glowered. Maria lurched slightly in front of Clarice and her left breast hung out of her very low-cut dress. "Go on, Clarice," Maria hissed, her mouth swollen and pouting. "You know you want to touch it."

Clarice, also drunk, shook her head and shifted her eyes to Velvet. "What do you think?" she said.

Velvet made a face, as if uninterested. "Do what you please," she said. "After all, she's only a two-bit whore, and you do find them so attractive."

"Maria," Sophia called. "Maria?" But she knew Maria couldn't hear her. Caught up in the abandoned sexuality of the moment, Maria moved nearer to her quarry and then slid her arm around Clarice's waist and pulled her into her arms. Sophia watched helplessly as Clarice's stern lips opened to Maria's passionate kiss. She saw Clarice's hand go to Maria's breast. Involuntarily Sophia shuddered. So, that's what Maria wanted from me.

She retreated behind the doorway and measured this moment against the quiet dignified death that morning of the woman she had loved. That is how women should love each other, she thought. As Miss Trublood loved me. But this is disgusting. She felt her arms and legs quiver with horror. She turned on her heel and left. No point staying. No point at all.

She climbed into the car and began to drive aimlessly about the city. At some point she realized she was near Rollo's house. He had liked Miss Trublood and would be sorry. She stepped out of the car and was relieved to see that Rollo's study light was on. "She died this morning," Sophia said, standing forlornly on the front doorstep.

"I'm so sorry." Rollo drew her into the puddle of light in his hall. "Come in. I'll get you a drink."

Sophia followed him. The solution to life, she thought, is always a drink. Someone's born: have a drink. Someone's married: have a drink. Someone has a baby: have another drink. Someone dies: have yet more to drink. Maybe there's something in the idea of finding solace in a bottle. Maybe the secret of survival is to drink so much you are never quite sober enough to feel the real horror of life.

No, she thought as she trailed upstairs behind Rollo. That can't be the answer. Look at Maria.

Tonight an enormous chasm seemed to lie between herself and her friend—if Maria could be called a friend. She tried to communicate this complicated thought to Rollo. "You see," she said, her voice slurred from the effects of a double brandy and a wave of tiredness, "she isn't really my friend at all. Tonight she had nothing on her mind but trying to seduce Clarice."

Rollo's eyebrows flew up like startled pheasants. "What?" His voice sounded like a pistol shot in the quiet room. "Clarice Carruthers? That big English dyke?"

"Yes." Sophia swallowed another mouthful.

"Well, well." Rollo took Sophia's hand. "Darling," he said in his gentle English voice. "You must try to understand us. People like Maria and myself, I mean. Don't forget, you did seek us out. We didn't go looking for you. People like us don't have much to do with your sort usually, unless we want to rip them off. I don't mean to be unkind, and I do love you, Sophia, really I do, in so far as

I can love anything or anybody. But we are the lost ones. We don't feel like other people deep down in here." He put his hand on his breast. "In here, there is nothing. We live for the moment, for a new sensation. We can't help ourselves. Does that make sense?"

"As much sense as anything else, I suppose," Sophia answered slowly. She remembered the intensity of that moment when Clarice's mouth was on Maria's, and Clarice's trembling hand on Maria's exposed breast.

"Tomorrow Maria will have an awful hangover and probably won't even remember much of what happened. She will giggle and laugh a little, but that moment will be over. Old Velvet will create a bit, and Moira will witter and scurry about, but it was just one of those many nights when the unfeeling play games with the unloving."

Rollo walked across the study to a painting of himself at eighteen. "Come over here, Sophia." She obeyed. "Look." Rollo pointed to the picture. "See my face then?"

Sophia turned to look at the painting. Rollo had been a golden young Adonis.

"And look at me now," he said.

She studied Rollo's face. She could see lines traced lightly here and there and the promise of a chin that would sag within a few years. "Oh, Rollo!" she said crossly. "Don't be ridiculous. Old age is waiting for all of us. Think of Miss Trublood. She was never worried about gray hair or an extra wrinkle."

"But I'm not Miss Trublood," Rollo declared. He sat down again. "I dread growing old."

"Then what will you do?" Sophia felt curiously aware that she had her own secret plan.

"Live until the wrinkles become undeniable, and then I'll kill myself."

"Are you serious?"

"I am," he said. "You see, Sophia, the likes of me don't have much to live for, except our looks. Once they're gone, we're finished. I don't want to end up chasing little boys in an effort to find new weary pleasures. I couldn't bear to watch myself turn pathetic. I would rather die quietly in my bed and leave it all behind."

Sophia shook her head. "I don't know what to think any more. Today's been such a dreadful day."

"Come along," said Rollo. "You mustn't drive home tonight. You're far too tired and you've had a bit too much to drink. I'll take you upstairs and put you to bed. I'll telephone Misha and tell him you're staying with me."

"Thanks." Sophia was too tired to protest. The room was spinning around her. She felt Rollo lift her and carry her up the stairs to the top of the house. She let him gently remove her clothes and then slide her, naked, between clean sheets. "Good night," she mumbled gratefully.

He kissed her softly. "Good night, darling," he said. "Sleep well."

CHAPTER 94

Maria, overhung and burbling when Sophia returned to the house for a late breakfast, sat wrapped in her red silk dressing-gown, her small feet swinging under the table.

Sophia had a headache. She listened to the flow of words for a few minutes, then said, "Listen, Maria, I don't really care what Clarice said, did, or did not do. Miss Trublood died yesterday."

"I know." Maria was instantly contrite—too instantly. "I'm so sorry." Her eyes filled with tears. "Really I am."

For once Sophia did not react. She watched Maria and felt manipulated by a facile display of emotions probably not deeply felt. "Are you, Maria?"

"Yes," she gasped, her lip quivering.

Sophia sipped her cup of coffee. "Tell me, Maria, what did Moira do after you kissed Clarice?"

The cloud cleared from Maria's face as Sophia had expected. Maria leaned back in her chair and grinned. "Well," she said, "it was like this." She shook her head at the memory and giggled.

Yes, Sophia thought, watching Maria. Rollo is right: there are those who have no feelings, and Maria is one of them. Well, I'd better leave her out of my plans.

Leaving Chu Wing and One-Eyed Charlie meant leaving everything behind. It meant Sophia could not even contemplate notifying her family. The only people she shared her plan with were Misha and Mei Mei. Misha agreed with her. "We must go north," he said. They never spoke of their plans in the house, only outside in the open, where they knew they would not be overheard. But one day Mordecai came to Sophia and said, "I go with you, Miss Sophia. I make promise to Miss Trublood."

Sophia felt a momentary panic. How did he know she intended to escape? He could not possibly have overheard. Nevertheless, he knew. Would he report all that he knew to Chu Wing, sabotaging Sophia's plans before she had even begun to put them into action? Sophia was terrified, but from behind his spectacles Mordecai's eyes appeared to give reassurance. No, he never had been happy working for Chu, working against this family whom he actually seemed to care about. Yes, he too wanted to escape. Sophia believed she could trust him. "I'm glad, Mordecai," she said at last, "because I want Misha and Mei Mei to be able to settle down and have a family. I don't want them to be on the run for ever."

Mordecai smiled. "Don't worry," he said. "I Charlie's cousin. But I not say anything. I keep ears open. I hear moment when we can go. Some day Chu have hands full. Then we run through fingers."

Years went by before any moment presented itself. Sophia took her customers to the Golden Dragon. She was obedient and compliant. Chu was busy. The Japanese had actually invaded China, and all of Chu's time was spent trying to protect his assets and business interests from the Japanese conquest of one city after the next, throughout the country. Sophia continued to live in the same house as Maria but no longer felt close to her. Now she and Stanislaus concentrated on clandestine meetings in bazaars or tea-houses not frequented by Charlie's spies. "I love you," Stanislaus said desperately three years on.

"And I love you," Sophia whispered, holding his hands. Like the lovers on the blue Chinese plates, they had nowhere to go. Even to walk over a bridge together was for them too dangerous.

"We must wait," Stanislaus whispered in what had become a ritual reassurance that eventually they would manage to have their own lives together.

"I can wait," Sophia said. "I can wait for ever if I have to, but we will be free one day." Sometimes she believed herself; other times she did not.

At last the day came when the Japanese were on the outskirts of Shanghai itself. They had attacked before, but this time Shanghai had been bombed into submission and the city was sure to fall into Japanese hands. Chu Wing, the spider, would be caught in his own web, or so Stanislaus figured. Busy trying to save himself, Chu would be in no position to threaten targets abroad. Little Maria would be safe.

"Now's the time to make our move!" Stanislaus said on the telephone. "I'll meet you at Chusin. I have a second cousin there. He runs the Peking Restaurant in the middle of town."

Quickly Sophia rounded up Mordecai, Misha and Mei Mei. "We leave today," she announced. She felt a great weight fall from her shoulders. A ripple of excitement, like the blue flame of a gas-burner, ran around the little group. She, Misha, Mei Mei, Stanislaus, and Mordecai, having lived on the verge of leaving for so many years, were prepared. It was as if all those years of planning and hoping had come to a head in that moment when Sophia said, "We leave today." Like a well-trained army, they were ready to go.

Mordecai grinned. He had his canvas case all packed.

Hundreds and thousands of people were leaving Shanghai and making for the surrounding countryside. Many were going south, and some, like Sophia and Stanislaus, had heard there were parts of the North where groups of liberated Chinese had holed up and were trying to wrest a living from the earth, sharing all they had equally among themselves. Stanislaus was keen to join them. Long-prepared for this day, Sophia changed into her baggy blue trousers and flat black shoes. Blessing the fact that Maria was busy at the Golden Dragon, she wrapped a few clothes in her bed-roll. She, Mordecai, Misha and Mei Mei let themselves out of the house for the last time. The car would be much too conspicuous. They must take to the streets, walk to the city and mingle with the thousands who were streaming out on the north-bound roads. Sophia prayed that Stanislaus was correct in assuming that Chu and Charlie would be making frantic plans to secure their money. As they left the house, they heard the telephone ringing furiously behind them. They let it ring . . .

"Oh Misha! Will we always have to run?" Sophia sighed. She remembered the days of escape from St. Petersburg. "We had everything in front of us then, didn't we?"

"Come on," Misha said roughly. "We have everything in front of us again." He held Mei Mei by the hand. "Anyway, I'm longing to meet Mei Mei's family. Let's go." And the four of them began walking toward the city.

CHAPTER 95

Trudging along beside Mordecai, Sophia mentally ran through the contents of Elena's last letter. Little Maria, now into her teens, was away at boarding school and happy. Sophia told herself that it was best that her girl had been raised by Edward and Elena. She never could have given Maria anything resembling a secure life. It was a good thing she was not here, marching beside Sophia to nowhere in particular. At least I spared her that, she consoled herself.

In an odd way she felt grateful to Chu: her daughter was well taken care of. For now, and maybe for a long time, Maria and Elena would not know where she was. While traveling to their eventual destination they could not allow themselves the luxury of correspondence. Perhaps she would be able to write once she arrived. But then that would be dangerous, unless Chu and Charlie were destroyed once and for all in the coming holocaust.

As they crossed the city they saw row upon row of Japanese soldiers marching toward the center of Shanghai. They made no attempt to stop the fleeing Chinese. Of course, Sophia thought. Why should they? When Shanghai collapsed, yet again, into chaos and disorder, the Japanese would have fewer mouths to feed. And if thousands of Chinese died during their long marches back to their homelands, well, so much the better.

They walked on and Sophia glimpsed the roof of the Golden Dragon in the distance. *Goodbye, Maria,* she thought, imagining Maria's face when she returned to the empty house. How much time would Maria give them, she wondered, before telephoning Chu? Sophia's back prickled as she imagined the knife slitting her tendons. She grimaced. It wouldn't be the first strip for punishment, she thought. Running away was a betrayal of the first order. It would warrant the garrotte. A shiver ran through her body.

Mordecai gazed down at her. "Don't be frightened," he said. "Mordecai know where to go. Charlie smart, but Mordecai clever. In China we say: The higher the monkey climb up the pole, the more you see of his behind. That is Charlie." He beckoned Sophia and then hissed at Misha. "This way!" he said. They bent low to the ground and passed down a long alleyway that ran between rows of bombed-out buildings, then turned into another alleyway, untouched by the bombs, criss-crossed with lines of washing. The clean linen flapped in their faces. Underpants waved cheer-fully, women's baggy knickers, vests, brassières all danced in expected welcome to this long crevasse between teetering buildings full of people clank-ing and chattering.

For a moment Sophia forgot she was on the run and remembered what a naturally happy people the Chinese were and how much she had grown to love this fascinating country. For so many years Shanghai had been the city of 668 brothels, the city of foreigners, of Victoria Park, polo grounds, cricket pitches, the Long Bar propped up by red-faced barbarians, but also of streets such as this one where she now felt oddly safe.

As the blue fingers of dusk darkened the sky over the northern outskirts of the city, little lights began to glow and to flicker. Mordecai led them to an inn on the roadside. He took two rooms. "Here, Missie." He opened the door on a small square white-washed room. "I find you food and hot water." The room was hardly larger than a horsestall, but it was clean and the window behind the bed looked out onto green fields. There were two cows and a bull munching at the grass. As they chewed, the sour smell of milky green weeds spread across the field. Sophia smiled. What a change of smell from the hot dusty roads!

She sat on the little iron cot, swinging her feet. Looking at the roll of bedding on the floor, she smiled again. Why did she feel so excited? Why did she feel young and carefree? Perhaps it was because she had left behind her all the clothes, the lines of shoes, the drawers of silk blouses, and the vast hat rack. She did not want or need any of those things. She just wanted to be with Stanislaus. Was she really such a fool that this man mattered to her so much she was positively happy to give up everything, as long as she could be with him? Yes, she was. She could not imagine life without Stanislaus. You felt like that about Elter, she reminded herself. And look what happened.

I know, her other self argued. I know. But this time Stanislaus will survive. We'll both survive.

She jumped when Mordecai knocked on the door. "Your hot water, Missie," he said. "And food. Rice and black beans. Smell good?"

Sophia smiled and thanked him. "Well, Mordecai," she said, "this is not exactly luxurious, but it suits me fine, thank you."

Mordecai bowed and withdrew. She already looks ten years younger, he thought.

Sophia removed her clothes, dipped a flannel into the water and began to wash. She ran the hot flannel between her legs. The startling warmth rejuvenated her tired thighs. She lazily passed her hands backward and forward. The rough texture of the flannel excited her. She looked out of the window. The bull had raised his head. His big dark eyes, with long, long lashes, gazed back at her. His nostrils quivered as he smelled the unfamiliar smell of a woman excited. He swished his tail and snorted. Behind him the moon shone on his massive shoulders. The rays lit up his russet-red coat.

Sophia returned his stare. If only her lover was there. She understood Stanislaus's explanation that he wanted to stay behind, just to be sure no trail was left and no one would follow them, that he would join her in Chusin. She fiercely missed him, nonetheless. If only, she thought as she put down the flannel. If only, she prayed, dressing herself again . . . Too tired to continue, she sat in a chair by the window and watched the night, her hand guarding her vulnerable self.

CHAPTER 96

By the time they were approaching Chusin, Sophia's feet were exceedingly sore. The others, used to miles of walking, were sympathetic. Other than bandaging her feet in rolls of cloth steeped in red berry juice, there was nothing to be done. "Thank heavens you not have bound feet, like ladies over there," Mei Mei said with an inclined head. Sophia watched a small flock of fluttering Chinese women. They tottered in evident pain along the road beside her.

"Poor things," she said.

"When liberators free China, women never bind feet again." Mei Mei smiled. "We all be equal."

Sophia sighed. "I just want to see the Chus and

the Charlies of this world get what's coming to them."

"They will. They will." Mei Mei's face was stern. "Long time China ruled by foreigners and warlords. Now all change. Japanese here now, but we get rid of them. Somehow. Then we take China ourself. Misha and I will have children who will work on land. We be a family. You see. You like North. Very good, very green."

Sophia grinned. "And I will plant in the rice paddies, eh?"

"Yes," Mei Mei said simply. "You plant."

Sophia smiled and tried to ignore the red-hot needles running through her feet. By the evening we should arrive in Chusin, she thought. I'm going to make it. She called to mind a photograph of her daughter, Maria, that Elena had sent. She had grown into a beautiful adolescent. Her hair was no longer so blonde, more of a honey color, and she had Sophia's eyes and full mouth. She looked back at her mother from the flat paper of the photograph with an air of gentle unconcern. Her life was her friends and her ponies. She had lived with Edward and Elena for so long that she was really unaware of her mother, except as a vague absence and an occasional sense of emptiness in her dreams. Elena, to her sadness, was childless, so she clung to Maria as to her own daughter. According to Elena's last letters, the news from England was again mixed, with rumors of war and strife. The whole world was in upheaval, as different forces went to work to dominate the globe.

Sophia now counted each painful step. She

would not ask to be carried. She must make her way to the Peking Restaurant alone. One, two, she counted, watching the blood soak through her bandages. One, two, carry my shoe. Three, four . . . She counted faithfully into the thousands.

At last she saw the sign swinging in the dusk. She took Mordecai's arm and he led her half-fainting into the back of the shop. She fell onto a chair and put her head in her hands. She felt strong arms and firm hands pull at the bindings of her feet. She opened her eyes and saw Stanislaus's head bent in silent concentration. "Poor darling," he whispered, his soft brown eyes full of her pain.

"Stanislaus?" she said weakly. "But you were behind us."

"There are many roads." He smiled. "From what I could tell, it doesn't look as if you were followed at all. But let's see to these feet of yours." He swiftly unwrapped the bandages and put her feet into a bowl of hot frothy water. Sophia jumped and exclaimed at the heat. He held her feet gently. "Don't move," he said. "The pain will soon go. This is fresh mustard seed. It will sting for a moment, but it will take the pain away." He looked up at Sophia. "How are you? I've been counting the days."

Sophia smiled. "Oh, Stanislaus, we're nearly free."

He smiled back at her excited face. "Yes, I think so. But we have a long way to go still."

"And you're sure Chu's people aren't after us?" Sophia said anxiously.

Stanislaus shook his head. "Mordecai is out scouting, just to be sure. But I'd imagine they're all too busy saving their own hides to bother with us. We chose our time well."

The pain in her feet and her legs subsided. Stanislaus picked up first one foot and dried it, and then the other. Gently he kissed the sole of each foot. In an instant a memory flashed through Sophia's mind, an image of the dreadful Kaido on the boat from Japan . . . But this was different. This was tender. This was the man she loved. Sophia smiled.

"Come." He lifted her from the chair, holding her head lightly on his chest. "I'll carry you to our room." Sophia clung to him as he mounted the stairs.

They entered another neat little room, white-washed and starlit. Gingerly he lay her down on the bed. He sat beside her, his chin in his hand and his eyes alight. "The liberators are moving," he said.

Sophia, content at last, put her arm on his shoulders. "Darling," she said, "kiss me."

"Yes, yes." Stanislaus bent over her and gave her a peck on the cheek. "Sophia, you don't seem to realize the importance of this. For once, the Chinese people—the 'coolies' and peasants—are getting together to demand something of their own. To own their own land . . ."

"I know," Sophia said wearily. "That's all Mei Mei can talk about." She felt the silence. There was a distance in Stanislaus's eyes. "What's the matter?" Sophia asked. "Did I say something wrong?"

"No." Stanislaus shook his head. "Not really. I think it's because you and Misha are both Russian. Your revolution had the same ideals as that of the Chinese, but it was and is a separate story. Your revolutionaries fought for the mother country, to own Russia for themselves. I do understand. I'm Russian myself. But I'm also half-Chinese. And we Chinese . . . It is our own land we fight for, not the whole of China. I'm not fighting for Shanghai, or Tiensin, or even Tsingtao. I am fighting for my people in Shinsan. And we have much to do before the revolution succeeds, but it will come one day . . . I don't expect you to understand." He smiled a soft dreamy smile that Sophia loved so well. "You must be starving," he said. "I've ordered a small feast just for the two of us. A chicken, to tell you the truth, but it will seem like a feast."

Mordecai returned during the middle of the meal. Stanislaus poured Mordecai a glass of rice wine. "What's the news?"

"Look like no one follow us," he sighed happily, and gulped the wine. "I'll clear plates," he said.

"You've had many long days," Stanislaus said when Mordecai had left them alone. "Let me get you to bed."

"With the man I love at long last," she said, feeling well fed and sleepy.

"Sophia." Stanislaus pulled her into his arms and kissed her slowly and lovingly. "Let go of your mind and think with your body."

She smiled. "If I do that," she said, "we'll never get to Shinsan."

They made unhurried, luxurious, tongue-touching, finger-probing, skin-stroking love. And then they held each other, content under the dark Eastern sky.

❧ CHAPTER 97 ❧

Like many of the other groups and individuals struggling along the roads on their way across China, Sophia and Stanislaus, with Misha, Mei Mei and Mordecai, took nightly refuge in caves and ditches. By now they all felt like beasts of burden. Their clothes had long since disintegrated and in order to eat they had to rely on what Mordecai and Mei Mei could beg, find, or catch. Soup was often a lot of water with a little sorrel or grass and a few nuts. Sophia, to her horror, learned to eat fried rat. She remembered Elter's revelation that he too had eaten rodents when on the run. No one had shoes, for the soles had worn out long ago. Often Sophia would stretch out a foot and gaze at the thick calluses that had formed on her once lovely feet. "Will you love me anyway?" she asked Stanislaus.

"Of course," he reassured. Each night they lay in each other's arms, too hungry and too exhausted to make love, but they took strength in each other.

During this journey Sophia realized that she was learning to restrain her temper. Usually quick to anger, she developed, as they walked the dusty roads through the countryside, a resilient cheerfulness. "I think," she said to Stanislaus, "there's a sort of freedom in this gypsy life that almost suits me. I don't have to think about how or why I should be living. I don't have to judge myself against anybody else. As we walk down the road, you can't tell peasant from king."

"Or countess," Stanislaus chuckled.

The river they had been following turned into a gorge. So far they had been walking a hundred yards parallel to the river barges and junks, which were pulled by donkeys and mules. Now ahead of them they could see the river dip and sheer cliffs rise up high above the banks. Sophia stood in awe. She stared at the saw-toothed spikes of the mountains and then at the tiny paths carved into the steep sides. This was where they would climb. One slip and there would be no second chance. She would fall to her death, beaten bloody by the crags and boulders. She looked down the chasm ahead and saw the criss-cross of the huge ropes tied to the junks and to the barges. The donkeys were freed and trotted up the ancient paths behind their masters, who had the great ropes tied around their chests. Men and women pulled their belongings through the canyon. The collective sound as they labored through the gorge was like the breathing of some vast, heaving, lumbering animal. She forgot that it was the sound of many. Only the one sound dominated: a tearing sobbing sound, the cry of a creature in torment, of a country in turmoil, and ultimately of a people who would endure. She beheld the sight and marveled at the Chinese. An incredible people, she thought. Never in Russia, nor anywhere else, would one see thousands and thousands of human beings, like bees spread out across the mountains, all pulling together as one. Maybe Stanislaus is right, she thought. They will clear this country of their enemies. It will take time, years and years, but they will take back their heritage.

Stanislaus's eyes were shining. "Do you see what I mean?" he said. "Look at them!"

Mordecai approached with a long piece of rope. "We tie up," he said.

Sophia was roped to Stanislaus, then Mei Mei, Misha, and Mordecai last. As they approached the first slope, before the vertical path ascended the mountain and the river dropped away from sight, Sophia looked at Stanislaus with anxiety in her eyes, and he said, "Call for the Gorgon. He will help you."

Sophia smiled. So, Stanislaus was one of them. She closed her eyes. "Breathe," she heard the old Hermit order. "Breathe in the mountain and then let it out slowly. Breathe in the people and then release them one by one. Breathe!" he said harshly. "And don't stop breathing. Do not open your eyes. The precipice will know your footfall. Your feet have been this way before, have they not?'' Sophia stepped forward and they began the ascent.

If they slept at all it was standing up against the solid backdrop of the mountain. Others climbed past them, but sleep could only be snatched a few minutes at a time. They resembled flies crawling up dusty walls in the bars of the red-light district. Sometimes Sophia felt she was sane, and stumbled on with the voices of Mei Mei and Stanislaus in her ears. Mordecai said little, but passed out various wads of tobacco that even Sophia learned to chew to assuage the pangs of hunger. Finally, and after what seemed ages, they came through the pass. The ledge widened to a discernible road. Two hundred yards up they could see people sprawled on the edge of a muddy lake.

At last they untied themselves and lay down on the soft earth. Sophia found her head resting in the cold mud, her hair wet and sticky. Stanislaus stretched out beside her. They lay happy and comfortable together. His head touched hers and their eyes celebrated this great victory. "We made it," he whispered.

"Yes," she said, "we kept the faith." Tears came into her eyes. "Are we nearly there?"

"Very close now."

"Are we really going to live in a cave?"

Stanislaus nodded. "And I promise you will love it."

"I'll take your word for it." She turned her body and fell asleep, the brown muddy water lapping over her hair. Stanislaus stood up and shook out his limbs. His wrists were raw from the rope that had been tied around it, and he was hungry. But as he looked around, a fierce joy clutched at his heart. The people were marching, his revolution was starting, and he was here and alive to be part of it. The fear of Chu and his Tongs seemed infinitely distant. For the first time in many years Stanislaus felt free. Or was he? Would Chu's organization reach them even here?

He picked Sophia up in his arms and carried her to a grass verge. Gently he laid her down. Well, he thought, only time will tell. We should be safe in Shinsan. Mei Mei and Misha would travel to Mei Mei's village, Shintu. Mordecai would remain with Sophia. Maybe one day Sophia would leave him, Stanislaus reflected, and go away to England. For now they must all practice the Taoist theory of action by nonaction . . . Stanislaus sniffed the air. To hell with philosophy, he thought. I smell fish.

Sure enough Misha came waddling toward them, his arms full of silver catfish. "Mudfish," he grunted, "but good eating." He squatted beside Sophia who stirred in her sleep. By the time she awoke it was night and the fish had been cleaned and gutted. No one spoke much, but they ate, pulling the many bones out of their mouths, and hummed with pleasure. "Tomorrow," Misha said, the fire gleaming in his eyes, "we'll go this way." He pointed toward the north-west. "And you'll go that way." His finger indicated north-east.

The moon beamed down on the little party sitting cross-legged around the fire. All about them other groups of refugees were huddled around camp-fires. Many were asleep on rags, many sat contemplating the horror of the journey recently undertaken. Small children ran bare-bottomed around the fires and their even younger sisters and brothers slept on drooping backs, like living knapsacks, with pancake faces and tired heads rolling to the rhythm of their mothers' bodies as they laid fresh branches on the fire, causing sparks to rise like fireworks. Sophia sighed. "I'll miss you both," she said, "but we will see each other again."

"Of course," Misha mumbled. "Of course."

Their last night together they all slept in a familiar tumble of bodies. And then in the thin early morning sunlight, they parted. "Goodbye, Misha." Sophia hugged him. She was too spent to cry. The months on the road had exhausted her reservoir of feelings. For the moment she just lived to survive.

"Goodbye, my nightingale," he said, recalling the years of her childhood, when she lived in the splendor of a Russian palace and sang with the joy of innocence in the adoring presence of her parents, sister and grandmother. Misha and Sophia stared at each other for a moment, his round eyes brimming with tears, both sharing this sacred memory. He hugged her, his stiff hair brushing her face. "Goodbye." He broke away, wiping his hands over his face. "Come, Mei Mei," he said, taking her hand. "We must go now."

Sophia watched the dear dwarfed man, whom she had known since her life began, shuffle down the long road ahead of him. She felt a searing pain that she recognized well, for she had grown accustomed to sorrow and loss, and had learned endurance. But now I have Stanislaus, she comforted herself. At least I belong somewhere. Hand in hand, with Mordecai bringing up the rear, Stanislaus and Sophia walked the last few miles of their journey.

Soon they would reach the village where Stanislaus had aunts and uncles, peasants who came into these mountains across the border from Mongolia many hundreds of years ago. They too had fought and fled their enemies—in their case, the Mongols. Finally Stanislaus's ancestors had settled in the mountains north of Shansai province. In the big caves they built their war-like homes. It was to those caves that Stanislaus was now heading. His Mongol blood had been diluted with a mixture of Chinese and Russian. Now he wanted to be part of the new China. As he hurried forward he blessed his good fortune: he had with him the woman he loved. Sophia would be happy here. He knew she would.

Mordecai scurried behind them, not so sure. But then, Mordecai argued with himself, why should I know what a woman wants?

To Sophia's surprise the so-called peasants were much more organized than she had expected. Several sympathetic, idealistic Americans also lived in the caves, which were remarkably comfortable and homey, as well as a handful of missionaries. Soon Sophia was busier than she had ever been. The peasants, the first children of Mao's dream, arranged themselves into communes led by committees of villagers. They realized that their liberation and ultimately the liberation of the entire country, depended on education and on their own ability to supply and fulfill their day-to-day needs.

Sophia found herself tending pigs—big fat black animals that gazed at her with their super-intelligent eyes. Often exhausted after a day of teaching children in the commune schools, she sat on the fence and scratched the backs of her other charges, the pigs. "I do love Stanislaus," she told her special pig, whom she called Emile. Emile lifted his snout toward her in understanding. Stanislaus was besotted by *The Cause.* "I can't live for causes," she confided in Emile, who grunted and rubbed his bristly back against the fence-rails. "At least not for ever. And if I ever leave this place," she told her faithful pig, "I know Stanislaus won't come with me." She sighed. "He says the Party is more important than his life, or any one life."

Presently her commune was organizing the making of lamps, oil, and other goods to fill the newly opened shops. Sophia helped most of the afternoons in the fields. She stooped and planted rice, her ankles awash with mud and water. Alone in the evening, she sat in her cave, aware that Mordecai next door was cooking. Mordecai knew that in this new world he must consider himself her equal, but for Mordecai the instinct to serve his mistress was too strong. He cooked not only for himself but also for Sophia and Stanislaus.

On a calm summer evening after a solitary dinner waiting for Stanislaus to return after yet another commune meeting, Sophia was submerged by a wave of loneliness. Yes, the new way was a much better way. Thanks to men like Stanislaus, the peasants in the northern area were not starving. Women were teaching other women to use contraception, so no longer did women die from repeated pregnancies that left them old before their time. But Sophia had to admit to herself that she did miss Maria and Rollo. She even remembered Clarice Carruthers with something approaching fondness. She sighed. I miss their humor, she thought, their ability to laugh at the dark side of life. Here, among the cheerful diligent workers, all was innocence. And work was so hard that making love with Stanislaus became rare. He usually came home exhausted and sweat-soaked. Tonight was one of many nights when he returned at midnight, took off his long boots and fell asleep beside her. Sophia kissed his forehead. She missed Elter. And somewhere in England she had a daughter. At least my Maria will never know that her mother was a prostitute. She dropped into a deep sleep.

Tomorrow's agenda included making candles. She moaned in her sleep. Her once silk-soft hands were rough and chapped from working in the fields. What a long way from the Golden Dragon . . . In her dreams the dragon writhed and roared, but Sophia slept on until the cockerel crowed outside her cave and Mordecai pushed open the wooden door, letting early dawn rays light up the huge cave. "Breakfast," Mordecai said. He carried two bowls of steaming gruel.

Sophia grinned. "No eggs and bacon?"

Mordecai shook his head. "No bacon *yet,*" he said, his eyes twinkling.

Sophia laughed. "You'll not get your hands on Emile. He's a stud boar. He has a nobler destiny than to end up as someone's breakfast." She reached out for her bowl. "Leave Stanislaus asleep," she said softly. "He needs all the rest he can get."

Mordecai bowed and left the cave. Sophia sat up in bed, quietly savoring the hot oatmeal boiled with garlic. Who is this woman I've become? she reflected. What has happened to the woman I used to be, who once played in a palace with her twin, and now lives a world apart from her beloved sister? What will happen to me? Stanislaus was making his way up in the Party, but Sophia was, at best, a keeper of pigs. She smiled as she looked down on Stanislaus sleeping so innocently beside her. A keeper of pigs, she thought . . .

She stood up, aware that she must leave her bed and go to the commune. A keeper of pigs is a more honorable profession, she decided, than placating swine at the Golden Dragon. The day would come, she promised herself, when Charlie and Chu would be swept away, as would the hundreds of brothels that made Shanghai a city of sin. The thought comforted her and she hurried into her padded clothes and stepped from the cave.

The breezy morning air was invigorating. All about her other caves disgorged women and children, the children off to the primitive school collective and the women to work in the fields. Sophia smiled. All this talk of liberation, she thought.

Here we are, women in the fields and the men on tractors. Nothing changes. She grinned. Especially not men. They never change.

A keeper of pigs is fine, she thought. But the children. There is so much more to be done with the children . . .

ANSWERS

"Pigs indeed!" The old woman laughed. "Though there's nothing undignified about tending pigs. That's one thing I learned. Emile remained my friend for years. But there were other, more valuable things to be done. Particularly with the children. How was China to have a future if its children were not equipped to create that future?" The Snow Leopard fell silent. She stared unblinking at Natasha, who waited patiently for more words to come.

The sky and sea outside the bedroom window were darkening to a starless winter's evening. The room inside remained bright, lit by polished brass lamps. Natasha felt as if hardly a moment had passed, though many hours had.

Half-way through the telling, the old man had entered to give the Snow Leopard her lunch, a blue porcelain bowl of rice and noodles, gentle to a delicate and ailing digestive system. He had sat himself down to listen and remained for the rest of the story, nodding and bowing in all his favorite parts. And when something made him chuckle, he put his hands over his mouth so as not to insult the Snow Leopard by showing his teeth, a habit he had not lost since those long years in China.

Natasha had sat enraptured, each word seeming to complete in her soul infinitesimal gaps whose existence she had hardly detected. She felt completely sure that she had found her grandmother, an absence in her life that she had always accepted as natural. "Why do you stop there?" she said at last.

The woman said, "There's not much left to tell. That is the story of the Snow Leopard, or at least of the person I thought the Snow Leopard was meant to be."

"But you became so much more afterward, didn't you?" Natasha did not want to overtire the woman, but she longed to know everything.

"Strange," the woman said. "While I was in Shanghai, I called myself the Snow Leopard. The name gave me strength and confidence and, in my young woman's imagination, mystery. But it was only when we reached the commune in Shinsan that I really began to choose what I would be. No one knew me there. In a way, I put my past behind me. The people of the commune accepted me as *Shie Bao*, the Snow Leopard. But the Snow Leopard was not the woman I had first imagined. No killer was she, no dangerous creature of the night. The real Snow Leopard was destined to nurture cubs, the children of the commune. That was the destiny that had awaited her all her life. The rest was mere preparation."

"It was for your work with children that you became famous in China?" prompted Natasha, though she already knew this to be the case.

The old man opened his mouth. "Too modest!" he laughed, wiping the thick lenses of his spectacles with a handkerchief. "Too modest!" His old golden skin wrinkled in great furrows around his slanted dark eyes. His thick lips quivered with delight.

"Mordecai," said the Snow Leopard. "You were always one to speak up for me."

He spoke with affection evident in his eyes. "I tell. Snow Leopard famous not only in commune, but in whole Shansai province, whole region, whole of China! First she make commune school, then start more schools in region, and help make new system for little ones everywhere in country. China love her. Call her mother of modern education. You go China now, you still hear little school children sing song about legend of Snow Leopard. 'Other beasts hurt and kill,' song say, 'but we have Snow Leopard who love and give life.' Snow Leopard not just famous, Snow Leopard hero! You go China, Missie Natasha. You hear song!"

"They have not sung that song for many years," the Snow Leopard said sadly. "You must not forget that."

"Mordecai not forget," he said with a shake of his head and a reddening of his cheeks that bespoke an anger that would never leave him. "Never forget."

"I don't understand," Natasha said. "What do you mean?"

"We mean, Jiang Qing," the Snow Leopard ex-

plained, "the wife of Chairman Mao. Great vision-
ary though Mao was, Jiang Qing was never anything but a petty, vicious, jealous woman. She
could not bear the fact that another woman—a
Russian woman—should gain fame in the China
she believed to be her own. She saw me as an
enemy. And when Mao himself was too old and
feeble to stop her, she and her gang staged their
so-called Cultural Revolution. Whatever else it
was, it was Jiang Qing's chance to avenge her
grudges. People may treasure ideals and dreams
and visions, but politics always ends up as a personal affair. I was high on her list, one of the first
to be declared an enemy of the people's republic,
all because a spiteful woman—and an actress at
that—would not share her spotlight!"

"And you left China?" said Natasha, trying to
piece together the last details.

"Always the journalist, aren't you? Ever the professional," the Snow Leopard said with a smile.
She was tired. Her face was pale, but her eyes still
bright. She willed herself to continue, wanting her
life-story told to the end.

Mordecai rose and poured her a glass of water
from an enameled jug. The old woman drank and
lay back against her cushions. "You see, I was
warned. Stanislaus told me I was to be arrested."

"Stanislaus?" Natasha was shocked.

"Yes, Stanislaus. He was my friend. Always my
friend. And a good companion. There had been
years when I thought I loved him. But he was one
of that rare species who are more in love with
causes than they ever can be with people. His love

for the cause was greater than his love for me. I suppose I always knew that."

"Stanislaus good man," Mordecai interrupted.

"Yes," the Snow Leopard agreed. "A good man. It did not take many years, after the communist revolution at the end of the forties, for Stanislaus's goodness to be noticed by others. He rose quickly within the Party; having been one of the heads of the commune, he was appointed a member of the board for our region. And then he was called to represent our region in the central government in Beijing—that is what we have learned to call Peking. I missed him when he went to Beijing, but I knew he had to go. We could no longer be lovers but our friendship was strong. So you see, Stanislaus was the true dignitary. And when the Cultural Revolution first started, he had word that I was on the list of enemies. He did me the kindness of warning me. He said there was nothing he could do, and I believe there wasn't. So I had a choice. I could stay and be imprisoned, or escape and leave behind the life I had made for myself."

Mordecai bowed his head, a gesture of pain shared with the Snow Leopard. "And Jaggers save us!" he said, raising his face suddenly.

The Snow Leopard continued. "Stanislaus warned me long enough in advance for me to get a message through to Jaggers, who, I found out, was in Hong Kong at the time. Mordecai and I packed up the few possessions we had—everything in this room—and we were fugitives again. Running away. Always running. We made our way to the coast where Jaggers, God bless him, met us and took us away on the *Elizabeth.*"

At last the pieces had come together. The Snow Leopard's story had become Natasha's story. Natasha felt a warmth, a wondrous sense of belonging, suffuse her whole body. What had started as an almost fantastical tale was real, part of her own life. Natasha said, looking into the woman's eyes, "I remember the *Elizabeth.* And I feel I almost remember Jaggers. A big man with a huge laugh. I was very young then, five at the most. But I remember my mother and I, together with my great-aunt Elena and my great-uncle Edward, sailing on a beautiful old boat with a man called Jaggers."

"No doubt you do," the Snow Leopard said, putting out a hand to touch Natasha's arm in the chair beside her bed. She had sensed from the very first moment of seeing Natasha that this was the granddaughter she had longed to see, if only once. "By this time, when Jaggers came to get me, neither of us was any longer young, but we were and still are very good friends. The *Elizabeth* was his. That was what Elena and Edward left him, when you got the rest of the legacy. The Monastery had long ago been sold, but the money was part of the estate you received."

Natasha did not know what to feel. Part of her wanted to cry for the past that had been annihilated by a flying bomb, and part of her wanted to laugh, to hug the woman before her in joy. "Did you know about me?"

"Jaggers told me on the boat, when we made our way here. And I was shocked. I did not know

I had a granddaughter. You see, I never set eyes again on my daughter, Maria, your mother, after she went as a baby to England with my sister. For years she was all I could think of. And then I worried that she would not want to know me, because of what I had become." Color rose in her cheeks. "But I remained determined to see her anyway. Stanislaus and Mordecai and I made our life in the commune, with Misha and Mei Mei nearby, and then what had started as the Japanese invasion became a world war. You can imagine the impossibility of letters from China finding their way to England, or from England to China, during that time. And there was no way to escape. Not then. But I always dreamed I would."

The Snow Leopard stopped. Tears filled her eyes. "And then came the awful day when word came from England. It came, as news did then, through people who knew people who had friends who knew someone else . . . I was told that my sister and her husband were dead. And worst of all, my daughter, my child. Though by then she was a grown young woman. I did not know about you."

Natasha touched the yellow cheek.

"I'm so sorry, but I had no way of knowing. In fact, it was not until Jaggers told me—more than twenty years later on the boat—that I found out it had been a flying bomb that had killed them. All I had been told was that they were killed in an explosion in London. And I blamed myself." She began to cry, shaking her head. "I thought Chu had killed them. I thought he was punishing me for leaving Shanghai. It was a guilt that stayed with me."

"It wasn't your fault. And how you must have suffered," Natasha said.

"I thanked God the day Jaggers told me. The truth was that very soon after we left Shanghai, when the Japanese took over, they found Chu—and Charlie—and gave them what they deserved. They are not ones to let something pass, the Japanese."

"Not like to lose face," Mordecai said with a triumphant grin of vengeance.

"They had learned long before," the Snow Leopard continued, "that it was Chu Wing and One-Eyed Charlie who had stolen their gold. They bided their time—such patient people they are!—until they could get Chu in his own city. Word of this reached Shinsan, but I thought Chu had given the orders to kill my family before he himself was killed. Still I blamed myself. Do you understand?"

"What did the Japanese do to them?" Natasha knew that her grandmother wanted to tell her.

The Snow Leopard wiped her cheeks. Her eyes held a glitter of pleasure. "They cut off their heads, just as they had done to my Elter."

"My grandfather," Natasha said.

"Your grandfather." The Snow Leopard nodded. She looked up at Natasha and saw in the young woman's face something of her former lover. For the first time since losing her baby a lifetime ago, she sensed that she had recaptured a cherished part of her past.

"You know," the Snow Leopard said, "he was

the only man I ever really loved." She shook herself. "And when I heard that my family was dead, well, I had no more reason to dream of coming to England. The war was won, and then came our revolution, and all I could do to live with the guilt I felt was to pour myself into my work. I worked for the commune. I worked for the children. And that, in the end, was the Snow Leopard's true destiny, the destiny that Lau Tchi had promised. When Jaggers told me about you, the inheritance was yours and you had disappeared. You had begun travels of your own."

All that time, Natasha thought, when I was in Barcelona, and Lisbon, and Paris, my grandmother was here. I never knew.

"Even the Snow Leopard," the woman said with a smile, "could not find you. I prayed some day you would come."

"You speak of yourself as if the Snow Leopard is someone else," Natasha said. "But *you* are the Snow Leopard."

"As I told you, a name exists to hide behind. When Jaggers brought me to England, he set me up in this house, here in Cornwall. He said I would find the climate gentler than up north at Hartland Point, where he still lives with his son on their farm. He is an old man, as I am an old woman. But he still manages to bring the *Elizabeth* down from time to time and visit me. He knows me for who I am. Not the Countess Oblimova, not the Snow Leopard, simply me, Sophia. But I'm now in the habit of hiding, always hiding from my own past. So the villagers here know me as the Snow Leopard. And I remain in hiding. Only you know who I am."

"You're my grandmother," Natasha said. She raised the woman's hand from the bed and held it to her lips.

"A happier name I will never hear." Sophia smiled. She pulled Natasha's hand to her own lips and returned the kiss. "And," she said, "if I may be allowed a grandmother's luxury of giving advice, you too have a destiny that you must not run from. It would seem that you have spent your whole life running, hiding, hesitating. Enough. Don't be afraid to love. Embrace your destiny, and then your life will really begin. Colum, you say? Such an interesting name."

She let her arm drop and lay back. "On that note," she said, "this interview shall end. You may switch your handy tape-recording machine off."

"You knew?"

"I'm not a fool," Sophia said with pride.

"But you told me your story anyway," Natasha said.

"I told *you.* I did not tell the world, or your magazine, or your readers. I have no intention of doing so. I was speaking to my granddaughter, not to a journalist."

"I . . ." Natasha paused. "That is, Natasha Waldbauer, no, Natasha Oblimova, my name before a husband gave me his—I feel as though I've discovered the world today. I've found you, and my grandfather, and my mother . . . You've completed something in me." She looked deep into the woman's eyes. "I also have a job to do. And it would mean a great deal to me, to be able to write about you, and let people know . . ."

"And take away my secrets," the Snow Leopard said. "Perhaps I was right all along. Perhaps you have come to assassinate me with your pen."

Mordecai felt an uneasiness threaten. He wanted to spare his Snow Leopard any threat. "Please," he said to Natasha. "It is late. She rest."

"I'm so sorry," Natasha said sincerely. "This is what I'd like to do: during the weekend I'll write up the story. On Monday I'll come back and show you. If you don't like it, I won't send it in. Not until you're satisfied with it, anyway."

"You will do what you must do," Sophia said. "And not another word said." The whisper of tension left the air as Sophia's face softened and her eyes gazed at Natasha with a powerful, loving, wistful tenderness. "Now come and kiss your grandmother goodbye."

Natasha leaned over and pressed her lips to the soft cheek that smelled of jasmine and honey. Finally pulling herself away, she said, "I'll be back on Monday."

The face of the Snow Leopard was beautiful. The mouth smiled and the eyes were proud. "Goodbye, Natasha. I'm pleased we met. Mordecai will see you to the door."

It was Sunday. Natasha sat at the desk of her room at the Holiday Inn in Plymouth, an oasis of luxury and comfort in the bleak gray sea-winds of the English coast. All weekend she had struggled with her article, but it refused to come out right.

Natasha made her decision. She typed quickly into the computer before her. Moments later the built-in printer regurgitated a page of neat print. She switched the machine off, took a shower, and dressed herself. She ripped away the printed page and descended in the lift to the hotel lobby.

"Could you please have my car brought up?" she asked the receptionist.

He nodded and rang for a doorman.

"And," Natasha said, "would you cable this off to New York?" She held out the sheet of paper, addressed to her editor. The message read:

> Sorry. False lead. Snow Leopard not at address given. Neighbors say might be in South of France for winter. Not sure when due back. Perhaps try another time. Return to New York soon. Natasha.

Her rental car appeared at the front door of the hotel. Natasha climbed into it and pulled away. She caught the ferry at the Plymouth docks and crossed to Tor Point. The cable, she knew, would be at the office when they opened up tomorrow morning. She rode along narrow Cornish roads through a sea-fog that clung to the land. She could not wait to tell her grandmother.

Mordecai's face at the door had lost its tawny golden glow. "Too late," he said. "Snow Leopard dead."

Natasha shook her head incredulously. The

woman who only days ago had spoken with her had seemed alive, strong, immortal. "When?"

"She knew time to go," Mordecai said, once again leading her down the corridor to the bedroom. "This morning she say, 'Mordecai, go to church.' I always go to church on Sunday. But today I not want go. She looked bad." He stopped at the door. "Yes," he turned to Natasha, "I *always* go to church." His tear-soaked eyes squinted in a sad smile. "Miss Trublood win."

He opened the bedroom door and stepped in beside Natasha. On the bed lay Sophia, her eyes closed, her face entirely peaceful. Together they stood looking at the woman who was no less beautiful in death than she had been in life. Her skin was a gentle color which somehow made her appear younger than her years. Natasha could see the striking young woman that Sophia had once been.

"And miracle!" Mordecai said softly. "I go to church. Not want upset her. And sermon was miracle. God talk straight to Mordecai. Preacher read from Bible, book of Jeremiah. Favorite verse of mine. 'Can the Ethiopian change his skin,' " he quoted, " 'or the leopard his spots? Then may ye also do good, that are accustomed to do evil.' I hear preacher, and I know. God tell me Snow Leopard dead. I come back here, and she lie like this. She with God now. And with people she love."

Natasha looked at the old man. She could see he yearned to cry, but open weeping was not his custom.

"You pardon me," he said, turning from the room. "I go my room. Please. You stay. Not worry. I make arrangements already. Please pardon." And he shut the door behind him.

Natasha sat in the bedside chair that she had sat in only days before, listening to this woman tell the story of her life. For many hours she sat and pondered.

She did not feel grief. Sitting in the silence of this wonderful room full of treasures from another world, Natasha did not cry in sorrow; instead a new and thrilling elation filled her heart. She had found the Snow Leopard, and her grandmother would be with her always.

Hours later, the last light of day struggled to penetrate the fog that had settled over the sea. Natasha raised her eyes to the window. There, just past the shore, in the strengthening pink glow of a clearing dusk, she saw an apparition so lovely and yet so strange that she wondered whether she was awake or dreaming. Its prow breaking through the mist, its shape clear in the ever-brightening light of sunset, the *Elizabeth* steamed into view. The anchor was lowered and in a moment two men could be seen setting a rowboat into the water and rowing to shore. This was no dream.

Natasha went outside to greet them. "Jaggers!" The old man embraced her and introduced her to his son. Mordecai had telephoned and spoken of her. Jaggers remembered her well. From now on, he promised, they would never be out of contact again. Together they went inside for Jaggers to pay his last respects to the woman he had loved.

That night, sitting with cups of tea at the table in the cottage's small dining-room, Jaggers and his son talked with Natasha and Mordecai. "Sophia," said Jaggers, still strong after a lifetime of salt air and sea winds, "was one of a kind. Women like that just don't exist any more."

"Plans made?" Mordecai asked.

"I've telephoned Stanislaus," Jaggers said. He turned to Natasha. "He's very senior in the Chinese government now. One of the old guard. Says the days of the Cultural Revolution are past. Everybody does their best to forget and pretend it never happened. Funny how fickle countries can be." He looked at her with pride clearly visible in his old but sharp eyes. "They want to give her a proper state funeral. And the Chinese government has invited me and my son to go with her. It seems right somehow, for her to go back. China was her only real home. She made it her home. And the China she helped to build wants her back."

Natasha found herself sharing in his pride.

"We leave tomorrow," Jaggers continued. "We'll sail on the *Elizabeth* to Plymouth. From there we'll take the train to London and then fly on to China . . . Strange to be going back, after all these years." He shook his head. "A long, long journey home."

The next day, a day so bright and full of sunlight it was hard to believe that Plymouth had ever been covered by cloud, Natasha left the hotel and started on her own way home. She would make New York her home. And when she got back, the first thing she would do would be to see Colum. She had much to say.

She chose the road that took her past Plymouth's wharves. Reaching the waterfront, Natasha stopped the car. Out to sea, the *Elizabeth* could be seen heading for the dock. The Snow Leopard's life had come full circle.

Natasha started the car and drove to the road that would take her to Heathrow Airport. On the passenger seat, her handbag held the tapes. The Snow Leopard's secrets would be preserved. Natasha would treasure the tapes for herself. She would keep the story, the words, the voice itself—that beautiful, singing, full-throated Russian voice.

Far away, his soul as old as China, Lau Tchi the Hermit softly put his forehead to the stone floor of his room. His work complete, his eyes rolled back in his head. He died unto this world for the last time, his ancient lips tracing an eternal smile.

Erin Pizzey is the author of four previous novels, THE CONSUL GENERAL'S DAUGHTER, FIRST LADY, IN THE SHADOW OF THE CASTLE, and THE WATERSHED. Well-known for her work with battered wives and their children, she is an accomplished journalist and has written a number of non-fiction books as well. She lives in Cayman Brac with her husband and children.